BLOOD FLAG

BLOOD FLAG

A Paul Madriani Novel

STEVE MARTINI

WM

WILLIAM MORROW

An Imprint of **HarperCollins***Publishers*

BLOOD FLAG. Copyright © 2016 by Paul Madriani, Inc. All rights reserved. Printed in the United States of America. No part of this book may be used or reproduced in any manner whatsoever without written permission except in the case of brief quotations embodied in critical articles and reviews. For information address HarperCollins Publishers, 195 Broadway, New York, NY 10007.

HarperCollins books may be purchased for educational, business, or sales promotional use. For information please e-mail the Special Markets Department at SPsales@harpercollins.com.

FIRST EDITION

Library of Congress Cataloging-in-Publication Data has been applied for.

ISBN 978-0-06-232896-0

16 17 18 19 20 DIX/RRD 10 9 8 7 6 5 4 3 2 1

Dedicated to the members of the US Army's 45th Infantry Division, the men who fought their way through Europe, liberated the concentration camp at Dachau, and occupied the City of Munich at the end of World War II

ONE

For most human beings, what to do with our hands is an issue. Until we need an opposable thumb to pick something up, our hands have the social utility of an inflamed appendix. Once upon a time we busied them by smoking. Bogart and Bacall taught us how to do this with style. Now that that has been declared unhealthy and a universal stigma, we employ our idle fingers fondling our cell phones.

It is what Sofia, my new legal assistant, is doing as I watch her sitting on the couch in my office. She is off to the side and behind my client, an older woman who is pouring out her soul, the painful details of her legal problems, from the client chair across from me. Sofia's attention is riveted on the small screen in her hand. A tiny charm dangles from the cell phone on a chain plugged into the iPhone's headphone jack. The charm, a minuscule chrome copy of the Eiffel Tower, signifies dreams of future travel. If she can stay on track between work and school, Sofia has already given me notice. She plans a trip to Paris with friends next summer. Ah, to be young and free—and utterly cavalier concerning assurances for continued employment.

Sofia came to us bearing three impressive letters of recommendation from social heavyweights in the community. I had to wonder how she knew these people. When I asked, she didn't bat an eye. Instead she admitted that she had never met any of them and that, in fact, a mutual friend whom she did know and who ran in their circles, a person she had been acquainted with for some time, had requested the endorsements on her behalf. She offered nothing regarding the identity of this individual and I didn't ask. The letters were very carefully crafted. None of them actually stated that they knew her. Instead they relied on her academic record and her reputation for hard work. I was impressed by Sofia's honesty, that she didn't lie about it. That and the fact that there was just something about her.

Her thumbs work on overdrive—enough speed to type out a Ph.D. thesis. I can be pretty sure she is not tapping out a transcript of my client's words. It's probably a text message confirming a date for tonight.

Sofia is our latest hire, a paralegal sidetracked on her way to law school, a hiatus to earn money and get some experience. She is twenty-six years old, and her real name is Sadie Leon. Someone, I think it was her father, tagged her with the nickname Sofia and it stuck. She is the spitting image of a young Sophia Loren. Tall, stately, beautiful, a little ungainly, like an adolescent doe. She is learning how to fend off the insecurities of youth, but still needs to hide on occasion behind the refuge of her phone. For me she is becoming an emotional stand-in for my daughter, Sarah, who, for the moment at least, is living in Los Angeles. Joselyn, my better half, has already taken Sofia under her wing. They spend a good amount of time laughing together. I suspect some of it is at my expense.

Sofia's hire, along with several others, was made possible by a huge financial windfall from our last case—like winning the lottery. Harry Hinds, who is my law partner, and I have netted millions. We have yet to stop counting it all. The money pours into our business account and from there into a burgeoning investment portfolio. It is the result of a federal whistle-blower statute. With the help of our client we were able to identify a small brigade of offshore tax cheats, some of whom were hiding millions in secret numbered bank accounts overseas—to be specific, Switzerland. The IRS and the Treasury Department rewarded our client and he, in turn, showered us with enough money in the form of fees for Harry and me to retire. But we didn't. Instead we doubled down, hired more help, and went back to the gristmill trying to rebuild our practice. As I listen to our prospective client from the chair behind my desk, I begin to wonder why I am not fishing off the deck of a gleaming motor yacht somewhere in the Lesser Antilles.

"I don't know how they could possibly think I killed him," she says.

Emma Brauer is sixty-three, has never married, and has no children. She has disheveled brown graying hair and a face like a pedigreed bulldog, which is etched with lines of worry that allow even the casual observer to suspect that this is not the first time she's fallen victim to anxiety. "They can't really think I did it," she says. "I loved him. He was all I had."

"That's why they think you did it," says Harry. "The motive for a mercy killing is usually love, though not always." Harry is seated in the other client chair in front of my desk playing devil's advocate, the devil in this case being the cops and the county's district attorney. "Let me ask you," he says. "Did you by chance come into any kind of an inheritance as a result of your father's death?"

"Only the house," she says. "And some money."

"How much money?"

"About two hundred and seventy thousand dollars."

Harry winces.

"They can't possibly think I killed him for that. He was already dying. Why would I kill him when all I had to do was wait? And besides, I loved him."

"Prosecutors have twisted psyches and hyperactive imaginations," says Harry. "Maybe they think he was about to change his will."

"He didn't have one. I was his only child."

"Maybe he was about to write one?" Harry's plumbing all the possibilities.

"Not that I know of," she says. "The police didn't say anything about any of this when they talked to me."

"They wouldn't," Harry tells her. He looks at me. "Dad was in a nursing home." Harry looks down at the open file in front of him on the desk. "Robert Brauer, eighty-nine years old, smoked like a chimney almost till the end, according to the notes. They haven't released the toxicology report or precise cause of death from the postmortem, but rumor is he was helped along."

"Why would I do that?" she asks.

"Your father was suffering, I take it?" I look at her.

"He was in some pain. He was old. Of course he was suffering."

"Diabetes, emphysema, COPD—chronic obstructive pulmonary disease . . ." says Harry.

"He smoked all his life," she says. "It was the only pleasure he had left. I couldn't bear to take them away from him. His cigarettes, I mean. Is that what this is all about? Because I didn't take away his cigarettes?"

"We can hope so," says Harry, "but I doubt it. According to the doctor's reports, Robert—"

"Bob. Nobody called him Robert," she corrects him.

"Bob's breathing was chronically labored," says Harry.

"Like sucking air through a straw," says Emma, "if you know what I mean. He had been using oxygen for a couple of years at the house before he went into the hospital."

"So you saw all of this?" I ask.

"Of course. I had to take care of him."

"Was that a burden?" asks Harry.

"It wasn't easy," she says.

All the possible motives. Harry glances at me.

"So I guess it looks bad for me, doesn't it?" This seems to dawn on her for the first time.

"We won't know until we see the evidence," I tell her. "Relax."

"It's hard enough to lose your father, but to have the police say I killed him . . ." Brauer looks down at the surface of my desk and begins to tear up.

Before I can search for the box of Kleenex, Sofia is off the couch and finds it on the credenza behind my desk. She dangles two from her fingers in front of Brauer's watering, downcast eyes. Emma takes them and mops up her tears.

Sofia's cell phone is still in her other hand, her gaze continuously on its screen as she navigates flawlessly in the blind, back to the couch. The girl must have learned multitasking in the womb. Quiz her after the client meeting, she'll be able to repeat almost verbatim everything Brauer told us. I know this because I've tested her before. A mind like a police scanner.

"I didn't do it," says Brauer. "Why do the police think I did something wrong?"

"Don't know," says Harry.

But it's clear that they do. Several of Emma's friends, one of them a neighbor, were interviewed by the cops. They were asked questions about hypodermic needles and medications and who administered them, with particular emphasis on Emma. One of her friends told Emma she would be wise to get a lawyer. It's the reason she is here this morning.

"Did you ever administer medications to your father?" I ask her.

"Sure, when he was home. But not after he went to the VA. After that, the nurses did it. After they finally took him in. Had to fight like hell to get him there. They said they would contract out for a private nursing home. They put him on a list and nothing happened. Weeks went by. You know, I'm thinking that if Dad died of some kind of problem with his medications, maybe they screwed up. The VA, I mean. They're known for it. I should have never let him go there."

I look at Harry. I can tell by the way his eyebrows arch, the familiar wrinkle across his forehead, that this is the kind of pregnant thought that might breed a theory of defense. "We'll look into it," he says.

"All the problems started after Dad received that damned package," she says.

"What package?" I ask.

"You mean medications?" says Harry.

"No, it wasn't medicine," she says. "It was a small cardboard box. Came in the mail, in brown paper wrapping. Dad said it was something left to him by a friend, a buddy from his army days. I thought it might be jewelry, you know, the size and shape of the box and all. It had Dad's name and address on the wrapper. Inside was a key. It looked like it belonged to a safe-deposit box. You know the kind, flat metal with no grooves on the sides."

I nod. "Go on."

"That box was no end of troubles. Inside, in addition to the key, there was a piece of paper folded up with a name on it, and a picture. It looked like it might have been a copy of an ID. It was military but not US. I don't think, anyway. The words printed on it weren't in English. I asked Dad what it was. He said he didn't know. But I think he did. Just the way he looked. He knew something. All the trouble started after that."

"What trouble?" says Harry.

"Phone calls late at night. A man's voice asking for Dad. Whenever I asked for his name on the phone he told me, 'I'm a friend of your father's. He'll know who I am.' Wouldn't give me his name. Dad would take the phone and send me out of the room while they talked. When the phone calls ended, Dad looked worried, you know what I mean? He was sick, getting sicker each day. Now whoever was on the phone was making it worse. Adding a ton of stress. Over what, I don't know. But it had to do with the key and that piece of paper. Of that I'm sure. Dad didn't need the aggravation and I certainly didn't. After the third call I stopped putting them through. I told the guy on the phone that my father was out and I hung up. Dad got scared. Told me I shouldn't have done it. He told me to put the box with the key and the paper in my safe-deposit box at the bank. He wanted it out of the house."

"Why?" says Harry.

"I don't know. But that was before the burglary," she says.

"When was this?" I ask.

"About five months ago. One afternoon I took Dad to the VA. We came home and the house had been turned upside down. Everything dropped out of drawers all over the floor. Dishes broken. The place was a mess. Upholstery and mattresses were all cut up, slashed and ripped. You know what I mean?"

"Like somebody was looking for something," says Harry.

"Exactly."

"Where's the box now?" I ask.

"Still in the safe-deposit vault at my bank."

"You have the key?" says Harry.

"At home hidden away, in a safe place. They didn't find it."

"Did you report the burglary to the police?" I ask.

"No."

"Why not?"

"Dad didn't want to."

"Did he say why?" I ask.

"No. Instead we called in some friends. They helped us clean up. Dad told them it was probably kids. But he and I both knew that it wasn't. Two weeks later Dad was admitted to the VA and he never came out."

"And he never told you who was on the phone?" says Harry.

"No."

"Do you know who sent the box to your father?" I ask her.

"No. But I think there was a return address on the wrapper."

"You saved it?"

"Dad folded it up and put it in the box under the key and the ID. I saw it in the box when I took it to the bank, but I didn't think anything of it."

"And you think whoever burglarized your house and called your father might have killed him?" I look at her.

"I don't know. All I know is he was scared."

Before Harry or I can say anything more, there's a rap on the door. It opens and Brenda, my secretary, sticks her head in. "Sorry to interrupt but there're two detectives here to see you. They say they have an arrest warrant for Ms. Brauer."

TWO

He was parked at the curb looking through the open window on the driver's side. The tiny rented Kia Rio was about a hundred and fifty yards down Winona Avenue from the small single-story house, the center of all the commotion across the street. It was a ranch-style bungalow like most of the others, gray stucco siding with a composition roof. There was a small single-car garage tacked on to the front of the house. Two fair-sized palm trees poked out of the planter bed that bordered the six-foot strip of front lawn that ran to the concrete sidewalk out in front.

A cop was busy tying off yellow plastic tape to one of the palm trees. He snaked the tape three times back and forth between a fence near the adjoining property and the tree, forming a barrier to keep the growing band of nosy neighbors at bay.

"Damn it!" He looked at the computer printout lying on the passenger seat next to him hoping that maybe it was the wrong house. It showed the street view from Google Earth. There was no question it was the same house, correct address, palm trees and all. Two police cars were parked on the street in front. There was a white official van of some kind backed into the driveway. The question was, what to do now?

He reached into the backseat, grabbed a backpack, and pulled out what looked like a short telescope. He popped the lens cover off the spotting scope, eased the rubber cover from the eyepiece, and steadied the tube of the scope on top of the exterior side-view mirror on the car. Then he adjusted the zoom and focused in.

The scope was capable of showing .30-caliber bullet holes, about a third of an inch across, on a target a thousand yards away. From where he was parked he could read the names of the officers from the name-plates on the front of their uniform shirts. The lettering looked like a highway billboard. He adjusted the magnification down to reduce the shake on the scope and focused in on the white van parked in the driveway. Blue letters on the side read: SAN DIEGO POLICE CRIME SCENE INVESTIGATION.

"What the hell is going on?" He talked to himself. This wasn't unusual. Lately he'd been scratching his head about a number of things. He wondered if the police were looking for the same thing he was. Unless the old man left something in writing or talked to someone before he died, which was not likely, there was no way for the police to know.

He settled in as he watched the front of the house. He sat there for nearly two hours as they carried cardboard boxes and a number of plastic bags out of the house. He could only guess at the contents. The bags were sealed and the transfer boxes were covered. He assumed that maybe there were papers in most of the boxes, but there was no way to know, not a clue as to what the cops were looking for. At one point they came out with a desktop computer tower and some other electronics too big for a box. One of them carried a house phone with one of those base stations that probably recorded messages.

He was relieved that he had never attempted to contact the old man by e-mail. Nor had he left any voicemail messages on his phone. The only connection between them were two brief telephone conversations for which there were a dozen plausible explanations. That is, if anyone ever came asking questions. Unless the old man had recorded their conversations or taken notes, which was highly unlikely, no one could possibly know what they talked about. He knew the man would never tell his daughter. He would have had well-founded and serious concerns for her safety.

Rumors were now floating, information leaked into some dark crevices in certain correctional halls where twisted cretins lurked in the shadows. Word was that the thing actually existed. It had survived, and with the right information it might be found. Some of these people were crazy. All of them were dangerous, many of them ethnic fanatics, nut-cases who would kill in a heartbeat if they thought they had the slight-est chance to lay hands on it. Then there were others, people who might pay vast sums if only to lock it away behind glass in the confines of a private collection. Something to share over evening cocktails in the in-timate gathering of other affluent friends. It was, after all, one of a kind, an original, like a Monet, only more lurid. A vivid and well-recorded piece of history. As to its ultimate monetary value? Who could say? It depended on the bidders, how many, who they were, the depth of their pockets, and perhaps most important, the intensity of the dark impulses that drove them to have it. The trick for any seller was to get it and to stay alive long enough to deal with the right people.

At the moment what was gnawing at him was the possibility that the police might stumble over the key and take it by mistake. If they found it they might assume that the box it opened could contain evi-dence they were searching for. They would take the key and worry about finding the bank and the box it belonged to later.

It would have been nice if the police had waited one more day. By then he would have been in and out of the house, had what he wanted, and been gone. There was more than a fair chance that once inside he could locate the key. Unlike the others, the stumblebums who couldn't wait and who trashed the place and terrified the old man, he knew exactly what he was looking for. He would recognize the toolmaker's stamp the instant he saw it. That is, if the key was still there.

He watched the house as police kept coming and going. He thought about getting out of the car and wandering up to mingle with the neighbors to see if any of them knew what was going on, why the cops were there, what they were looking for, and when they might be done. He quickly dismissed the idea. He noticed two of the uniforms were working the small crowd with pens and notepads. They were talking to people, taking names, and jotting down notes. Why? He didn't know and he didn't want to find out. Better to remain anonymous, keep his distance, wait, and hope for opportunity.

It didn't take long to present itself. Just before three in the afternoon the cops wrapped up. The last bag of stuff came out of the house and one of the uniformed officers started cutting and pulling the yellow tape from around the tree and off the fence. One of the squad cars pulled a U-turn and headed out the other way. A few minutes later it was followed by the van.

The dwindling bunch of neighbors that remained began to break up. They drifted back toward their homes and the dull existence of normal life. Only the one squad car remained, two of the uniformed cops left behind to close up.

He zoomed in with the spotting scope on the area around the open front door. He was wondering how they had gained access to the house, whether the daughter had let them in, though he hadn't seen any sign of her. Or had the cops taken the door down, broken the lock, or called in a locksmith? The answer came almost immediately. An older woman was standing near the front stoop with the two cops. She had a small dog in her arms. She leaned over, pushed the door, and kind of pitched the animal into the house as one of the cops quickly closed the door behind it. As it shut the push-button lock swung out of the indoor shadows and into bright sunlight. The woman leaned over, studied it for a second, and then began to press the four-digit code into the keypad. He watched through the scope as her finger moved over the buttons, then pushed the lock button. She waited a second, then checked the latch. It was locked. The neighbor woman must have let them in to save the door from being destroyed by the cops.

He grabbed a pen from his pocket and made a quick note on the palm of his hand. He looked at the time: 3:28. By six thirty it would be dark. He could move the car farther back and watch to see if the police set up a patrol. If so, he wouldn't go near the place. He could watch to see if anybody came and went, neighbors looking out their windows or checking on the house, and whether the daughter came home. He wondered where she was.

He started the engine and pulled away from the curb, drove quickly past the parked patrol car, and headed down the street to look for a better location to watch the area. He was approaching the intersection with Forty-Ninth Street, about eight houses down, when he saw them. A rusted-out Chevy Chevelle, a muscle car from the seventies. Two white guys with shaved heads were sitting in the front seat. The driver looked at him, direct eye contact as he drove by. The driver showed tracks of gang tattoos all over his face, ink like a Maori warrior running down his neck disappearing beneath the collar of his shirt. He didn't have to take a second look at the swastikas, the numbers 14 and 88, to realize that others were scoping out the house and to know who they were. Police patrols in the area might not be a bad idea.

THREE

Emma looks at me with large oval eyes. The warrant for her arrest and the two detectives waiting in our reception area test the limits even for the queen of worries. Her face has now collapsed into a mask of angst. In too much shock even to cry, she looks at Harry, then back to me. "What do I do?"

"Nothing," I tell her. "Relax. Let us handle it. Don't say anything." I look toward the door and Brenda. "Tell them to wait, she'll be out in a minute. Tell them she is conferring with counsel and that we will surrender her momentarily." Brenda closes the door. "Have you talked to any other lawyers?" I ask Emma.

She shakes her head. "I wasn't . . . I didn't think I needed one; at least I wasn't sure. Do I have to go to jail?"

"It appears so," says Harry. "Lemme go check, see what they got." He's out of the chair and headed for the door, then slips out and quickly closes it behind him.

"The important thing is to keep calm and don't say a word. They will book you, process you into the jail, take a couple of pictures, do your fingerprints."

Now she starts to cry, a river of tears. Sofia grabs the box of Kleenex and hands it to her. She's put her phone away and for the first time even Sofia looks worried.

"We'll handle it," I tell Emma. "See if we can get bail. If so, you'll only be there a short time. If they put you in a cell with anyone else, be friendly, polite, but quiet. Whatever you do, don't talk to them about your case. If they ask why you're there, tell them you don't know what's going on, your lawyers are handling everything. And don't talk to the cops. If they ask you anything beyond the spelling of your name, your date of birth, and home address, you tell them to talk to your lawyers. Got it?"

She looks at me with a frantic expression and nods.

"I've never been in jail. I've never been in any kind of trouble before. Last traffic ticket I got was so long ago I can't remember."

"Getting arrested is not a crime," I tell her.

The door opens quickly and Harry slips back in and closes it. He hustles to the empty client chair with a fistful of paper. "Looks like one count, voluntary manslaughter." He glances up at me, a puzzled look on his face. "It doesn't make sense."

"No murder count?" I say.

He looks through the papers, checks one more time, and then shakes his head.

"What does that mean?" she asks.

"Means you're eligible for bail," says Harry. "Do you have a passport?" he asks her.

"No. Never needed one."

"Then we won't have to surrender it," says Harry. "There's also a search warrant for her house." He looks at me. "Apparently they're searching as we speak. That's how they found her with us. One of the neighbors must have told them where she was."

"What are they looking for?" I ask. A search warrant has to be supported by probable cause, an affidavit sworn to by a law enforcement officer setting forth in sufficiently specific terms the nature of the evidence being sought and the reason to believe it's to be found at that location. Police cannot simply come in and ransack a residence looking for whatever they can find, though at times it happens.

Harry scans the document quickly. "Medications, any toxic substances or materials, medical implements, any and all medical prescriptions, electronics including any computers, data disks and drives, telephone recordings and records, any and all documents relating to the estate of the decedent, and any and all financial records belonging to the decedent and/or to Emma Louise Brauer."

"They're leaving the door open," I say.

"What do you mean?" asks Brauer.

"They may amend the charges later, depending on what they find," I tell her.

"You mean murder?"

I nod. "It's possible. We'll have to wait and see. In the meantime we'll work on bail."

I'm guessing that the cops are also looking for evidence in two areas. First, medications that might have been stored at the house and allegedly used by Emma to kill her father. This would establish the necessary evidence of planning, the element of malice aforethought and premeditation for a charge of first-degree murder. Second, they're looking for evidence that money may have been the motive. If so, they can jettison the theory of a mercy killing, ratchet up the charges to first-degree murder, and top it off with the special circumstance, under California law, that personal financial gain was what prompted her to act. This would open the way to a death penalty or, at the very least, a life term without possibility of parole.

"And, of course, the two dicks outside brought the media sharks to document the arrest," says Harry.

It's election time and the D.A. is running for a third term. Even if it's not a capital crime, allegations of a mercy killing at a local hospital are likely to catch a premium spot on the local nightly news. This is free face time, worth a million dollars in campaign ads.

"Do you have any cash in the bank?" Harry asks her.

"Yeah," she says. "I don't know how much of it I can get at. Most of it is in Dad's account and could be tied up in probate for a while."

Of course. Dad died intestate, no will.

"It could be tied up for months," says Harry.

In perpetuity if they convict her.

"And the title to the house?" asks Harry.

"In Dad's name. If you're worried about your bill, I can pay," she says.

What Harry is thinking about is bail, the 10 percent cash payment for the surety bond to get her out of the bucket.

"Why worry about it?" I wink at Harry.

Harry looks at me, thinks about this for a second, then smiles. "Of course, we can front it."

It's difficult to break the habits of a lifetime, a criminal defense practice run on the edge of a dime. At the moment, Harry and I have enough cash on hand to buy a casino in Vegas. And it's not as if Emma Brauer is going to jump a jet to Brazil. For a number of years Harry and I maintained a small criminal defense practice in Capital City. We moved south to Coronado and have made this our home for almost two decades now. Until the whistle-blower's windfall we maintained a small practice. Most of our clients had few resources, like Emma, and often-times couldn't pay. Now the world is a wild and woolly new frontier with opportunities, and no doubt our share of pitfalls. We are treading on unfamiliar ground.

"It's time to go," says Harry.

"Maybe she'd like to freshen up before she leaves," says Sofia. "Would you like to go to the ladies' room?"

"That would be nice. You're so sweet." Emma turns and looks at her. "Don't know what I would do without all of you. Will they wait?" She's talking about the detectives in the lobby.

"I doubt if they'll leave without you," says Harry.

"If they don't mind," says Emma.

"And even if they do," says Harry.

"I must look a wreck." She reaches for her purse.

"Let me take that." Sofia is up off the couch, takes the purse, and opens it up on the top of my desk. She fishes inside. I am wondering what she's looking for. "You did drive here, didn't you?"

"Yes."

Sofia comes up with a set of keys and asks Emma, "Where's your car?"

The little details.

"Oh my God. I forgot all about it," says Emma. "It's down the street at one of the parking meters on this side." She gestures. "A blue Prius. Do you know how to start it?"

"Electronic key," says Sofia. "Just push the button, right?"

"You've driven one before?"

"My mom has one."

"Oh, that's great."

"We'll park it here in the lot behind the office. It'll be fine until you get out," I tell her.

"Is there anything else in your purse you want to leave with us?" Harry is not as diplomatic as Sofia. The way he puts the question makes it sound as if he's offering to stash any spare hypodermic needles Emma might be carrying.

"Not that I can think of. Unless you think I should leave my wallet and checkbook?"

"Keep them," says Harry. "They'll prepare a receipt for everything. It's better to have ID and the usual sundries. Otherwise they'll wonder where they are and come looking."

Sofia takes the smart key for the Prius off the ring and drops the rest of the keys back in Emma's purse.

"And if they ask you about your car or how you got to our office, don't answer, just refer them to us. We'll answer any questions," I tell her. They'll probably want to vacuum her car as well, looking for any evidence. But that can wait.

Harry and Sofia ease Emma out of the chair and toward the door. I get up to follow them.

"As soon as we can get a judge to set bail we'll file for a bond and move to get you out," says Harry.

"How long will that take?" she asks.

"A day, maybe two," I tell her. "One of us will see you at the jail in the morning to check on you. We should know more by then."

She turns as if to thank me and then suddenly stops in her tracks and says, "What about Dingus? I forgot all about Dingus!"

"Who's Dingus?" I ask.

"Dad's dog. He's a miniature schnauzer. Tiny little thing. He's not been the same since Dad died. Who's gonna feed him, watch him while I'm gone? He'll die."

"I'll take care of him," says Sofia. "Don't worry. But I'll need your house key to get in."

Emma says, "No, you won't. I have one of those push-button locks on the front door." She gives her the four-digit combination and Sofia taps them into the notes app on her phone.

"I can go to the house and get him this afternoon. Will he be OK until then?"

"He'll be fine. I don't know how to thank you." She gives Sofia a big hug. "You're so sweet. Wish I had a granddaughter like you."

"I'll take care of him until you get out, or I'll find somebody who can."

"He barks a lot, but he doesn't bite. Don't let him scare you."

"Not to worry." Sofia smiles. They're out the door.

Harry runs interference as the two women head for the ladies' room.

"Hold on. Where're you going?" One of the detectives tries to step around Harry to stop them.

"She's going to take a pee. You want to watch?" says Harry.

"You said you were gonna surrender her. That was five minutes ago. We're not gonna wait forever!" The detective starts jacking his jaw in Harry's face, up close like he wants to chest-butt him.

"You want to have a mess all over the backseat of your car, go ahead, pull her off the commode," says Harry. "I'll catch the video on my cell phone. We can put it on YouTube and take odds on how many million hits we get."

Outside the entrance to our office I can see the camera crews. Harry has apparently forced them out of the office onto the path out in front, where they're setting up to film the capture of Public Enemy No. 1.

The other cop steps toward me and whispers up close: "I take it there's no other way out of there." He tilts his head toward the bathroom. He's getting nervous, wondering whether maybe Emma might shimmy up an air vent in the bathroom and disappear. With the cameras all primed outside that wouldn't make a happy sound bite or a winning picture.

"Only one door," I tell him.

"What about windows?" The detective thinks I'm giving him a lawyer's answer.

"One little six-incher, high on the wall," says Harry. "So unless she's gone on a crash diet and learned how to fly in the last minute or so . . ."

"You must spend a lot of time in the ladies' room. You know so much about it." The antsy detective is in Harry's face again.

"Relax, Dick. Give it a break." His partner nudges him away before it bubbles over.

"Dick, is it?" says Harry.

"What's it to you?" says the angry cop.

"Just wondering," says Harry.

"Wondering about what?"

"How parents can be so prophetic when naming an infant."

"You wanna talk about that outside?" says the cop.

"Why not?" says Harry. "We can bring the secretaries. They can bring their cell phones. And you can get airtime." Harry starts to take off his jacket as if he's about to go ten rounds with the guy.

"Harry!" I look at him.

"I was only kidding." He smiles. "Dick knows I respect him. We were just having some fun."

"I wasn't," says the cop.

"Jeez!" says Harry. "And here I was thinking you had such a great sense of humor."

FOUR

One of the things garnered by our windfall whistle-blower award is that Harry and I are now the proud owners of an online political news tabloid in D.C. called the "Washington Gravesite." I am busy going over a spreadsheet showing monthly overhead costs and revenue, a business enterprise that appears to have been largely a labor of love for its prior owner.

It's a long story, but the short version is that a young reporter, a friend of my daughter, Sarah, a kid named Alex Ives, who worked for the site and whose down-in-the-heels drunk-driving case resulted in our financial bounty, needed a job when the case ended. His boss, Tory Graves, who owned the site, had been murdered. So Harry and I bought the thing and installed Ives as the managing editor. It was probably a mistake, but we did it. It's the problem with money. You spend it. Sometimes in foolish ways. But it didn't feel right putting Alex out on the street when we had benefited to such a great extent from his case.

Neither Harry nor I know squat about publishing. We would give the thing to Ives for a dollar, but he lacks the capital to keep it running. So for the time being, Harry and I are owner and publisher. The blind leading the stupid. We have laid down one rule: Ives is to send us any story that offers up even the vestige of a whiff of defamation. This much we know. Libel is that red line you don't want to cross. If Harry and I can't tell exactly where it is, we can find another lawyer in town with a plumb bob who can.

We have made a lot of enemies in and around Capitol Hill: members of Congress and their staff, powerful people. Some of their friends were outed to the Treasury and the Internal Revenue Service, found holding offshore bank accounts that were undisclosed for purposes of US taxes. They have been busy answering questions; some of them have been closeted before federal grand juries, trying to explain where the money came from and for what purpose it was paid. The back taxes and penalties that are still being tabulated are the source of our client's whistleblower award and our windfall legal fees, that and a mammoth fine that was leveled against the Swiss bank that was involved.

The money is good. The ill will from high places is not. It has us periodically looking over our shoulders wondering when the knife is coming and from which direction. Having wealth makes you a target for hired legal guns, get-rich courthouse sharks looking to fatten their wallets and perhaps cozy up to powerful political players. This is something we never had to worry about when we were impecunious, which is lawyer jargon for "broke." People wanted to kill us. But that was different. This is personal.

There is a comfort factor in being judgment-proof, a certain peace of mind that comes from knowing that you lack the value of a meatless sun-bleached bone, something that two junkyard dogs might want to fight over in a civil courtroom where the only issue is money. You have it and they want it.

Most criminal defense lawyers aren't worth the time or trouble of a civil suit. In a malpractice case it's tough finding a sympathetic jury where the plaintiff seeking money damages and crying that you blew his defense is a career felon with a record longer than a laser beam. Odds are that if he didn't do the last three crimes, he did the six before that.

Besides, the most pressing remedy for malpractice in a criminal case is a petition by way of appeal for a new trial. Anything to get out of the joint. Sue your defense lawyer for damages and he will probably sanitize your trial file. Doctors bury their mistakes. Lawyers shred them. I can't remember the last time a criminal defense attorney was sued for malpractice. I suspect it happens, but with the regularity of an ice age.

But now that we have money, we worry about this, along with everything else. Harry tells me he's not sleeping as well at night. He is already starting to hate other lawyers, and not just criminal prosecutors.

There is a gentle rap on my door. It opens. Sofia smiles her way into my office and closes the door behind her. "Joselyn just pulled into the lot. She'll be here in a minute."

I check my watch. We have a date, my significant other and me. We have talked about getting married but we're afraid it might ruin the deal. Formalities like familiarity breeding contempt.

Sofia has finished shuffling the cars behind our office and lays my car keys on my desk. "I parked her car in front of yours. Is that OK? It was the only space available." She is talking about Brauer's Prius.

"It'll have to do."

She glances at me as she messes with Emma Brauer's smart key from the car. "I have to go get the dog. I'll leave this with you." She sets the key on the desk. "You wanted to have Herman take a look at her car, maybe get some pictures in case the police come to take it away. What are you guys gonna see tonight?"

"Don't know. Joselyn always chooses movies with Fandango," I tell her. "The little bar code on her phone. It's magic for tickets."

"QR code," says Sofia.

"What?"

"It's called a QR code: quick response code," she says. "You're going to have to learn to do tickets. Otherwise you're gonna spend your life watching chick flicks."

I look up at her. She winks at me. Twenty-something going on forty. The young men she is dating don't have a chance. In terms of maturity, she has twenty years on them, all wrapped up in a package the maker designed for male seduction. Nature's most efficient lure.

"I don't mind," I tell her. "Romantic comedy is my speed."

"My kind of date." She smiles. "The guys I used to go out with were into heavy action."

The way she talks about her dates, in the past tense, makes me wonder if she's joined a convent.

"All that fast action on screen gives me motion sickness," I tell her.

"It wasn't the action on screen I was worried about. It was their hands I had to watch," she says.

It seems we're talking at cross-purposes. The age-old conflict between men and women, that blurring boundary line between lust and love.

"You should try streaming some movies on your iPad," she tells me.

"I don't have an iPad."

"Why not?"

My door starts to open.

"I wouldn't know how to use it."

"Tell Joselyn to buy you one. I'll set it up, show you how."

"She has one," I tell her.

"What do I have?" Joselyn breezes through the door and closes it behind her.

"An iPad," I say.

"Then she can show you how to use it," says Sofia.

"Yeah, I love it." Joselyn crosses the room and gives me a kiss. "What are you two up to? If I didn't know better, I'd be jealous."

"I have to go pick up a dog."

"Are you getting a dog?" asks Joselyn.

"It's a long story," I tell her. I look at my watch. It's almost five. Joselyn and I have dinner reservations at six.

Sofia shouts: "Damn it!" Her hand goes to her mouth as she sucks the tip of her finger.

"What's the matter?" Joselyn turns.

"Broke a nail."

"Oh, jeez! Let me see." Joselyn is on her like a mother hen examining her finger. "Ouch, that's bad."

If I had a coronary I would have to wait. Female code blue. Bring on the crash cart, nail files, and emery boards.

Joselyn wastes no time. She digs in her purse. "How'd you do that?"

"I don't know. I think I snagged it on that ring from Emma's keys. Getting the key to her car off of it."

"Who's Emma?"

"Part of the long story," I tell her. "I'll fill you in over dinner."

Joselyn comes up with a package of those little wooden sandpaper files from her purse and goes to work on Sofia's finger.

"Those things are treacherous. With nails like these what are you doing messing with key rings? You should let Paul do that." Joselyn is looking at the wounded appendage, but she's talking to me.

"Sorry. I didn't realize," I tell her.

"You think the police will come looking for her car? You said the police might impound it," says Sofia.

"Almost five o'clock, they won't come again today. Which reminds me. When you get to her house, if the cops are there, they could still be executing the search warrant." We haven't yet seen a warrant for her car. "Give me a call on my cell if they're still there."

"Sure."

"If they give you any trouble, take one of your business cards, tell them you're with the firm and that you're there to pick up the dog. There shouldn't be any." I am guessing if the young men in blue are still there, she and Dingus will get a police escort to the car, with the cops all collecting business cards. I am hoping that they haven't already called animal control. If so, we will have to retrieve the pooch from the pound.

"There you go. Best I can do," says Joselyn. "How's it feel?"

"Fine. Thanks." Sofia gives her a hug and says, "Bye! Have a good time at the show," as she heads for the door.

"Drive carefully," I tell her. "You have her address, right?"

"Keyed it into my iPhone. Trust me, I won't get lost."

By all rights I should have Herman doing this. He's the firm's investigator, a burly six-foot-three black man who's been part of the firm's family for more than a decade. But he's out of the office this afternoon, working another case.

"Give me a call if there's any problem. I'll leave my phone on vibrate just in case."

"I'll be fine. See you Monday morning," she says.

"And Sofia!"

She turns to look at me.

"Thanks, you were a huge help. Brauer was upset. She didn't expect to be arrested, not here, not today. You being here made it easier on all of us."

"Thanks." She beams a smile at me from the open doorway. It melts me in my chair. Then she's out the door. A few seconds later I see her jogging, long-legged in her short skirt, down the walkway out in front toward her car.

FIVE

The female voice from the maps on the iPhone told her that she had arrived. Her destination was "on the right." It was a good thing. Sofia was having trouble finding or reading any of the numbers on the houses. The single cone of light, the naked ray from a vapor lamp that hung off one of the telephone poles halfway down the street, offered little relief.

What poor illumination punctured the darkness came here and there, soft yellow emissions filtered through slatted blinds and closed living room curtains from the houses that lined both sides of the street. The homes looked as if they were shoehorned onto the narrow lots and piled up against the wooden fences or the occasional brick walls that separated them.

Once she confirmed the address from the four brass numbers on the wall next to the garage door, Sofia swung her car into the narrow driveway. She put it in park, turned off the engine, and doused her headlights. It had taken her more than an hour to follow the snaking directions north from Coronado. She had been bucking the end of the traffic bulge from the evening rush all the way out, and she was tired. She was anxious to pick up the dog and get home.

As she stepped from her car, the flicker from a television screen in one of the houses across the way stabbed the darkness with blue flashes. Like distant lightning, the thunder followed. Climactic bars of muted music from the sound track and the noise of canned explosions carried on the cool evening air. Signs of life in the suburbs.

None came from Brauer's house. Like its owner, the place looked every inch its age, worn and forlorn. It stood deserted and dark behind the small island of dying Bermuda grass. Two dead and fallen palm fronds lay in the planter bed between the grass and the front of the house. Emma wasn't much of a gardener, it seemed.

Except for the fact that Sofia had talked to one of Emma's neighbors during the drive from the office, she would never have guessed that little more than an hour earlier the place had been crawling with cops. Emma had given her the neighbor's phone number as she and Sofia chatted in the bathroom before the police took Emma away.

And a good thing, too. Because when Sofia called, the neighbor told her that the police, who were just finishing up their search, were making an issue over the dog. They insisted that Dingus had to be taken by animal control to the pound.

The neighbor offered to take charge of the dog and to care for it until Brauer came home. But the police said no. This was out of the question. Protocol required animal control to take custody unless the owner gave express authority in writing to transfer the dog to someone else. There were no other family members living in the house, so that was it. They told her that Brauer or anyone she designated could pick the dog up at the pound later, as long as they did it within thirty days. After that the dog would either be put up for adoption or be put down.

Sofia's blood was up. They were not taking the dog. Not if she had anything to say about it. She could have called the office for instructions, but she didn't. Harry had left in the afternoon and by now Paul would be at dinner. She had Madriani's phone number, but why bother him? She could handle it. Sofia told the neighbor to grab one of the detectives in charge and have him come into her house and get on the phone.

She licked her dry lips and took a deep breath as she waited. When the cop came on the line Sofia identified herself, and then in a cold, measured tone she told him: "I'm with the law firm of Madriani and Hinds. I am informing you now that under the terms of a signed retainer agreement *our firm* represents Emma Brauer. I understand you've got a problem with Ms. Brauer's dog."

"No problem," said the detective. "It'll be taken care of by animal control."

"I am instructing you now that when you have completed your search of the premises you are to leave the animal in the house and lock the door. Do you understand?"

There was no reply from the cop.

"The firm has made arrangements to have the dog picked up and to provide for its care. Do I make myself clear?"

Mostly what the detective heard was the level of assurance and the command tone coming from the other end. His cop's ego wanted to tell her to go to hell, to call in the pound and let them take the dog. Better yet, he could have shot the beast while the mouthpiece on the line listened to it yelp.

He didn't need the grief. Not over a yapping four-pound ball of fuzz. He waited a second and then genuflected. "Fine! It'll save us the trouble of a phone call and we won't have to wait for animal control. But understand that if something happens to the dog, it gets killed or lost, once we leave here it's no longer our responsibility. It's on you. Do I make myself clear, counselor?"

She wasn't responsible for the man's sketchy assumptions. Sofia never told him she was a lawyer. So before he could ask how to spell her name, she said, "Thank you, Detective," and hung up.

She listened as she stood out in front of the house. There was no sign or sound of the dog. Still, unless the cop got pissed off after they talked and had second thoughts, Dingus should be somewhere inside the house.

Sofia walked to the front door. She used her phone like a flashlight to illuminate the buttons on the touch pad for the lock. As soon as she hit the first one the pad lit up. She punched the other three numbers and watched as the little green light flickered. She heard the locking mechanism as it released and turned the knob sliding the dead bolt back. She tried the latch and the door opened.

Inside it was pitch black. She closed the door and waited for her eyes to adjust and listened for the dog. Nothing. She wondered if maybe there was a doggie door in the back, in which case it might be out in the yard. If so, she wondered why it didn't bark when she pulled up into the drive.

Sofia didn't want to turn on too many lights in the house and risk drawing attention, in case neighbors saw it and called the police. The one neighbor, the woman she talked to earlier, wasn't home. She had an appointment and was already running late when Sofia talked to her. Otherwise the woman would have taken the dog herself, gathered everything else, and held it for Sofia until she arrived. As it was, Sofia was on her own.

She pressed the button on her phone and used the light to navigate past the opening to the living room and down the hall toward what looked like the kitchen, at the back of the house. The leash and the dog food were supposed to be there in a cupboard on the right-hand side near the kitchen table. Emma may have been frazzled but her directions were spot-on. In less than a minute Sofia found everything she was looking for, including the dog's bedding, one of those padded igloos.

But still, there was no sign of Dingus. She called for him and listened. She heard nothing except the hum of the motor from the refrigerator on the other side of the kitchen. Sofia was getting worried. Maybe the cops left a window open and the dog got out. She remembered the ominous words of the detective that the animal was now her responsibility.

There was a doggie door at the back of the house. She looked through the kitchen window into the tiny yard outside. It was nothing but concrete with a small strip of grass. She flipped on the back porch light and peered out through the window. No sign of the dog. The yard was enclosed by a six-foot cinder-block wall. Unless he was an Olympic-class jumper there was no way he could have gotten out there.

She headed out of the kitchen, down the hall, and checked the two bedrooms she had passed on her way in. The doors were both open. If he was there he could have come out. Maybe he was locked in one of the closets. Dogs get into trouble, especially small ones.

The first room obviously belonged to Emma. Her clothes were in the closet, but no dog. Sofia checked under the bed, flashed her light just in case. She checked the other room. There were items belonging to a man inside: a few shirts and trousers and some old shoes on the floor. It felt a little eerie standing there knowing that the old man was dead. Maybe the dog was hiding under his bed. She checked. No Dingus.

Sofia's worry was approaching panic mode. How would she tell Paul that she lost him? Who was going to break the news to Emma? Sofia should have allowed the cops to take the dog. Instead she had played smart-ass with the detective and now she and the dog were paying the price. She wondered if the cop had turned him loose out of spite. She should have used a friendlier tone, less authority, more warmth. Then she thought, Why would he do that? It was her fault for assuming the responsibility. At the very least she should have called Paul for instructions.

The thought that she could get fired flashed through her brain for an instant, then was quickly extinguished. She knew they wouldn't can her, not for this. Nonetheless, she didn't like it.

Along with native good looks, Sofia was armed with a well-tuned antenna for assessing people. It wasn't reserved for men, though they were often quicker to gauge and more susceptible, the same way you can sink a ship faster when its radar is blinded. Harry would give her a star for jerking the cop around on the phone. Paul might tell her to call him next time. But that would be the end of it.

They had reputations as tigers in the courtroom, but outside the railing, their claws were generally retracted. You could post placards on their desks, one reading "easygoing" and the other "forgiving." It came with the turf. It's tough to be an unremitting boss when you spend your days like a priest dispensing absolution to people accused of committing crimes. Sofia was a quick study. She already knew the secret pass phrase to the defense bar—"who among us has not committed sin?" The difficulty was in converting others to the cult: the jurors and the occasional judge. She knew that before she could open her mouth to say she was sorry, Paul and Harry would be churning excuses in their brains to forgive her. And it would have nothing to do with her gender or her looks. They would have done the same for the bearded lady in the circus.

At the moment, Sofia was the one kicking her own ass. She had volunteered to do something and had failed. If the dog was lost, she was the one who would have to tell Emma. She let them all down, the two partners, the people who gave her a chance and the client, a woman behind bars whose dog was now missing. She would have to make it up. Find the dog or burn every spare moment of her time looking for it.

With visions of her weekends spent stapling signs with Dingus's picture over half of San Diego, she headed out of the bedroom and checked the bathroom across the hall. He wasn't there. She stormed back down the hall toward the rear of the house. She flipped on the outside light once more, unlocked the door, and stepped out.

As soon as she did she heard the sound: barking, somewhere off in the distance. Then a reply, a deeper bark that seemed to come from another direction. Then quickly in succession, two more. Neighbors' dogs. Then the first barked again. It sounded like a small dog. But it was too far away to be Dingus, unless, of course, he got out and ended up trapped somewhere else. She thought to herself, There must be at least a dozen dogs in the neighborhood. It was hard to tell which direction it came from.

She looked toward the wall on the far side of the yard. The top of the concrete blocks was obscured by a large wandering wisteria. It clung to several metal pipes protruding up through the center wall. The pipes were bent so that they leaned over the edge of the yard. Between them were strung heavy strands of galvanized wire, supporting the tangle of tentacles from the vine as they spread across the top of the wall. The concrete pad underneath was piled inches deep in dead, dry leaves as if it hadn't been swept in recent memory.

Sofia stepped to the right, away from the mess at the foot of the wall, and walked around the corner of the house. There she found a closed wooden gate. She checked it. It was shut tight and latched. Even in five-inch heels she could just barely reach the toggle to the latch on the other side, over the top of the gate. She pressed on it, but it wouldn't open. It was either frozen with rust or locked. She peeked through a crack in the wood. Beyond the gate was a concrete walk that led along the side of the house. It disappeared around the corner of the garage and out toward the street in front. If Dingus had gotten beyond the gate he was long gone. Again she heard the high-pitched bark. It seemed a little more distant now.

As soon as she turned at the corner of the house and headed toward the back door she noticed that the yap got louder. She realized that it was coming from somewhere beyond the concrete wall on the far side of the yard. Maybe there was a dog run on the other side. If so, there was no gate. At least none she could see.

She listened for moment. It barked again, then a crescendo of deeper and louder replies. No question it was a small dog. But it was too far away to be coming from just beyond the wall. Sofia took a tentative step in that direction, then another. She was three feet from the cinder-block wall, toes deep in dead leaves, when the dog barked again. It was then that she noticed the slight muffled echo, something almost tubular in the quality of the sound, or maybe subterranean, as if the dog were in a tunnel somewhere underground. If so, he might be closer than she thought.

SIX

ofia stepped back a few feet away from the wall and looked up toward the top of the cinder blocks. Through the tangle of wisteria and the dark night she could just barely make out the roofline of the house on the other side of the wall. As she peered through openings in the vegetation and followed the ridgeline of the roof in the direction of the street out in front, she realized that the structure beyond the wall didn't belong to a neighbor at all. It was part of Emma's house, an L-shaped wing that wrapped around behind the concrete wall. It connected to Brauer's house on the far side of the kitchen.

The adrenaline rush had her moving at a run, clicking high heels over the dead leaves as she headed across the concrete toward the back door. A heel turned and Sofia went down onto the hard cement. She sprawled on one knee, both hands out in front of her to catch herself. Her cell phone skittered across the concrete like a hockey puck and slammed into the cement step leading to the back door.

Damn it! she thought. This was not what she needed.

Her knee burned, along with the palms of both hands, which had taken the brunt of the fall. She stayed on the ground for a long moment and waited for the pain to pass. Slowly she lifted her hands one at a time and checked her palms to see if they were bleeding. Except for a few abrasions, some ground-in dirt, and the broken nail from earlier in the day, they looked OK.

Sofia reached back and touched her knee. The second she did she felt it burn. Her fingers gently plied the raw skin. She knew that by to-morrow she would have a lump like an egg, with a bruise the color and size of a thundercloud to go with it. She looked back and saw her shoe, the high heel that turned on her foot. The heel had broken off. It was hanging from the shoe by a torn strip of fabric.

"Get what you pay for!" she whispered under her breath as she slowly began to rise. Sofia had bought the heels at a discount shop two days before her interview at the firm, thinking she got a deal. Instead what she got was a banged-up knee. It was all she could afford. She was staring at college loans and car payments, as well as rent with two friends in an apartment in the Gaslamp Quarter that she couldn't afford without help.

The source of that help was a secret. No one knew, including her parents. They were not rich. They couldn't assist her any longer, not financially. Her father lost his job as a bookkeeper during the recession. At fifty-eight he was working two part-time jobs trying to pay off the mortgage on their house, which they had borrowed against when he got fired.

Sofia and her roommates kidded each other that at some point when they were older and established, driving around in Mercedes and living in suburban splendor, they would look back at this threadbare period as "the best of times."

None of them believed it. Sofia knew she couldn't pay for law school without more help. Her life was in a holding pattern until things could be worked out.

She took a deep breath and stood there balanced on her good right leg, using the injured one as an outrigger to keep herself from falling over. She waited a few seconds and put her bare foot flat on the cold concrete. She took a few tentative steps, tested her banged-up knee, and hobbled on the single five-inch heel on her other foot. From what she could tell, nothing was broken.

Sofia took off the good shoe and picked up the broken one, the heel still dangling from the torn faux leather material. She walked toward her cell phone, which was lying screen-down on the cold concrete, and picked it up. The plastic protector on the back was nicked and scratched along one side. One corner was dented.

When she turned the phone over, her heart sank. Cracks spread like a spiderweb across the tempered glass screen protector. Under it there were several nicks and what looked like a hairlike crack in the screen itself. She wondered if the phone would work. She hit the button at the bottom and the backlit screen fired up. She held her thumb to the button until it read her print. The icons assembled under the fractured glass. She touched the screen with her finger and tried to flip the page to the next screen, but it didn't respond. She was sick. Maybe they could fix it.

The phone was Sofia's prized possession, that and her car. She wanted to cry, but she couldn't find the tears.

The dog barked.

Sofia turned and looked at the wall in the yard as if she wanted to kill the pooch. She knew it wasn't to blame, but still. Instead, she slipped the shattered phone into her jacket pocket and stepped toward the door. Next to it was a trash can. She lifted the lid and dropped her shoes onto a couple of plastic bags of trash in the bottom of the can and put the lid back on. Dejected, she headed into the house.

Inside the kitchen Sofia headed straight toward the closed door next to the stove. She opened it and looked down the dimly lit hallway. There was another bathroom at the far end. The door was open. A window there allowed in some light.

She took out her phone and turned on the screen to add a little illumination, then headed down the hall. In front of the open bathroom door she turned right and saw another door, closed, about ten feet away. In the distance she could hear the dog yapping. Finally! About time, she thought. She opened the door. The barking got louder, but the dog didn't come out.

"Where the hell are you?" She called him by name several times. "Here, Dingus!" All she got in reply was more barking. She flashed the light from her phone around the room. The dog continued to bark. If he was there he was hiding.

The room looked like a study, a man's office. Sofia figured it must have belonged to Emma's father. There was a rolltop desk against the far wall and an old swivel-back wooden chair in front of it with some filing cabinets against the side wall on the left. The window was covered by what looked like an old olive-drab army blanket, dusty with cobwebs clinging to it.

In her bare feet, Sofia was careful where she put them. She glimpsed a wooden yardstick next to the desk, shined the light on it, checked it for spiders, then picked it up. Using it like a sword she pulled the blanket off the curtain rod and suddenly the room came to life. Light from the house next door streamed in.

The room was a mess. There were papers all over the floor, dust and cobwebs everywhere she looked. The trash in the can next to the desk was overflowing. Against the wall behind her was a gun rack. It held several rifles, all of them covered with dust. Everywhere she looked was a filigree of spiderwebs. A map on the wall to her right looked like Western Europe. She recognized France. There was a door next to the map that was closed.

It had to be a closet, since there wasn't room for much of anything else. Just beyond the room in that direction was the concrete wall outside. Next to the closed door, sitting on the floor, were two pairs of black leather boots, old and cracked, abandoned as if someone had forgotten to put them away, maybe fifty years ago. There was no doubt about it, the sound from the barking dog was coming from beyond the closed door.

Sofia kept her eyes on it as she drew near. She held the light from her phone toward the opening side of the door, reached over, turned the knob, and pulled. As it swung open she expected to get her first glimpse of the dog as he came rushing out. But he didn't. The closet was empty except for a few items of clothing on hangers. They looked like assorted pieces of old military uniforms. She could hear the dog more clearly now. It was coming from somewhere down, beneath the floor. He couldn't be more than a few feet away. The barking was incessant, almost constant. To Sofia it sounded like a dog who had gotten himself in trouble. Wherever he was, he wanted out.

She flashed the light toward the floor inside the closet and saw the inlaid brass finger pull. It was countersunk into the thick hardwood flooring. She ran the light across the floor to the other side of the closet and saw the brass hinges on the back of the trapdoor.

Sofia wasted no time. She stooped over, reached down, put her finger through the loop in the brass, and pulled. The door was heavy, three foot square, solid wood, three inches of oak flooring and subfloor. She jerked it with all her strength and slowly it started to come up.

It was a good thing Sofia didn't have to lift it out. She could never have done it alone. It was all she could do to raise the door on its hinges and lean it against the wall on the other side of the closet.

As she looked down into the darkness she could hear the dog yapping wildly. She shined the light down into the yawning hole. Two gleaming eyes set into the black fuzzy face shined back at her. Dingus bounced and barked like a rubber ball all over the concrete floor in the cellar. Sofia didn't have to be a dog interpreter to realize he was overjoyed that someone was finally coming to get him.

"How did you get down there?" She looked at the fixed ladder, almost vertical, straight up and down. There was no way the dog could have climbed down. The drop to the floor below was at least ten feet. The fall onto hard concrete would certainly have injured him. She assumed there had to be another way into the cellar, but Sofia wasn't going to waste any more time looking for it.

"Give me a second."

Now that the door was open and Dingus could see the way out, he wanted to be there immediately.

Sofia had to free up her hands to use the ladder. She slipped the phone back into her pocket. Then, holding on to the frame at the edge of the closet door, she carefully eased her foot into the gaping darkness beneath the floor. She felt with her foot until she found the top rung of the ladder, put her weight on it, and started down. The rest was easy. A few seconds later she was standing on the cold concrete down below, looking up at the square of light above her. Dingus jumped almost up to her waist. He pawed and scratched her legs as he barked.

End of a perfect night, thought Sofia. She could have been out for drinks with friends. Instead here she was down in a dark hole trying to rescue a dog who was scratching her legs all to hell. She reached down in the darkness, got her hands around him, lifted him up, and tucked him against her chest, holding him tight with her left arm. Reaching out with her right hand she grabbed the ladder. Phantom vision from the fine nerves in her face sensed something up close as it penetrated the zone in front of her sightless eyes. It tickled the tip of her nose and the tiny hairs on her right ear. Sofia stopped for a second to scratch her face and rub her ear in case it might be a spiderweb. But it wasn't . . .

SEVEN

"id you give Sofia the day off?" It's Monday morning and Harry is standing at the front counter in the office as I come through the door.

"No." Coffee in my hand, briefcase under my arm, I'm running late. It's already after ten.

"Well, she's not here. She's supposed to do the filings at the courthouse. Be nice to have them done before noon," says Harry.

"Where is she?"

He shrugs a shoulder.

"I've been calling her since just before nine. There's no answer." This from Sally, our receptionist.

"Try it again," I tell her.

"I have. Several times. It rolls right over to voicemail. She's either on the line talking or she's turned off her phone."

"Well, check it again. Maybe she hung up," I say.

Sally punches the number for Sofia's cell on the reception console at her desk, waits a second for the auto dial, then slowly shakes her head as she listens through the headset. "There's no answer. Just 'leave a message.' I left one earlier." She hits the button and hangs up.

"Does she have a home number?" I ask.

"If she does she never gave it to me," says Sally.

"Shoot her a text message," I tell her. "Ask her to call in."

I glance at Harry. "Don't look at me. You're the one who hired her."

Harry is still searching for his own assistant. I suspect this could take a while. When it comes to the office Harry's like a cloistered monk. He doesn't like strangers invading the sanctuary of his secluded contrarian monastery down the hall, even if they're trying to help him. Strike that—*especially* if they're trying to help him.

"It's not like her to be late," I say.

"How would you know? You keep banker's hours," he says. "You'll have to give her a little more time before she's gonna have you properly trained." Harry gives me an I-told-you-so smirk and goes right back to the question of the day: "In the meantime, who's gonna do the filings?"

"How about Selena?" Selena Johnson is Harry's secretary.

"She's busy!" he says. Harry is giving me a message: Sofia is my hire. I created the problem, so now I own it.

During all of this, Brenda Gomes, my secretary, has been standing, peeking over the wall of her cubicle like a spotter checking to see whose target's been hit. As I lift my eyes she drops down behind her carpeted barricade faster than a doughboy nailed by a sniper.

Before I can even ask her, Harry says, "Fine, let's have Brenda do it!" Ever helpful, he's quick to give me a hand, making points with my secretary. I will owe her a lunch, and Sofia, when I can get her to call in, will owe her an apology.

I finish dictating some letters into the computer behind my desk and check my watch. It's just before noon. I'm thinking of grabbing Harry and getting some lunch when the phone on my desk rings. I turn and look. It's the com line. I pick it up. "Yes?"

Sally's voice: "There're two detectives here from the sheriff's department to see you."

For a moment I think maybe I've blown a scheduled appointment. It wouldn't be the first time. I check my watch to see if it's stopped and glance at the calendar. But both my watch and the clock on my desk say no and my calendar is clear.

"What's it about? Did they give you a client name?"

"No. Just a business card."

"Ask 'em for the client's name and pull the file, please," I tell her.

She checks. I hear the muffled voices as she covers the mouthpiece with her hand. When she comes back on the line she says, "It's not about a client. It's something private. They want to talk to you."

The way she says it triggers an alarm in my head and acid in my stomach.

"Show them in." I hang up, turn, and dim the screen behind me. Before I can swing back around there's a rap on wood from the outside.

"It's open."

As it does I look up. A hulking shadow in a dark suit stands there filling my doorway. He's big enough to play linebacker for the NFL but looks old enough to be retired. I'm guessing in his early fifties, close-cropped hair, something between an old flattop and a butch. What's left of it is losing the battle to the rebels in the war between the brown and the gray.

"Mr. Madriani?"

"Come in. Have a seat."

As he clears the door I can see the other one, younger, more dapper, blond, tall, and lean in tan slacks and a dark polo shirt. He strolls in and navigates around the mountain that is his partner. His unbuttoned blue blazer flashes open so that he gives me a peek at the bulge of brown leather and black gunmetal threaded onto his belt. It's accented by the glint of brass from the shield on his other side.

The older man in the wrinkled serge suit says, "I take it you are Paul Madriani?" They don't sit, they just stand there looking down at me. The dour expression on his face, his tone, the way he looks at me like an insect under glass, cause me to wonder if they're about to arrest me.

"I am. Is there something I can help you with?"

"I'm Detective Brad Owen. This is my partner, Jerry Noland. We're with the sheriff's Homicide Unit. I'm afraid we have some bad news for you. You have an employee by the name of Sadie Maria Leon?"

The flood of adrenaline to my heart gives birth to a surge of panic. I read it in his eyes, hear it in the undertaker's tone of his voice, a message he has delivered a thousand times. The oracle of pitiless loss. I know what is coming, but I don't want to hear it.

"No. No. The girl who works here, her name is Sofia." I shake my head. "You've got the wrong person." I want them to go away.

He looks at a notebook in his hand. "Name on the driver's license reads Sadie Maria—"

"Our girl uses the name Sofia."

"She did," says the younger cop. "But not anymore. She's dead." He drops Sofia's business card on my desk directly in front of me. Disbelief slams at light speed into the wall of reality. "We found that one and several more just like it in the purse near her body."

The brief moment of premonition is not enough to dampen the shock. I sit there as my paralyzed brain tries to cope. Denial and desire freeze time as my mind scrambles madly to swim back up the river to those golden seconds of safety before they knocked on my door.

EIGHT

A re you all right?"

My eyes wander from the business card on my desk to the sea of blue serge standing in front of me. When I look up, the older cop, the one named Owen, is staring at me.

"Are you OK?"

"Yeah. I'm fine." I lie to him. I am breathing hard. Beads of cold sweat are erupting like popcorn from the flesh on my forehead.

"Can we get you anything?" he asks.

"No."

"Do you take any medications?"

I shake my head, though at the moment I could kill for a sleeping pill, anything to knock me out so that when I wake this nightmare will be over.

"A glass of water?" he asks.

"No." It's strange but the only thing I can think of right now is how I am going to tell Joselyn. I look at the cop, try to collect myself, and finally come up with a cogent question: "How did it happen?"

"We're not sure." It's the younger cop, the one named Noland, who speaks. "A jogger found her body early this morning out off Highway 94 in the El Cajon–La Mesa area. Do you have any idea what she might have been doing out there?"

I shake my head.

The older detective says, "When's the last time you saw her?"

I try to think for a moment, clear my head. "It was Friday, late in the day. I'm not certain of the time. Probably around five thirty. I'm not sure."

The older one starts to take notes. "Where was this?" he asks.

"Here in the office," I tell him. "She was headed out on an errand."

"Where was she going?"

"To pick up a dog. Was there a small dog with her?"

"Not in her car or anywhere near the body," says Noland. "Where was she supposed to pick up this dog?"

"Client's house. I'd have to get the address," I tell him.

"We'll wait," he says.

"I'm sorry. I need to think. I'm a bit rattled."

"We understand." The older man seems sympathetic. The younger one, not so much.

"You're sure it's her?" I ask.

"No one has formally identified her yet," says Noland. "And the face was a little distorted. But there's no question it matched the picture on the driver's license."

My heart sinks.

"This house she was going to. Where was it located?" asks Owen.

"I'm not sure how much I can tell you. The client was gone and there was no one else living in the house, so someone had to pick up the dog."

"We need to have that address," he says. "If that's where she was headed, we're gonna need to check it out. Was it in the El Cajon or La Mesa area?"

"I don't think so. I'm not sure. Tell you the truth, I've never been to the house." Brauer's file is still on my desk, but I don't want to reach for it and open it in front of them. The fact is, I have no idea where she lives. But the second they leave I intend to find out.

"Can you give us the name of the client that owns the house?" asks Noland.

"If I was going to do that, I'd just tell you where she lived."

"Why don't you help us?" says Owen. "We're trying to find out who killed the girl. You do want to help us, don't you?"

"I'd love to, but I can tell you that my client's not involved, if that's what you're thinking."

"How can you be sure?" says Noland.

"Because she has a ironclad alibi."

"How can you know that unless you know the time of death?" he says.

"Trust me, I know. Where exactly did they find the body?" I ask.

"Make you a deal," says Noland. "You tell us where the house is, we'll tell you where they found the body. Then we can compare notes."

I consider this for a moment. Emma Brauer couldn't possibly be involved. She was in jail before Sofia left the office, and she remains there this morning. Harry is still working on bail. If somehow her house was involved in Sofia's murder we need to know about it before anyone goes back in and fouls the evidence. The place has already been searched by the city PD in Brauer's case, and it's not likely that the two sheriff's detectives are going to find anything relating to Robert Brauer's death since they aren't even looking for it and are not involved. I look at them. "Better yet, tell you what: I'll take you to the house on one condition."

"What's that?" Noland looks at me.

"You take us to the crime scene where you found the body, myself, my partner, and our office PI and let us look around . . ."

"Can't do that," says Noland. "Can't have you tramping through the evidence."

"We won't. We'll keep our distance. We can probably help you."

"How?" says Owen.

"What was she wearing when you found the body?"

He scratches his head. "Yellow dress of some kind and a jacket."

"It sounds like what she had on Friday afternoon when she left here. But I can't be sure unless I see the body, as it lies." I want to know who killed Sofia and why. The place where she was murdered might give us some answers.

The two detectives look at each other. "He could identify the body," says Owen. "Save her parents some grief."

"I can do that," I tell them.

"Why not?" says Owen.

Noland's not sure. "We need to check with the lieutenant. We'll call you a little later. They'll still be working the scene. First we have a few questions."

"Go ahead," I tell him.

"This client of yours is a woman. You said 'she' has an alibi."

"Slip of the tongue," I tell him. "She was in jail all weekend since Friday afternoon. She's still there."

"And you say there's no one else living in the house with her?" asks Noland.

"As far as I know. That was the reason Sofia was headed to pick up the dog."

"But you don't know if she ever got there?" says Owen.

"One way to find out."

"What's that?" he says.

"See if the dog's still there."

This catches their attention. They look at each other as if it hadn't dawned on them.

"Could be dead by now," says Noland. "Three days without food or water."

"We don't know that. But I'll be sure to find out, and when I do, I'll let you know."

"If that's a crime scene, you'll need to stay away from it," says Noland.

"We're not gonna know that until we go look."

"Let me ask you," says Owen. "Did you hear anything from the girl after she left the office on Friday?"

I shake my head. "No. As far as I know, no one else in the office did, either. We were worried about her when she didn't show up for work this morning. We called her cell phone several times, but there was no answer. Did you find her phone?"

"We're still looking," says Owen.

"About your client," says Noland. "You say she was in jail. Is she married? Any boyfriends, any males who might have had a key to her house, maybe lived there with her at one time?"

"She's not married and has no boyfriends that I know of."

"You're sure of that?" says Owen.

"As sure as I can be."

Noland asks: "What is she in for?"

"That I won't tell you. But I'm sure you'll find out, sooner or later."

"How long did Sofia work for you?" asks Owen.

"Eight months, maybe nine. I'd have to check our records."

"Who sent her after the dog? To the woman's house?" asks Owen.

This is a sore point. Ever since they walked in and told me what happened I've been asking myself the same question. Did I send her out there? "I'd have to think about that," I tell him.

"What does that mean?" says Owen.

"I'm not sure if anyone actually sent her."

"Are you telling us she went out there on her own?" says Noland.

"No. Not exactly. You had to know Sofia. She was a self-starter. If something needed to be done, she did it. She didn't ask. It was one of the things I liked about her. You didn't have to sit there and tell her what to do. But . . ."

"But what?" says Owen.

"Like every other good thing in life, it had its downsides. There was always the risk that she might take on more than she could handle."

"Did she?" asks Noland.

I think about it for a moment. "Nothing serious. Couple of times. Little things I don't even remember now. Occasionally I'd keep an eye on her. But she was learning fast. And I am gonna miss her."

"But you say you didn't send her out to the house to get the dog?"

"I knew she was going out, if that's what you mean. I told her to be careful."

"Why would you say that?" asks Noland.

I think about it for a second and then I lie. "Because she'd put in a long day at the office. She was probably tired. I didn't want to see her get into an accident."

A politician might call this spin, but I know better. Traffic was the least of my concerns. I was worried she might get tangled up with the city PD and their search of Brauer's house, overextend herself, and get into trouble. But the bigger reason for cautioning her was probably embedded in my subconscious. It was never stated when I said goodbye to Sofia and she walked out of the office and disappeared down that path. But it looms large in my mind at this moment: the burglary, the one Emma told us about during her interview in the office. If there were people breaking into her house looking for the package, the small box, the key, and the piece of paper she described as an ID, then I should have known better. We all sat here and listened to her, Harry and I, and

Sofia. We all heard it. But Harry was gone when Sofia left. I was the one who was here. I should have stopped her. Why the hell did I let her go? The answer comes bouncing back almost immediately. Because of the dog. If it had been anything else at that house we would have left it until this morning. It was a job for Herman, and then maybe only if he was packing heat. I wonder if Sofia thought about it. I will never know.

NINE

I n a way it would be much easier if the cops determine without any question that Sofia was killed in some other place and for some other reason, that she never made it to Brauer's house. I know it sounds selfish but I would sleep easier at night if I was sure that the hand of fate had intervened to lift me off the hook of guilt.

"Can I ask how she died?" I ask Owen.

"The medical examiner's still out there with the body," says Noland. "We don't know yet."

"Did you see her?" I look directly at Owen.

He glances up at me and nods.

"Then you must have some idea. What did your eyes tell you? Bullet wounds? Stab wounds? Blunt trauma?"

"Ligature marks around the throat, signs of cyanosis around the face, some swelling," he says.

Sofia was strangled.

"Like I say, we won't know for sure until the ME produces a report," says Noland. "Where were you Friday night?" he asks.

Finally we get down to cases, clearing suspects, looking for alibis. "Is that when she was killed?" I ask.

"Answer my question," says Noland.

"We're not sure," says Owen. "The two girls she lived with said she never came home Friday night. They didn't see her Saturday or Sunday. No sign of her or her car around the apartment all weekend. According to them, the last time they saw her was Friday morning when she left for work."

"Sounds like you've narrowed it down then."

"Unless somebody snatched her and held her captive, in which case they could have killed her anytime over the weekend," says Noland. "Which brings us back to the question, where were you Friday night?" he says.

"My girlfriend and I went to dinner and then took in a show. We had reservations for dinner at six. The name of the restaurant is on my calendar if you want to check. I'm sure I have a copy of the credit card receipt. We saw a movie. My girlfriend got the tickets on Fandango, paid for them with her credit card. I'm sure you can check that as well."

"What did you see?" says Owen.

"Latest James Bond installment." I give them the name of the theater and the location.

"What time did you get home?" he asks.

"I think it was about eleven thirty."

"Did you go home alone or did you get lucky?" he says.

"I'm always lucky. We live together," I tell him. "Going on five years now."

"But you're not married," says Noland.

"Is that all right with you?"

"Absolutely," he says. "That way there's no marital privilege. She can be compelled to testify against you. What's your girlfriend's name?"

I give them Joselyn's name, the fact that she's a lawyer but doesn't work for the firm, and some background on the Gideon Foundation, where she's employed. "You seem to be working the theory of the jealous or jilted lover," I say. "Can I ask why?"

"You saw the girl. She was a looker," says Noland. "She have any boyfriends?"

"She was a sweet kid," I tell him. "She was trying to work her way to law school."

"Then she couldn't have been that sweet," says Noland.

"Cut it out, Jer." Owen shoots him a look. "Do you know if she was seeing anyone steady?"

"I don't know. She had her share of dates. Who they were, I couldn't tell you. I didn't pry into her private life. You might check with her roommates."

"How did they get on, your Joselyn and Sofia?" Noland is relentless.

"I could tell you that Joselyn liked her, but that would be a lie." He sits up in the chair and looks at me. "*Liked* is too mild a word. They bonded the minute they met. Birds of a feather, I suspect. They had a lot in common. They were both smart. Both of them came up the hard way. Poor families, worked hard. Joselyn is a lawyer. Sofia wanted to be one. They were supposed to go out to dinner tonight. Joselyn had a surprise she wanted to share with her. I'm afraid Joselyn might call before she comes by. If she does, I'm not sure I can take the call. I don't want to have to tell her over the phone . . ." My voice starts to crack as it trails off.

"I understand." Owen, his immense frame sitting in the chair, his head hung low, looks at me like a bear.

"What was this surprise?" says Noland.

"What difference does it make now?"

"I'd like to know."

"You're not going to like it." Given his attitude toward lawyers.

"Humor me."

"Joselyn was going to tell Sofia that she and I were willing to spring for a three-year scholarship, a full ride through law school, anyplace Sofia was accepted."

"And you agreed to this?"

"Yeah."

"What would something like that cost?" he asks.

"I don't have any idea."

"Then how did you know you could afford it?"

"I hate to break this to you, but money is not a problem," I tell him.

"You must either have a thriving practice or you just bought your own printing press?"

"Something like that."

As I sit there bantering with him, my mind turns over the constant question: How am I going to tell Joselyn that Sofia is gone, that she will never see her again?

"So what you're telling us is everybody loved Sofia?" says Noland. "Someone musta had a problem with her."

"You had to know her," I say.

"Sorry I missed the chance."

"So am I." I look past him to the couch against the wall and think to myself, It was only three days ago she sat there fidgeting with her phone, fiercely independent, competent and confident, perhaps to the point of foolishness. We'll never know. I can still see her, the ghost of Sofia, her gaze riveted on the tiny screen in her hand, the lost little girl struggling to get out, striving to grow, but now frozen forever in time.

TEN

Like the country it served, the headquarters of the Mossad, Israel's principal intelligence agency, was small. It consisted of a collection of modern high-rise buildings, dark obelisks, each connected to the other like modules on a space station. It was located in an agricultural area of orchards and farm fields south of the city of Tel Aviv, not far from the Mediterranean coast.

The agency itself was highly compartmentalized. Many of its functions and units operated from outstations spread throughout the country as well as abroad. Operational personnel from these outliers seldom mixed with people from headquarters. Israel didn't possess a Cheyenne Mountain, so dispersion was the standing rule. It not only facilitated mission secrecy; it also made it far more difficult for an enemy to destroy or completely blind Israel's intelligence apparatus with a single devastating blow to one central facility.

The lights often burned late at night and into the wee hours at the offices atop the warehouse on the old quay at Haifa Harbor. It was more than fifty miles north of Tel Aviv. Above the docks, the company's name in faded black paint was sprawled across the rust on the corrugated metal on the side of the building. Right to left in Hebrew it read: "Yamat and Co. International Traders."

Up the rickety metal staircase at the outside of the building, the company's managing director, Uri Dahan, waited for his assistant, who was down in the bowels of the warehouse running an errand.

At fifty-two, Dahan looked every inch the harried businessman. He studied his reflection in the dark window overlooking the harbor. His once-thick black hair receded from his forehead like the tide pulling out ahead of a tsunami. The face peering at him out of the glass was etched with age lines on their way to becoming valleys. His two deep-set dark eyes resembled swirling black holes that could easily swallow any messenger bearing bad news. This was the only feature of his face he favored. At times a serious dose of intimidation was needed if you were going to get the job done. He paced the room and waited.

Dahan was a former fighter pilot and veteran of the Israeli Air Force who spoke three languages, including nearly perfect American English. He held an aeronautical engineering degree from the University of Colorado, and at one time attended the US Army's War College at Carlisle Barracks in Pennsylvania. After his flying days ended, Uri joined the Aman, Israel's military intelligence agency. Six years later he was recruited by the Mossad.

Now he was head of K, one of the principal outstations located in northern Israel. K Station functioned under Mossad's "Collections Department." As such, it was engaged in overseas espionage as well as counterterrorism. Though very few even within the Mossad knew where the station was located, and almost none knew the identity of its personnel, there were some who believed that it had connections with "Kidon," part of the Mossad's Caesarea branch.

Kidon was rumored to handle overseas "wet work," foreign assassination whenever such was deemed necessary. Not much was known about the secretive unit or whether it even actually existed other than in name, which was bandied about in the spy press from time to time. Officially the Israeli government denied its existence or that they ever sanctioned assassinations. But then, of course, so did nearly every other government on the planet.

Dahan heard the elevator as it opened onto the hallway outside. Seconds later the door opened and Josef Tal, his assistant, came in. He was breathless, holding what appeared to be two pages in his hand, printouts from the code room downstairs.

"Did they find it?" Dahan's dark eyes bore down on his young assistant.

Tal looked at him, grimaced, and then shook his head. "No."

"Why not?"

"There was interference," said Tal. "Someone else was there. According to the cable from Ari, our man was not alone."

"What?"

"Someone in the house."

"Who?"

"I don't know. He doesn't say." Tal glanced down at the pages in his hand. "All he says is that someone else got in the way. He doesn't say who. But he says he thinks he knows where it might be."

"I should hope so by now. He's been there twice. He should have gotten it the first time," said Dahan. "Instead he tore the place up and came out with nothing. Who hired this guy?"

"Ari."

"One more time on his background?" said Dahan.

The man assigned to enter the house was a private contractor, not a Mossad agent. Intelligence agencies almost always used cutouts on dirty work, breaking and entering and pilfering things their handlers wanted. If the burglar got caught in the act, it was much less embarrassing for the country involved.

"We talked about it."

"I know," said Dahan. "Tell me again."

"He's former US military, navy, if I recall correctly. He does private security work when he can get it, which apparently isn't often. He works cheap, but according to Ari seems to know his way around."

"Yes, and he's failed twice now," said Dahan.

"And as we discussed previously, he has a record, one prior arrest for burglary, no convictions. He got off on a technicality when the evidence of the theft was suppressed due to a bad search."

Uri nodded. "Yes, I remember." It was the reason Dahan instructed Ari to hire the man. The Mossad had a source who worked at the California Department of Justice. The source had access to the department's criminal records system. Not only was Ari able to make certain that the record of the arrest was in the database, but his source who worked in the department's information technology unit verified that the date the information was entered into the system corresponded to the actual date of arrest. It was not something keyed in more recently as part of a burglary sting for a police officer working undercover.

The Mossad couldn't afford to have Ari, who was attached to the Israeli consul's office in Los Angeles, scooped up in a burglary sting.

"I warned you there would be others looking for it," said Tal.

"Yes. Yes. I know," said Dahan. He wondered who they were. "Was our man compromised in any way? Can anyone identify him?"

"I don't think so. The man told Ari he went to great lengths to make sure."

"What does that mean?" said Dahan.

"I'm not sure. Ari's language from the cable is in quotes." Tal looked down to check the words on the page one more time.

"We can't afford to have an international incident," said Dahan. "If the Americans find out . . . if local authorities pick him up, he is on his own. Does he understand that? We cannot come to his aid."

"He has been told," said Tal. "There's nothing in writing that can be traced back to us. And even if he talks, the man has a record of arrest for burglary. They're not likely to believe anything he says. A dog crapping in the park once is likely to do it again."

Dahan nodded. Even if the man tried to finger Ari, it would be his word against an attaché to the consul general of Israel in Los Angeles, an Israeli citizen with diplomatic immunity whom they could not arrest in any event. So why make a stink? They were probably safe.

"The guy wants to go in again. Should we let him?" asked Tal.

The man was being paid a bonus if he succeeded. No doubt this was motivating him. "I don't know. For the moment tell him to hold off. I need to think about it. How did Ari send the cable?" Dahan was worried about eavesdropping.

"Just as you instructed. Diplomatic pouch to the embassy in Mexico City, encoded and sent by way of secure channel to the institute." The institute was Mossad headquarters in Tel Aviv. "They relayed it here. That's why it took so long."

"That's all right. Better to be safe." Dahan didn't trust the normal encrypted channels out of the States any longer. The US National Security Agency had long ears and a nose that was in the middle of everyone else's business. To Dahan and his colleagues at the Mossad, the White House no longer cared about Israel or its security. They paid lip service to get Jewish votes and money. But if the administration got caught snooping at the embassies in Mexico City, that could carry serious domestic political implications for the Hispanic vote in the United States.

It was the world gone upside down. On the domestic side, after nearly sixty years of relative racial peace, the United States was beginning to pick at the wounds, and sores were starting to open once again. On the foreign front the supposed leader of the free world was going through a foreign policy convulsion on the order of a Venusian eruption. No one, not even its closest allies, had a clue as to what it might do next.

Some observers believed there was a mad grab for power going on inside the country, a naked attempt at permanent one-party rule that involved a rapid, almost overnight change in the nation's demographics, the theory being to open the southern border and invite in the flood, one massive final push to get the party over the top.

Dahan didn't know if this assessment was accurate. What he did know was that he and others at the Mossad could not alter the course of US history. They would be far too busy in the maelstrom that was coming, doing everything they could just trying to save their own country.

For a long moment he stood there staring at his own reflection in the dark glass.

"What are you thinking?" said Tal.

"I'm thinking there's a lot of chaos out there. Enough problems for a troubled world that it doesn't need this one. Suppose it was ISIS."

"What?"

"Whoever was at the house," said Dahan. "With a few connections over the Internet and some domestic on-site help they could have mounted an attempt."

"It's possible, I suppose. Of course, that assumes they have a lead on it," said Tal.

"We did. They could have gotten the information from the same dark sources. If they get their hands on it, you can be sure they'll use it, the masters of manipulation that they are. Given what's happening in the US and elsewhere, the deep political divisions, the pent-up emotions, the racial angst, the armies of tattooed lunatics searching to find some point of ignition, if ISIS finds it, they'll use it to try to set the world on fire."

"Do you think the Americans know it's out there?" asked Tal.

Dahan shook his head slowly. "They think it was destroyed in a bombing raid."

"Why don't we tell them?"

"They'll laugh at us," said Dahan. "Even if they believe us, they won't see the danger."

"They're about to get a rude awakening. So what do we do?"

"We follow our marching orders. We find it as quickly as we can," said Dahan. "And we destroy it!"

ELEVEN

Once the two sheriff's detectives started questioning our staff, word of Sofia's murder spread through the office like a kerosene-fueled fire. There was sobbing in the hallway outside my door. Secretaries and some of the part-timers were reduced to tears.

Everyone had the same questions—above all, how did it happen and why? For the moment there are no answers. Harry and I can be sure that the minute they find out where Sofia worked, the media hounds will be jamming our phone lines and knocking on our door. As it is, Sally is having a difficult time keeping it together just to answer the phones.

The detectives pitch the usual questions about Sofia, who were her friends, where did she party, was she aware of any threats, were there stories of unrequited affections or twisted admirers? One by one, as the cops finish with them, I send our people home. Harry and I have decided to close the office. We figure to give it a day or two, let things die down, give everyone time to adjust to the awful news.

I have Sally roll the phone lines over to the answering service and tell them to take messages. Harry and I have a mission. We need to get out of here, over to Brauer's house to see if there's any connection between it and Sofia's murder.

Noland, the detective, is dragging his feet, refusing to say whether he will allow us to visit the crime scene.

Coward that I am, I send a text message to Joselyn telling her that her dinner with Sofia is off, canceled, that something has come up and that I will explain later. I tell her I am tied up outside the office all afternoon, unavailable. "See you at home later this evening. Love you!" I sign off. I dread the moment.

Joselyn isn't likely to hear about Sofia's murder over the airwaves since the police won't release the victim's name until they notify next of kin. That will take a while. According to our records, Sofia's mother and father live up north, somewhere off the beaten path in the gold country near the small town of Sutter Creek. I would call them, but to what purpose? I have never met them, and the authorities have no doubt already informed them or are in the process of doing so.

I envision it in my mind's eye, the creeping black-and-white as it pulls up slowly to the sidewalk in front. A uniform, perhaps two of them, will get out. Then the solemn trek to the door as if marching to the meter of a funeral dirge. They may doff their hats as they ring the bell, anything to telegraph the message before they have to deliver it. I want to warn the people inside. "Don't open it!" But they will, only to be consumed by the blast of the life-altering message. Your child is no more. Sofia is dead.

I think to myself, What if it was Sarah? What if it was my own? I expel the thought from my brain, stamp it out before it can take root. Even in the abstract the pain is too great. Hollowed out as I am by the death of Sofia, how could I ever bear that? How can any parent?

The detectives save Harry for last. They question him as to his whereabouts on Friday evening. It seems that Harry was having dinner and drinks until late into the night with a friend. When they press him, Harry finally admits that he was with a woman. Noland and Owen take this in stride. But you could have knocked me over with a feather. They demand to know the lady's name. Harry tells them to jam it.

Noland launches into him instantly: "In other words, she's married."

Harry says no.

"So then why not give us her name?"

Harry refuses. He says he has his reasons.

"What you're telling us is you don't have an alibi?" says Noland.

"You asked me what I was doing. I'm telling you."

"Where did all this take place?" Noland pushes him.

"At a restaurant in the Gaslamp Quarter. We had dinner."

"Maybe you can give us the name of this restaurant?"

Harry does, and Owen writes it down.

"Where did you go after dinner?" says Noland.

"Her place." As Harry says it, he glances at me sitting on the couch in his office.

"Which is where?" Noland is standing, leaning over Harry's desk. Owen, the other detective, sits in one of the client chairs quietly observing.

"Up near La Jolla." Harry is in his chair behind the desk.

"That's a big area. Maybe you can narrow it down with an address?" says Noland.

"Can't do that," says Harry.

Noland turns toward me and says, "You might want to advise your partner to cooperate. It'll go a lot easier and faster. That is, if he has nothing to hide."

"His interview," I tell him.

"Fine!" He turns back to Harry. "So what's the problem here? You tryin' to tell us you don't kiss and tell? The gentleman's code? That you're trying to protect the lady's honor? Is that it?"

"Something like that."

"That's a luxury you can't afford. Not in a situation like this. You say she's not married. So what has she got to hide?" says Noland. He thinks for a moment, then turns back to me and asks, "Could it be that your partner is humping a client? That is a no-no, correct? I'm told the bar frowns on it, right?"

He doesn't really expect an answer and I don't give him one. Besides, I know better. What's beginning to bother me more is Harry's silence. I'd expect him to be on top of the desk with both feet by now, snarling in the cop's face. A lawyer who suddenly goes quiet when confronted with this kind of an accusation has a reason for biting his tongue, especially if it's Harry. Like the cops, I'm left to wonder what he's hiding. I shudder to think.

Noland looks Harry up and down, the wrinkled shirt, a spotted trail of grease across his tie like a map of the Sandwich Islands, the shadowed beard under Harry's repentant gaze, lawyer looking for a rock to crawl under. Suddenly it dawns on him. You can see it like a lightbulb as it flashes on over his head.

Who the hell would ever go out with this guy? What woman in her right mind? To the blond cop, the blue-eyed trendsetter, it is obvious. If Harry had a date, especially if he is trying to keep it quiet, it could only mean one thing: Harry had paid for it. "Did you find her on one of the services or did you pick her up in a bar? How much did she cost you, counselor?" Noland smiles and waits for an answer.

There is none. Harry looks down at the surface of his desk as he nibbles a little on his upper lip. It is a nervous tic Harry falls into whenever he is in trouble. I am beginning to worry.

"Seems we caught him in the act." Noland turns and glances toward his partner. "How's that for bad timing? Man needs an alibi and all he has is Shady Sadie who, for a few dollars more, will spin any lie you want." Back to Harry. "If that's your alibi, it ain't worth spit. That's not an alibi a jury is likely to believe."

"You're not gonna tell us the lady's a hooker?" says Owen.

"That or a high-priced call girl," says Noland.

I'm thinking, No! Not Harry! He would never . . . But Harry is saying nothing. Instead he just sits there chewing on his lip. I start to think. For the first time in his life, Harry has more money than he knows what to do with. I slap myself for the thought. But it's true. People with too much money do stupid things. All too often it doesn't buy happiness. But Harry with a call girl?

Noland bears down: "How much did you pay her? You know it's gonna come out sooner or later."

Harry gives me a soulful look, and then before I can think he says, "What do I do? Should I tell them?"

The moment he says it, my heart drops into my stomach. "I don't know. Up to you." Finally I recover and say, "Maybe you shouldn't say anything. Just keep quiet."

"I knew it," said Noland. "Don't you love it? The mouthpiece needs a mouthpiece. Come on, cough it up. Gimme her name, otherwise you've got nothing," he tells Harry. "You go right to the top of the list, number one on the hit parade, person of interest. Like a thirsty dog I'm sure it's not the first one you hired. We'll find 'em. We'll dig 'em up. Get their names. Do you have their numbers in a little black book? Or maybe they're in your computer? Try this on. Let's say you get tired of paying for it. You see this young new stuff in the office. You make a move to dip your quill. And she says no. You don't like it. Maybe it's the way she says it. You left the office early Friday, didn't you?" They already know he did. It's on the calendar. Harry left the office at about three. "Let's say you followed her. Caught her somewhere off the road. She fought back. You panicked. Is that what happened?"

"Go screw yourself," says Harry.

"In a situation like that, a guy's gonna panic. I can understand that," says Noland.

"Don't say another word," I tell Harry.

"An alibi, even a bad one, is better than nothing," says Noland. "Who knows, maybe we'll even believe her. And even if you lose your ticket for pandering, there are worse things."

"Don't say anything," I tell him. "Keep quiet."

But Harry's not listening. "I'll tell you what. Why don't I call her, and you can talk to her over the phone, but no names. How's that?"

"What, do you think I'm nuts? I'm gonna swallow an anonymous alibi from some bimbo who sells herself a trick at a time over the telephone? Not on your life," says Noland. "Not a chance."

"What do I do?" Harry looks at me, mournful eyes, then turns to Owen and says, "I was hoping I wouldn't have to tell my partner."

"It's time to pay the piper," says Owen. "Besides, you'll feel better when it's over. You know you will."

Harry falls silent for a moment, then looks at me and says, "I blew it."

"Shut up!" I tell him.

"I'm sorry." Then he turns to Noland and asks, "Can't we keep this private?"

"Her name?" says Noland. He has one cheek on the corner of Harry's desk, pen poised ready to take notes on the little pad in his hand.

"Her name is Gwyneth . . ." says Harry.

Noland writes it down. "I'm sure that's her real name. Sounds pricey. Gwyneth what? And I'll need a phone number!"

"Gwyneth Riggins," says Harry.

Noland writes for a second and then stops abruptly, as if his brain has seized. With the pen frozen over the pad he glances sideways at Harry and says, "You mean like the . . . ?"

"Yeah," says Harry, "like the Superior Court judge. And spelled the same way."

Noland has this quizzical look, wondering, I'm sure, what call girl is sufficiently stupid to be using the judge's name—or if he's just being jerked around.

"I don't know how I'm gonna break the news to her," says Harry.

Noland is sitting there perched on the corner of Harry's desk looking at him, not sure if he should ask, but curiosity gets the better of him. "What news?"

"That you think Gwyn looks like a hooker."

"Who are we talking about?" says Noland. "Are you talking about the judge?"

"Who else? That's the only Gwyn Riggins I know."

"I never said she looked like a hooker!"

"Now I suppose you're gonna ask me if I stayed there all night," says Harry. "Whether we got down and did the big naughty. I can't lie to a law enforcement officer," says Harry. "I was there all night. And we did in fact—"

"So that's why you had to affidavit her?" I cut him off. Harry has been dropping paper on Riggins for weeks. I wondered why. He moved to disqualify her every time he found himself in front of her on the bench. Whenever I asked him why, he brushed me off. Harry told me he had a problem with her. It wasn't serious. He was working it out. So I let it slide. Figured it was his problem.

"OK, so I lied," says Harry. "I never actually affidavited her. She recused herself. She had this problem, call it a conflict."

"You were sleeping with her?" I ask.

"Yeah, well, that's what ultimately caused the problem," says Harry.

"Yeah, I'd say that's a conflict! Why didn't you let me in on it?"

"For the same reason I didn't want to tell them."

"Hey, I'm your partner!"

"What are you worried about? She did the right thing. No crime, no foul," says Harry.

I can't tell if he's talking about Gwyn's recusals or the fact that she's sleeping with him. He gives me a sheepish look. "We've been dating for a couple of months now. She didn't want the world to know. Can you blame her?"

"Congratulations!" I say. "But you can tell her it's out of the bag now."

"Yeah. Congratulations!" At the moment Noland looks sick.

"Thanks," says Harry, "but we still need to work this out, the three of us, you, me, and Gwyneth."

"What do you mean?" says Noland. "Work what out?"

"Maybe it's her makeup or the way she dresses," says Harry. "Perhaps if we get together you can give her some pointers, so next time you won't mistake her for a hooker."

"I never said . . . I didn't say that . . . I never said anything about the judge. You heard me." Noland looks to his partner for help.

Owen puts both hands in the air, palms out. "I'm not involved in any of this. I never said a word."

"Forget the whole thing." Noland rips the page out of his notepad as if to emphasize the point.

"I thought you weren't supposed to do that," says Harry. "Aren't your notes subject to discovery?"

"He's not. And they are," says Owen. "But in this case I think we can make an exception."

"I think we're done here." Noland lifts his ass off the desk and starts to move toward the door.

"No. No." Harry stops him in mid-stride. "Now that you pushed me to the wall, forced me to give up Gwyn's name, outed her, so to speak, you're gonna have to talk to her to verify my alibi. I insist!"

"I believe you," says Noland. "I'll take your word for it."

"I wouldn't," says Harry. "That's not good process. You have a job to do." He plucks the receiver off the phone on his desk and starts to punch in numbers to dial: "Let me call her. I'll get her off the bench, talk to her, tell her what you said, and then you can get on the line."

"No. No," says Noland. "No need to bother the judge. I'm sure she's busy." He moves away from Harry's desk like it's radioactive. "I'll call her later. I'll check it out myself. I promise," he adds.

"Or I can have her call you," says Harry.

"No, I wouldn't do that. I'll take care of it. I said I would, and I will."

"Are you sure?" says Harry.

"I'm sure!"

"Fine. Then for the moment I suppose, we can let that slide." Harry lays the receiver in the cradle and says, "So now let's talk about Sofia."

"What about her?" says Noland.

"I understand you have some reservations about our visiting the scene."

Noland thinks for a moment, glances at the phone on the desk, and finally says, "No. There must be some misunderstanding. I don't have any reservations. Do you have any reservations?"

He looks at Owen, who shakes his head. "Fine by me. Whatever."

"There you are, see? No problem. You can come by and take a look anytime you want. Your convenience. Just give us a call." Noland reaches into his pocket, pulls out a business card, and drops it on Harry's desk.

"No need for that. Why wait," says Harry, "when we can do it right now? We can swing by our client's house, see if Sofia ever arrived, and then go directly from there out to the scene." Harry makes a note on a Post-it slip, tears it off, and hands it to Noland before he can pull his hand away. "That's the address to our client's house. We'll meet you there in forty-five minutes. You will be there?"

Noland stands there looking at him.

Harry picks up his card. "In the meantime I'll just hold on to this, in case I have to pass it along to Gwyn, see if she wants to call you."

How could he say no?

TWELVE

Harry and I locked up the office and headed out. We picked up Herman Diggs, our investigator, on the way. The cops are no doubt going to want to question Herman at some point. He's the only other male in our office. But after tripping over Harry, I suspect they may want to do a backgrounder on Herman's dating habits before they brace him.

The three of us drive forty minutes through midafternoon traffic until we find ourselves on the street in front of Emma Brauer's house. By the time we arrive it's almost three. Owen and Noland, the two detectives from the sheriff's Homicide Unit, are sitting in the "black beast," their unmarked Dodge Charger that no one can miss. It's parked at the curb waiting for us.

As soon as I pull into the driveway, they get out. Harry leads the way since he has the four-digit code to get into the house. He also has directions from Brauer as to where she hid the key to her safe-deposit box, the one holding the small cardboard box with the other key and the paper she said looked like an ID.

If we can grab her safe-deposit key without the two detectives seeing us, we'll do it. Otherwise we'll have to come back. Emma's key itself is not evidence of anything. We can't even be sure if it's still here. The police may have found it during their earlier search. What's in her safe-deposit box could be evidence depending on where it leads us. Right now the first order of business is to check on the dog, see if he's still at the house. If he's gone, it's a fair assumption that Sofia got this far before she was killed.

Harry steps to the front door and punches the code into the lock.

"I don't hear any dog, do you?" says Owen. The big detective is right behind Harry. "If somebody is at the front door, it's usually gonna bark."

Harry opens the door.

Inside, from what I can see around the hulking form of Owen, the entry area is dark. The blinds across the front windows are all drawn.

"What's the dog's name?" says Owen.

"Dingus," says Harry.

"Here, Dingus! Come on, boy!" Owen slaps his open palm on the frame of the front door and calls the animal's name, loud enough to be heard in the backyard this time. We wait for a few seconds. Not a sound. Nothing.

Harry steps into the entryway, Owen right behind him. We start to follow.

"Hold on a second." Suddenly Owen stops just inside the door. Noland and Herman bump into him like cars on a train. "If this is an active crime scene we shouldn't all go tramping through it," he says. Owen checks with Harry to make sure we and he have permission from the owner to be in the house. He wants to make sure he doesn't need a warrant.

Harry assures him that he's authorized to enter.

"Then I'm gonna ask you three to stay here." He looks at Harry, Herman, and me. "Don't touch anything. My partner and I will take a look around."

Just as he turns to walk away a female voice from the bright sunlight outside says, "Can I help you?"

Owen looks out the door and says, "Who are you?"

"I might ask you the same thing." She's older and a bit cranky, in sweatpants and a top that's bulging in all the wrong places with a hairdo like Cruella De Vil trying to decide which color it wants to be next.

"Sergeant Brad Owen." He flashes her his badge.

"When are you people gonna be finished?" she says.

"What?"

"Hi. I'm Paul Madriani. I'm a lawyer. I represent Emma. You must be her neighbor?" End of the train, I step out to shake her hand before Owen or Noland can ask any more questions.

"When's she gonna be home?" says the woman.

"Probably tomorrow." I look up at Harry.

He nods.

"About time," she says. "Poor woman. Why don't they leave her alone?"

"She's in the bucket on a homicide charge," says Noland. "Maybe we need to talk a little more about this."

Apparently the two detectives have been on their radio or a computer in the car on the way out here. Once we gave them Brauer's address they called it in and checked her out. They probably know as much as we do at the moment.

"We can talk about their client later. First things first. Let's find the dog," says Owen. "Any idea where her dog is?" he asks the neighbor.

"What do you want with Dingus? I suppose you want to arrest him, too?" she says. "He's fine. He's with me."

Noland turns to his partner and says, "I told you. It's a goose chase. Nobody's been here."

"How long have you had him?" asks Owen.

"Since Friday night," says the woman. "I heard him barking so I came over and got him."

Owen steps out into the sunlight. "Did you see any sign of a young woman here, brown hair, pretty, in her twenties? She was supposed to come by and pick the dog up."

"That must've been the one I talked to on the phone," she says. "She called but she never showed up."

"When did you talk to her?" says Owen.

The woman thinks for a moment. "Must've been around five thirty, maybe six o'clock."

"This would be Friday evening?" says Owen.

"Yeah. She said she was gonna come by and get Dingus. But she never showed."

"Did you get her name?" I ask.

She thinks for a moment, shakes her head. "I can't remember if she gave it to me. If she did I forgot. She said Emma gave her my number. She said she worked for a law firm."

"That would be her," said Owen. "Did she say where she was calling from?"

The woman thinks for a moment, then shakes her head again. "But it sounded like she was in a car. You can always tell."

Owen is thinking what I am. Except for her killer, the woman standing in front of us may have been the last person to talk to Sofia alive.

"Did she say anything else?" says Owen.

"Not that I recall."

"The call. Did you take it on a cell phone?" he asks.

"No. The only phone I have is the landline in the house."

"How about caller ID?"

"You think I can afford such luxuries? You try living on Social Security."

It seems her only luxury is gossip. A cell phone would have easily kept a record of incoming calls. It would have shown Sofia's number and the precise time that she called. If Sofia called from a cell phone, the authorities could trace the call and discover which towers it went through, which would give them an approximate location of where Sofia was when the call was made—that is, when the two women talked. If the cops have Sofia's cell phone, which they aren't saying, they'll be working this angle already, seeing if she called anyone else.

"So I take it you had the code to get into the house?" Owen asks the woman.

She nods. "Whenever Emma is away I watch her place. Take care of things, you know? Pick up the mail, put out the garbage, water a few plants, that kinda stuff. She does the same for me. Sometimes I watch the dog, but usually she takes him with her."

"And you never saw this other woman come by to pick up the animal?"

She shakes her head.

"Have you seen anyone else around the house?" asks Owen. "Say since Friday evening?"

"No."

"We're wasting our time," says Noland. "Why don't we go out, show 'em the scene before it gets too late." He's looking at his watch. "Another half hour and we're gonna get tied up in traffic."

"Sounds like a man in a hurry," says Harry. "What's the problem, you got an early date?"

"No. Nothing like that. But if you want to see everything in place we should move. Once the forensics people finish processing the area around the body, the ME's gonna pick her up and move her."

Owen turns to the woman and says, "Thank you. I appreciate your help." He takes her name, address, and phone number and writes it down, turns to me, and says, "You wanna take the dog?"

The thought of what to do with the dog hadn't entered my mind. Before I can open my mouth the neighbor says, "He's fine with me. And you said Emma's gonna be home tomorrow anyway . . ."

"If you don't mind," I tell her. "That would help. If there's any problem with Emma I'll give you a call." I also get her phone number and give her my business card.

Harry locks the front door and we head to the cars. I slip behind the wheel. Harry and Herman get in. As I wait for their doors to close I take a deep breath, an effort to steel myself. My hands are shaking on the wheel as I think about the dark task ahead. We asked for it and now we must do it. I back out into the street. As Noland pulls away from the curb I fall in behind him. We follow the black beast as it drives slowly down the street, the sorrowful sojourn, the lonely caravan on its way to find Sofia's lifeless body.

THIRTEEN

For the first twenty minutes we drive in silence. Noland was right. The traffic is bumper to bumper. A few miles farther on, Harry finally kicks in. "This doesn't make any sense."

"What do you mean?" I say.

"Well, look where we are."

I've been on autopilot since leaving Brauer's house, my eyes glued to the unmarked police car in front of us, not paying much attention. I look at one of the overhead road signs as we approach it at walking speed. It's the interchange from I-8, turning south onto State 125.

"What was she doing way out here?" says Harry. "You said when Sofia left the office on Friday she was headed directly to Brauer's place?"

"That's what she said. In fact, as I recall, she was in a hurry."

"Could it be she had another stop to make?" says Herman.

"I don't know."

"Maybe that's why she was in a rush?" Herman sits in the backseat looking at my eyes in the rearview mirror.

We drive on, another twenty minutes in grinding freeway traffic to where Highway 94 turns into a divided four-lane road. Noland keeps going. We pass through a mixed area, houses and retail, an occasional restaurant and some light industrial plants along the road. Here the development starts to turn spotty. There are open areas of chaparral where the excavators have not yet found their way.

I notice some flashing lights up ahead, two California Highway

Patrol cars parked on the side of the road, one of them blocking a dirt easement into an area of undeveloped land. Noland slides into the right lane. I stay right behind him. He hits the emergency lights in the beast and the strobe starts flashing. Cars around us immediately slow down. One of the patrol officers jumps in the car blocking the dirt road and pulls forward just enough for us to pass behind him.

Noland guns it and we follow him down the dusty road. He disappears in the billowing cloud that boils up in front of us. I slow down so as not to pile into him from behind. I see his brake lights go on as he rounds a bend, and suddenly we're there.

It's a wide spot on the road carved out by the bulldozer that graded it. Washboards cut into the sandy soil from the last heavy rains, now more than two years ago, indicate that the road has been here awhile. Parked on top of the ripples at the edge of the road on the other side is the coroner's wagon. Next to it is the forensics van. There are three other patrol units and another unmarked car parked up ahead. On the road off to one side a flatbed tow truck is winching a vehicle onto its tilt tray, getting ready to haul it away.

I glance over. Harry sees it, too.

I hear him sigh. It's a hollow sound I've never heard from Harry before, like the vapor of a ghost as it leaves his body.

Until this moment I suspect that each of us, Harry, Herman, and myself, perhaps the women in the office, each of us without saying a word, fed the famished shadow of a chance that somehow the cops were wrong. That it wasn't Sofia who was lying out there on the parched ground under that hot sun. That a merciful God would spare us the pain and offer up some other lost child. But now as we sit here listening to the hum of the car's air conditioner, all hope dies. Its spirit ascends on a roiling cloud of dust as the truck moves toward the highway carrying on its back the little blue car, Sofia's Kia Rio, which every day for months now had been parked like an old friend in the lot behind our office.

I turn off the car's engine and the three of us get out. Overhead I can hear the rotors of a helicopter as it circles like a vulture a few thousand feet above us. One of the local television stations no doubt following up on a lead from their police scanner.

We walk to the other side of the road and join up with Owen and Noland. A few feet away, yellow tape anchored to several steel stakes marks off the immediate crime area. Beyond the tape, about forty feet away and up a slight incline, they have erected a small white tentlike cabana maybe eight or ten feet square. Under its shade, two figures, each of them down on one knee, are working. They are wearing coveralls looking like surgeons. I know that Sofia is there, though I cannot see any part of her.

Owen buttonholes one of the forensics guys as he walks by headed toward their van. "What do they have, anything yet on time of death?"

"Best they can figure, by the time they found the body she'd been there at least two days, maybe longer."

"So they don't think it was Saturday or Sunday?" says Owen.

The guy shakes his head.

"You think they'll get anything more precise when they do the autopsy?" asks Owen.

"Not likely. An animal of some kind got at her. They aren't gonna find any stomach contents. And the core heat from her body is long gone. It gets cold out here at night. Any radiant heat coming out of her now is coming from the sun. They figure she's been here at least two days, from the insects and the ground underneath her."

"That means Friday night," says Owen.

"It looks like it."

"Any shoe prints or tire tracks?"

The guy shakes his head. "Ground's too dry. Too much sand. Couldn't get a thing. They're still checking for hair and fibers around the body. Then we'll move her. They bagged her hands and they'll check under her nails when they get her to the morgue. We might find something there. One of her nails is broken."

"Which hand?" I ask

"Index finger on the right. Who are you?"

"She broke it in the office Friday afternoon," I tell him.

"Who's he?" the guy asks Owen.

"This is Madriani," says Owen. "The lawyer she worked for."

"What's he doing here?"

"ID'ing the vic," says Owen.

The other guy nods.

This at least is the official justification for our presence here. The real reason they are letting us get this close to the scene is to silence Harry. Owen doesn't want my partner gossiping with Gwyn regarding Jerry Noland's loose lips. Get on her wrong side and she might flame the two detectives the next time they find themselves in her courtroom. Homicide is a small world, and in San Diego County, Gwyneth Riggins owns a chunk of it. Become a liability to prosecutors in court and homicide detectives, even seasoned ones, can find themselves back doing snatch-and-grab misdemeanors and traffic cases.

"Sofia broke her nail in the office Friday afternoon," I tell them. "I remember because she complained about it; my better half tried to help her fix it. She filed it and touched it up with an emery board."

"If she did we'll see it under the scope. I'll make a note," says the tech.

"We thought it would be easier for them to ID the body than to drag in the family," says Owen.

"That's fine. Just watch where you walk and don't get over the body where you might drop hair or fibers. Go suit up. Put your name on the list and sign off so we can clear you if they find anything later." He nods toward the van.

We do it, Harry and I. The two cops are uneasy allowing Herman near the scene until they have an alibi for him. Herman doesn't fight it. He says he'd rather remember her as she was, the last time he saw her in the office.

We don the white polypropylene coveralls with hoodies. They are disposable and cheap, a pack of twenty-five, one size fits all, in this case 3X. We roll up the pant legs and tape them, then do a little tuck and roll with tape on the sides so we don't swim in them. We cover our shoes with blue booties, snap on a pair of latex gloves, and march toward the short path beyond the yellow tape.

One of the assistants to the medical examiner leads the way. Owen is geared up and following behind us. We walk up the rocky path. It's covered in splinters of shale sharp enough to pass for broken glass. As we get closer I can see her on the ground, sprawled in the shade under the white tent. Her feet are toward us. She is still wearing the bright yellow dress, tight, and short above the knees, though it has been pushed up and is now stained, either by dirt or blood, I can't tell which. As we get closer, the medical examiner, who is still huddled over her, sees us approach. Quickly he grabs a large white towel and drapes the entire midsection of her body with it.

"I understand you're here to make the identification." The ME stands up.

I can barely force myself to look at Sofia's face. It is badly swollen, her lips parched and split. Her once-beautiful hair is now tangled and littered with dry leaves and twigs from the brush around her. Her eyes are open, bulging, staring out at nothing, a horrified gaze fixed on infinity. Around her throat is a deep ligature wound, like a black tattoo cut into the flesh, a quarter of an inch or more in width. I try to blot out the fact that I am looking at Sofia, concentrate on the details in front of my eyes, try to stay objective. I know I will never get another chance.

Whatever the killer used for the ligature was sufficiently thick and strong to complete the job. Anything more fine would have either snapped or cut the flesh, resulting in external hemorrhaging. The only bleeding around her throat appears to be under the skin. The solid unbroken line around the front of her throat leads me to believe that whoever did it came at her from behind.

Harry and I introduce ourselves to the ME. Harry is still looking. He can't take his eyes off Sofia on the ground.

"Do you recognize her?" asks the ME.

"Barely," I tell him. "But it is her. It is Sofia."

"Who?" He looks at me and then back at the clipboard in his hand.

"Sorry. Her legal name was Sadie Leon. We knew her by her nickname, Sofia. She worked for us at the firm."

"Should I include her nickname as an alias?" he asks.

"I would. Her family called her that and a lot of her friends knew her only as Sofia."

He makes a note. "Is there any doubt or question in your mind as to her identity?" he asks.

I shake my head.

"How about you?" He looks at Harry.

"No. It's her." Harry seems devastated. No stranger to crime scenes, this one hits where it hurts.

"She's still wearing the same outfit she had on Friday afternoon at work," I tell the ME. "Same dress. Same jacket."

He makes another note. "When was the last time you saw her?"

"We already have all of that," says Owen. "I'll send you a copy of my notes when they're printed up."

"Good," says the ME.

There is a spot like brown rust on a sliver of the yellow fabric near Sofia's knee. It peeks out from beneath the edge of the towel covering her midsection. The knee itself appears to have suffered some kind of an abrasion but no apparent bleeding. This means that the blood is coming from somewhere higher up on her body.

"What about that?" I point to the spot of blood.

The ME follows the line of my eye, sees where I'm looking, and says, "We're pretty sure it's all postmortem. Probably a coyote or an abandoned dog. It happens. She's been here awhile."

I'm still looking at the spot on her dress.

"Trust me, you don't want to see it," he says. "We won't know for sure until we finish the postmortem, but I doubt it has anything to do with the cause of death."

"So you're pretty sure she was strangled?" says Harry.

"That's our best guess. Fortunately we found her before the animals could finish the job. Otherwise we might never know. Listen, thank you for your help. I'm sure her family will appreciate it." The ME gestures with his head toward the cop that it's time for us to go, that he has work to do, and then he quietly steps away.

"Where are her shoes?"

"What?" The ME turns back to look at me.

"Her shoes? Did you already bag them up?" I scan the ground around her. They are nowhere in sight.

"No. As a matter of fact, we didn't. Do you know what they looked like?" he says.

"High heels, stilettos, maybe five inches high. They were shiny, off white, what you might call cream-colored. They looked like patent leather, but I'm sure they weren't. They were probably vinyl, plastic of some kind. She wore them almost every day no matter what outfit she had on."

"We used to kid her about them." Harry's voice catches. "She said she'd get a new pair for Christmas. Now I guess she won't." Harry the stalwart, the old warhorse, starts to tear up. "Sorry." He wipes it away with the sleeve of the Tyvek suit.

"It's all right," says the ME. "We wouldn't be human if we didn't do that once in a while."

"Where are they?" I ask. "Her shoes?"

"We don't know," he says. "They weren't in her car. We know that. And we didn't find them here."

"It's possible the animals might have carried them off," says Owen.

"Both of them?" says Harry.

"Or chewed them up," says the cop.

"In which case forensics would have found little pieces all over the ground," I tell him. I take a few steps back toward the path leading toward the tape and turn. The bottoms of Sofia's feet are perhaps the only part of her body that seems untouched. Except for some ground-in dust they are remarkably smooth. I look at the path that Harry and I walked up to get here and then check the bottom of my left foot. The blue bootie covering my shoe has been punctured and shredded in at least one place by the sharp pieces of shale along the path.

"One thing is certain. She didn't walk up here barefoot," I tell him.

"No. We don't think so, either."

"She was killed somewhere else and her body dumped here," I say.

"Not necessarily," he says.

"How else do you explain it? She didn't fly here."

"No, but she might have walked."

"Explain?" says Harry.

"It's possible she knew her killer, maybe someone she trusted. Maybe they came here to talk out a problem. Whoever killed her walked her up here with her shoes on, strangled her on the spot, and then took her shoes."

"Why?" says Harry. "Why would he do that?"

"We don't know. We're not sure. Perhaps as a trophy," he says.

"A foot fetish?" says Harry.

"We've seen it before," says the ME. "About four months ago. Another young woman, strangled the same way, her body was found on the beach near Oceanside. Her shoes were missing. High heels," he says. "Some men get off on them."

"I don't buy it," says Harry.

"It's the third time we've seen this in the last two years," says the

ME. "All the victims were young, pretty women, shoes missing, high heels."

They think it's a serial killer. Catch whoever it is and they can close three files.

"Is it likely Sofia would know a serial killer?"

"Why not? It happens all the time. They walk among us every day," he says.

"If that's the case wouldn't it be more likely it was somebody who was stalking her?"

"That's possible, too," says the ME. What he means is that anything's possible. But they are already launched on a convenient theory, the danger of which is that they may have already stopped looking for anything else.

"Come on, we gotta go. Leave the man alone, let him get back to work. You've seen all there is to see." Owen ushers Harry and me away from the body, back down toward the path. We leave her there on the ground under the tender mercies of the medical examiner and head back toward Herman and our car on the dirt road.

FOURTEEN

Back at Emma's house, Harry leads the way, down the hall and through the kitchen. Herman and I follow. Emma told Harry where to look for her key to the safe-deposit box during their meeting at the jail this morning before Owen and Noland showed up with the awful news. We're hoping the key is still there.

We reach the room at the back of the house. It's dusty and dark, a few papers on the floor. The folds of an old army blanket lie like the undulations in a pastoral landscape under the muted light from the window.

"This has gotta be it," says Harry. "She said it was the old man's study."

There is a rolltop desk against one wall, some large maps on the other.

"Some old stuff," says Herman.

As I turn around he's looking at some rifles in a rack on the wall behind me. "Garand and an M-1 carbine, need some cleaning, but they look like they're in pretty good shape. Man needed a maid," says Herman. "Somebody to clean house."

On the wall next to the guns is a small glass display case. Inside is a mounted pistol, what looks like a Luger, and under it two military patches. One of them has what looks like an American Indian motif— a gold thunderbird set off against a diamond-shaped field of red. Under it is a label that reads: "45th Infantry Division—US Army." But it's the other patch that catches my eye. It's the same color combination, gold on red, but the symbol is a swastika.

What the hell? Who was this man, Bob Brauer? "Is that real?" I ask Herman as I tap the glass over the Luger.

He takes a close look. "I'd say so. And probably worth a good piece of change . . . if it's authentic. I mean vintage German, from the war."

"Then what's that?" I ask. I point toward the patch with the swastika.

"Maybe it came with the gun," says Herman.

"Same color as the other patch? That one says US Army, 45th Infantry. What was up with this guy?"

Harry's in the closet at the side of the room. He pulls out a couple of pairs of old army boots and tosses them onto the floor. "I'm getting tired. It's been a rough day. It's time to be home."

"You sleeping alone tonight or do you have plans?" I ask.

Harry gives me a look as if to say, "Don't push it!"

"You just can't help but pick at it, can you?" he says. "At least I don't have to go home and tell Joselyn why I turned off my phone—why I wasn't taking her calls."

Harry knows how to slip the knife in. I had forgotten about it. Now it comes back with a vengeance. Joselyn will be waiting at the door when I get there. Unable to reach me, she's probably been calling Sofia's cell number for hours, trying to find out why dinner was canceled.

"Gimme a hand here," says Harry. Herman goes over to help him in the closet. There's not enough room in the closet doorway for the two of them.

"Let me get it," Herman says.

Harry doesn't argue with him. He steps out of the way and lets the man do it. Herman reaches down and lifts the heavy trapdoor back on its hinges like it was made of cardboard. "You sure this is it?"

"That's what she said," says Harry.

"Damn dark down there. She tell you where the light was?"

Harry looks down at the hole and then back at Herman. Apparently not. "Anybody got a light? Never mind, I'll just use my phone."

We're learning how to spend money. Recently we all got new smartphones and linked them on the company network.

"Did she tell you where the key was?" I ask.

"She gave me some vague directions," says Harry. "She said she kept it on a nail behind one of the posts under the house. But she couldn't remember exactly which one."

"Great! That means we'll have to crawl under the house and check 'em all."

"No, she said it was in one of the corners. You could reach it from down in the cellar if you stood on the bottom shelf against the wall. She said it was behind the post."

"Let's hope the cops didn't look there with their search warrant," I tell him.

Harry starts down the ladder. "Don't let that thing come down and hit me in the head." He flashes the light from the phone's screen on the bottom of the open trapdoor.

"I got it," says Herman. He holds it with one hand as he helps Harry down into the hole with the other. "Watch where you step. Can you see where you're goin'?"

"Not if I'm gonna hang on to the ladder." Harry puts the phone between his teeth as he places both hands on the ladder and disappears down the hole.

I give him a couple of seconds. "What's it look like down there?"

"Shit!" says Harry.

"In other words, the same as up here," says Herman.

"No, I mean I stepped in shit," he says.

"You sure?" Herman looks down the hole.

"I know dog shit when I step in it. More particularly when I smell it. You got a handkerchief?"

"Not for that," says Herman. "You already have my phone." He looks at me. "What are you contributing to this party?"

"Nothing that I'd want to put back in my pocket." I look around, see the blanket on the floor, walk over, and pick it up. "It's pretty dirty."

Herman snaps his fingers for me to toss it to him. "That's all right. It's gonna be a lot dirtier when he's finished with it. Watch your head," he says. And he drops it down the hole.

"God damn it! Now I got dust all over me," says Harry.

"Always complaining, never satisfied," says Herman. "Wipe your shoes and then turn the blanket over so you can cover whatever's left on the floor. That way I won't step in it when I come down." Herman smiles at me and winks.

"Screw you," says Harry.

Herman laughs. "Do you see the light switch?"

"Is it fresh?" I ask.

"Is what fresh?" says Harry.

"What's on your shoe."

"I don't know. Why don't I get down and lick it," says Harry. "Or if you want to know if it's fresh, you can come down and check it out yourself."

"If it's fresh there must be another way into the cellar besides the ladder. Otherwise how would the dog get down there?"

"No other way I can see," says Harry. "Just a dark hole down here, cement on four sides. There's a crawl space under the house, but it's a good six feet, maybe seven to the top of the concrete on the walls. A small dog is not gonna try and jump that, even if he found a way under the house from the outside."

"You sure it's from a dog?" says Herman.

"Let me smear some on the light from your phone. I'll send it up and you can smell it."

"Don't you do it," says Herman. "I'll drop the door, put the desk on top of it, and we'll leave you there."

"OK, I see the light switch," says Harry. "Hang on a second."

"Watch where you step," says Herman.

"Trust me, I got that figured out." A couple of seconds later the light comes on.

"OK, time to go down," says Herman. Quickly he's onto the ladder heading down. His beefy bulk barely fits through the open square in the floor.

I follow him. At the bottom I step off the ladder and onto the blanket, very carefully.

Harry is already groping around in one of the corners looking for the key, feeling around behind the post set on a concrete pier. The post supports one of the joists under the first floor. You can smell the moist earth from the undisturbed soil under the house.

Herman heads to the opposite corner. He's tall enough that he doesn't need to step on anything to feel around behind the post.

I take the third corner. The concrete walls of the cellar are lined with shelves and an occasional warren of boxes filled with assorted rusty nails, nuts and bolts, small pieces of old machinery, discards you never want to throw away because you might need them one day. On the floor by the blanket, like a black snake maybe three feet long, lies an old V-belt, broken so that it no longer makes a loop. The air compressor that it once ran sits in the corner near Harry's feet, its motor covered with dust and cobwebs.

I look down, put my foot on the bottom shelf, and step up so that I can reach behind the post. I feel around trying to find the key or the sharp prick from the nail that it's hanging on. It takes a couple of minutes to do a complete frisk of the post.

I finish up and step off the shelf onto the floor when Herman says, "I got it!"

By the time I turn to look, he's standing there holding a small key between his giant finger and his thumb. "This gotta be it. Looks like every other safe-deposit key I've ever seen."

He's right. It's cut from a brass blank, no grooves on the sides, just deep teeth along the top edge, with a wire key ring through the hole to hang it.

"Let's check the last post just to be safe," says Harry. "In case there's more than one key hidden down here."

Herman pockets the key and checks the last post all the way up and down with his hands on the back side. "Nothing."

"Then that's it. We're good to go." Harry starts up the ladder. He can't wait to get out of here.

I follow him.

Herman turns off the light and trudges up the ladder behind me. We lower the trapdoor, put the boots back in the closet, and head out. Harry is out in front walking down the hall toward the kitchen when suddenly he stops and whispers: "What was that?"

"What was what?" I say.

We stand there for moment, frozen in the hallway, the three of us, looking through the door into the kitchen. And then I see it.

"That!" says Harry. "Did you see it?"

"Yes." Somebody is flashing a light outside in the yard. "Herman?"

"Yeah."

"By any chance are you packing? Please tell me that you are."

"That's the problem with guns," he says. "You never have one when you need it."

"Shit!" I say.

"That's an idea," says Harry. "I could throw my shoe at him."

"Gimme a second." Silently Herman disappears back down the hall toward the old man's study.

"What's he gonna do, hide in the cellar?" says Harry.

"Not without me."

A few seconds later Herman comes back down the hall looking like Rambo. He's carrying a rifle the size of an elephant gun, enough wood under the barrel to make a sequoia. It's one of the military pieces from Robert Brauer's gun rack.

"Is it loaded?" I ask.

Herman shakes his head. "Couldn't find any bullets in the rack or the desk drawers."

"That's all right. You get out there behind him and pound his melon with that and I doubt if he's gonna argue much," says Harry.

"How's he gonna know it's empty?" says Herman. "You didn't."

"You point that at him and he's either gonna crap and die on the spot or, if he has a gun and he's feeling stupid, he's gonna shoot you," says Harry. "Either way, why don't you go first?"

Herman steps around us and into the kitchen, headed toward the back door. For a big man he can move quickly, quietly, and with unusual grace. Without a sound he unlocks the door, opens it, and in one fluid motion, raises the muzzle of the rifle toward the source of the light.

I hear her scream almost immediately. "Don't shoot! Take what you want and go." It's the old lady, the neighbor from this afternoon. I recognize her voice.

"Oh jeez! I'm sorry." Herman lowers the gun. "Didn't mean to scare you. It's me," he says. "Remember? From this afternoon."

A string of profanities come out of the old lady's mouth—"shit," "damn," "piss"—take your pick. "You scared me to death!" For a moment I think perhaps she's not exaggerating. She grabs her chest as if she's about to go to her knees. Harry and I step out the door around Herman and get ahold of her arms to steady her before she can fall.

"Are you all right? It's just us," I tell her. "We needed to pick something up for Emma."

"I thought people were robbing the house," she says. "I was gonna call the police, but then I thought I'd better take a look, and a big black guy comes out the door and points a bazooka at me. Oh, my God!" she says.

"Relax," I tell her.

There's a lawn chair a few feet away. Harry grabs it, puts it behind her, and we ease her into it.

"Are you OK? Would you like a glass of water?" says Harry.

"No. No. Just let me rest for a minute."

"Take your time," he tells her. "Make sure you're all right."

"I'm sorry. I didn't mean to scare you." Herman has stashed the gun. He comes out the back door, walks over and puts his big hand on her shoulder, then squats down next to her so he can talk to her at eye level. "We thought the same thing you did. We saw the light in the backyard and thought somebody was trying to break in. The gun wasn't even loaded."

"Oh, boy," she says, "I'll tell ya. You could've fooled me. I was ready to let you take everything in the house."

They talk. He laughs, then massages her arm a little. "You sure you're OK?"

I step away for a moment as she and Herman talk. I walk toward the back door. Harry is standing there just staring down at the ground.

"Are you all right?"

"I don't know. I'm not sure," he says.

"What's the problem?"

"That, right there." He points toward the ground right at the concrete footing along the back of the house.

At first I don't see it. I try to focus my eyes, but they are tired. It's been a long day. I bend down to take a closer look. There, on the cement in the shadows, is a tiny chain. It is delicate and light, like a piece of lace. At one end is a small plastic fitting. It's shaped like the plug to a set of earbuds, only this one doesn't pipe any sound. I stand there staring at it like Harry. I am mesmerized because I know that the last time I saw this, which was Friday morning, it was being used to anchor the miniature chrome trinket, the replica of the Eiffel Tower on the other end of the chain there on the ground, to the headphone jack on Sofia's iPhone.

FIFTEEN

How did you know Sofia didn't come by?" I'm talking to Emma's neighbor, still sprawled in the lawn chair in the yard.

"Because the dog was still here."

"So you weren't watching for her?" I ask.

"I wasn't here."

"What?"

"I wasn't home. I had an appointment. I told her on the phone, the girl from your office, that I wouldn't be here. Otherwise I would have given her a hand with Dingus."

"Why didn't you tell that to the police?" says Harry.

"They didn't ask me. I came home, I guess it was about ten o'clock. The dog was barking. I came over and picked him up. What was I supposed to think? Sure didn't seem like she had been here—the dog still being home and all . . ."

She has a point. It's hard to blame her. She made the same mistake we did, the two detectives, Harry, Herman, and I when we all came out earlier in the day. We assumed that if we found the dog here it was conclusive evidence of the fact that Sofia never made it to Emma's house. When we discovered that the dog was with the neighbor, that was the assumption we made. And we were wrong. The discovery of Sofia's cell phone trinket, the miniature chrome Eiffel Tower, proves it. She was here. So why didn't she take the dog and leave?

Harry, Herman, and I start looking, searching the house for anything else that might give us a clue. Herman is going through the bed-rooms. Harry is checking the kitchen, back in the study, checking the desk.

I'm still in the yard with the neighbor, who wants to help. I start to think, If the trinket was on the ground, the iPhone may not be far away. That's when I notice the trash can against the house near the back door. I walk over, lift the top, and look inside. It's empty.

"They picked up the garbage this morning," the neighbor says. "I al-ways take it out and bring it back in when Emma's not here."

"Any chance you might have looked inside?"

"No. Why would I do that?"

"No reason," I tell her. "Just wondering." If Sofia's phone was tossed in the trash it is long gone now. There are applications built into devices for locating lost or stolen cell phones or tablets. I am wondering whether Sofia might have activated this feature on her phone. My guess is that she did, for the reason that she prized it so. The question then is how to use this feature to find it. The cops would know. They would go either to the carrier or the manufacturer. I make a mental note. The two detec-tives may already be working on this. I am hoping. But if the phone is in a landfill, or worse, at the bottom of the ocean, we can forget it. If, on the other hand, the killer took it, we can only pray that he did and if he's not too adept with cutting-edge electronics, we can punch a button, check the map, and find Sofia's phone, and we will have found the bastard who killed her.

Harry wanders out through the back door. He's got something in his hand.

"What have you got?"

"I was wondering," he says, "about the dog. What he was doing down in the cellar?" Harry looks down at his shoe. "Remember?"

I nod.

"So I went back down. Took a look around to see if there was some other way he could have gotten down there."

"Did you find one?"

"No," says Harry.

"Is the dog a climber?" I ask the neighbor.

"What?"

"Doofus," says Harry.

"You mean Dingus?"

"Yeah."

"Not that I know of."

"Then I suppose he wouldn't be able to climb down a ladder into the cellar under the house." I look at her.

"I didn't know there was a cellar. But I doubt it. Do you want me to get him and try?"

"No, not now," I tell her.

"So if that's the case," says Harry, "what was he doing down there and how did he get there?"

I shake my head. I don't have a clue.

"How do you know he was there?" she asks.

"That's a story for another time," says Harry. "I wonder maybe if you should go back, check on the dog. We're gonna lock up and leave in just a couple of minutes."

"You're right. It's getting late." She picks up her flashlight. We thank her for her help and she heads toward the gate at the side of the house.

"Can you get out that way?" I ask.

"I left it unlocked when I came in," she says. "Good night."

"Good night."

Harry waits until she's gone and he hears the gate latch shut. "I was thinking what if Sofia came by and the dog was in the cellar?"

"Why would he be there?" I ask.

"Suppose someone was in the house and the dog was making too much noise. So whoever was there put him down in the cellar to try to keep him quiet."

"Go on," I tell him.

"Sofia comes in, looks for the dog, can't find him, but then she hears him barking . . ."

"So she looks," I say, "finds the trapdoor, opens it, sees the dog down below. She goes down to get him."

Harry's nodding, his hands behind his back. "And she runs into the killer in the dark." He brings his hands from around. He is holding the torn V-belt, from down in the cellar.

"I know. I saw it. But it's too wide." The outer band on the belt is at least three-quarters of an inch in width.

"Yes, but if you flip it over . . ." says Harry. He turns the belt toward the inside where the wedge-shaped V takes it down to no more than a quarter of an inch. Here solid hard fiber was designed to grip down deep in the pulley on an air compressor, while the half-horse electric motor turned the belt and provided the power. It was these forces that ultimately tore the backing and the snapped belt. But twisted in the grip of a pair of human hands and looped around a pretty throat, the fiber belt had more than enough strength left in it for that.

As I enter the kitchen at our house Joselyn is standing at the island in the center, chopping onions on the wooden board. There is a salad already on the table and stir-fry steaming on the stove. She looks up at me. Tears from the onions are already in her eyes—this is the moment.

"Where have you been?"

"Busy," I tell her.

"So I gathered. I've been trying to reach you all afternoon. Your phone is turned off."

"I know."

"You send me a text message, tell me that dinner with Sofia is off, that you're out of the office. I call there, I get the answering service, who tells me they don't know where you are. I call Sofia, there's no answer. I have no idea when you're going to be home . . ."

"Honey . . ."

"What?"

"We need to talk."

"What is it?" She lays the knife on the board next to the chopped onions and wipes her eyes with the bottom corner of her apron. Then she looks me straight in the eyes, weighs my somber expression, and says: "Don't tell me it's another woman. I don't want to hear it. Don't you dare . . ."

"It *is* another woman, but it's not what you think."

"It never is," she says. Joselyn starts to take off her apron, probably getting ready to throw it at me.

"Come here," I tell her. I open my arms. "Please. There's some terrible news I have to tell you."

The anger dissipates, replaced by a look of puzzlement around the eyes.

"Sofia is dead."

She stands there for a moment, frozen in place behind the granite island, her soft features framed by the cauldron of steam hissing from the stir-fry on the stove. "What? What do you mean?"

I move around the island, take her by the arm, and turn off the burner.

Her eyes are following me.

"Let's go sit down."

She looks dazed, as if I just sucker-punched her.

"Come on." I guide her by one arm and grab the box of Kleenex from the countertop as we pass by. Through the dining room I ease her into the living area and we settle on the couch.

As I turn my head to look, she's still staring at me, waiting for an answer.

"Two detectives came to my office this morning. They told me that her body was found by two joggers early this morning, off a road out near El Cajon."

"Was she hit by a car?"

I shake my head. "She was killed."

"You mean murdered?"

The word I can't bring myself to say.

A look of agony suffuses her eyes as she reads the answer from my face. "No—no." She shakes her head, looks at me again as if perhaps I'll give her a different one if she waits long enough. When it doesn't happen she collapses against me, her sharp fingernails digging into the back of my shirt as I feel the warmth of her tears flood my neck. She sobs. "How? Who did it?"

"They don't know."

She continues to cry.

I try to hand her a Kleenex. She shakes it away, buries her head in the open collar of my shirt, sobs some more, and then says, "When did it happen?"

"Best they can figure, Friday night."

She is silent for a moment, anguish giving way to calculation. "But we just saw her at the office . . ."

"Yes, earlier in the evening, just before she left."

She eases her hold on me, retracts the claws, sucks up some tears, and finally takes the Kleenex from my hand. "They must have some idea who did it? What did they tell you?"

"I'm not sure you want to know the details."

"Tell me!"

"They believe she was strangled. It's not clear exactly what time. But the marks on her throat would indicate—"

"Did you see her?"

I nod.

"Was she raped?"

"I don't think so. They won't know all the details until the coroner finishes his examination. But I don't think that was the motive," I tell her. "Of course, I may be wrong."

"What do the police think?"

"It's not entirely clear. Harry and I suspect they may be headed in the wrong direction."

"What do you mean?"

I tell her about Sofia's missing shoes, the theory voiced by the medical examiner that the case may be tied to a series of murders where the victim's shoes disappeared.

"Maybe they know something you don't," says Joselyn. "You know as well as I do that the police hold back details. Maybe there's something else that links them besides just the missing shoes."

"It's possible, but . . ."

"What?"

"Remember Sofia's iPhone?"

"Yes."

"Remember the little metal charm, the Eiffel Tower that was attached to it?"

"It's called a dust plug," says Joselyn. "She bought it online."

I open my hand.

She looks down. "Where did you get that?"

"In the backyard of Emma Brauer's house. Remember the woman I told you about, the one charged with the mercy killing?"

She nods.

"That's where Sofia was going when she left the office Friday night . . . to pick up Brauer's dog because Brauer had been arrested earlier that day. She was in jail."

"Who else was at the house?"

"No one, as far as we know. According to Brauer, she lives alone."

"Then you have to tell the police what you found."

"I intend to first thing in the morning." I have been trying to reach Noland and Owen ever since finding the trinket in the yard. They are off duty and their phones roll over to voicemail. I left a message. Harry and I debated whether we should take the tiny Eiffel Tower from the site where it lay and decided it was wise to do so. Otherwise the neighbor or a gardener might come along, sweep the yard, and throw it in the trash. I had Herman take several pictures of it on the cement where Harry found it. We placed a quarter next to it for scale and then I picked it up and put it in my pocket. If we have to, we can all sign an affidavit as to where we found it.

"Let me see it," she says.

I hand it to her. She looks at it.

"That's hers, I'm sure."

"How do you know?"

"Well, because Sofia and I talked about it. And I saw it on her phone."

"Do you know where she bought it, what site?"

"No. She didn't say. But who else could it belong to?"

"I don't know."

"Then tell the police to look at Sofia's phone. If the dust plug is missing, it's hers."

"I asked them about her phone. They were a little cagey," I tell her.

"What do you mean?"

"They didn't want to say anything. I'm wondering if they have it. I'll find out tomorrow."

"Who else would have it?"

"Whoever killed her might have taken it," I tell her.

"So you think Sofia was killed at this woman's house?"

"If the charm is hers, then we know she got to the house. We also know that she didn't take the dog, because it was found barking in the house later that night by a neighbor."

"So she was killed before she could get the dog," says Joselyn.

"That would be my guess."

"And her body dumped where the joggers found it."

"Yes. You know, I think maybe we should grab a bite and call it a night. Talking about this is not good for either one of us. We're tired and hungry."

"I'm not hungry. I've lost my appetite. I want to understand what happened," says Joselyn. "If someone killed Sofia I want to know why."

"So do I."

"Why would he move her body?" she says. "Unless it was somebody who lived there."

"No. No one lived there but Emma. We checked with the neighbors and they confirmed it. Emma's in her sixties. She doesn't have a boy-friend. From everything we've seen, what we know, she's very quiet."

"So we cross that off," she says. "OK, let's assume it was a burglar and he panicked. Sofia walks in on him and he kills her. Why would he take the time or the risks involved in moving her body? That's not protocol, is it?"

"I don't know."

"Well, you're the defense lawyer," she says. "Help me out here." She brushes the last tear from her cheek. She might cry later tonight, but for the moment the best painkillers are answers.

"All right. He wouldn't move the body. Not if he was just a burglar. A burglar with a dead body would run. If he had a brain he might slow down long enough to make sure he wasn't leaving a name tag behind."

"All right, so we can cross that off," she says. "What's left?"

"Well, we have to assume he moved the body for a reason."

"Obviously," she says. "I know that. The problem is we don't know what the reason was."

"Perhaps we have a guess," I tell her.

"What's that?"

"He didn't want the police locking the house down as a homicide scene."

"Go on."

"You sure you want to do this tonight?"

"Unless you want to sleep on the couch." Joselyn wants it all, every-thing I know.

"All right. Let's say he was there looking for something. She comes in, interrupts him, maybe traps him in an area of the house where he feels threatened. He can't be sure if she's alone, or maybe he thinks she's meeting somebody there. He kills her. Now he has a problem. If he leaves her there and somebody finds her, the police will throw a blanket over the house. He can't keep searching because he can't be certain someone else won't walk in on him. So he takes Sofia's body and her car, drives and dumps them—"

"Sofia's car was near her body?"

"Yes."

Joselyn is trying to make a mental picture in her head, the body dump and what it might have looked like.

"He walks a few miles back, either thumbs a ride someplace where he can get a cab or calls one. He gets back to the area where his car is parked. Probably a little ways from Emma's house. But he still hasn't found what he's looking for."

"How do you know that?"

"Because I have it."

"What? What is it?"

"It's a key to a safe-deposit box. Inside the box is another key and some papers. Beyond that we don't have a clue. Call it a work in progress. But if you give Herman and Harry claw hammers and a few seconds alone with the cretin who killed Sofia, I'm sure they'll be able to give you some answers in short order."

"Is that how the law works these days?" She finally gives me a small smile, Mona Lisa. "Come on, let's go get some dinner."

SIXTEEN

Tuesday morning is spent at the courthouse. Harry and I spring Emma from jail. The judge sets bail at one hundred thousand dollars on the single count of voluntary manslaughter.

There is no euthanasia law in California. Assisted suicide is a crime. The state can charge either murder or manslaughter, depending on the circumstances. Though we don't have access to all the state's evidence yet, the charge doesn't seem to make sense. Voluntary manslaughter is generally reserved for cases involving a homicide committed on the spur of the moment, in the heat of passion, where there is no evidence of premeditation or malice, like stabbing a person in a bar during a fight, especially if the knife just happens to be on the table.

If Harry and I buy it, which we don't, that means the police believe that Emma killed her father using some means that conveniently presented itself in his hospital room, that she did it without prior planning, in a moment of weakness, where the element of heat of passion might have been supplied by her inability to tolerate the pain he was suffering.

It's a creative theory, the kind you might expect from a defense lawyer in a closing argument after he spent a year or more thrashing out the evidence, and going toe-to-toe with prosecutors on motions to suppress, and arguments to exclude or narrow the testimony of expert witnesses.

But to have it presented in criminal information in the charging document as the state's opening shot leaves little ground to bargain down unless they want to say it was an accident, that she hit him with her bumper on the fourth floor in the geriatric unit, and treat it as a traffic infraction.

We listen as the deputy D.A. does a verbal dance with the judge on the terms of bail. Emma can't leave the county without notification and approval from the police. At no time is she to be within less than ten miles of the Mexican border. No trips on any waterborne vessels. No air travel, not even a hot air balloon . . .

I stand at the counsel table jacking my jaw like a wooden nutcracker: "Yes, Your Honor. We understand, Your Honor. No objection, Your Honor."

Harry pens a note on a yellow pad and eases it across the table in front of me. "They intend to amend." He underlines the word *amend* twice and then slips the pen back into his vest pocket.

Harry is right. And there is nowhere for them to bump it except up—to murder. If that's the case, the question is, why are they are letting her go? Murder is a nonbailable offense. I'm wondering why they're not charging her now and getting it over with.

But I don't ask. Instead I thank the judge, smile at the prosecutor, and glance at the two city PD homicide detectives sitting in the back of the room.

"Next case," says the judge.

Harry tells Emma we'll see her downstairs. We drift away from the table as a sheriff's deputy takes her back to the lockup to remove the waist chain and cuffs and get her street clothes in order to process her out. I sign the papers with the clerk on the bond and she gives me a receipt. Harry and I are now on the hook for ten grand, the premium on the bond if Emma goes on the lam, not that I'm worried.

"Why are they waiting to file?" says Harry.

I shake my head. I don't have a clue.

"Unless they're still going through evidence trying to bake up a theory and they've run into a problem," he says.

"Or there's something else we don't know." Harry and I have spent the better part of the morning trying to tell the sheriff's homicide detectives what we found at Emma's house—namely, the cell phone trinket with the Eiffel Tower from the backyard and the dog feces in the basement. I tried to get through to Owen, but he wasn't available, so Noland took the call.

I told him that we were wrong, that we made a mistake, that the trinket belonged to Sofia, and that I had seen it attached to her phone the Friday she disappeared. He asked me to describe it. I did. Noland said he was familiar with them, that his daughter had two just like it.

"They make a million of those things," said Noland. "And they all look alike. Why don't you check with your client and make sure it doesn't belong to her?"

I asked him if they found Sofia's phone.

He said they haven't. So of course they can't check to see if the chain with the little Eiffel Tower from her phone is missing.

"You don't understand," I told him. "The neighbor, the woman we talked to, do you remember?"

"Yeah, I remember."

"She wasn't home that evening, Friday evening, when Sofia was supposed to come by to get the dog. The woman had an appointment and she didn't get home until ten o'clock that night."

There was silence from the other end.

Finally, I thought, I made a dent, until Noland said, "So?"

"So she couldn't know whether Sofia got there or not. Don't you understand? We relied on the fact that the neighbor didn't see Sofia arrive at the house, but she *couldn't* see her because she wasn't there. She was out until ten."

"Yeah, but the dog was still there, right?" said Noland. "Otherwise how did the neighbor get him?"

"Yeah, the dog was there, but—"

"That means your girl never got there."

"Not necessarily. What if—"

"Listen, we're on top of it. We've got some fresh leads. We'll keep you posted."

"Yeah, but the dog was in the basement . . ." The line went dead. I looked at my cell phone. Either the signal was dropped or Noland hung up. I dialed again. It rang three times and rolled over to his voicemail—"Leave a message at the tone."

I did.

That was three hours ago, before Harry and I headed out to court for the bail hearing. Noland hasn't called back, and when I call him now, I get the same message. He's not taking my calls. I call Owen. His phone is turned off.

"Can't you smell it?" says Harry. "They're launched on a mission. In their minds they've already solved it."

Harry and I are waiting downstairs for Emma to come out of the jail. I call Herman on his cell. He answers on the second ring.

"Yeah?"

"Where are you?"

"At the office," he says.

"Good, I want you to get some help."

"What kind of help?"

"Contract PIs," I tell him. "Can you do it?"

"How many?"

"I don't know. Four or five, unless you think you can get more."

"Depends what we're paying," he says.

"What's the going rate?"

"Depends how fast you want 'em, for how long, and where," says Herman.

I look at my watch. "Tell them we need them in ninety minutes on the street in front of Brauer's house. Tell 'em we need them to canvass the neighborhood. It should take no more than two hours, depending on how many we get."

"You want 'em to drop everything and come right now, it's gonna cost you at least seventy-five, maybe a hundred dollars an hour," says Herman.

"Do it," I tell him. It's nice to have money. "Give them the address and then wait for me at the office."

"Got it," he says, and I hang up.

"I'll get the car," I tell Harry. "You stay here and wait for Emma. I'll pick you up. Tell her we have one errand to run, then we'll swing by the office, pick up her car, and then take her home."

"Why are we taking her if she has her own car?" says Harry.

"Because I don't want her there alone."

Forty minutes later we're back at the office. Herman is waiting for us.

"How many were you able to get?" I ask him.

"Six. It was the best I could do on short notice," he says.

"Good." I fish through the drawer in my desk until I find the key to Emma's car. I flip it to Herman. "You drive the Prius; take Emma. Harry and I will meet you there."

"How is Sofia making out with Dingus?" When I look up, Emma is standing in the open door to my office.

"The dog is fine," I tell her. Harry and I haven't told her anything about Sofia, not yet.

"Do you think she might be able to bring Dingus home later?" she asks.

"Dingus is already there," I tell her. "He's with your neighbor."

"Aw, she's so sweet. Tell her thank you for me. Is she here in the office?" Emma steps away and looks down the hall.

"No. No. No. She's not here."

"I'd like to get her a present. Do you have any ideas?"

I glance at Herman, who is standing there looking down at the carpet.

"I'll need to think about it," I tell her. I'll break the news to her when she's home. But I don't want to tell her that I think it happened at her house. I'll leave that for later, and only if it becomes necessary.

Harry steps into the office. "Are we ready to go?"

"You and I are gonna stay here. Got some things to do. We'll go out later. For now Herman can take care of it. But I wonder if you could take Emma out to the car, start the engine and the air-con, get her comfortable. Herman will be out in a minute. There is something he and I need to discuss."

Herman hands the car key to Harry and he and Emma head out. Just before Harry gets to the door I whisper: "And Harry, don't stop at the front desk on the way out. We don't need Emma talking to the girls out front about Sofia."

As soon as they're gone I turn to Herman. "Here's what I want you to do. Have your guys canvass the neighborhood around Emma's house. Talk to all the neighbors, anyone who was around on Friday afternoon and evening. Ask them if they saw anyone around the house, any strangers or cars they didn't recognize. See if any of them have surveillance or security cameras on their houses that might have video of the street.

Oh, and by the way, while your guys are checking, call the city and see if they have any security cameras on any of the power poles in the area."

Herman looks at me and says, "Who's gonna tell Emma about Sofia?"

"You want to draw straws?"

"That's beyond my pay grade," he says.

"I'll take care of it later when I come out. But check and see if any of your people there have licenses to carry. If so, we're going to want them to get armed and keep an eye on the house and on Emma." If Sofia was killed there, anyone staying in the house would be in danger. "They won't be there long," I tell him, "because Emma is probably headed back to jail. She just doesn't know it yet."

As soon as Herman steps out, I check the item in my pocket. The errand, the stop we made after leaving the courthouse, was to Emma's bank. We used the key from her basement to open her safe-deposit box. Inside was a small cardboard jewelry box.

I take it out of my pocket. It looks as if it might have been white at one time. It has seen a lot of wear and now looks more gray than anything else.

I lift the small lid. Inside is a key similar to the one we found in Emma's basement that we used to open her box at the bank. It clearly belongs to another safe-deposit box. Where this one is located is anyone's guess. Under the key are two pieces of folded paper. One of them is the brown wrapper that originally covered the box. The other is the document that Emma described as an ID. I take it out, unfold it, and spread it open on my desk.

Harry comes through the door. "What's that?" He looks at the small scrap of paper.

"I don't know. It looks like German, maybe Dutch." There is a picture, a photo ID, maybe an inch and a half square, like for a passport. It's a head shot of a man in what looks like a brown or perhaps a gray uniform. It's hard to tell because the picture is black-and-white, and old. The only thing I can make out is the name: "Jakob Grimminger." And under it: "SS Standartenführer."

"Who is he?" says Harry.

"I don't know. But whoever he is, he's German."

SEVENTEEN

We are not paying you to play bull in a china shop," said Ari. The Israeli attaché sat across from Nino, elbows propped on the table, his gold cuff links dangling over the beef and chopped liver on rye that lay open on the plate in front of him, untouched. The man had a face and fingers like a corpse.

Nino figured the Jew either had ulcers or a tapeworm. Whenever they met it was always the same. Nino wouldn't get the call until just before the meeting. Ari would name the place, and Nino would have to hustle and would get there in a flop sweat.

Ari thought he was calling a pay phone at a location selected by Nino. But he wasn't. Nino used a cell phone with a disposable prepaid SIM card from one of the major US carriers. He would buy a new SIM card and give Ari the number at each meeting, leaving the Israeli to believe he would be calling a different pay phone. Why should Nino race all over town being jerked around at pay phones when he could sit in a local bar and wait for the call?

The cadaver would greet him without a smile, hug him as if he was feeling him up, looking to see if Nino might be wearing a wire. The Jewish consul's gofer was trying to be careful. But he was never happy. He would order a sandwich and either leave it on the table or drop it in the trash on the way out. Nino wanted to tell him there were children starving all over the world, but he knew the guy wouldn't care.

"Twice you have been there now. And twice you have failed."

"Not entirely," said Nino.

"Oh, you mean you found it?"

"No, but I narrowed it down."

"I would hope so," said Ari, "seeing as you destroyed most of the furniture in the house on your first visit. What are you planning next, a fire? Is it necessary to remind you who I work for? We cannot afford an embarrassing incident. Particularly one that can be traced back to me or, more important, to my employer."

Nino guessed that the man would slide under the table with a stroke if he knew the whole story, the details that Nino hadn't told him. Still, he was hoping that today the man might be in a better mood, seeing as he picked a kosher deli for their meeting. But it didn't seem to help. The sandwich was still going in the garbage. The guy had a perpetual hot wire up his ass. He needed to find a more peaceful line of work. If he kept doing this much longer it was going to kill him.

"Why should we give you another chance?" said Ari. "Tell me."

"Because I know where it is," said Nino.

"Do you?"

"Yeah."

"Well, then enlighten me."

"Why would I wanna do that? If I tell you where it is, you're just gonna hire somebody else to go get it."

"You mean someone with skill," said Ari.

Nino looked at the pickle on the guy's plate. He was wondering if the man was going to eat it or if he would fight for it if Nino reached over and harpooned it with his fork. Nino's mind was occupied, plotting the trajectory across the table.

"Listen to me, Jimmie." Ari leaned forward.

Nino's eyes suddenly diverted to the man's face with the thought, Who the hell is Jimmie?

"Stop eating for a moment and listen to me."

Nino put the fork down. This was getting hard, trying to remember the false names under which he was operating, let alone keeping them matched with the right clients. It would have been easier to run for office. There all you had to worry about was forgetting the names of the fools who gave you money. Nino had to worry about forgetting his own. Answer to the wrong name with some business tycoon who went to the trouble to check out your rap sheet just to see if you had the credentials to off one of his partners, and what do you do then? Some of these people had money, more than enough to hire some wiseguy to erase their mistake. Nino could end up on a rolling cart in the morgue with somebody else's name on his toe tag.

"We are on thin ice here," said Ari. "You and me. The people I report to are not happy. They are telling me that I hired an amateur. I'd like to tell them that I didn't. But at the moment I'm not sure. Did I?"

Nino shook his head slowly.

"I hope not. For your sake as well as my own. The burglary was clumsy. You know that. To break in and do all that damage . . ."

"It's a very small item. You're the ones who told me what to look for. There's a lotta places you can hide something like that. It wasn't an easy search. Sometimes that means breaking stuff. After that, well, it was necessary to make it look real. You know, teenage vandals."

"Teenagers are one thing. Visigoths are another," said Ari. "And then when you left, you didn't take anything. For crying out loud . . ."

"Why would I want to take any of that old crap?" said Nino. In point of fact he had taken only one item, a document that he had no intention of sharing with the Israelis.

"That's not the point," said Ari. "Teenagers would have taken something. Even some idiot burglar your age would have grabbed a few small things of value."

Nino wanted to tell him, "Yeah, that's how their stupid asses end up in prison." But he didn't. The only reason he took the job in the first place was that he had two other clients looking for the same item. One of them he had on the hook advancing his costs. He was a guy who was married to money with a shaky marriage, and he wanted a backup plan in case of a divorce. Each one of them had given him differing slivers of information, where to look and what to look for. When he found it he would haul it away, find out who else was interested, hold a private auction, and sell it to the highest bidder. The money would be wired into a numbered account in Aruba.

He found the other clients the same way he found Ari. By flying under false colors, posing as someone he wasn't. In this case it was a former navy petty officer, third class, James "Jimmie" Pepper. Pepper came out of the navy with a drinking problem and not much else. He lived on the streets and panhandled for booze. When Nino found him he was standing under a highway overpass with a banged-up shopping cart.

He was about Nino's height with the same dark hair, holding a cardboard sign that read: "Former Navy—Need Help." Nino tossed him into a rendering tank at a small tallow plant near Miramar, but not until after stripping his clothes, lifting his wallet, and scouring the shopping cart for any other identifying information. It was one of the advantages of helping yourself to the identity of the homeless. They were rarely missed, and usually everything they owned was with them. In Pepper's case this included some navy papers and a jail release form showing that the former petty officer had been booked for burglary. By now, molecular particles of Pepper were probably gracing ladies' luxury facial soaps on shelves in a half-dozen western states.

"So now, because of your bungling," said Ari, "they know that it wasn't a burglary. They know you were looking for something specific, and because you didn't find it, they can go to much greater lengths to hide it. So tell me, what happened the second time?"

"I was interrupted," said Nino. "I didn't get the chance."

"I thought the place was empty."

"So did I."

"Who was it?"

"I don't know."

"Can they identify you?"

"No. You don't have to worry about that. Listen, the old man is dead," said Nino, "and the house is empty because the daughter's in jail. Let me go in one more time."

"*Was* in jail," said Ari. "She has been released on bail. And we have to assume that by now she is probably back at her house."

EIGHTEEN

The photo of the German on the ID looks as if it could easily date back as far as the early forties, World War II. From everything Emma has told us, Robert Brauer served honorably in the war, saw combat in Europe, and was present there on V-E Day in 1945. Beyond that we know nothing.

Harry and I are alone in my office. I tell him about the Luger in the display case in Brauer's study and the military patch, the gold and red thunderbird with the label "45th Infantry Division" under it, and the swastika. Harry was busy working the trapdoor when Herman and I were looking at them.

"I saw them later when I was going through his desk. I wondered the same thing," says Harry. "You think Brauer was a closet Nazi?"

"Who knows?"

"That might explain why he was afraid," says Harry. "Maybe he got tangled up with some skinheads."

I turn to the computer, punch up Google, and type in "45th Infantry Division."

In seconds the site list pops up. There're a bunch of sites. I open one of them. It spills across the screen, a map of Western Europe with text underneath in big letters.

"The 45th Infantry Division drove on Munich in the closing days of the war and, in the process, it liberated the Nazi concentration camp at Dachau. The division crossed the Danube River on 27 April, 1945, and liberated 32,000 captives of Dachau on 29 April. The division captured Munich during the next two days, occupying the city until V-E Day and the surrender of Germany. During the next month, the division remained in Munich and set up collection points and camps for the massive numbers of surrendering troops of the German armies. The number of POWs taken by the 45th Infantry Division during its almost two years of fighting totaled 124,840 men."

"Dachau concentration camp," says Harry.

"I see it."

"You think Brauer was there?"

"I don't know."

"We could ask Emma."

"She says she doesn't know anything. According to her, her dad never talked about the war. All she knows is little bits and pieces from letters he'd written to army buddies and a few telephone conversations she overheard. Whenever she asked him about the war, the men he served with, he'd go silent. Didn't want to talk about it. She assumed it brought up bad memories, so she never pressed him."

"It is possible the swastika on the wall is something Brauer captured, like the pistol. Maybe they go together," says Harry.

"Herman looked at the Luger and said he thought it was authentic." I punch up another site, wait a couple of seconds, and sit there staring at it. "I'll be damned."

"What is it?" says Harry.

"The unit emblem for the 45th Infantry Division of the United States Army."

"What was it?"

"Come take a look," I tell him.

Harry steps around the desk so he can look over my shoulder. It's an item from the 45th Infantry Division Museum, their online site, an organization dedicated to the history of the unit.

I know from other readings that the symbol in question has a history dating back thousands of years. It is formed by an equilateral cross, the outward legs of which are bent at a ninety-degree angle. It has been used by various cultures and religions from time immemorial, including Hindus, Buddhists, and followers of Jainism. In ancient Sanskrit it was known by the word *svastika*. We know it as the swastika.

According to the article from the 45th Infantry Division Museum, the unit wore the swastika on their divisional arm patch for a period dating from around 1920 until 1933. To the unit it was an ancient American Indian icon, a symbol of good luck.

The 45th was headquartered in Oklahoma City and trained at Fort Bliss. It was made up of recruits mostly from Oklahoma, New Mexico, Colorado, and Arizona. This was Indian country for many of the western tribes, so according to the article the symbol made sense.

From reading we find out that the problem arose when the swastika became known worldwide as the symbol of Hitler's Nazi Party in Germany.

Apparently the 45th abandoned the swastika in 1933. They wore no arm patch insignia until 1939. After much thought and a contest to come up with a new insignia, the army settled on another American Indian motif. It was gold and red, the same colors as the old patch, but this time it was the Thunderbird—the symbol of the "sacred bearer of happiness unlimited." They marched with it on their shoulders through World War II and the Korean War.

The 45th Infantry Division was deactivated in 1968 and rolled into the 45th Infantry Brigade along with its battle flags, storied history, and Thunderbird shoulder insignia.

"That proves what they say," says Harry.

"What's that?"

"There's nothing stranger than history. Could have knocked me over with a thunderbird feather. We can forget the theory that Brauer was a Nazi."

"Looks like it."

"Where did they end up?" says Harry.

"Who?"

"The 45th, at the end of the war?"

I look through some of the materials online. "Looks like Munich. Why?"

"Munich was a hotbed," says Harry. "It's where Hitler got his start. The Beer Hall Putsch, remember? Early twenties."

"That was before my time," I say, and start to smile.

"I know it's fashionable to be ignorant with regards to history," he says, "but the Millennials will end up reliving it if they aren't careful.

Our own American version of Hitler. Country's in trouble, in case you haven't noticed. And most people haven't a clue as to current events. They know even less about history."

He's getting wound up. I can tell. Harry's lecture series, new season, episode one.

"If a nuclear war happened before four o'clock yesterday, they don't know about it. If another one is scheduled for tomorrow, the only question they'll ask is whether they can catch it on YouTube. The definition of being cool. The younger generation is ignorant," he says.

"You tell my daughter that, tell Sarah that the next time she's down, and I'll take odds she hits you with a book."

"You can bet it won't be a history book," says Harry.

I start to laugh.

"It's not funny," he says. "The world's coming apart and the kids are gonna inherit it."

"You did pretty well last year. Have you checked your portfolio balance lately?"

"I'm not talking about money," says Harry. "Forget the money. Do you realize you'd have to dig up at least three generations of elementary school teachers in any major city in this country before you find one who knows what World War Two was and when it happened? I'm not kidding. Stop anybody on the street under eighty and ask them who Stalin was, and they'll tell you it's a rock group. We're gonna wake up someday and find his clone sitting with his feet on the desk in the Oval Office," he says.

I need to buy Harry a bullhorn and sandwich board so he can go out on the street and scream at the kids. See if all those noise-canceling headphones really work.

"They can either learn it or relive it," he says.

"Well, I suppose every so often the world needs a refresher course," I tell him.

"That's not funny," says Harry. "That's not funny at all. That's learning the hard way."

"Yeah, well, maybe it's a lesson they won't forget," I tell him. I have my back to him looking at the screen. "Can you find that little box with the key? It's on the desk there somewhere."

"What, this?"

I turn. "Yeah. There's another piece of paper folded up inside. Take it out and take a look."

He does it.

It's the brown wrapper. "Do you see a return address on it?"

"Yeah, there's a small sticker."

"What does it say?"

"Law Offices of Elliott Fish. There's a P.O. box, Oklahoma City, Oklahoma, and a zip."

"It was sent from a law office?"

"Looks like it," says Harry.

Harry gives me the name again and I punch it into the computer. Sure enough, I find a website with a phone number. I pick up the phone and dial. A receptionist answers: "Elliott Fish Law Offices, can I help you?"

"Is Mr. Fish in, by any chance?"

"Who may I say is calling?"

"Attorney Paul Madriani, from Coronado, California."

"Just a moment please." I get an earful of elevator music.

A few seconds later a male voice comes on the line. "This is Elliott Fish. Who am I speaking to?"

"Mr. Fish, this is Paul Madriani. I'm a lawyer out in California."

"Yes, what can I do for you?"

"I have a client whose father received a small package from your office. His name was Robert Brauer. Can I ask who you represent and why you sent it to him?"

"Do you represent Mr. Brauer?"

"No. No, I'm afraid Mr. Brauer is dead."

"Oh, I see. Do you represent his estate?"

"I represent his daughter, Emma Brauer."

"May I ask when Mr. Brauer died?"

"About six weeks ago."

"And may I ask how you know about the package?"

"It's sitting here on my desk right now."

"I see. Then you should be able to tell me the contents of the package."

"A key. Looks like a safe-deposit key. And some kind of an ID, very old. In German, the name Jakob Grimminger."

"Yes." He clears his throat. "I'm sorry, but I can't help you."

"Am I correct in assuming that you sent the package to Mr. Brauer?"

"I did."

"Was it on behalf of a client?"

"It was."

"May I ask who the client was?"

"That I can't tell you."

"May I ask why?"

"It's confidential lawyer-client information," he says.

"Well, let me explain. Mr. Brauer's daughter, Emma Brauer, is my client. She has her own set of problems at the moment."

"Yes?"

"Well, she's charged with homicide. Mr. Brauer, who was quite ill before he died, was in a VA hospital out here, and it seems the authorities have reason to believe that he may not have died of natural causes. They seem to believe that my client may have put him out of his misery in a mercy killing."

"I see."

"At the moment it's a single charge of voluntary manslaughter, but I'm concerned that if I can't determine what's happening here it could become more serious."

"What makes you think that the package has anything to do with your client's case?"

"Before Mr. Brauer died, his home was burglarized. Whoever broke in was looking for something. Mr. Brauer told his daughter that he was fearful both for himself and for her, and told her to place the package in a bank vault for safekeeping."

There is a lot of heavy breathing on the other end of the line.

"Last week an employee of my office, a young woman, went to Brauer's house on an errand for the office. Ms. Brauer was not there because she was in jail. That employee was found murdered Monday morning. We have reason to believe that she was killed at the house and that her body was deposited at another location."

"I'm sorry to hear that," he says. "But if, as you say, Ms. Brauer placed the package in a bank vault and it wasn't in the house, how can you be sure that it's in any way connected to the death of your employee?"

"The placement of the package in the bank was a private matter known only to Mr. Brauer and his daughter."

"I see. This does complicate things," says the lawyer. "I'm not certain whether I can disclose the identity of my clients."

The way he says it makes it clear that there is more than one.

"When did you say Mr. Brauer died?" he asks.

"About six weeks ago."

"Do you have a death certificate?"

"I can get one."

"You might send me a certified copy," he says. "He would have been the last."

"Last what?"

"I'm sorry, I can't say. But I should advise you that there may be other claimants."

"Claimants to what?"

"I can't say. But you should be aware that since you hold the box and its contents you may be on the receiving end of one or more lawsuits."

"For what? By who?"

"By persons with a valid legal claim to the item in question."

"What's the item?"

"To tell you the truth, I don't know the answer to that myself. I'm simply carrying out the instructions of my clients."

"Can you tell me when you were hired?"

"The specific date? I'd have to look, but it was several years ago."

"Can I ask you—and you don't have to answer if you can't, but I'm really up against the wall here. I'm assuming that whatever's going on here has to do with Mr. Brauer's former military service with the 45th Infantry Division in Europe during the Second World War."

Nothing but breathing and silence from the other end.

"Hello?"

"I'm here," he says. "There is one peculiar thing."

"What's that?"

"You did say that the police believe that Mr. Brauer may not have died of natural causes, is that correct?"

"That's right."

"It's a strange coincidence."

"Yes, what's that?"

"There's another individual out here in Oklahoma City who says his father died under similar circumstances. He was in a nursing home. And according to what I've heard, there is at least one person who doesn't believe he died of natural causes. He's requested an investigation by authorities, but so far they have no evidence to establish foul play."

"Am I to assume that this other individual, the man who died, is somehow connected with Mr. Brauer?"

There is no reply from the other end of the line, but I can still hear him breathing. In this case I construe silence as assent.

"Was he by any chance a member of the 45th Infantry Division?"

More silence. "You put me in a very difficult position," he says.

"You don't have to answer. My client told me that the package came from one of her father's military buddies. That's what he told her before he died. The wrapper has your return address on it. So I have to assume that the group you represent consists of Mr. Brauer's former military associates. I would further assume then that whoever is raising questions about the man's death, the gentleman back there in Oklahoma City, must be a relative or a friend of one of these men?"

More silence.

"Let me ask you, do you have an attorney-client relationship with the individual who is complaining about the death of this gentleman?"

The lawyer finally exhales and says, "As a matter of fact, I don't." He seems almost relieved to give up the information. "Do you have something to write with?"

"I do."

"His name is Anthony Pack." He gives me the man's phone number and address. "I think if you contact him, he may be able to help you."

"Thank you very much." I hang up.

NINETEEN

Early Wednesday morning and Herman is in my office first thing. He is looking tired, haggard, and unhappy.

"Did you get Emma settled in?"

"Yeah. We've got security watching the place."

Late last evening before I went home I trekked out to Brauer's house and gave her the bad news about Sofia. She took it hard. Herman had brought the dog over so Emma wouldn't talk to the neighbor before I got there. It took her a couple of minutes to get the bottom line. She looked at the dog, thought for a moment, and then asked me whether Sofia ever made it to her house. I didn't lie. I told her the truth, that the cops were operating on the theory that Sofia never got there. We talked for a few more minutes and I asked her if she had a cell phone. She said no. Said she wouldn't know how to use one. I asked her if she had any relatives or friends who might have had one and used it in her backyard recently. She looked at me and asked why. I took a chance, pulled out the Eiffel Tower charm, and showed it to her. I told her we found it in her yard and wondered whether it might belong to someone she knew. She looked at it, shook her head, and said no. The fact that it doesn't belong to her or a friend is a sword that cuts both ways. No doubt Noland would pounce all over the fact that she didn't remember seeing it on Sofia's phone in the office on Friday, either.

"So what did you find?" I look at Herman.

"You want the truth, it looks like we wasted a lot of their shoe leather and your money." He plants himself in one of the client chairs and opens his notebook. "We covered Brauer's neighborhood, both sides of the street all the way to the next intersection in each direction, north and south. We couldn't find a soul who saw anything unusual at her house Friday night. There was one older couple said they walked by the house about eight o'clock. They don't recall any vehicles parked out front, none in the driveway. They didn't notice extra lights on in the house."

He glances down at his notepad. "One neighbor on Brauer's side of the street, two doors to the south, says she thought she heard the dog barking, but she didn't bother to look, cuz she said the dog barked all the time."

"Did she say what time?"

"She couldn't remember. But she said it was dark so it must have been later."

"What about cameras? Do any of the neighbors have security videos?"

He shakes his head. "We found four or five, but none of them close enough to catch anything at Brauer's house. One of them might have picked up a narrow slice of the street out in front. We're checking to see if we can get a copy of the video. There's a slight chance, very slim, it might have picked up somebody driving to or from the house assuming the motion of the car was close enough to trigger the camera. Even if it did, you won't be able to see Brauer's place. The camera was one of those little pinhole security jobs. It was across the street, on a front porch, but about four houses down."

"Any chance it might have night vision?"

Herman looks at me and chuckles. "Why don't you ask for the Hubble Space Telescope while you're at it. Not according to our man who looked at it. Said it looked like one of those forty-nine-dollar specials."

"Let's see if we can get the video and look at it."

"We're on it," he says. "One other thing. We took a report from a neighbor down the block, lives about six houses to the north. She and her husband saw a car parked in front of another neighbor's. It wasn't in front of Brauer's house. This would have been down the block a ways, parked at the left curb going the wrong way. And it wasn't Friday. It was Thursday night."

"Go on."

"They got curious because they saw it parked the wrong way, parking lights on and the engine idling. The husband wanted to go check it out. She wanted to call the police. She said it was an old beat-up car, all rusted out."

"Any make or model?"

"Old is all she said. Anyway, the husband went out the door. She didn't want him to go alone, so she grabbed her phone and followed him. She said that as they approached the car along the sidewalk from behind, the driver saw 'em in the side-view mirror, threw the car in gear, and pulled away. According to her he left enough smoking rubber on the road for a lifetime supply of erasers."

"Did they get a look at the driver?"

"White, is all she said. Two men. Driver and one passenger in the front seat. She said the one driving had a tattoo."

"Where, on his arm?"

"Back of his neck and the side of his face. In the mirror she said she could see a metal ring, maybe two, she wasn't sure, through the corner of his lip."

"Sounds like they were fortunate not to make it all the way to the car. Any chance they got a license plate?"

"I knew you would ask. They got a partial rear plate, one number and two letters. Five, a space, the letters *PU,* and three more letters or numbers, they weren't sure."

"California?" I ask.

"They think so."

"Then the last three ought to be numbers. Correct?"

"Assuming they got everything in the right order and it's a California plate. The old man was trying to read it, but according to her it was moving pretty damn fast. And there wasn't much light. She got a picture with her cell phone. The investigator got a copy, but it looks like nothing but fuzz to me."

"Send it out to a lab, see if they can do anything to enhance it. Check the video from the home security camera and if there's anything on it, do the same. I take it there's no chance the husband or wife can identify the car?"

"All she said was it was big, fast, and had a lot of rust."

"OK, well I guess that's it."

Herman is up out of the chair, headed to the door.

"Oh, what about the other thing?"

"I'm working on it," he says.

"Let me know when it's up and running."

"Will do." Herman barely clears the door and Harry comes in.

"Have you seen anything from the medical examiner on Brauer yet? Autopsy or toxicology?"

I shake my head. "No. Did you check the front desk?"

"It's not there. I'm getting worried," says Harry. "Where is it? You know they had it before they filed, so why haven't they produced it?"

"Let's not be in a hurry. You can bet the minute they give it to us they're going to bump the charge to murder one and take Emma back into custody."

"If they're gonna do it, may as well do it now. At least then we'll know."

"Yeah, but a few more days might give you time to get ready."

"Ready for what?" says Harry.

"I told Emma that if she has to go back in, you'd take the dog."

"What?"

"You can't imagine how relieved she was when I told her. Don't get me wrong, she's still frightened by the prospect of going back to jail, but telling her that you'd take care of Dingus made a huge difference."

Harry makes one of those strange expressions, halfway between a smile and a question mark. "Yeah, right."

"We can't send the dog to a kennel, not after what he's been through. And besides, Emma's baking you a cake. She said she'd bring it by to-morrow. She likes you. She trusts you. I didn't say anything to her, but we both know Dingus will feel much more at home sleeping in your closet, with your shoes."

"Bullshit!" he says.

"No, same material but from a different species," I tell him.

"You didn't. I don't believe you," he says.

"I hope you like German chocolate."

"I don't care whether you told her or not. I'm not gonna do it. I won't. I'm not some hired dog sitter."

"No. I told her you'd be happy to do it for free. You know what she said?"

"I don't care what she said."

"She said you and Sofia were the two nicest people she'd ever met. That's what she said. And then she started to cry. I'm telling you she cried like a baby."

"I don't care. I don't believe you. And even if it's true, I won't do it," he says.

"What's your problem? You know what I think?"

"I don't care what you think."

"I think Gwyn doesn't like animals."

"You know, you know," he says, "that's not even funny."

I glance at the yellow pad on my desk. "Maybe we should continue this over lunch. I've got a phone call I have to make. Do you mind closing the door on your way out?"

Harry stands there looking at me, seething. He'd like to laugh it off. But he can't. It's that little ember of doubt, the hot cinder caught in his throat that tells him maybe he'll have to go into hiding to avoid Emma and her dog. Finally he turns, walks out the door, and slams it behind him.

I laugh. If Harry can drill my noodle with his lame lectures on history and politics, I can return the favor with a head job on him from Dingus. Tonight I'll heat up the cinder with the bellows, pick up a cake at a local store, slip it onto a nice dish I'll buy, and put it all in the middle of Harry's desk. I'll pen a note with my left hand. "I don't know how I will ever be able to thank you for taking care of Dingus. If I must go back, it will take some of the pain out of my long days and nights in jail. It means so much to me that someone who cares is looking after Dad's dog. I know that my father is watching from heaven and blessing you for your love of helpless and dumb animals. Yours truly, Emma."

I'd add a postscript, "Be careful where you step," but it would totally destroy the effect.

TWENTY

It's a 405 area code. I pick up the receiver and punch in the number for Mr. Anthony Pack, the name given to me yesterday by the lawyer, Elliott Fish, in Oklahoma City. I tried to call Pack late yesterday but there was no answer. When it rolled over to voicemail I decided not to leave a message.

This time it's answered by a young female voice. "Hello."

"Hello, is Mr. Pack there by any chance?"

"Dad, it's for you. Just a minute, he'll be right here." *Clunk* in my ear as the receiver gets dropped on a hard surface. "Dad! Someone's on the phone for you."

"Who is it?"

"I don't know. Some man."

I hear footsteps, the receiver rattles. "Hello."

"Hello, is this Mr. Anthony Pack?"

"Yes. Who is this?"

"My name is Paul Madriani. I'm a lawyer in California. I am calling because I was given your name by someone in Oklahoma City who told me that it's possible that you and I might have an interest in sharing some information."

"In what regard?"

"I represent a woman, a client here in San Diego, whose father, I believe, may have served in the army with someone you know. It would have been many years ago, during World War Two in Europe."

"What is your client's name?"

"Her last name is Brauer. Her father was Robert Brauer. Do you know the name?"

"Did you say *was*?"

"Yes. He died recently."

"May I ask how he died?"

"We're not entirely sure. That's part of the problem."

"I never met the man, but I know the name," says Pack. "He served with my father in the 45th Infantry in France and Germany during the war. They were in the same platoon. You say you can't tell me how he died?"

"The authorities think someone may have killed him."

"I knew it," says Pack. "Damn. I've been trying to tell the police here in Oklahoma City for almost a year that someone murdered my father. They just won't listen."

"How did he die?"

"They say natural causes. But I don't believe it."

"What evidence do you have?"

"None. That's the problem," says Pack. "There was no autopsy."

"Why not?"

"My dad was in his eighties, though he wasn't in particularly bad health for a man his age. He needed help caring for himself. He couldn't cook, needed help getting dressed at times. He was under the care of a physician. I guess they don't usually do an autopsy in his type of situation, not unless there's a reason. Then all of a sudden, one day he doesn't wake up, he goes into a coma. The doctor's can't figure out why, there's no indications of a heart attack or a stroke, and within a matter of hours he's dead."

"Sounds like good reason for an autopsy."

"That's what I thought," says Pack. "I was busy talking to the authorities insisting that they do one. Before I knew it, the body was released to a funeral home. Within an hour my dad was cremated. There was nothing I could do about it. Whatever evidence existed went up in smoke with him."

"Maybe they just screwed up, released the body prematurely. It happens," I tell him.

"Except for one thing: my dad was Roman Catholic. He would never have authorized cremation. I know that. I examined the signature on the form. It wasn't his."

"Did you tell the police?"

"Oh, yeah. They said people's handwriting often changes when they get older, especially if they're sick. According to them, it has to do with loss of coordination, microvascular problems in the brain. They had a dozen explanations. The fact is, they didn't want to be bothered. Someone killed him and they burned the body to destroy the evidence," he says. "And that's not all. I know there was something wrong because at the end he was very frightened. In the last month before he died he was scared. And that wasn't like my dad."

"Scared by what?"

"I'm not entirely sure. But it had to do with his time in the army. I know that."

"What did your father do in the army?"

"He was a medic. When he came out of the military he finished college and went to medical school on the GI Bill. He became a doctor, general practitioner, internal medicine. People here loved him. He'd been in practice almost forty years. How much do you know about what's going on here?" he asks.

"Not much," I say.

"Has Mr. Brauer's daughter been able to tell you anything?"

"No, only that her father was also scared, quite afraid, before he died. And like your dad, it wasn't in his nature. Whatever it is, it seems to be contagious," I tell him.

"And terminal," he says. "In case you're wondering, they weren't alone. From what I understand, and I don't know all the details, there were seven men in the platoon originally. At least that's what my dad told me. He used to talk when I was a kid about his experiences in the war. If I remember right, two of the men died in combat. I don't have their names, but I may be able to find them. Two others died in a traffic accident in Munich where they were stationed after the war waiting to come home. It sounds like all of them may be dead by now."

I suspect that Pack is correct. Fish let slip during our telephone conversation that Brauer was the last survivor.

"Do you know," he asks, "if there was anything that happened that caused Mr. Brauer to be frightened?"

"I'm not sure. I'd have to talk to his daughter." Until I know more, I want to be careful how much information I share.

"By any chance did he receive a small package?" asks Pack.

"What kind of a package?"

"A small cardboard box. The kind you might get if you bought a small bracelet."

"He may have," I tell him. "Why do you ask?"

"Because my father got one."

"When?" I ask.

"About a month before he died. And it scared the hell out of him."

"I see. Do you mind telling me what was in it?"

"A key and something else, a piece of paper. I'm not sure exactly what it was. Whatever it was, my father destroyed the paper. He burned it in the trash can in his office. I watched him do it."

"What happened to the key?" I ask.

"I don't know. I never saw it again."

"Do you know where the package came from?"

"Yes. I picked it up at the post office box the day it arrived. It came from a lawyer here in Oklahoma City."

"Elliott Fish?"

"How did you know?" he says.

"I talked to him on the phone yesterday afternoon. That's how I got your name."

"I hope he's been more helpful with you than he's been with me," he says. "I've talked to him several times, asked him for information, and have gotten nowhere. He says his lips are sealed. Lawyer confidentiality."

"He told me the same thing. I got your name only because you weren't a client."

Pack has already answered one question, how the lawyer came to find out about his father's death, that and the fact that the son was pounding on the police for answers.

"I'm not sure it's wise to discuss details over the phone," I tell him.

"I agree," he says. "I think it might be better if we got together and compared notes."

"When and where?" I ask.

"Where are you located?"

I tell him, give him my address and phone number.

"What's your schedule look like?" he asks.

"Right now I'm up to my teeth," I tell him. "I could come out there, but I'm not sure when. I could send an investigator if that would work."

"No. If we're going to do this, we need to do it one-on-one," he says. "In fact, I'd like to meet your client, Ms. Brauer. She may be the one I need to talk to."

"That depends on her schedule," I say. I don't want to tell him that unless we hurry up, any meeting with Emma may be behind bars. I don't want to scare him off.

"Tell you what, how about if I come to you?" he says. "At the moment it sounds like you're busier than I am. Then, if we need to meet a second time, the travel will be on you. How's that?"

"Fair enough," I tell him.

"Now to the calendar," he says. "Let me see. This is Wednesday. What does your schedule look like?"

I take a look in the computer. "I'm in court Thursday. Friday I'm tied up all morning, a matter that may go into the afternoon."

"What's your weekend look like? I assume lawyers don't like to work on the weekend. But how about Saturday?" he says.

"No, I'm sorry. That won't work. I already have a commitment." My calendar is blocked out—"Sofia's memorial service."

"Then it looks like Monday," he says. "Do you want to pick the time?"

"When would you be coming in?"

"Figure late Sunday. I'll have to check the airline schedules. If I have trouble booking a flight, I'll call you back. Give me your number," he says.

I give him the office number and my cell so if he has to, he can catch me on the fly.

"Let's do it Monday morning," I tell him. "Say ten o'clock, here at our office. How does that sound?"

"Sounds good. No," he says. "Actually that sounds great. I'm relieved."

"How's that?"

"For more than a year I've been fighting this thing all alone," he says. "I feel like a hermit wandering in the desert. The police won't help. They think I'm crazy. I've been searching for answers and getting nowhere. At least now maybe I have someone else I can share it with. Someone else who's crazy."

"Thanks," I tell him.

"Listen, I don't want to scare you away. You're the first glimmer of hope I've had. I look forward to seeing you on Monday."

"See you then." And we hang up.

TWENTY-ONE

The old 1970 Chevelle SS 454 looked a wreck. Its rusted-out body and torn upholstery were well past their prime. The car had seen better days. The overhead cloth liner on the inside of the roof was long gone, showing bare metal with sharp edges on the ceiling. The backseat had disappeared, leaving an opening that a man could crawl through into the trunk.

Still, looks could be deceiving. Under the hood the old LS6 had a rebuilt Holley four-barrel carburetor and a modified 454-cubic-inch V8 engine. It allowed the beast to put out 450 horsepower on the open highway. That and a set of street-legal high-performance racing tires made the old Chevelle more than a match for any local cop cars or highway patrol pace vehicles on the road. The vintage muscle car was immune from the pit maneuver, since few cars could ever catch her and the ones that could would be too light to flip the heavy beast around if they ever nosed into her.

If anybody wanted to shoot it out, the trunk held an arsenal of weapons, including a Remington pump twelve-gauge, an assortment of 9 mm and .45-caliber semiauto handguns, and two M16A1 carbines offering triple-shot full-auto fire, borrowed from a National Guard armory in Fresno. The car and the two men in it would be one badass experience for anybody stupid or unlucky enough to tangle with them. And they looked every inch the part.

Zach, behind the wheel, was thirty-two. At six one, 220 pounds, he was a bundle of white fury, a bristling package of bigotry hardened by a prison record showing years of gang play in institutions across the Southwest. His face, neck, and upper body bore the tribal markings of the Aryan Nation. The flesh on his body, face, ears, tongue, and nether parts had more puncture wounds and piercings than the average target on a pistol range.

Jess, the animal sitting next to him, was older. He had long, stringy gray hair pulled back in a ponytail. The deep-set slit of his eyes, the lean angular shape of his face, and the squared-off jawbone under his ears gave him the appearance of a pit viper. The look earned him his nickname, "the Snake."

The two of them sat in the car, the engine rumbling on idle in the parking lot outside the Robber's Roost, a bar in the desert not far from Murrieta, off Highway 215.

A few minutes later two bikers rolled in on choppers. They pulled up in front of the building. One of them goosed his engine as they shut down the bikes and leaned them over onto their kickstands. They studied the car for a second and then took off their helmets, stingy domes just big enough to meet the requirement of the state's vehicle code. One of them, the fat one, had his road name emblazoned on the back of his denim jacket: "Ditch Shit."

They took off their gloves, put them inside the helmets and laid them on the seat of their bikes, then walked toward the car. The two bikers were part of the Aryan Nation, couriers who carried messages.

The driver rolled down his window as the tall, slender one approached.

"The fuck's goin' on, man?" said the biker.

"Well, we're still above ground," said Zach. "And being as you're here I have to figure another nigger's dead, so it must be a good day."

They laughed. The two of them touched skin as the bikers' eyes cruised over the interior of the Chevelle before they came to rest on the dark cavern in the backseat leading to the trunk. "Have you got it yet?"

"Not yet. But we will."

"Man's gettin' impatient," said the biker. "Not gonna wait much longer. We mean to have it."

"We will," said Zack. "Only a matter of time."

"How much time?"

"Few days."

"You better not take too much longer. Belongs to us. Nobody else," said the biker.

"I know it, man. Whadda you think we been doin'?"

The fat one wandered around to the other side of the car and glanced through the passenger-side window.

The Snake held his hand down in the dark crevice between the side of his seat and his locked door. The .45 auto he was holding was already chambered and cocked in case he needed it.

"Supposed to give you a message," said the one on the driver's side. · "We just got word there's some ragheads lookin' for it, too," said the biker.

"Where'd you hear that?" Zach looked at him.

"We got ears. ISIS, ISIL, whatever they're callin' themselves today. Somebody told 'em. They got people lookin'. Word is, they think if they can get it, they can use it to recruit. Turn us or some of the others into lone wolves to do their bidding. Must be crazy," said the biker.

"That's what they say," said Zach. But he knew better. Aryan Nation had become a world of splinter groups. Some of the groups had been penetrated by FBI moles and riddled by informants. One of the factions had struck a deal years earlier to form an alliance with Osama bin Laden's Al Qaeda. If they could do that, they could do anything. The thought made him mad. "Tell them not to worry," said Zach. "Kill them if we have to, but we'll get it."

"Good. I'll pass the word. Take care of yourself, bro."

"Will do." The driver gunned the car and popped the clutch. The Chevelle screeched out of the parking lot, across a dirt strip, and out onto the highway.

The two bikers stood there looking as the car with the California license plate 5QPU783 disappeared through the veil of dust.

"You think they'll get it?" said the fat one.

"If they don't, we will."

TWENTY-TWO

aturday midmorning, and the mist has yet to burn off along the coast by the time Joselyn and I arrive in La Jolla. We drive the curving streets, following the directions from my cell phone until it tells us we've arrived at our destination. The address on Camino De La Costa is a large private home, right on the ocean, the location of Sofia's memorial service. I am surprised. I had expected a park or a church or some other public venue. "Who owns it?"

"I don't know," says Joselyn. "I guess someone who knew Sofia."

Joselyn has been communicating with Sofia's parents, Frank and Ida Leon. Her mother remains in the family home, in shock, devastated, barely able to function. Her father flew in last night, stayed in a hotel. We asked him to join us at our house but he said no. He is headed back up north tonight. I have yet to meet him.

One of Sofia's roommates, Tess Zavala, has taken the lead in putting together the small memorial service. She included the location, time, and other details in an invitation she posted on Facebook.

According to Tess, Sofia's family wanted to keep it small. The larger funeral will take place up in Sutter Creek in a few days.

There is no parking on Camino, so I turn right, drive up a block, park, and we walk back. By the time Joselyn and I reach the house a small van is in the driveway, a local florist delivering flowers, three large arrangements. One of them, I know, is from the firm. We follow the florist up the steps and through the front door, which is already open.

There is no one there to greet us, so we just keep going through the expansive living room, across a sea of cream-colored carpet and gleaming mahogany. Through windows I can see out into the yard. A few people are already gathered.

It's a mixed crowd, some gray hair in dark suits and dresses, a few younger people in more casual attire, guys in jeans and white shirts wearing ties. They stand around in small clusters, like pilgrims on a barren prairie, desolate souls searching for comfort.

Herman is suited out in his best Sunday wear just outside the door. He is leaning against the side of the house like a mountain holding it up. Brenda, my secretary, is talking with him.

Selena, Harry's secretary, and Sally, our receptionist, have put themselves to work handing out programs just inside the door leading out into the yard.

"Good morning." Selena reaches over and gives Joselyn a hug and a peck on the cheek. "Can I take your coat?"

"I think I'll keep it for a while," says Joselyn.

"I know, we were hoping for better weather." Selena hands each of us a program.

It is a single sheet, letter-folded in thirds. On the outside fold, in an arc across the top, are printed the words A CELEBRATION OF LIFE. Under this is a full head-and-shoulder shot, a color photo of Sofia. Her sunny smile seems caught by the camera's lens, teetering on the crest of laughter. Her dark, sparkling eyes soar from the paper as the wave of her shimmering brown hair frames her shoulder. It is the image seared in my mind of that bright spirit whom I allowed to go from my office on a stupid errand of mercy and who, as a consequence, never returned.

"That's her dad."

"Excuse me?" I am wrenched from the nightmare by Sally, who whispers something in my ear.

"The man outside, that's Sofia father." She gestures toward a man who is standing in the yard off by himself. His hands are folded in front of him as he stares at the three floral arrangements as if looking right through them.

"He looks like someone who could use a friend," she says.

"You're right."

I lean into Joselyn's ear. "Be back in a minute." I walk out the door and turn toward the man, who has his back to me. I'm only a few feet from him when I say: "I hope Sofia would have liked them. Do you know what her favorite flowers were?"

When he turns, I look into his face, stretched by sorrow. His eyes are two dark sockets, like bottomless pits of agony. "You must be Mr. Leon, Sofia's dad," I say.

"Yes."

"I'm Paul Madriani. I worked with Sofia."

"Oh. Oh, yes. I think I talked to your wife on the phone." He wipes his hand nervously on his pant leg, then shakes my hand. "I hate to say it but I don't know what her favorite flower was. I'm sure her mother probably knows. But the ones your people sent, I saw the card, they're beautiful," he says. "Can I ask what they are? So I can tell her mother when I get home."

Usually I wouldn't know, but in this case, I ordered them. "Lilies and hydrangeas, mostly," I tell him. "Lilies are the flowers of innocence. Hydrangeas for emotion, or so I'm told."

"I see."

"Mr. Leon, I don't know how to say this. Words don't mean much at a time like this. But I am sorry for your loss, so sorry. Both for you and your wife. And sorry for all of us as well. Because we miss her so," I tell him. "She was an incredible young woman. But then, you know that."

"Thank you," he says. And he starts to tear up.

"Any parent would have been proud."

He wipes the tear with the back of his hand. "She told me a lot about you," he says. "She loved working with you. And she learned a lot in such a short time. She was looking forward so much to going on to law school."

"I know. We talked about it, she and I. She would have been a fine lawyer." I would love to tell him that Joselyn was getting ready to spring her surprise, but it would only serve to worsen the pain.

"Her mother wanted to be here today but she couldn't," he says.

"I understand. There's no need to explain. I have a daughter. She and Sofia were just about the same age. I have no idea how I would cope, where I would go to get the strength. I know now why Sofia loved the two of you so much. The fact that you're able to be here for her, so soon after what's happened. You were her anchor."

"No. No, I wasn't," he says. "If I were, she would have been away at law school already and none of this would have happened. But we couldn't afford—"

"You can't look at it that way," I tell him. "If she had been at school she could have been hit by a bus crossing the street. You can't account for the vagaries of life. None of us can." And yet I know what he's feeling.

"Maybe you're right. But still, I should have done more."

"You can't blame yourself."

"Do you have any details about what happened?" he asks. "Do they have any idea yet who did it?"

"No. And now is not the time. There will be time for that later," I tell him.

"Promise me one thing."

"What's that?"

"That you'll help find the man who did it."

"That's a job for the police," I tell him.

"Yes, but sometimes, you know how that works. And she trusted you. Promise me you won't let them drop it."

"You can count on it," I tell him.

"Good," he says.

"Why don't you come over and meet some people from our office."

"I'd like that."

I lead him over to Joselyn and the secretaries. They are standing just outside the door. Herman has now joined them. I introduce them to Frank Leon.

"So you're Herman Diggs," says Frank. "Sofia told me all about you."

"God, I hope it was good," says Herman.

"She said you were a big guy. But I had no idea. She said you were full of what she called PI war stories. She loved to talk about them."

"That's not all he's full of."

When I turn, Harry is standing behind me and he's not alone. I step to one side to make room so they can join the circle. "Frank, let me introduce you to two more people. The homely one here is my partner, Harry Hinds. The attractive lady standing next to him is the Honorable

Gwyneth Riggins, judge of the Superior Court. Your Honor, it's good to see you." I take her hand.

"On weekends, and for those who are outside of my courtroom, it's Gwyn," she says, and smiles.

Message received. As a result of Harry's judicial incest, I'm now banished from her courtroom as well. Unless she and Harry own up, the county bar can conduct a pool and take bets as to which one of us is sleeping with her.

They shake Frank's hand. He seems befuddled, surrounded by all this power. "Sofia's father." I mouth the words to Harry and Gwyn.

"Oh." Riggins draws back a step and puts on a more sober expression.

Jolting music, blasting horns, and a bass drum makes us all jump. Somewhere there's a sound system. Powerful speakers under the eaves of the house blast down on us. Aaron Copland, "Fanfare for the Common Man." It's a nice tune, but not at this volume, and certainly not something Sofia would have picked.

I look over and one of her roommates, Tess, I believe, is telling someone inside the house to turn it down. A few seconds later the ear-shattering noise quells to background music. We can hear ourselves again. Copland on the quiet. Tess must know the owner of the house. Maybe it's her family.

The program begins. The pastor of a local church starts things off. A few homilies about the inevitability of death and the way station that is this brief life. You could set his words to music. He didn't know Sofia but "she must have been a wonderful girl."

It's the kids who get the emotions flowing, several of her friends, one in particular, who came south with her and knew her since grade school, stories of kindergarten and how they met. I have a hard time grappling with the image of Sofia at five, a bundle of wiggling energy and gap-toothed laughter.

Next Frank Leon tries to say a few words, but he can't. Two sentences in, he locks up, loses it, and breaks down. He is comforted by the pastor while I go up, take the mic, and introduce myself as Sofia's boss and friend. I put my arm around her dad's shoulder. "To feel that kind of pain you have to know what it is to be a loving father," I tell them. "There are only two people in this world who have been with Sofia since that moment, that second when the nurse or the doctor held her by her feet, slapped her on the rump and she cried and took her first breath. They have been with her every step of the way since. That is the measure of love that only a parent knows. And the portion of pain that is felt when that child is lost. What is left, the difference between the two, are the memories, the happy times that only they know. The recollection of an infant taking its first step, uttering its first intelligible word, followed by the second—the universal 'no.' "

This draws some smiles and a little laughter from some of those assembled.

"Her mom and dad hold memories of Sofia's childhood frolics that none of us could ever imagine, the inimitable intimacies of a tightly woven and loving family. The wonder of life in their daughter's eyes, a treasure beyond any wealth on earth. The rampaging adolescent with its quickening mind, the gangly teenager whose knowledge is infinite and whose poise evaporates like steam. A parent sees it all and at times struggles to keep up. But there is always the reward. It's called love. And it pays huge dividends to parent and child alike. Savor the years. The Sofia that we all knew and loved may be gone, but we can cherish the memories and relive the moments in our hearts. The richest of them all are the memories held by her family. They are special, they endure, and it is where Sofia now lives."

The pastor takes the mic while Herman and I walk the stricken father away from the crowd, across the yard and toward the house. Inside we find a spacious library off to the right of the living room, secluded and wrapped by shelves of leather-bound books, the kind people show but never read. We guide him to a large cushioned club chair near the desk, something gilded and French from the period before the tumbrels rolled and the guillotine blade fell.

"You must have children?"

It's a voice from behind that I can't see. When I turn and look, there is an elderly gentleman standing in the doorway, well dressed, suit and tie, assisted by a walking cane. A woman about the same age stands next to him.

"I have one child, a daughter," I tell him. "She's grown."

"I could tell. But then they're never really grown up. Not to us." He smiles as he steps into the room. "If Sofia's father needs something to drink there's liquor in the cabinet against the wall." He gestures with his free hand toward the cabinet. "Please help yourself."

"Is he all right?" the woman asks. "Does he need a doctor? There's one right next door, our neighbor. I'm sure he'd be happy to come over."

Herman asks Frank if he would like a drink, but Leon shakes it off and says, "No."

"He's fine," Herman tells the couple. "He'll be all right. He just needs to sit for a few minutes."

"Take all the time you need," says the old man.

"I take it you're the homeowner?" I ask him.

"Yes."

"If he'd like to lie down there's a couch in the other room," says his wife.

"Are you related to Tess?" I ask.

"Who?" says the man.

"Tess Zavala, Sofia's roommate."

"Oh, no. But she's wonderful, isn't she? They all are. So energetic, full of life. To be young again," he says.

"And you are?" I ask.

"Theo Lang," he says. "My wife, Claudia. We simply wanted to help out."

"Kind of you to offer your house," I tell him.

"It was the least we could do. She was such a lovely young lady."

"Then you knew Sofia?"

"Hmmm?" He looks at me. "Oh yes. It's terrible," he says. "Absolutely terrible. And look what it's done to her family, her mother and father." He wrings his hands while still holding on to the cane. "She was such a wonderful young person. What's the world coming to?" he asks.

I nibble around the edges of this question myself as I wonder how an old man, so gentle and austere, the very image of aged sobriety, can stand there and tell such a bold-faced lie. Theo Lang never met Sofia. I know this because she told me herself. Lang is a successful industrialist, scion of a wealthy family, a name you couldn't miss if you lived in the area for any length of time. He and his wife support every worthy cause in the community. Among his other good deeds, he is one of the three men who signed letters of recommendation for Sofia, men she told me herself she never met. The letters were obtained by an intermediary whom Sofia didn't identify. At the time I didn't press the issue. Now I'm beginning to wish that I had.

TWENTY-THREE

onday morning just before ten, I have my secretary show Anthony Pack into our conference room the moment he arrives. Harry and Herman want to meet him, but I don't want to overwhelm him with numbers until I've had a chance to feel him out. He may be reluctant to talk in front of a crowd.

Inside, I offer him coffee, bottled water, or a soft drink. He takes a Diet Coke and we settle into two chairs at the corner of the big table to talk.

"Thank you for coming all this way."

"It's not a problem. I'm happy to do it," he says. "I just hope we can help each other."

He's a big man, tall, rangy, ruddy complexion with sandy-colored curly hair, a little gray at the temples and around the ears. He has an affable smile, something of the Irish if I had to guess.

He's put a thin zippered leather folio on the table in front of him. From the look of it he hasn't come burdened with a load of documents.

"Have you heard anything more from the authorities regarding Mr. Brauer's death?" he asks.

"No. We're still waiting." I don't tell him that Emma's been charged. I'll break that to him later.

"Tell me about your father," I say. "You said over the phone, if I heard you correctly, that there were seven members in the platoon originally, but only three survived the war and that your father stayed in contact with the other two over the years."

"That's right."

"What was your father's name?"

"Edward. Everybody called him Ed. Even most of his patients. He wasn't one to stand on formalities."

I make a note on the legal pad in front of me. "Edward 'Ed' Pack = Army Medic."

"Was there any kind of a designation for the platoon that you know of?"

"I'm not sure. They were part of Company C, I know that."

I write it down. "Was there a brigade or a regiment?"

"I don't know. Is it important?"

"Probably not, unless we need to do research."

"I can check to see if it's in any of my dad's old papers at the house," he says.

"Let's put it aside for the moment. You said there were three survivors. Your dad, Bob Brauer, and a third man."

"Walt Jones," says Pack. "Walter. He was the sergeant in charge of the platoon. He and my dad stayed in contact over the years. They both lived in Oklahoma City. The 45th was a National Guard unit. It was federalized when the war came. It was headquartered in Oklahoma City. Most of the men who served came from that area. But during the war they drew recruits from all over, mostly the Southwest. They did basic training at Fort Sill. My dad said that after that, they went all over the place, Texas, Massachusetts, Virginia. That's where they shipped out, Hampton Roads. They ended up in North Africa, and from there they went to Italy. They saw a lot of action in Sicily and later Salerno."

"But they ended up in Germany, right?"

"That's correct."

"So I take it they were at Normandy on D-Day?"

"No. The 45th came up through southern France, the area around the Riviera, part of a diversion to draw German troops away from Normandy. When I was little, my dad and I used to look at maps of the Mediterranean and Western Europe. We actually took a trip some years ago. The entire family. He showed us where they fought."

"Hell of a way to see St. Tropez," I tell him.

"That's what he said. Almost his exact words." There's a smile and a twinkle in his eyes as if this brings back happy memories.

"They actually landed a little to the west of there and fought their way north through France. They had to push through the Maginot Line from the west and later the Siegfried Line, crossed the Rhine, and took Nuremberg."

"Sounds like you memorized it."

"I used to move toy soldiers on the map spread out on the floor in Dad's study. Little green plastic G.I. Joes," he says. "I knew every city on that map."

"Somewhere I read that they liberated the concentration camp at Dachau."

"That's true. Dad never talked much about that. I asked him several times and he didn't want to discuss it. It was the one thing that was off-limits."

"Well, I'm sure you can imagine why," I tell him. "I've only seen old film and that was enough. I can't imagine being there."

"Yes. No question about that," he says. "But I've always wondered if perhaps there was another reason."

"What do you mean?"

"Well, twice there were units of the 45th that came under investigation for war crimes."

My ears perk up.

"There were soldiers in the division charged with executing German prisoners. Of course, my dad never told me about this. I found out about it on my own, doing research when I was older. One of the episodes involved Dachau," he says. "Charges that German guards were shot while trying to surrender. Estimates of those killed as high as fifty. And that some of the wounded Germans were denied medical treatment by US soldiers."

"You don't think your father was involved in any of that?"

"I'd like to say no. I'd find it hard to believe. But the fact is, I have no idea. War does funny things to people. It's what he always said."

I make a note to check it out.

"In the end it probably doesn't matter, because the investigation all came to nothing," he says. "The division captured Munich near the close of the war and that's where they stayed when it ended. General Patton became the military governor of Bavaria. He had been itching to bury the investigation from the start. When the charges from Dachau ended up on his desk, that's exactly what he did. They buried Patton a short time later after a traffic accident and the rest is history. The division was highly decorated. A number of them got the Medal of Honor. According to my dad, the worst part of all came after the war when they were stuck in Munich. They were there for months. They were bored and they wanted to come home. There was nothing to do but drink, get plastered. That's how two of the men from the platoon died in the front seat of a jeep. To my father, that was the real tragedy because there was no reason for it. It was a total waste. He kept in touch with the families of those two men for years after the war. To my dad, it was like he was still serving with them. He was their medic. Strange thing is, years later, several of the family members, the survivors, became patients in his practice." Pack looks up at me. "Well, that's it. That's all I know. What I want to know is who killed my father and why. Not that he had a lot of years left. But whoever did it had no right," he says. "Not to take the life of a man who lived like that."

"You're right," I tell him. "You're absolutely right." I sit back and look at him. "Have you had anything to eat?"

"A cup of coffee and a roll early this morning," he says.

"Why don't I take you to lunch. Let me grab some people. I want you to meet my partner and a few of the others. We'll go next door."

Twenty minutes later we are huddled around one of the larger tables at the Brigantine. Harry and Herman are on one side, Pack and me on the other when Joselyn walks in. Apparently one of the secretaries told her where we were. "Joselyn, I'd like you to meet Anthony Pack . . ."

"Tony," he says. "Please. You keep saying Anthony. I'm looking around wondering who you're talking about."

"Let me start over. Joselyn, I'd like you to meet Tony Pack. Joselyn is my better half," I tell him.

"His only half," says Harry. "The empty-headed fool left a cake on my desk the other night trying to convince me it came from somebody else."

I ignore him.

"Tony's from Oklahoma City. He flew in last night and he's hungry," I tell her. "So join us."

Ignoring Harry never works.

"By the way, we enjoyed the cake," he says. "But next time you might try chocolate mint. That's Gwyn's favorite."

"I hope she's fond of dogs," I tell him. "I'll lodge your request for mint with Emma."

"I must have missed something," says Pack.

"In our office you need a roster to know the players," I tell him. "I'll bring you current later."

Joselyn sits down at the end of the table right next to me. She already knows who Pack is because I've told her. If it has to do with Sofia's murder she wants to know about it. From the little we've gleaned at Emma's house, it may. I tend to think there's some connection between the little box and its contents, the key in Emma's basement and Sofia's death. If it's true, whatever Tony Pack's dad knew may be one of the yellow bricks in the road that leads to her killer.

We order drinks and then lunch. When the cocktails come and as soon as the waitress has laid them all out, I ask Pack, "Mind if we make it a working lunch?"

"Not at all," he says. "Let's not waste time."

"One person we haven't talked about is Walter Jones, the sergeant. I assume he's dead?"

"Of course," says Tony. "How could it be any other way?" He offers up a cynical smile, then sips around the ice from his Scotch and soda. "It's very convenient how they all died in such quick and orderly succession. It's something I brought to the attention of the police, and which they immediately dismissed. Their answer? 'They were all old.' "

"How did Jones die?"

"He was killed crossing the street by a hit-and-run driver five weeks to the day after my dad passed. The police never found the driver."

"I can see how that could be considered a geriatric disease in certain police departments," says Harry.

"This was in Oklahoma City?" says Joselyn.

He nods. "That's where he lived, just like my dad, his entire life."

"And then Brauer," I say.

"Let me ask you. Do you see any kind of pattern here?" says Tony.

"The police can be obtuse sometimes," I tell him.

"That's a polite way of putting it," says Harry. "Why bring the hospital's problems down to the precinct house when you can avoid all the trouble by checking the little box that reads 'pneumonia.' "

"If you had to make a guess—and I know you don't have any evidence—but if you had to guess, what would be your best flying leap as to the cause of death in your father's case? You saw him, I take it, in the final throes?"

"Oh, you bet I did. And it's a good question. I've put it to myself many times. I've spent hours bent over the computer looking at the screen searching for the answer. And it always comes back the same."

"What's that?"

"Insulin overdose," he says.

"Your father was a diabetic?" I ask.

"No. But it fits the symptoms and it's the perfect substance for murder. The victim goes into hypoglycemic shock, followed by deep coma, which, if it's not diagnosed quickly and treated almost immediately with the appropriate countermeasures, results in brain death. Hospitals sometimes fail to diagnose it. According to the literature it's one of the favorite ways the elderly use to commit suicide. Massive insulin overdose. Do it in a facility where the prime mission is residential assistance and you can forget it. My dad was on the floor for hours before they found him, and he still lingered. But they couldn't bring him back."

"Best of all," says Harry, "in most states insulin doesn't even require a prescription. You can buy it over the counter and nobody will ask any questions." How does Harry know this, you ask? From the boarding-house case across town where the little old landlady was knocking off tenants in order to cash their Social Security checks. It's been in and out of the news for weeks.

"Does Oklahoma require a prescription?" I ask Tony.

"I don't know. But what difference does it make? It's a short ride across any border to the next state."

"Good point." The fact is, it's a readily available medication.

TWENTY-FOUR

D r. Edward Pack, Walter Jones, and Robert Brauer, unless I miss my guess, are the three clients who hired the attorney, Elliott Fish, in Oklahoma City. Fish couldn't reveal their identities, not because it was a national security secret, but because it was confidential attorney-client information. What services he provided to the three men we don't know. Except for the fact that he sent out the small box and its contents, we wouldn't even know about him.

If he sent them to Brauer and Ed Pack, we can assume that Walter Jones may have received one as well. Is it possible that the keys fit a three-lock box and that all three are required to retrieve whatever is inside? If so, it's a problem because we don't know what happened to Dr. Pack's key or the one that may have been sent to Jones. It's also possible the keys fit three separate boxes, in which case whatever is being stored could be in pieces or parts. Maybe you have to assemble the whole to have anything?

If it's a cache of valuables—say, precious metals or gems—then it's possible it may have been divided into thirds. But if that's the case, why did the receipt of the tiny box and its contents strike such fear in Ed Pack and Bob Brauer, men who fought through the war and survived combat? It seems each new discovery brings with it only more questions. And why would something sent by their own lawyer, whom they retained, cause concern?

We settle back into the conference room after lunch. Now there are five of us, Joselyn included. Tony Pack seems comfortable with the group. If he's holding back anything, there's certainly no sign of it. In fact, I'm beginning to feel guilty. I have said nothing about Emma and the fact that she is charged with her father's death. Nor have any of us said anything in front of him about Sofia's murder. It's time to share some information.

"Let's assume there were three boxes sent out, one to each of the survivors from the platoon. The question is, did each little box contain the same items, a key, perhaps the same key, and the antiquated ID with the passport photo?"

"What ID?" says Pack.

"That's right, you didn't see the paper, the one your father burned?"

"No."

I fish in my jacket pocket and take out the box. I lift the lid and remove the copy of the ID. I slide it across the table to Tony.

He unfolds it and takes a look.

"Would you recognize the key?" I ask.

"I might."

I take it out of the box and hand it to him.

"It certainly looks like the one my dad had. Same style, shiny brass. I remember it was smooth on both sides, no grooves. It looks about the same size as the one I saw. I remember when I saw it I thought, That's a safe-deposit key."

"That's what we're thinking," says Harry.

"So you're wondering how you're gonna find the bank and gain access," says Tony. He's already ahead of us. "It won't be easy unless you have the signatory on the box, the person who rented it, or a court order."

"How do you know about that?"

"Because it's my business. I own a small bank." Pack is still studying the key. When he glances up he notices Harry and me looking at him. "Oh, if you're thinking it's there, you can forget it," he says, and smiles. "This key wouldn't fit any of the boxes in our vault. We use an entirely different blank. Grooved keys and much heavier stock. This is old, I'm guessing before my time."

"Yes, but maybe you can help us find out where it came from," says Harry.

"Won't be easy," he says. "There's no stamp on it, not even a box number. You sure there was no key ring with it? Maybe a brass number label?"

"What you see is what we have," I tell him.

He shakes his head and hands it back to me. "I wouldn't know where to begin."

"Have you looked for your father's key?" I ask.

"I have. High and low. No sign of it," he says.

I'm thinking that if the doctor burned the paper, maybe he destroyed the key as well, or tossed it.

"Look again when you get home," I tell him.

"I will."

"If we can compare them, the cuts on the teeth, we'll know if they're the same key. If they're not, then we're dealing with something more complicated, and the chance that we're missing a third key."

"The one to Jones," he says.

"Yes."

"There's one person who might know," says Tony. "The lawyer."

"Fish? Forget it," I tell him.

"There must be some way we can get him to talk."

"How?"

"Sue him," says Pack.

"For what?" says Harry.

"Withholding information."

"Quaint theory." Harry smiles. "Stick with your banking day job. We couldn't get him near a courtroom unless we could show damages, some legitimate cause of action."

"We argue that whatever is in the box is valuable, that it belongs to us. You have the key," says Pack.

"The problem is we don't know what's in the box. Even to file a lawsuit we'd have to put a value on it. What do we say?" says Harry.

"We make up a figure," says Pack.

"And what if the box is empty?" says Harry.

"Then we say we're sorry."

"That assumes that Fish knows where the box is and that he has access to the vault," I say.

"Of course," says Tony.

"In which case you're dealing with the Holy of Holies," I tell him.

"What do you mean?"

"The attorney-client privilege, what he hid behind on the phone when I talked to him. I got the definite impression that he was operating based on specific instructions from his clients."

"Yes, but from what you're saying they're all dead," says Tony.

"That doesn't matter if he's signed on to the vault, the signatory on the box. That is what you're assuming?"

Tony nods.

"Then he has constructive possession of whatever this key represents. One or more boxes we don't know because we only have one key. If we drag Fish into court he'll assert that he can't disclose anything without violating client confidentiality. Unless I'm wrong, he'll present the judge with a set of written instructions, what he is operating under, and demand that the court review them in camera."

"What does that mean?" says Pack.

"The judge will read the instructions in chambers by himself. We'll never get a chance to see them because the instructions themselves would be covered by the privilege—they're confidential."

"Case dismissed," says Harry.

"All I can say is you damn lawyers, you're all the same." Tony smiles and looks at Joselyn. "What do you think about all this?"

"I think we ought to have Herman get his gun, stick it in Fish's mouth, ask him where the bank is that that key belongs to, and tell him that if he doesn't sign us in we're going to bounce a bullet off his tonsils."

Harry looks at Tony. "Did I forget to tell you? Joselyn's a lawyer, too."

"She's hired."

"Yeah, but she doesn't do trial work," I tell him.

"That's OK, I like her attitude," says Tony.

We all laugh. Except for Joselyn. She smiles mildly and glances at the key in my hand, smoldering dark eyes and tawny skin. I wonder if push came to shove and we ran into a stone wall on Sofia's murder, if she thought the answer was in that box, whether she might just do it.

"OK, so what's this all about?" Tony picks up the piece of paper from the table in front of him. It's the copy of the ID. "Who is this guy?"

"Don't know. It came in the box."

"Jakob Grimminger." He reads from the paper. "SS Standarten-führer. It's German."

"We thought so, too," says Harry.

"SS . . . an officer of some kind. I'd have to look it up."

"How is it spelled?" asks Joselyn. She pulls her iPad from her bag. Tony spells it as she taps it into Google.

"It's a Nazi Party rank. Used by the SA and SS. They commanded units known as *Standarten,* between three and five hundred men."

"Yes, but what's the significance?" says Tony. "Why is his ID in the box with the key?"

"You got me," I tell him. "Unless . . ."

"What?" he says.

"You think he might have been at Dachau?"

Tony looks at me and thinks about it. "You mean . . . ?"

"Yes."

"What are you talking about?" says Joselyn.

"Give us a minute," I tell her. None of them know what Tony told me this morning, about the allegations of war crimes brought against American soldiers following the liberation of the concentration camp at Dachau, that GIs were accused of shooting German guards who were attempting to surrender.

"It's a possibility, I suppose," says Tony. "Still, I don't get it."

"Nor do I."

"What's it all about?" says Harry.

"Some charges brought against soldiers in Brauer's division back during the war. The charges were eventually dropped. But there's still a record of them, I suppose?" I look at Tony.

"Yeah, online," he says. "That's where I saw it. It's mentioned in some of the articles on the Internet."

"Where do you think they got it?" I ask.

"I imagine from action reports in military archives and histories that have been written, you know. Charges like that don't just go away."

"You have to cut them some slack," I tell him.

"Who?"

"The older generation. Your father and his band of warriors. Especially at a place like Dachau, given what they found. Emotions had to be running high. Piles of bodies, women and little children."

"Yeah. And we tried some of them at Nuremberg after the war. Convicted and executed them. But if it happened—the shootings, I mean—you can understand why people might say that not everything America does is good."

"Yeah, well, let 'em go live in Russia," says Harry. "Besides, shoot 'em there or hang 'em later, what's the difference? Whether it was a speeding bullet or a slow rope, the people who ran that place got what they deserved. I wouldn't lose any sleep over it." And Harry wouldn't. Do it on a Saturday when he's free, and he'd be happy to pull the trigger for you.

"We could turn the information on this guy, what's his name?" says Harry.

Tony looks down. "Jakob Grimminger."

"We could hand it off to Ives in D.C. Have some of his researchers check army records. See what he finds. We're paying them anyway." Harry is talking about the staff at the "Washington Gravesite," the Internet news blog that we now own.

"Or we can look right here." Joselyn is looking at the screen on her iPad. She taps it to enlarge something, then flips the screen around so we can all see it. "This guy right here"—she points with her fingernail—"in the black uniform wearing the helmet, standing right next to the open car. According to the information under the picture, that's Jakob Grimminger. This other man standing up in the car with his arm in the air looking like a deodorant commercial, that," she says, "is Adolf Hitler."

"No shit," says Herman. "Let me see that."

She hands him the iPad.

Up to this point Herman has been sitting quietly listening to everything, sucking it all up. Now he looks at the screen. "That's the man," he says.

"What does it say?" I ask.

"Jakob Grimminger, born twenty-five April, 1892, Augsburg, Bavaria. Died twenty-eight January, 1969, Munich, Germany. The car looks nice. One of those big open-top six-wheel Mercedes, large engine, get you two hundred feet to the gallon."

"Tell us about the man," I say.

"Sorry. Where was I? Oh. Yeah, born in Augsburg, let's see, entered the Imperial German Army at sixteen. Served in World War One as a mechanic in an air regiment. Fought in Gallipoli, served in Palestine, discharged in 1919. Joined the Nazi Party in 1922, became a member of the, I can't pronounce it, SA. Took part in fights in Colburg in 1922 and the Munich Beer Hall Putsch, 1923. Served at general headquarters, became a member of the SS, 1926. Eventually reaching the rank of, I can't pronounce it, equivalent of a colonel. Had the honor of carrying the Blutfahne, whatever that is, won a lot of medals. Put on trial after the war, 1946, for being a member of the SS. He didn't go to prison, but had his property confiscated. He attempted to enter politics after the war, served as councilor in Munich but it says here his past prevented him from continuing his career. He died in obscurity in Munich in 1969. That's it."

"So what's he doing standing next to Hitler?" I ask.

"I don't know. Maybe he just happened to be there."

"Let me see that." Herman hands me the iPad.

There's a knock on the door.

"Come in," says Harry.

It's Harry's secretary. She whispers in his ear. Harry says, "Sign the receipt and I'll be out in a second." He takes a deep breath and stretches. "Why don't we take a short break?"

"Sure," says Tony. "Where's your restroom?"

Joselyn points the way.

Harry slips around the table, leans over, and whispers, "We need to talk."

"What is it?"

"ME reports have been messengered over. Two of them, Brauer and Sofia." Harry had put in a request for the autopsy report on Sofia. We didn't expect to receive it this quickly. "They must be burning the midnight oil," he says.

I leave the iPad on the table and Harry and I head to the outer office. The messenger is just leaving. The reports are in two separate envelopes. Harry grabs them and we head to my office. Inside we close the door.

I hand him the letter opener from my desk and he slits open the envelopes. He hands me one of them and opens the other himself.

I read from the top of the form, "Sadie Marie Leon, aka Sofia Leon." I scan it quickly. "Cause of Death: Asphyxia." The box labeled "Homicide" is checked and next to it the words "Strangulation by Ligature." No surprises. Typed below is the more detailed report. "Evidence of sudden and violent compression and restriction of the airway . . . U-shaped ligature marks . . . abrasions . . . contusions . . . fingernail marks believed to be from the victim evidences a brief struggle to remove the ligature . . . Ligature appears to have been pulled tightly from behind . . . upward sloping ligature wound indicates that the perpetrator was considerably taller than the victim."

According to the report they took scrapings from under Sofia's fingernails and found microscopic evidence of cellular tissue. Whether it belongs to Sofia or to her killer will have to await DNA testing. They have sent the material out for profiling.

I read on. "Internal examination reveals fracture of the thyroid cartilage and hyoid bone as well as compression of the carotid artery." Whoever did it was strong. It appears that he overpowered her and crushed her windpipe almost immediately. I take some solace in the fact that death must have been quick.

"You have to wonder if there's some contagion going around," says Harry.

"Why is that?"

"Cause of death. According to the coroner, Robert Brauer died of cardiac arrest, but here's the kicker. It was induced by insulin poisoning, believed to be a massive insulin overdose, resulting in hypoglycemic shock, coma, and collapse of the functions within the brain stem. Where have we heard this before?"

I hear him, but I'm not listening. Instead my eyes are fixed on the four lines toward the bottom of the ME's report on Sofia, grouped under the heading "Additional Findings."

"Blood screening panel detected elevated levels of the hormone HCG, indicating that the victim was approximately eight weeks pregnant at the time of death. Internal examination confirmed the existence of an intrauterine pregnancy, embryo approximately 1.6 centimeters in length recovered."

TWENTY-FIVE

This morning Zeb Thorpe was meeting with some of his section chiefs within the Counterintelligence Division of the FBI. Thorpe was executive director of the FBI's National Security Branch, otherwise known as the NSB. He held a broad portfolio that ranged from weapons of mass destruction and counterterrorism to counterintelligence and espionage.

Today Thorpe had been tipped off by one of his assistants that he might find himself tripping through a political minefield, something he hated. According to the assistant there was reason to believe that Israeli intelligence might be working an active espionage operation on US soil out of their Los Angeles office.

Foreign intel operations were not uncommon, though most of the time they did not show up on the six o'clock news or in the next morning's newspaper. Often they were run out of foreign embassies and consulates, as this one apparently was. In most cases the incident was disposed of quietly and at a low level. The foreign operatives would be identified. Their diplomatic credentials would be canceled and they would be invited to leave the United States. Of course, this would depend on the nature of the relations between the two countries and the size of the bone over which they were fighting. Normally it was industrial, high-tech, or national security secrets. If true to form, the foreign nation would then, in order to save face, retaliate by expelling one or more American diplomats from the US embassy in their country, at which point things would then go on as before. It was a time-honored and tested process.

The problem in this case was the deteriorating nature of relations between the Israeli government in Tel Aviv and the US administration in Washington. What to do when old friends have a falling-out?

Israel was a long-term US ally with close ties to the American military. The two countries often shared critical intelligence. The United States supplied arms and Israel shared research and development in weapons as well as other fields.

For decades Israel was considered one of the principal islands of American interest in a troubled and increasingly chaotic area of the world. It was a region in which American influence was now seen by many as being in decline. Perhaps it was only natural then that there were increasing voices in Tel Aviv wondering whether, if it came down to a battle for Israeli survival, the Americans would have Israel's back. Add to that the feelings of Jewish-American voters and the issue had the potential to become a powder keg.

Thorpe already had standing orders from his superiors at the Justice Department to run everything they turned up in the investigation past political operatives at the White House before taking any action. He hated it, and at this point he didn't even know what was going on.

Thorpe settled into his chair, looked at the men around the table, and said, "So what do we have?"

One of the men across the table, a special agent from Los Angeles, handed him a small clear plastic evidence bag large enough to hold a fifty-cent piece. Inside was a tiny glass vial of some kind. It was about the length of two long grains of rice and about the same diameter.

"What is it?"

"It's a human microchip implant," said the agent. "It contains an integrated circuit device, RFID, radio frequency identification. The transponder is encased in silicate glass. It's implanted under the skin by injection using a special syringe, usually in the fleshy part of the hand."

"Go on."

"It runs wirelessly through a noncontact radio system. The microchip can provide automatic identification as to the owner or it can be used for tracking as well as other information. It depends on how it's programmed. That one was set up for identification only. It was found embedded in a bar of shaving soap by a gentleman in Sandpoint, Idaho. Fortunately for us, the man was a bit of a conspiracy theorist. He'd seen pictures of them on the Internet and thought someone might be trying to spy on him. He called the local police. They took the bar of soap and ran the implant by their tech people, who called us.

"When our people saw it they got suspicious."

"Why is that?"

"There's not a lot of private employers or public agencies that use them, and the few that do employ them have high security needs. We sent it to our lab and they checked it. It came back as part of a batch that was sold to the US government. In the meantime we had our lab check the soap. They found traces of human DNA. Not enough to establish a profile for identification, but we know that the manufacturer uses beef tallow—"

"You think the body was dissolved," said Thorpe.

"We think there's a good chance."

"The DNA could be from the guy in Idaho," said Thorpe. "Maybe he sneezed while he was shaving, or cut himself. Hell, it could be from sloughed-off skin cells."

"We don't think so."

Thorpe was getting a queasy feeling in his stomach. The next thing they'd tell him was that it belonged to a CIA agent who disappeared after having lunch with the Israeli ambassador.

"We had our people check government purchase orders and discovered that this particular implant was part of a shipment that went to the navy. We sent the implant to them. They checked it with their equipment and it came back as having been implanted three years ago in one James Arnold Pepper, a former chief naval petty officer, part of a team that was assigned to a special project being run by DARPA."

That got Thorpe's attention. DARPA was the Defense Advanced Research Projects Agency, a black-bag research arm of the Defense Department. Whatever they worked on was normally top secret.

"This particular project dealt with subsurface drones, antisubmarine warfare. They wouldn't tell us anything more because we weren't cleared. But they did tell us that Pepper had access to highly sensitive information. It was the reason he was ultimately dropped from the project and discharged from the navy."

"Why was that?" said Thorpe

"He had a drinking problem."

"Oh, wonderful."

"And it gets worse," said the agent.

"It usually does," said Thorpe. "Go on."

"The navy had no record of Mr. Pepper's whereabouts. All they had was his date of discharge and the name and phone number of next of kin, a sister in Washington State. We contacted her. She hadn't seen or heard from her brother in more than two years. So we started looking, checking for phone records in his name, running the computer on licensing and driving records. We ran the URC database and found one arrest for burglary in Southern California but no conviction. And then we made a hit, a credit card in Pepper's name on an account in San Diego opened about five months ago using Pepper's Social Security number. The statements on the account go to a PO box. So far the bill is being paid regularly by cash at the bank, no checks, even though there was a checking account in his name. The deposits into the account are all in cash, no checks. All of them under ten thousand dollars. To date just under thirty thousand dollars."

"What are you saying? They're structured payments?" said Thorpe. "Are you suggesting we pick the man up for money laundering and sweat him?"

"If we could find him," said the agent. "We think there's a good chance he's dead."

"Why, because of the trace DNA?"

"If not, how did his microchip get into the bar of soap? Tallow plants have been used in the past to dispose of dead bodies."

"I know," said Thorpe. "I read the same stuff in the Bureau histories." The mob was believed to have done it for years in the area around the Chicago stockyards.

"So you think somebody killed him and is borrowing his identity," said Thorpe.

"We think it's a possibility."

"Why? To what end?"

"We don't know," said the agent.

"What does this have to do with Israeli intelligence?" He was hoping it was just a flat-out murder, in which case they could drop it back on the locals and tell them good luck.

"I'm getting to that," said the agent. "The credit card in question, it was used to purchase additional minutes on some prepaid SIM cards for a cell phone. We checked with the carrier that provided them. They were able to pull up records of incoming and outgoing phone calls under the assigned phone numbers. There weren't many," said the agent. "No more than two or three under each card before the number disappeared from their records. Almost all the phone calls were incoming, from a cell number in Los Angeles. The number belongs to a man who has a diplomatic passport issued by the state of Israel. He's an attaché to the Israeli consul's office in L.A."

Thorpe looked down at the table and thought, Shit!

TWENTY-SIX

try to convince Joselyn to stay at the office, that I will call her when I finish talking to the man, but she will have none of it. Almost from the very moment she found out that Sofia was pregnant when she was murdered, Joselyn was out the door and headed for the car.

"You can stay here or you can come," she tells me, "but either way, I'm going." She wants to hear it from the horse's mouth. Theo Lang, the old man whose grand house in La Jolla hosted Sofia's memorial service, has some questions to answer. He lied to me about meeting Sofia. We know that. What we want to know is, who brokered the letters of recommendation given to Sofia, one of which he signed?

"You can be sure it wasn't just casual sex," says Joselyn. "Whoever it was. Whoever was the father, it was someone she cared about. You know that and so do I. The person who got her those letters was connected, older, and powerful. Why would the old man lie, unless he was trying to protect someone?"

"We need to think about this before we go blundering in," I tell her.

"You can think about it in the car as we drive," she says. "You saw the report. Sofia was two months pregnant. That means she knew, and she was probably scared. It doesn't take a rocket scientist," says Joselyn. "Whoever got her those letters runs in the same social set with Lang. That means he's rich, he's powerful, and he's probably married. Sofia goes to him and tells him she's pregnant. What do you think he's going to say?" She stops on the walkway outside the office and looks me dead in the eye.

"You may be right," I tell her.

"May be?" she says.

"Probably. It's entirely possible."

"The immaculate conception was possible. This is etched in stone. You know it and I know it. Men are all alike," she says.

"Present company excluded, I hope."

"I'll let you know about that later," she says. "First let's go talk to Lang." She starts to walk again.

"Let's assume you're right."

"Assume, my ass," she says. "I know I'm right."

"In that case we should take it to the police, tell them what we know, and let them deal with it. This is a whole new angle. The pregnancy. It's not something they know about."

"What do you mean?" She stops again. "It's *their* medical examiner, *their* report. They know she was pregnant. Or they would if they bothered to read it. They certainly weren't interested in Sofia's telephone trinket in your client's yard. What if he followed her there?"

"It's possible."

"Damn right, it is."

"The cops don't know about the letters, the fact that they were brokered by someone who got them for Sofia. They have no leads. No clue as to who the father is."

"Neither do we. So let's go find out," she says. She starts walking again. Before I can catch up to her she's at the car door, tapping the toe of her high heel on the concrete, boring holes through me with eyes that look like hot coals, waiting for me to unlock the car.

I push the button on the key fob. She gets in and slams the door. If she had a gun I'd be worried.

I go around and get in on the driver's side.

"Let me have your phone," she says.

"Why?"

"Please. Don't argue with me. Just give it to me. It will get us there faster." Joselyn is afraid that I might take the long way around, a drive through the park to try to cool her down. She can read my mind. She punches up the maps on my phone, finds Lang's address from Saturday, and before I can say another word, the phone is instructing me to "proceed to the route."

I pull out of the lot and turn onto Orange Avenue, and we head toward the bridge.

We left Harry and Herman to finish up with Tony Pack. He offered to hold over, but I told him no. We have inconvenienced the man enough. He was interested in only one piece of information after we read the autopsy reports: the news that Robert Brauer died of insulin poisoning. For Tony this was the lynchpin. It confirmed everything he suspected about his father's death and drew up the knot even tighter that all three of the men, Ed Pack, Brauer, and Walter Jones, were murdered. Why? We don't know. But it settles any question as to whether there was ample reason for them to be afraid.

Joselyn and I cross over the Coronado Bridge and head north up I-5. Three miles on and my mind is turning over with all the options. "What if it isn't a man?" I say.

"What?" Joselyn looks at me.

"What if it was a woman who got her the letters? It is a possibility."

She thinks about it for a moment and then says, "No. It's not. It doesn't make any sense."

"Why not?"

"If it was a woman, why would she be hiding?"

"Who's hiding?"

"We know one thing, whoever it was, they were not at the memorial service on Saturday. Otherwise we would have met him. He would have come up and introduced himself."

"What? You mean, 'Hi, I'm John. I was Sofia's lover'?"

"Laugh if you want. But I met almost everyone who was there. And I didn't see anybody who fits this bill."

"What bill is that?"

"You know."

"No. Tell me."

"Older, dashing, tall, perhaps a touch of gray at the temples. I'll let you know the second I see him."

"You have to remember there were two other letters of recommendation. They weren't there either. I checked the list of names in the guest book."

"And for good reason. They didn't know her. Remember? They never met Sofia. Why show up at a memorial service for a perfect stranger? But the person who got her the letters . . . he knew her. He was her lover, her friend, or he was posing. Maybe he was trying to show off. Show her how important he was, that he could get her endorsements. He had important friends. Young women are impressed by that, and she was a child in so many ways," says Joselyn.

"If that's the case, why was Lang there? He didn't know her, either."

"It was his house."

"Yeah, but he didn't have to be there. And he had to know he was taking a chance. Lying about knowing her."

"How could he possibly know that Sofia would tell you the truth? But then, of course, she didn't," says Joselyn.

"What do you mean? About the letters? No, she told me right up front that she never met any of them."

"Yes, because she was protecting someone."

"No, I don't think that was it at all. I think she was just being honest."

"That's what you'd like to think," says Joselyn. "Let me ask you a question. You wanted to hire her, didn't you?"

"What do you mean?"

"When she first walked into your office. When she sat down. When you started talking to her. How long before you decided you wanted to hire her? And if you tell me it took more than two minutes, I'll tell you you're lying."

"OK, so she made a good impression."

"Why?"

"She was smart," I tell her.

"Smarter than you realize," says Joselyn. "And pretty."

"OK, fine. She was both. What's your point?"

"What a smart girl always knows," says Joselyn. "That a pretty smile, a flash of thigh will usually get what she wants, and if it doesn't, a quick display of honesty is sure to close the deal."

"You're saying she played me?"

"Like a harp."

"You're wrong."

"What you construed as honesty, the reason you hired her, was, in fact, manipulation," says Joselyn. "Don't get me wrong. I loved her. You know I did. But if I had to guess, I'd say she was probably afraid that you might call the people who signed those letters. Talk to them to draw them out. It would have been the natural thing to do. You saw those letters," she says. "They were all so generic and vague. It would have been the height of incompetence not to check them. What if you called and one of them slipped up? What if they mentioned the man's name, the one who got her the letters? Wouldn't you wonder why he hadn't given her a letter himself?"

She has a point. "I probably would have."

"Sofia wasn't going to take that chance. Instead she gave it all up, knowing that with the truth, the fact that the letters were worthless, you wouldn't pursue it further. Her lover was safe. I'm guessing that by that time in the interview, she already knew she had you on the hook."

"Am I that transparent?"

"Ask yourself the question," she says. "Did you rely on those letters when you hired her?"

"No, of course not. I just told you . . ."

"Oh, but you did."

"What do you mean?"

"It's just that Sofia found a better way to use them."

Son of a bitch, she's right. I am a piece of cellophane. Maybe it's something only a woman could see. At least I hope so.

"Child she may have been," says Joselyn. "Sofia was one smart cookie."

This time we don't park a block away and walk. Instead we pull into the driveway, the big house overlooking the ocean in La Jolla. "Do me a favor," I tell her. "Let's not go in there angry. If we do, he may not let us in at all. Or he may call the police and have us tossed out. We need to get him talking."

"I'll let you take the lead," she says. "But if he starts to lie I'm not going to sit there and listen to it."

"All right."

We step out of the car and walk toward the house. I ring the bell. It takes a while, maybe half a minute, before someone comes to the door. When it opens there's a man dressed in dark livery, Asian, tall, powerfully built with an angular face. I don't remember seeing him at the memorial service on Saturday. "Yes?" he says.

"Is Mr. Lang in, by any chance?"

"Is he expecting you?"

"No, but he knows us . . ."

"We're friends," says Joselyn. "We were here on Saturday for the memorial service."

"Who is it, Chin?" I hear Lang's voice somewhere off in the distance.

"I don't know, sir. What is your name?"

"It's Paul Madriani, Mr. Lang, and Joselyn. We met on Saturday at the service."

"Oh, yes, I remember. Show them in," he says.

"This way." The heavy door swings open.

We step in and the footman closes it behind us. We follow him down the hall. He doesn't take us toward the living room. Instead we turn toward the study, the room where Frank Leon sat recovering in one of the large chairs Saturday morning. Suddenly it dawns on me. Who is going to tell Frank about the autopsy report, the fact that Sofia was pregnant with their grandchild? It would be cruel to allow him and his wife to find out by reading it. I make a mental note to call Harry and get their number from the office, to call them as soon as I can. Another crushing blow. They will be left to wonder, when will it stop?

When we reach Lang's study the old man is already seated in one of the overstuffed club chairs waiting for us. "What can I do for you? Come in and sit down. Would you like something to drink?"

"No. We're fine," I tell him.

"Please sit. Come join me."

We do.

The servant waits by the open door. I glance at him over my shoulder and Lang says, "It's all right, Chin. You can go."

"Call me if you need anything," says Chin.

"I will." As soon as he disappears down the hall, Lang says, "Chin has been with me for years. At times I think perhaps he's a little too protective."

"I understand entirely," says Joselyn. "One can never be too careful.

Especially living in a big house like this on the beach. There're a lot of bad people around. We know." She smiles at him. "Paul's practice is full of them," she says.

Lang looks at her, gives her a half-baked paternal smile as if he's not sure whether to laugh or hide. Then he says, "What can I do for you?"

"It's a simple matter," I tell him. "We'd like to know who the middleman was."

"I'm sorry. I don't understand."

"You wrote a letter of recommendation for Sofia."

"You know I did. We talked about it the other day."

"We'd like to know who obtained it for her," I tell him.

"I don't know what you mean. She was a lovely girl, a hard worker, a good student . . ."

"How would you know? You never met her," says Joselyn. "You didn't know her."

"I think you should go," says Lang.

"She told me the day she interviewed with me that she never met any of the three people who wrote the letters recommending her. They were obtained by a friend," I tell him. "It's a simple question. We want to know who that friend is."

"So obviously she didn't tell you."

"If she had we wouldn't be here," says Joselyn.

"I'm afraid there's nothing more to talk about," says Lang. "If you'll excuse me I have some things to take care of." He starts to get up.

Before he can do it Joselyn reaches over and grabs his walking cane, which is hooked on the arm of his chair. "You're going to talk to us whether you like it or not," she says. "I can understand why the man who asked for those letters might be in hiding. But you're going to give us his name. You may as well accept that fact."

Lang struggles to get out of the chair. She puts the point of the cane against his stomach and pins him there. It doesn't take much.

"Joselyn, don't."

"Don't try to get up," she says. "You might fall and break something. Old people sometimes do." Joselyn bounces the rubber tip of his cane on the hardwood floor as if to emphasize the point.

He settles back into the chair and looks at the open door. Lang is about to call for Chin.

"Did you know she was pregnant when she was killed?"

This distracts him. He looks at me wide-eyed. He doesn't say a word, but I can tell from his stark expression, this comes as a surprise. He finally says, "No. I didn't. How do you know this?"

"The autopsy report," I tell him. "We received it earlier today. She was two months pregnant. Eight weeks along. That means the medical examiner has an embryo. A budding fetus probably not much bigger than a kidney bean, but large enough to extract a sample of DNA for a profile. The police are going to want to know who the father is."

"I see," he says.

"Can you think of a better motive for murder?" says Joselyn.

"I don't understand. What does this have to do with me?" he says.

"You wrote the letter as a favor to the man she loved," says Joselyn. "Correct me if I'm wrong. Young woman, older man, married, I presume?"

He doesn't say it but he nods, just enough so that there is no doubt.

"Let me guess," she says. "He came to you for the letter telling you he wanted to break it off."

He takes a deep breath and sighs. "How did you know?"

"It's a classic tale. What was the problem? Was she getting too clingy?" asks Joselyn.

"He wanted to tell her but he didn't know how. He thought if he helped to find her a job . . . Well, you know."

"She might disappear." Joselyn finishes the thought for him.

"I don't think that was it at all. I think he was hoping she might make a life for herself, perhaps find someone else her own age. He's not a bad man. I know what you're thinking. But he didn't kill her. I know that."

"How do you know?" I ask.

"I just don't think he could do something like that. He's not the type."

"Who is he?" says Joselyn.

"If I were to tell you, what purpose would it serve?" says Lang. "She's dead. My telling you is not going to bring her back. It will only serve to cause more pain. The man has a wife and a family, children," he says.

"Are his children older or younger than Sofia?" Joselyn puts it to him like a knife.

"You think he's my age. He's not. He's a much younger man."

"I'm not looking to date him," says Joselyn. "I merely want to introduce him to the police."

"You're a hard woman," he says.

"You don't know the half of it," she tells him. "You can talk to us or you can talk to the cops."

He looks at her, lips drawn tight.

"You should remember there are two other people who wrote letters for Sofia. They are strangers as well. She never met them. She told me as much. We can go to them," I say, "put the same question to them. I'm guessing that one of them is probably going to be smart enough to avoid a possible indictment."

"What do you mean?" he says.

"Accessory after the fact of murder. If the police find out that your friend killed Sofia and you covered for him, acted to conceal his identity, what do you think they're going to do?"

"Tell him, Theo." It's a woman's voice, feeble and subdued. It comes from the doorway behind us. I turn and see his wife, frail and bent standing there in a nightgown. "I heard your voices," she says. "So I came to see. We both knew that sooner or later someone was going to come knocking. Now you're here, and it's time. So tell him."

I look back at Lang. He's slumped in the chair, all ninety-eight pounds of him, his face etched with lines of grief. "I warned him. I told him not to get involved. It was foolish. He asked me, he came to me and asked if I would have the memorial service here," says Lang.

"That was big of him," says Joselyn. "What was the problem? Was his place too small?"

"You can make fun of it if you like, but he was shattered. I never saw a man look that bad."

"Juggling women will do that to some men," she says. "Tell me, did he attend the memorial service, was he there?"

"How could he?" Lang looks at her, eyes pleading.

"Told you." Joselyn looks at me. "Of course not. How could he explain the outing to the wife and kids? I understand."

"Did he know she was pregnant?" I ask.

"I don't know. If he did, he never told me. Still, he looked like death warmed over," says the old man.

"He couldn't possibly have looked worse than Sofia," says Joselyn. "So what is this saint's name?"

"Ricardo Menard," he says.

TWENTY-SEVEN

t is just after noon when Harry, Herman, and I meet in the conference room to talk about the latest information gathered by Herman's small army of investigators. A photo lab has managed to enlarge and enhance the cell phone shot taken by Emma's neighbor of the car seen loitering in the neighborhood the night before Sofia's murder. It was the old rusted-out car the elderly couple described.

The digitally enhanced photo allowed Herman's people to make out that the car carried a California plate. It also captured enough of the letters and numbers on the rear plate that the investigators have now been able to reduce the number of variables to three possible combinations. Herman assigned investigators to run license checks with the DMV on all three.

"One of them was an older-model 1973 Olds," says Herman. "It caught my eye because of the vintage. I thought it might be our vehicle. But it turned out to be a salvage car. It was declared totaled by the insurance company a couple of years ago after an accident. It's been junked out, maybe shredded by now, we don't know for sure. According to the DMV, that particular plate number is not assigned to any vehicle currently registered on the road."

"So we can scratch that one," says Harry.

"Not necessarily," says Herman. "Old plates from salvage yards sometimes find their way onto other vehicles, especially if they're gonna be used to commit a crime. They may change out the plates several times before the car is abandoned or dumped in a lake somewhere."

"You said there were three?" I ask.

"One of the cars was resold to a new owner. The plates were changed and the old plates retired. The last one is a later-model Toyota Celica. It doesn't fit the description of the car the neighbors saw that night. But here's the interesting thing. The Celica was last registered and licensed three years ago. Later that year it was totaled in an accident and hauled to a wrecking yard. But when the report got to the DMV, the vehicle's VIN number, the vehicle identification that's stamped inside the door or under the hood, didn't match the old plate number. According to DMV records, the car showed a different plate."

"What does that mean?" says Harry.

"We don't know. It could just be that the DMV screwed up, an error in data entry. Or maybe the wrecking yard sold the plates to somebody else. What we do know is that there's no current registration under the old license number. It just seems to have disappeared."

"If a traffic cop saw it on the street, especially if the license didn't have a current tag, they'd run a check right from the squad car," says Harry. "They'd nail them on the street."

"I was thinking the same thing," says Herman. "Remember the neighbor? The woman said the car looked like a wreck, all rusted out. A car like that would be a ticket magnet."

"It doesn't sound like there's much else to go on. So maybe we work that angle." I look at Herman. "Can we have the investigators run a check on moving and parking violations, say San Diego County, for any citations issued under that license number?" Herman has laid a DMV form on the table with the subject plate number.

"Might need some authority," he says. "A subpoena would help."

"We can issue it as part of the discovery in Emma's defense. Do it," I tell Harry.

"Got it."

I look down at the plate number printed on the form, 5QPU783, and wonder if it's connected to Sofia's killer.

TWENTY-EIGHT

t's after hours and the office is locked up. Harry finds me at my desk checking voicemail messages.

He sticks his head in the door and says, "Got a minute?"

"Come on in."

"I've been researching the Internet. Something caught my eye. You remember the article from Joselyn's iPad, the piece on Jakob Grimminger?"

"Yes."

"There was something in the article, a word in German, that got lost in Herman's translation when he skimmed the piece in our meeting."

"What was that?" I place the receiver back on the phone's base.

"I went back and read it," says Harry. "It was the word *Blutfahne*. According to the piece, one of Grimminger's duties was to carry the Blutfahne during ceremonial functions. And that wasn't all. At the end of the article, Herman skipped something I think may be important. He read from the article that after the war Grimminger was put on trial for being a member of the German SS, that he wasn't convicted, but they took away all his property anyway."

"I remember."

"But there's more. There were two charges brought against Grimminger, according to the article: his SS membership *and* the fact that he carried the Blutfahne for nineteen years."

"Well, don't keep me in suspense," I tell him.

"The word *Blutfahne* means 'Blood Flag' in English."

"What? You mean like waving the bloody shirt?" It's a tactic on the part of some politicians to refer to the blood of martyrs and heroes, often in the form of dead soldiers, to silence their opponents.

"In a way," says Harry. "But in this case it was more than a metaphor. The item was real. You remember from the article, Grimminger goes way back. He had a long history with Hitler. What do you know about Adolf's rise to power?" he asks.

"Not a lot. He rose up out of the Depression. Took power as chancellor after Hindenburg died. Took over two or three countries before the war started in '39 with the invasion of Poland."

"Before that," says Harry. "The early days."

I shake my head. "Is it important? Otherwise I've got some things . . ."

"It is if you want to know what we're looking for. It's very important," says Harry.

This stops me cold in my tracks. I look at him. He is dead serious. "Go on."

"Before the First World War, Adolf was a homeless itinerant. Transport him to modern times and he'd be sitting on a sidewalk outside a mall with a cardboard sign and a plastic bucket panhandling for change.

"He was a failed artist. He wandered from the small town where he was born in Austria to Vienna, the capital. There he was denied entrance to art school at the university. It was a rejection that many of the highborn Viennese would come to regret. He went from there to Munich, where he worked as a laborer, sold watercolors on the street, and survived in flophouses.

"Hitler didn't find any kind of a groove until the First World War, when he joined the German army. There he found a cause even though he was Austrian, not German, by birth. During the war he served as a messenger on the front lines. He was wounded several times, won the Iron Cross, but never advanced beyond the rank of corporal, even though he was offered a promotion. He turned it down. Why? Nobody knows for sure, but according to some it was because he hated authority. That's ironic, isn't it?" says Harry. "The ultimate authoritarian rejecting a share of authority."

"Maybe he didn't want it unless he could have it all," I tell him.

"Ah, so you did read history," says Harry.

"No, psychology of the warped mind. Go on. I assume this is leading somewhere?"

"Bear with me," says Harry. "Near the end of the First World War, Hitler gets gassed in the trenches. He loses his eyesight for a time. He's sent to an army hospital for treatment, and while he's there convalescing, the war ends. Germany surrenders, followed by the onerous Treaty of Versailles, where the Allies, mostly the French and British, take their pound of flesh from the Germans in the form of huge reparation payments and the transfer of territory. They set the table for World War Two.

"The German people were bitter. There was high unemployment, their economy was ravaged by hyperinflation, and in 1929 it went over the edge and into the abyss with the Great Depression. It became the perfect backdrop for the rise of a tyrant," says Harry.

"But long before that, Hitler was given a job by the army. Way back when, in 1918, after the war, he had recovered his eyesight. He was still a corporal in the army. He was sent back to Munich. The army was the only place he'd ever been semi-successful. It was the only home he had, so he wasn't about to muster out voluntarily. They needed to find him a job. You know what they say, idle hands are the devil's workshop. In his case, they would have been wiser to chop them off. The job they found for him ultimately led the world to disaster.

"They assigned Hitler to an army intelligence unit. They sent him out to spy on various rabble-rousing political groups that were cropping up around the city of Munich.

"There was a lot of angry talk about how the army had been stabbed in the back by the politicians who sued for peace and signed the treaty. The German people were angry about how the war ended. So was Hitler. So it shouldn't have come as any great surprise when Adolf showed up at one of these meetings and decided that he agreed with the fanatics who were up on the stage.

"They wanted to overthrow the government—the new Weimar Republic. Hitler figured why not, but only on one condition: if he could lead the parade. Hitler came to realize in a short time that he had an exceptional gift for speaking before large groups. He was especially skilled in the dialect of demagoguery. He could appeal to the basic instincts of the human heart in a single sentence, stick his tongue directly in the bull's-eye and wiggle it.

"With a little manipulation and backstabbing, Adolf took over the group. At the time it was called the German Workers Party, the DAP. Later, he and some followers changed the name to the National Socialist German Workers Party, known to history as the Nazis. Hitler used his artistic skills to craft its emblem, the black swastika in a white circle on a red background. It's rumored that he designed and commissioned the original flag himself.

"In 1919 he left the army and went to work full-time for the party. He spent the next four years speaking in beer halls where the group met, increasing its numbers, inflaming its members and organizing.

"By early November of 1923, he was getting impatient and ready to act. He had watched Mussolini take over Italy the previous year and thought he could do the same. Hitler decided to take over the German government by force, starting with the city of Munich. He planned out the coup, brought in a few necessary allies, including Ludendorff, a general from the First World War, and appropriated a couple of machine guns from a local armory. He had some former disaffected soldiers man the guns.

"Then Hitler, with a pistol in his hand, stormed a beer hall where the titular head of the Bavarian government and his entourage were meeting. He took them captive and tried to convince them to join his movement. When they pretended to negotiate but then escaped, Hitler didn't have a lot of options left. He was already committed. He and his followers, including Grimminger, marched on the city hall in an attempt to take it over.

"They didn't get far. The Munich city police opened fire on them in a narrow street. Thirteen of them were killed. Hitler went to the ground, his arm dislocated, when the man next to him was shot. The flag they were carrying, the one Hitler designed, fell on the street and was stained with the blood of one Andreas Bauriedl, who fell mortally wounded on top of it."

"The Blood Flag," I say.

Harry nods. "Hitler escaped, but he was caught two days later hiding in a house with a woman, the wife of one of his wealthy supporters. He was arrested and put on trial for treason. He used his skills as an orator to turn the trial into one against the government, and himself into a folk hero. As a result he received a very light sentence, just over a year in Landsberg Prison. He spent his time living in relative comfort with aides while he wrote his memoirs, *Mein Kampf*, meaning 'My Struggle,' in which he gave the world's leader fair warning about what was to come. Of course, they didn't listen to him. They never do.

"When Hitler got out of Landsberg, there was a gift waiting for him. One of his followers had managed to find their flag, blood and all. They presented it to Hitler as a memento of the Beer Hall Putsch, the incident that brought him to national prominence. To Hitler the putsch became a seminal event in terms of personal loyalty. Those involved with him were considered the patron saints of Nazism.

"In the early thirties, after his rise to power, Hitler used the flag as a talisman during the giant Nuremberg rallies, when he performed seeming acts of voodoo. He would grip the bloodstained flag in one hand while he touched the various flags of SS units in order to consecrate them. He would present a wreath to the immortal thirteen who died, shot down by the police. God help anyone who didn't genuflect," says Harry.

"The bloody shirt," I say.

"In a word," says Harry. "There were some who theorized that the entire ceremony was the result of Hitler's own sense of guilt, because he not only survived the putsch, he ran. As for Grimminger, Hitler steered him away from brown-shirted SA to black-uniformed death's-head of SS just in time. As a result, Grimminger survived the 'Night of the Long Knives,' which took place in June 1934. Hitler and his SS purged the SA and assassinated most of its leaders. But he saved his old comrade from the beer hall days, and then assigned him to carry the Blood Flag. There are pictures all over the Internet of Grimminger, standing like a statue, holding the flag at ceremonies and meetings. It's a wonder pigeons didn't crap all over him."

"What happened to the flag?"

"Nobody knows," says Harry. "Or if they do, they aren't saying. According to what I could find, the flag was stored in a special area, a flag display in the Brown House, the Nazi headquarters in Munich. The building was bombed by the Allies in the late summer of 1944. The structure was heavily damaged. From that point on the flag disappeared.

After the war, the Allies and the German authorities assumed that the flag was destroyed in the bombing. As far as they were concerned, it was good riddance. They didn't want any Nazi shrines or relics to give rise to a Hitler cult. But it's possible that they were wrong."

"What do you mean?"

"There have been rumors, very persistent rumors."

"Rumors of what?"

"They date back to the end of the war," says Harry. "And it's possible that at the time, they had no idea as to the significance of what they found. But there are stories that American GIs who occupied Munich in the days following the German surrender found the Blood Flag and took it as a war trophy."

TWENTY-NINE

For several days Nino had watched the house on Winona Avenue in hopes of going back in. But there were problems. The woman, the homeowner, was now represented by a law firm. Nino knew this because he had seen the lawyer's name in the newspapers. His office was somewhere over in Coronado. Lawyers were always a pain in the ass. Her house was also now being watched by security. Nino had seen the cars drive by on a regular schedule, overhead light bars and the company's logo on the doors.

There was another one in the house, a suit. When the man walked in front of the open blinds in the living room with his coat off, Nino could see the shoulder harness and what looked like a Glock in the holster. Unless he missed his bet, they probably installed new security gear as well, silent alarms and the little pinhole cameras that you could never find. Nino would have to do a fan dance to keep his face off the video while he sprayed every crevice in the house with paint just to have a shot at getting in and out unseen. The place looked like a fortress and smelled like a trap. This told him that what he was looking for was no longer there.

Either the lawyer had it or the cops did. If it was the police, Nino could forget it. The game was over. He could go home. Assuming, of course, that they knew what they had. If the lawyer had it, that was another matter. In this case, the item was still in play. Getting it might be a little difficult, and it might mean a little blood. Nino didn't particularly mind as long as it wasn't his own. That was the price of doing business.

For the moment he was behind the wheel doing close to eighty, down the South Bay Expressway east of San Diego. It was a toll road with almost no traffic this late at night. It was almost ten. Nino was gambling that at this hour, with sparse traffic, the CHP wouldn't waste much time on patrols way out here.

Ari had called him thirty minutes earlier thinking that Nino would have to haul ass just to get there on time. As it was, he'd have an edge on the Israeli, arriving early. The meeting site was a barren area of rolling hills out in the middle of nowhere. The change of venue away from a public place and the late hour could mean that they were going to give him bad news, no more attempts on the house. The job was over. Break my heart, thought Nino. Only the mentally challenged would go back into that place after what he had seen. Or it could be they had something else in mind.

Whatever it was, he didn't like it. He wouldn't have been here except for the fact that they owed him money. Ari said he'd have it tonight. Nino made a point of never leaving money behind. If you were gonna do that, then you had no business being in the business.

He took the San Miguel Ranch Road exit from the highway and followed the road. It wound up into the hills off to the right of the highway. Nino had already taken a good look at the terrain on Google Earth from his phone, so he had a heads-up as to the lay of the land.

When the asphalt road turned to dirt he flipped off his headlights, slowed down a little, and felt out the road with his parking lamps. It was dark, no moon. Without the light pollution from the city, he could see the Milky Way spread out overhead like a flickering blanket.

A few hundred feet farther on, the road forked. Nino went to the left. In doing this he bypassed the road to the meeting site given to him by Ari on the phone. He climbed higher into the hills. As his eyes adjusted to the darkness he picked up speed. About a mile on he found the spot he was looking for.

It was a flat area off to the right of the road and as long as two football fields and about sixty yards wide.

At the far edge on the right, if the Google satellite image was accurate, the ground fell away at a steep incline. It was a ridge overlooking the location where Ari told him they were to meet.

He didn't want to drive any closer to the overlook. The ground was flat enough, and hard, but he didn't want to take the chance that someone down below might see or hear the car. For all he knew, Ari was already down there. He pulled to the side of the road, turned off the engine and the parking lights, and put the car in park. Then he got out, closed the door quietly, and walked to the rear. From the trunk he grabbed a large pair of binoculars and started to move in long, quick strides over the flat ground. Someone had graded the area with a bulldozer.

It took Nino less than two minutes to traverse the sixty yards, reaching the crest of the ridge where he could look down. He quickly scanned the area below with the thermal imaging night vision field glasses. If the little prick thought he was going to set him up, he had another thing coming.

From here he could see everything. The flat area below was mostly barren, and in places graded. It didn't provide a lot of cover for hiding. That was good, or maybe it was just intended to make him feel safe. There were no vehicles, none that he could see, and no places he could see to hide them. Ari's wasn't there. He checked his watch. It was still early.

What he didn't like was the road leading in. If someone came in from behind and blocked him, there was no way out. The possibility bothered him. If they tried it he could grab Ari and put a pistol to his head until they backed off, then take the little fucker for a ride. But that was a low-percentage play. And besides, the people with Ari might not care. They might shoot them both and sort it out later.

The smarter move was to wait until Ari arrived, watch him for a while, make sure he was alone, and then go down and block the road himself. When Ari got tired of waiting and tried to come out, he could grab him, get his money, and find out what was going on. At this point it really didn't matter much to Nino whether they wanted to fire him or not. As far as he was concerned, Jimmie Pepper had pretty much used up his nine lives. It was time to move on, another identity, another name.

Nino studied the area carefully for several minutes but saw no sign of any green flares, heat registers from human bodies or hot engine blocks. There were little pockets of brush here and there, what the locals called chaparral, mostly sagebrush and manzanita. He was just about to lower the field glasses when something caught his eye. It was a flick of greenish light in a brush about three hundred yards to his right, halfway down the slope. Something had moved just enough to allow the glasses to pick up the glow. Nino focused in on it.

Whatever it was, it was putting out heat. There was no question about that. He could see it. But he couldn't make out the shape. The object was stationary, unmoving. It could be an animal, like a dog or a deer. Or it could be a sniper set up in a blind, waiting for his target to appear.

Nino crouched down, then got flat on the ground, just in case it might be human with a thermal scope, something that could pick him off the ridgeline before he could blink. He watched the glowing image for several seconds, trying to make out the dimensions and the outline of the form. But the brush broke it up. He glanced at his watch. Unless he was late the Israeli would be arriving any minute.

Ari felt the wheels of his car as they left the pavement and ran onto the dirt. He left his headlights on as instructed and followed the road to the right. It was narrow, wide enough only for a single car until it reached an area where it widened out. It was the spot where they were supposed to meet. He took a deep breath, then turned off his lights and killed the engine. He waited for the dust to settle, then looked around. There was no sign of another car. He checked his rearview mirror for the glare of headlights coming up the winding road behind him. But he saw nothing. Ari wondered if he'd made himself clear regarding the directions.

The man he knew as Jimmie Pepper could be dense at times. But Ari knew now that was probably a ruse. Thanks to a flare sent up by the FBI, Israeli intelligence was aware that the American government believed that James Pepper was dead. The FBI had put out a bulletin notifying local law enforcement that Pepper was missing, believed to be deceased, and to be on the lookout for any person or persons using his identity. Tel

Aviv picked up the bulletin almost immediately from Interpol and noti-
fied the consulate in Los Angeles.

Ordinarily the Israelis would have contacted the FBI and had Jimmie
picked up. But these were not ordinary times. The man calling himself
Pepper had managed to penetrate an Israeli intelligence operation. Israel
wanted to know who he was, who he worked for, and what he was up to.
On such matters the Israeli cabinet was no longer sure they could trust
the American government.

So two days earlier the Israeli military had dispatched a Hercules
C-130 from Nevatim Airbase in Israel directly to northern Mexico. It
was refueled three times in flight by a KC-130 tanker. The plane carried
thirty-two Israeli commandos and a four-wheel-drive pickup with California plates. The commandos were sufficiently well armed to protect
the plane while on the ground, though if they had to leave in a hurry,
they could be airborne within minutes. The plane landed at a private
airstrip on a ranch a few miles from the Tijuana-Mexicali highway in
the countryside east of Tijuana.

The commandos secured the area and sent a two-man sniper team
north in the pickup truck. Both the driver and the passenger, sniper and
spotter, carried valid US driver's licenses and US passports, all of them
good for the reason that both men held dual citizenship, US and Israeli.
They crossed the border into the United States at San Ysidro less than
two hours after landing. The Americans were right about one thing:
their border was porous.

As Ari sat in his car and glanced at his watch he already knew that
the Israeli sniper team was somewhere on the hillside above him. He
had been in touch with them on a crypto-capable satellite phone that allowed him to communicate not only with the sniper and his spotter but
with the plane on the ground in Mexico.

The plan was not to kill the man known as Jimmie, but to take him
down with a dart, drug him, and then bundle him across the border,
onto the C-130, where he could be flown back to Israel for interrogation.
There were fears that he might be working for ISIS or possibly Al Qaeda
in the Arabian Peninsula. If so, they needed to know if he was part of
a broader network, and if he was, had they penetrated any other Israeli
operations or the intelligence operations of any of Israel's allies?

Ari checked his watch again. Jimmie was now running late. More than ten minutes. Perhaps the phone call had scared him off, made him wary due to the remote location. Under the circumstances it couldn't be helped. It was a risk they had to take. Ari reached over and grabbed the satellite phone from the seat next to him. He punched in the number and waited. When the voice came over the line it was a hushed whisper. "Eagle here."

"Eagle, this is Cable. Any sign on the road?" said Ari.

"Negative."

"I don't think he's going to show."

"Sit tight. Turn it off. Eagle out."

Ari could tell from the aggravation in the man's voice that the military pro up on the hillside did not consider Ari to be part of their team. Patience was the name of the game. Snipers and spotters could lie in the hot desert sun in camo gear and ghillie suits for hours, sometimes days, and barely take a breath, just waiting for a shot. Here he was, sitting in a comfortable car, sweating blood because the man was ten minutes late. He tried to calm down, took a stick of gum from his pocket, unwrapped it, stuck it in his mouth, and started chewing.

The instant the man stirred to adjust his headset, the brush moved and Nino got a good look at him. There were two of them. The spotter was bent forward low to the ground, kneeling on one knee, the spotting scope in front of him. The sniper was lying prone, the stock of his weapon just touching his shoulder.

Nino took a quick glance up the hillside behind the two men. It was immediately apparent why they had picked that location. A cleared firebreak ran up the hill behind them, all the way to the top of the crest, on the level where Nino was lying in the dirt. That's when he saw it.

A dark vehicle that looked like a pickup was parked right near the edge of the crest, just at the top of the firebreak. Nino hadn't seen it because, with the naked eye, in the darkness it was too far away. He was lucky. If the two men had stayed with their vehicle up on the ridge he would have run right into them. Walking across the open ground from his car they couldn't have missed him. They would have nailed his ass.

He took another look at the firebreak. It had been graded by a bulldozer and wide enough for a good-size truck to drive on, though the grade was far too steep for anything but a tracked vehicle. Down the hill the break ended in a shallow gully where the team had set up. They were covered by the brush. Whether it was natural growth or if the two men had cut it and carried it in, he couldn't tell. They were perhaps no more than twenty feet above the flat area where Ari's car was parked. Anyone pulling up close to him would give them an easy shot.

He focused the glasses down on the car below. He could see Ari sitting there, behind the wheel, big as life, chewing gum, his cadaverous jaw moving up and down like a cow chewing its cud.

Ari wanted to pick up the satellite phone again and call them to see if they could spot anything out on the road coming in behind him. But he didn't dare. The sniper might put a dart in his chest just to put him to sleep. He thought about turning on the car's radio, some music, anything to calm his nerves, then wondered what the guys up on the hill might think when they heard it. Instead he fished in his pocket for another stick of gum.

He had it halfway out of the wrapper when the flash of light from the fireball up on the hill lit up the windshield of his car. Ari leaned forward over the steering wheel to see what was happening just in time to watch the flaming pickup truck start on its fiery trek down the hill. Fuel spilling from the vehicle's gas tank left a blazing track behind it on the bare earth as the truck streaked down the steep firebreak on the side of the hill. It moved with the speed of a meteor, silhouetting the two figures as they tried to scramble from their nest under the brush. The flaming missile slammed into the gully at the bottom of the break and exploded like napalm as the gas tank ruptured. The kinetic energy of the impact crushed the front end and sent the truck into a slow end-over. The flaming mass peeled itself from the gully and landed in a burning tangle of metal at the bottom of the hill. The rubber from its tires flared like fireworks.

Ari sat behind the wheel slack-jawed, looking at the flames, his gaze glued on the two mangled and charring bodies stuck like gummy bears to the grill and the mangled bumper. His mouth open, he tried to breathe, but his heart was pounding so hard that he couldn't. Finally he swallowed, looked away, and sucked in a deep breath of foul gasoline-scented air.

He collected himself and looked back toward the hill. The firebreak was ablaze, a straight line of fuel-fed flames pointing like an arrow back up the incline toward the top of the ridge. There, standing at the edge, he saw the figure. Ari knew instantly that he was in trouble. He glanced quickly at the satellite phone on the seat next to him and knew it was useless. The plane and its men were too far away to help him.

He tried to start the engine, fumbled with the key, then looked back up the hill. His eyes searched the ridge and he realized that the dark figure was no longer standing there. He tried again and the engine started. He slammed it into gear and floored it. As he pulled hard on the steering wheel the car spun a doughnut in the dry sand. The rear wheels, struggling to find traction, finally dug in and the car took off. Ari turned on his headlights and sped down the road.

Squeezing the wheel, hanging on tight, he kept glancing over his right shoulder up toward the hill where the road led. His heart was hammering, blood vessels pounding in his head. Ari was almost through the narrow area of dirt road when he saw the glare of the lights coming from somewhere high up on the hill. He tried to push the gas pedal through the floor. The car jumped from dirt onto the pavement as the tires grabbed asphalt. The car rocketed ahead down the road, around a curve racing for the on-ramp to the expressway. Ari could see it in the distance less than a mile away. He looked in the rearview mirror and watched as the halo of light in the night sky behind him faded and slowly disappeared.

By the time Nino reached the fork in the road he realized he was too late. Before he got to the expressway Ari would be long gone. Within a few miles he would be back on the freeway, where he could take any one of a dozen off-ramps and disappear. He looked in the mirror at the glow from the burning wreckage over the hill behind him. He thought about driving over to take a look, but then decided that wouldn't be wise. An explosion like that could be seen for miles, especially on a dark night like this. Instead he stepped on the gas and headed down the road. That's all right, he thought. The cadaver can run, but he can't hide.

THIRTY

Harry and I are huddled in my office going over hospital records and notes regarding Robert Brauer's care in the days before he died. The crucial issue is insulin.

According to the conclusions of the medical examiner in Brauer's autopsy report, "The cause of death is consistent with metabolic encephalopathy resulting from hypoglycemia believed to be induced by the administration of high levels of exogenous insulin."

In short, somebody shot Brauer up with an estimated eight hundred units of insulin, the daily normal being about fifty. The overdose caused the glucose in his blood to drop like a rock, putting him into insulin shock within minutes. He would have been unable to help himself or call for assistance. If anyone looked in on him they would have thought he was asleep.

According to the literature, insulin, which is sometimes used to attempt or commit suicide, is not considered a particularly certain method of inducing death. On the other hand, though, according to the report, if you're of a mind, eight hundred units should do it. Because of the volume there is no possibility of an accident. The syringe had to be filled at least eight times to get the job done.

"Whoever did it dumped it into the IV that was plugged into the back of his hand," says Harry. "The nurse had him on a drip to replace fluids. He was becoming dehydrated. The cops figure he was asleep, probably dozed off when the insulin was administered. The fact that it went directly into the vein instead of being shot into the fatty tissue of the stomach or the leg means it went to work much faster. There was almost no wait time for the effect."

"Where did they find the bottle?" I ask.

"In the trash can in the corner of the room along with the syringe. The bottle is how they know the dosage. Full, it would have had a thousand units," says Harry. "According to the nurses' notes it had nine hundred units remaining when she brought it into the room. There were a hundred units left when they found it in the trash."

The last hundred units the killer probably would have had a hard time getting out with the syringe. He wouldn't want to take the time in case someone walked in. He already knew he had more than enough. "Do we have a time frame on all this?"

"Estimates," says Harry. "It was the night shift." He paws through the pile of documents stacked on the other side of my desk. "According to the nurse, she worked a twelve-hour shift that night, seven to seven. She came into Brauer's room with medications and the insulin about seven fifteen. Emma was there at the time. Brauer had a set of tests late in the day. They just rolled him back into his room a few minutes earlier. They were going to bring him a late dinner. That was the reason for the insulin. The nurse had everything laid out on the bedside table and then there was an emergency, a code blue. She got called away. There was only one RN and an LVN on that floor that night. That was it."

"How long does she say she was gone?"

"According to her notes," says Harry, "a little over ninety minutes. About ten minutes in, she sent a nursing assistant back to Brauer's room to secure the meds and put a hold on Brauer's dinner until they could give him his insulin. According to the assistant she held the dinner tray outside the room and picked up the meds. All she saw were three small plastic cups with pills on the table next to the bed. There was no insulin and no syringe. Because the nurse didn't tell her what was there, she didn't look any further. She assumed that was it."

"And of course no Emma," I say.

"No, as she already told us, she went home."

Emma had been with her father all day, waiting for hours and sitting with him while they ran tests. She was exhausted. So when they finally got him back to his room to get him ready for dinner she stayed until the nurse left. She excused herself and went to the ladies' room, and when she came back, she said her father was asleep. She kissed him on the head and noticed that he was very cold. So she covered him with a blanket on top of the sheet that was already there. Then she left and went home.

"According to the CNA," says Harry, "Robert Brauer was sound asleep when she got to the room, so she didn't disturb him. She took the pills and stashed them back by the nurses' station. When the RN finally freed herself up, she went back, found the pills, and asked the assistant where the insulin was. They went down to the room, tried to rouse Brauer, but by then he was already deep in a coma. They tried resuscitation. Glucose countermeasures. Nothing worked. He died a little after midnight."

"Who else was on the floor that night? Any visitors?"

"Yeah, people coming and going," says Harry, "visiting other patients. No sign-in system, of course. They had security cameras but the one on the floor that night was out of commission. According to the staff it was down half the time. And even if it had been working, they said someone had disconnected the cable." Harry looks at me.

"Whoever did it wasn't taking any chances," I say.

"How could they know the camera was out?" says Harry. "According to hospital security they weren't terribly concerned, because they knew who did it. Emma was there when the meds came. She was gone and so was the insulin by the time the nurse's assistant showed up. And Brauer had just been given some bad news. He was going to have to get on a schedule with dialysis three times a week because his kidneys were shot," says Harry. "According to the nurse he was very upset. So was Emma."

"Why didn't she tell us about that?"

"Who knows? Maybe she figures, what's the diff," says Harry, "he's dead. It's the fact that the meds were available on the table along with the syringe, and that Emma and her dad just got the bad news about dialysis that put the hammerlock on the state's murder case. They'd have an uphill fight trying to show malice or premeditation. So the best they could do, absent other evidence, was a mercy killing—one count, of voluntary manslaughter," says Harry. "Let's hope they don't come up with anything else."

"That's the good news. Bad news," I tell him, "is there's no way to deal down from here. From their point of view they're going to be thinking Emma has already gotten all the breaks she's gonna get. And we still don't know how the pieces fit. We don't have a clue as to who killed her father or Ed Pack."

"Or Sofia," says Harry.

"Or Sofia."

"Are we thinking it's the same person?" says Harry.

"Pack and Brauer are becoming pretty clear. Sofia, I'm not sure."

"We have a common MO. Somebody injected both Brauer and the doctor with an ocean of insulin."

"Yes, but we can't prove it, not with regard to Pack," says Harry. "We only have Tony's opinion for it, and that's not evidence."

"All right. OK, fine. We know that both men, Ed Pack and Brauer, go back to the days of Adolf in the army, in the same platoon. They each received little boxes with brass keys. We know it scared the crap out of both men. They were together in Munich at the end of the war, along with Walter Jones. We know Brauer's house was burglarized."

"Yeah, but Emma didn't file a report with the police. You can't produce evidence of the burglary unless you put her on the stand. And trust me, you don't want to do that."

"So we have a few holes."

"That's not a hole. That's a chasm," says Harry.

"It's a work in progress. We know that whoever did the burglary ripped up the house looking for something,"

"We know about it, but we can't talk about it in front of the jury until we lay a foundation," says Harry.

"OK, fine. But you and I know they were looking for the little box, the brass key, and Grimminger's picture. With Grimminger's name and background, we discovered the Blood Flag."

"Assuming we can build an evidence ladder to crawl across and touch the flag, that might work," says Harry. "But only if."

"Listen, I grant that it's an unknown. But everybody loves a mystery," I tell him.

"Everybody but a judge. You try to mystify some Buddha in a black robe and he's gonna hit you with his hammer," says Harry. "What we need is evidence."

"We have the box, the key, and the ID as well as the return address for the lawyer in Oklahoma City who sent the package."

"Yes, but did you personally receive that package?"

"You know I didn't."

"Where did you get it?"

"I told you. From the safe-deposit box at Emma's bank."

"And who put it there?"

"Emma."

"So we're back where we started," says Harry. "Emma was there when her father received the package. She saw him open it. She saw the wrappings with the return address and she can identify the contents, authenticate them as having been in the package when it arrived. With that we can testify to a little judicious research under Grimminger's name and with that we arrive at the Blood Flag. With the Blood Flag we have a theory, one that perhaps we can sell to a jury. Come to think of it, it's a hell of a lot better than the theory in the O.J. case. 'You have to let our client out of jail so he can go chase the real killer.' The problem is we can't get to any of it without Emma."

"Maybe we can."

"How?" says Harry.

"What if we put Tony Pack up on the stand?"

Harry thinks about this.

"He identified the box and the key as being similar, if not identical, to the one that was sent to his father. He saw it personally, remember?"

"Go on."

"His father and Brauer were in the same platoon. They were in Munich together at the end of the war. Tony recognized Brauer's name. He can testify to that."

Harry shakes his head. "No, I don't think he can. He never met Brauer. He only knew the name because his father told him. It's hearsay," says Harry.

"Fine. We can get army records showing that the two men served together."

"We can do that," says Harry, "assuming the records still exist. But the link to the flag is Grimminger, the photo ID in Brauer's box. Grimminger is the one who carried the flag. Tony said he never got a good look at whatever the paper was in his dad's box. Without that we can't get to Grimminger. And without Grimminger we can't get to the flag. If we can't get to the flag we don't have anything. It's a quest without an object. A treasure hunt without the treasure. Not without putting Emma up on the stand."

"We may have to."

"The D.A. will eat her," says Harry. "The prosecutor starts pounding on her about her father, how much she loved him, how much she misses him, how much he suffered, and whether she saw it. How it made her feel. Go ahead, share it all with the jury. It's therapeutic. You'll feel so much better for it when it's over. Can't you hear him?" says Harry. "He'll drive her to tears and then he'll hand her Kleenex. She'll be a quivering mass of jelly in the box. That's when he'll hand her the syringe and ask her if she knows how it works. And we know that she does because she used to inject him when he was home. And that's the damage she'll suffer if she's able to stay on track. What if she makes a mistake? One little slip. And it's so easy. After all, the D.A. is only trying to help her. What if she opens the door to the possibility, even the shadow of an admission, that the thought of killing him might have crossed her mind at an earlier date, even if only to put him out of his misery? You know what they'll do," he says. "They'll move the court for leave to amend and they'll get it. They'll bump the charges to first-degree murder based on the evidence from her own lips that she premeditated. You can't put her on the stand," says Harry. "Because you know what will happen."

And he's right. Without Emma we can't get to the flag, and without the flag we have no defense.

THIRTY-ONE

L ate yesterday afternoon we received new lab results from Sofia's autopsy. They included a DNA report on microscopic tissue scraped from under her fingernails. The results came back showing her own DNA, unidentified animal DNA, as well as DNA from another, unknown person. The unidentified human DNA failed to produce a match with any profiles on record with the FBI or the California Department of Justice.

We are guessing there is a good chance that the animal DNA may match Dingus, Emma's dog. If so, it would unquestionably place Sofia at Emma's house prior to her murder. We are holding off on discussing this with the sheriff's department until we know more. The problem is that Sofia's murder is now inextricably tied up in Emma's case. Anything we discuss with the sheriff's department is sure to be shared with the police and prosecutors in Robert Brauer's homicide. The evidence speaks for itself, but our theory of defense does not. It's best kept to ourselves, at least for the moment, and probably through trial.

The fact that unknown human DNA was also found under Sofia's nails provides probative evidence as to the identity of her killer. It's probable that these microscopic tissue samples were the result of defensive efforts by Sofia when she scratched her assailant, who was in the act of strangling her from behind. She might not have seen her killer, but science can identify him, if he can be found.

To that end, Herman and a few of his minions have been combing the records gathering background information on Ricardo Menard, the man Theo Lang told us was having an affair with Sofia.

This morning Herman and I are strapped into our seats on the Boeing 737-300, listening to the whine of the jet engines as I pore through Herman's investigative report.

Menard is married to Paige Proctor Menard, twelve years his senior. She is the daughter of Henry Jason Proctor, a wealthy industrialist who controlled several corporations and amassed a fortune producing high-end medical equipment. He was widowed and then died three years ago, leaving his entire fortune, now estimated at more than $4 billion, to his only daughter, Paige.

Seven years ago Paige Proctor married Ricardo Menard, a twenty-seven-year-old Costa Rican whose family was well known in Central America. For several generations the Menard clan had been wealthy planters and plantation owners who were considered to be possessed of old money, most of it now gone.

According to Herman's reports, Menard played the part of Latin royalty, the eligible bachelor looking for a worthy princess, until he netted the gringo heiress. It was love at first sight. Paige Proctor was enamored with Menard's rugged good looks and trim body, which had been hardened by long seasons on the backs of polo ponies. Menard, his parents, and from all accounts the entire extended family were in love with Proctor's money.

The only one not keen on the match was Henry Proctor. He tried to bring his daughter home and put an end to it. When that failed, he insisted on a prenuptial agreement to be crafted by his own lawyers. Otherwise, he threatened to cut his daughter off financially.

According to reports, the agreement was signed by the couple, the terms of which remain private and presumably locked away somewhere by the lawyer who drafted it. It is safe to assume, however, that a divorce might very well leave Ricardo Menard high and dry in terms of any marital settlement. Henry Proctor was no fool.

The Menards are prominent members of the social set in Southern California. They have given generously to the local university medical center, as well as a long list of other charities. On society pages, pictures included, they appear to be the ideal couple.

Paige Menard serves on six separate boards of major public corporations. Ricardo serves on three, all of them smaller corporate entities, what appear to be the crumbs pushed off the table by his wife's family. I recognize one of these, Genantro Ltd., a plastic fabricating company. It was one of the lesser holdings of Henry Proctor's old empire. Sofia listed it as one of her prior employers on her resume when she applied to become my assistant. I assume it is where she met Ricardo Menard.

I am also guessing that it was Menard who told Sofia to come to the firm and look for a job. He would have known there was a good chance we'd be hiring. Harry and I were sitting on a pile of money from the IRS whistle-blower's fund. We had performed legal work for a client who outed US taxpayers with hidden offshore bank accounts in Switzerland. Paige Menard was one of them. She was sitting on a numbered account in her maiden name that had been opened before they were married. It totaled nearly $10 million, pocket change that I'm sure Ricardo didn't know about it until it was brought to his attention. It's the little things that pop up when you're working on a computer. In this case it was a global search under the name "Proctor" that kicked out a spreadsheet from the Swiss banking case.

The Menards maintain two homes: a large private estate overlooking the ocean in the hills above Del Mar, and another sizable palace on a golf course in Las Vegas. There is also a ranch in Santa Ynez where Ricardo runs a string of polo ponies.

Herman has provided overhead shots of everything so that I can properly assess their wealth. It's the funny thing about money. No matter how much you have, someone else always has more. I'm not complaining, mind you. Not with my own private army of investigators complete with an air force of aerial drones and cameras to get what I need.

THIRTY-TWO

I n less than an hour the wheels of the 737 touch down on the runway at McCarran International Airport in Las Vegas.

It wasn't hard to find Ricardo Menard. In a little more than a week Herman not only located him but discovered that the bloom was off the rose on the Menard marriage. It seems that Mrs. Menard occupies the house in Del Mar while Ricardo holds forth in Vegas. They get together for social and commercial obligations and that's about it. The marriage is one of convenience, each living a separate life. Ricardo flies his fast and loose, though well under the public radar. Not that his wife couldn't find out if she made the effort. I have to assume she doesn't care, as long as he doesn't land in the public square and become an embarrassment.

Herman and I step off the plane and down the jetway. Inside the terminal, past the security checkpoint, we see the driver with Herman's name on a white placard. Herman buttonholes the man and we head for the car. Neither of us is carrying luggage, except for my leather folio, which contains Herman's report. Traveling light. We hope to be back in San Diego by tonight.

Outside we climb into the back of the black town car. The driver in the front seat starts the engine and turns on the air. He already has the address.

"I was gonna do a stretch limo," says Herman, "but I thought it might be a tad splashy. Don't want to overdo it. Just blend in."

"What kind of security do they have?"

"My man saw some muscle," he says. "They're probably armed, but if so, they keep it behind closed doors."

One of Herman's investigators got into the place yesterday afternoon posing as a guest. He cased the place and reported back as to what he found. Herman wanted to know why I insisted on doing this myself. He and his investigators could have done it. I told him it was personal. Joselyn has no idea where I am. If she did, she would have insisted on coming. It would have been more than a little awkward.

"How far is it?"

"Half hour, maybe forty minutes, depending on traffic," he says.

We catch the highway and head east toward the hills above the city.

According to the investigators, Ricardo's Las Vegas home, the mansion overlooking the golf course, has eight bedrooms. He slept in none of them on seven of the nine nights that the investigators followed him.

Instead he stayed at a very large private estate in the hills above the city. From the air the place looks like a Bavarian castle. Something you might see overlooking the Danube. It has a spectacular view of the lights along the Vegas Strip at night. There is a long road leading up to the mansion through dense woodlands. The lush forest of large trees on the otherwise barren hillside makes clear that the property has been well watered and tended for years.

It was purchased from the estate of one of the major Hollywood stars who died a few years ago. According to our research, the buyers were a limited liability partnership, a joint venture on which Menard's name doesn't appear at all. On paper the sole asset is the mammoth house and the property surrounding it. The stated purpose of the business is real estate investment.

In point of fact, the only thing the partners seem to be invested in is flesh: hot and cold running women at all hours of the day and night. They show up in private vehicles, pass through the security gates, and disappear onto the twenty acres that make up the fenced compound.

We wouldn't have a clue as to what was going on inside except for the overhead drones. The area around the pool is an eye-popper. It was the video from there that gave me my first view of Menard in action.

Herman tells me to put my wallet and the leather folio under the seat in the car, and hands me another wallet. This one contains a New

York driver's license in the name of "Gerald Aims." It contains several credit cards and business cards, various other items, all in the same name. "Don't use any of the credit cards to pay for anything," he tells me. "If they require payment, I'll use mine."

"Why?"

"Don't ask," he says. "If they ask you who I am, I'm just doing my usual job. I'm your security. High-toned gentlemen who come here don't talk much," says Herman, "especially about their lives on the outside, business or personal. They won't expect you to, so don't. The wallet is just for cover in the event you get pressed," he says.

"Where did you get it?"

"That's the other question you shouldn't ask," says Herman. "The only thing you need to know, if they squeeze you, is that your name is Gerald Aims. You're the manager of a New York hedge fund. Take a look at the business card and try to remember the address. Don't worry about the office phone number. If they ask, tell them you never call it cuz it's programmed into your cell phone. If they ask you where your phone is, tell them you never bring it to places like this. They will expect you to protect your privacy. And they will probably expect you to be nervous, so don't worry about it. Half the guys who go to a place like this do it for the rush, then they don't enjoy it because they're sweatin' and shaking too much, worried that Vice is gonna drop in on 'em any second and put an end to their nice whitewashed lives."

I tell him, "No, we're not going to do it that way." Herman thinks we're going in undercover. "I intend to deal with him face-to-face. Tell him who I am, why I'm here, and see what he says." One of the many things I need to know is whether Menard knew Sofia was pregnant when she died. If so, it would elevate motive for murder considerably and perhaps bump him to the head of the list of suspects.

Herman and I tried to find other areas where we could approach and make contact with Menard, but it wasn't possible. Whenever Menard travels he's with security. They drive him everywhere. He never goes to town, visits the Strip and the casinos, or makes any other stops. His household staff, including two maids, a footman, and his driver, run all his errands and do his shopping.

"The man is more cautious than a mainline mobster," says Herman. "Why do you think?"

"I don't know. Maybe protecting his good name," I tell him. "The last thing Menard needs is the paparazzi shooting pictures of him with another woman."

"Oh yeah, that's the other thing," he says. "They're gonna pat you down, so be ready for it. And no cameras. They will tell you that. So if they ask, tell them you don't have one. Also they will run you through the magnetometer."

If even a whiff got into one of the Hollywood tabloids or some blog, and if Paige Menard got her nose rubbed in it by her society friends, I'm guessing that it would be back to Costa Rica for Ricky and an end to the Proctor money machine.

Last year he filed a financial statement for a loan on a $2 million Sun Ray Sundancer speedboat. Ricardo showed an annual salary of four and a half million dollars for attending twelve corporate board meetings. Harry and I figured it out. The pro forma meetings that required him to sign a few papers would have taken less than ten hours of his time in total. That's $460,000 an hour. I doubt if Ricardo could make that picking fruit back home. It begs the question why he couldn't pay cash for the boat. My guess is a good part of his cash flies south to take care of his family.

How Sofia penetrated his bubble of security is obvious. He saw something he liked and let her in—like a Venus flytrap.

We arrive at the front gate. Herman hands a slip of paper to the driver with the key code written on it. The driver punches it in and the gate opens.

"They change out the code every other day," Herman tells me.

One of his people picked the current code with a spotting scope yesterday morning when another guest arrived. We're guessing that the code is listed on an encrypted site on the Internet. You can't get onto the site unless you're registered and have a password. How they keep registered members from giving the gate code to others we don't know. But Herman's investigator had no difficulty getting into the main house last night once he punched through the gate. We're praying that the same thing happens today.

THIRTY-THREE

The driver has instructions to take the town car and wait for us in the parking area. Herman tells him we will try to be out in less than an hour. If we are not out in ninety minutes he is to call a number given to him by Herman. It is a call for backup, licensed investigators in Nevada who are armed and stationed just a few miles away, to come and get us out.

The driver pulls up in front of the main house and gets out. He opens the door for Herman and me and we climb out of the car. The building is Romanesque, with two cylindrical towers capped by ornate finials. Two security men in black suits are waiting for us on the stairs.

"Good day, gentlemen, how are you?" We exchange a few pleasantries and then they get down to business. "I take it neither of you is carrying any firearms or cameras?"

We both shake our heads, say no, and raise our arms; then they pat us down. As soon as they are finished, they step aside and wave us on up the stairs toward the main entrance.

Inside, the dark Jacobean wood paneling of the large entry hall seems to swallow up the light from the outside before the door even closes behind us. We are confronted by two other security guards, both in tight-fitting black suits, with bulging biceps and quads. "Is either of you a member?"

"We're guests," says Herman.

"In that case the entry fee is two hundred and fifty dollars each. You can pay by credit card or cash."

Herman takes out his card and hands it to the man.

He runs the credit card, looks at the receipt, checks the card again, and says, "We'll keep the tab open in case you want to order food, drinks, or anything else." It's the "anything else" that draws the wink from the man just in case we don't understand. "Just give whoever waits on you the name on the credit card and they'll add it to the bill. Private rooms are upstairs."

"How convenient," says Herman.

He gives the credit card back to Herman, then directs us to the security line across the entry area.

We get there and another one says: "You know the drill, gentlemen. Same as TSA at the airport except we don't grab you in the crotch. We leave that to the girls. Take off your shoes, belts off your pants, everything out of your pockets, watches off. Everything goes into the plastic tubs, then step through the machine one at a time."

It's not nearly as advanced as the airport. The gateway is a simple metal detector, though as Herman goes through he sets it off.

"Sorry about that. I should have told you, I got some metal in my hip," says Herman.

They send him back a second time. He sets it off again. This time they hold him on the other side and use a hand wand. It screams as it gets close to his hip. They frisk him and find nothing. "He's OK," says the guard. "Grab your stuff," he tells Herman and waves me on. I step through the magnetometer without mishap.

We start to gather up our belongings and the guard says, "No. There's no sense putting them back on. Just take the tubs into the dressing room, through the gallery." He points the way. "You're not allowed to wear street clothes beyond that point. They'll provide you with swimwear and sandals, robes if you want them."

He gives us each a pair of cloth slippers. We grab the plastic tubs with our stuff and start to slip our way across the cold tile toward the cavernous gallery. The Bavarian theme is carried on inside as well as out. Suits of armor and chain mail flank the wall on one side of the massive walkway.

On the right, high up on the wall above the display of armor, are tall Gothic windows. Through them I can see the upper parapets of an outer wall surrounding what appears to be an enclosed courtyard. Across the gallery on the other side is a fireplace large enough to swallow and burn an SUV.

Beyond the fireplace the wall is covered by bookshelves, leather-bound volumes stacked neatly behind closed cabinet doors. The carved filigreed wood is inlaid with diamond-shaped strips of brass. Whoever built the place spared no expense.

As we pass the bookshelves there are several large glass display cases spanning the wall to the end of the gallery. Behind the glass are mannequins in period costumes, Bavarian folk dress and military uniforms, some from earlier periods, some from the nineteenth century. One of the cases houses a German soldier complete with gas mask and helmet from World War I.

Herman nudges me with his elbow. "You see what I see?"

"I do."

We stop for a moment and look.

Standing alone in the last display case is a figure dressed in the black uniform of a German officer. Around the neck is the military medal unmistakable as the Iron Cross. Above the elbow, on the left arm, the tunic sports a red armband with the black Nazi swastika. The mannequin has its hands posed on its hips, its unyielding face and sightless eyes fixed on the wall at the other side of the gallery. Covering the head is an officer's cap with its shiny visor, and above it the death's-head insignia of the SS.

THIRTY-FOUR

The Israeli consul general's office was located in a brown high-rise office building at the corner of Wilshire and Granville in West Los Angeles. It was a large concave structure with smoked glass windows and a well-planted elevated plaza in front of the main entrance. Nino suspected that the plaza contained defensive obstacles for cars and trucks, to prevent bombs from being driven inside, though he didn't know for sure since he'd never gone over and picked any of the flowers.

He also assumed that the Israelis probably took up the entire top floor of the sixteen-story structure. He had never been inside and had no intention of going now. The place was an armed camp. It bristled with security, and for good reason. The building housed at least five foreign diplomatic missions. Besides the Israelis, there were the Brits, the Swiss, the Hungarians, and three or four others.

The parking structure in back had secured areas chain-linked off and closed to the public. Here they parked their black SUVs with the smoked windows. There were also a few armored limos, though from what Nino could see, they were not often used.

Instead the choppers flew back and forth, landing on the rooftop helipad right above the Israeli offices. Diplomats, even in America, had wised up to the fact that it was no longer safe to ride on congested freeways where bumper-to-bumper traffic could make them sitting targets.

Even an armored limo could be opened up like a soup can if you had the correct penetrating warhead on your RPG.

Nino sat under an umbrella outside a Japanese restaurant sipping green tea as he watched the front of the building from the other side of Wilshire Boulevard. Ari had an office inside. Nino knew it. And Ari knew that he knew it. The little Israeli cadaver wasn't taking any chances, not since failing to nail Nino with the sniper team.

Ari actually came out of the building several times on foot. But each time he had at least two security men with him.

Once, the day before, Ari and his entourage actually walked within three feet of Nino, down the sidewalk and directly in front of the table where he was now sitting. Nino could have reached out and smacked the little bastard with a fly swatter. But he didn't. Instead he looked down so that his face was covered by the brim of his large floppy hat. Nino stared at the sidewalk as the three men passed by. Fortunately he had shaved his legs the night before, at least up to his knees. Nino was almost disappointed when none of them even bothered to turn their heads and take a look.

Something told him that today would be different. Ari was a creature of habit. And that made him vulnerable. He almost always took a long lunch on Thursdays. He ate alone and he didn't walk. He drove about nine miles across town to what apparently was one of his favorite haunts. It was a small open-air diner near the tourist-congested stalls inside the old Farmers Market in the Fairfax District of L.A. The only question in Nino's mind was whether Ari was feeling safe enough to do it today.

He checked his watch. It was almost noon. He looked back toward the building. There was no sign of Ari's car coming out of the lot next to the building where it was parked. Maybe not today, thought Nino. He would just have to be patient. Sooner or later he'd get him, assuming he had enough time. After all, there was business to take care of. He couldn't constantly indulge his pleasures.

He got up slowly from the table, walked the few feet, and dropped the paper cup with the remaining tea and its bag into the trash. As he turned to come back to pick up the straw bag he glanced up and saw the car stopped near the corner of Stoner, about a block away. Ari was wait-

ing to make a left turn onto Wilshire. He was alone in the car, headed
for the 405 freeway on his way to lunch.

In the 1880s, before the village of Los Angeles became L.A., the area
around what is now Third and Fairfax was a dairy farm. In 1900 a
farmer drilling for water struck oil. Derricks went up almost immediately as far as the eye could see. As the city moved in around them, the
derricks had to give way. They were noisy, smelly, and a fire hazard. The
area fell into decline. In the 1930s, at the height of the Depression, two
businessmen decided it would be a good idea to develop a small village
where farmers from the outlying areas could come to town and sell their
produce. And the Farmers Market was born.

It has been an institution for locals and tourists alike ever since.
Usually crowded, largely open-air, it functions under a sprawling series
of connected roofs and intersecting walkways, a series of barns, sheds,
and other buildings constructed and patched together over the years. An
old wooden clock tower presides over everything. Today the farms are
gone and the market has gone high-tone. Starbucks presses cappuccinos
under the clock tower. Vendors and merchants still sell meats, poultry,
fruits, and vegetables, but much of it is shipped in from around the
world along with high-end gourmet goods and other trendy consumer
products. Step outside and there's a tourist tram and a multiplex theater
across the way.

But none of this meant anything to Ari. He was a traditional man.
He had come here for the first time in the late seventies as a little boy.
Brought by his grandmother, who lived in a big house on the corner of
Third and Hoover, he remembered the market as it was back then. And
he pined for the past. Ari had spent the first twelve years of his life in the
United States before moving to Israel with his parents. He held both US
and Israeli passports.

He stepped around all the glitz and headed for his favorite spot. It
was a small open-air place called Moishe's Restaurant at the far end of
all the stalls. It wasn't old, but it reminded him of the restaurants that
his grandmother favored. That and the fact that they had great kebobs.

He walked up to the gleaming stainless-steel counter under the old

green-and-white-striped canvas awning and ordered the usual: lamb kebobs with grilled tomato, peppers, and onions, a side of rice, and a sauce
to die for. He gathered up the plastic knife, fork, and a couple of paper
napkins and waited. Three minutes later the man behind the counter
handed him a plastic plate filled with steaming food.

Ari carried it twenty feet or so to one of the small round metal
tables up against a wall, where he was out of the traffic. The little round
tables were probably the same ones he and his grandmother sat at so
many years ago. He settled himself, back to the wall, in one of the three
mint green folding chairs that surrounded the table and started to eat.
He was enjoying the taste, savoring the flavors, halfway into the first
kebob when the old lady wandered up to the table. She stood there for
a second, looked in her bag, and then pulled the chair out next to him.
She put her large straw bag down on the seat and kept looking inside,
searching for something.

Ari didn't say anything, but he did look around at the two empty
tables just a few feet away. If she tried to sit down, he would tell her. But
she didn't. Instead she remained bent over, fishing for something in the
bottom of her bag. The woman had the hairiest arms Ari had ever seen.
When he glanced up he glimpsed the five o'clock shadow on the chin
and the Adam's apple. He didn't say anything. After all, this was L.A. No
one was surprised by anything anymore and correctness dictated that
you kept your mouth shut. Ari diverted his eyes and kept eating, hoping
she would take her bag and go.

A few seconds later something toppled out of the bag. Ari heard it
hit the chair and felt it as it bounced onto the floor and hit his foot under
the table. He looked down and saw a woman's hairbrush lying there. Ari
made no move to retrieve it. Instead he just sat there chewing, ignoring
that the item was even there. Dressing like a woman was one thing. Expecting a guy to act as if you were was another.

The gravelly deep voice said, "Would you mind?"

Ari fumed. He didn't look up. Instead he shook his head slowly and
leaned down to reach under the table. His fingers were inches from
the hairbrush. He strained to reach it. He was stretched out as far as
he could, his back under the small table, when he felt the shock of the
spring-loaded spike. It punched through his left side under his out-
stretched arm deep into his chest. As the needle-sharp tip entered his

heart, Ari's eyes opened wide. He leaned there frozen, paralyzed with pain.

Nino looked down and wiggled the handle on the stiletto's long blade. He watched as Ari's mouth opened. No words came out, only the gurgling sound of blood.

He moved the handle again, slid it out a few inches, and pushed it back in, all the way this time. He waited a couple of seconds and Ari's body went slack. A little shove by Nino and the dead man's upper torso was folded over, balanced perfectly on top of his motionless thighs and knees. Ari's hands dangled on the ground. Anyone looking would think he was doing stretching exercises.

No one at the counter or in any of the public areas behind Nino could see a thing. His dress with its billowing folk skirt of many colors blocked their view as he stood there leaning over the table. He wondered if he'd make a fetching appearance on the market's security cameras. Gypsy woman killer, he thought. Next time he'd wear cymbal rings.

He pulled the stiletto from Ari's body, pressed the button retracting the blade back into the long handle, then dropped it into the straw bag. He reached down, scooped up the hairbrush, and did the same. Nino pumped up his best falsetto voice and said, "Thank you." Then he gave a little curtsy, picked up the bag, and walked quickly away. Within seconds he had disappeared into the crowded shopping area.

THIRTY-FIVE

Y ou think maybe there's room inside that case back there for a
flag?" says Herman.

"I don't know."

Herman and I are thinking the same thing. Maybe Menard
was after something more than just Sofia?

We can hear women laughing and giggling, and the sounds of
splashing water beyond the maze of lockers in the center of the room
leading to the pool outside. The attendant comes by and hands us each
a pair of tiny Speedos.

Herman looks at his, holds it up, and says, "I know they stretch, but
I'm worried about if it snaps, goes off like a roadside bomb and kills half
a dozen innocent bystanders."

The guy laughs and says, "You've come to the wrong place if you
think there's anybody innocent out there. Help yourself to a pair of
rubber sandals. Robes, if you want them, but nobody ever does. Enjoy
yourselves."

Ricardo Menard, known as Rick to his friends, is everything Joselyn described in the car that day driving out to Lang's house. If she had given
it to the cops for a sketch she couldn't have been more dead-on. He is,
in fact, tall, dark, and handsome right down to the gray streak on his

temple. He even has a cleft that either his maker or some plastic surgeon chiseled into his chin.

But if, as Lang said, Menard was devastated by Sofia's death, it appears he's had time and found sufficient diversion to recover.

As Herman and I step out onto the pool deck I see, across the water, Menard frolicking. Under a striped canvas cabana, he has both hands full of women, two of them, each looking younger than Sofia. The girls are topless, wearing string bikini bottoms, a piece of floss up the crack and not much else. As for Menard, he stands there in the state of nature, what you might imagine Michelangelo to have carved had he hammered out a nymph under each arm for David.

Herman draws most of the looks as we enter the scene. The six-foot-four bald black mountain in the white terry-cloth robe, flip-flopping his way across the concrete, draws Menard's attention almost immediately.

"Like the man said, dress code's a little slack," says Herman. "Maybe we'd fit in better if we took it all off."

"The wallets, the IDs, and credit cards we can show them. The salami we keep under wraps."

"If I didn't know better I'd say you were scared," says Herman.

"I don't have your experience in these matters," I tell him. "Besides, if I end up without clothes, you're gonna have to be the one to explain it to Joselyn. You know, the part about how this was work related."

"I told you not to come. You sure that's all it is?" he says.

"What else would it be?"

"I'm thinking maybe you're afraid cuz you don't want to be standing next to me when the beast is out in the open."

"Well, that, too," I tell him.

"There you go. I knew it," says Herman, "all the tired clichés, the shopworn crap about black men and their prowess. How would you even know?" he says. "Have I ever whipped it out in your presence?"

"Not that I can remember," I tell him. "And if it's all the same to you we'll keep it under lock and key today."

"Fine by me," he says. "I don't need to prove anything."

Herman has abandoned the Speedo. He's wearing his boxer shorts under the robe, a concession to comfort.

"I'm just tryin' to let you know that if it comes down to it I'm pre-pared to go the extra mile, go all the way as they say, if it's necessary."

"We'll make sure it's not," I tell him.

"In case you're interested, see the guy behind Menard in the lounge chair, other side of the pool?" says Herman. "The one wearing the dark glasses, loafers, and the Speedo?"

"I see him."

"That'd be Menard's security."

"How do you know?"

"He's the only one wearing anything you could call clothes, along with street shoes. But I don't think we have to worry."

"Why is that?"

"Unless I'm wrong, that bump in his Speedo is not a gun. It's the good thing about coming to a place like this. It may not be wholesome, but it's hard to hide heat," says Herman.

There are six or eight other men sitting around the pool, all of them naked, several of them with their hands full of flesh. I am wondering if Menard is Jekyll and Hyde, and if so, how Sofia had her head turned.

I can't imagine her ever getting involved with the man had she known about this. I'm sure she didn't. Menard would never have brought her here. He would have taken her to the grand house on the golf course, shown her the city, told her how miserable his marriage was, and how he was on the verge of ending it. That he was about to become a free man again, and eligible. Sofia might have gone for that. She was a sweet kid, but she was also ambitious, harboring dreams of becoming a lawyer and spending holidays in Paris. To a young girl with stars in her eyes, Menard, I am sure, might have seemed the pathway to all of it. It was Joselyn who said young women are impressionable and sometimes naive. For Sofia, Ricardo Menard would have been a blind grasp into the dark distance, beyond the safety where she could see.

THIRTY-SIX

When we get close to Menard's cabana at the pool, Herman situates himself where he can watch Ricardo's security man, to pounce on him if he has to. Herman works his fingernails over with a small metal file as he stands there. The file has a sharp pointed edge at one end.

I approach the tent.

Menard looks at me. "Can I help you?"

"You're Mr. Menard, I believe?"

"Who are you?" He glances back at his security man, who struggles to get up out of the chaise longue.

"Relax." Herman freezes the guy with a stare. "We're just here to talk. Unless you wanna go for a dance over by the pool."

The guy stands there bent over doing the splits with the chaise longue between his legs. "You want I should deal with it?" he asks Menard.

"Little late." Menard takes one look at the size of Herman and the position his man is in and says, "No. Why don't you just go in the house?"

"Better idea," says Herman. "Why don't you lie down, go back to sleep again. We'll wake you when we're done." Herman doesn't want any surprises coming out of the house.

The security man looks at Menard, who nods. The guy sits down.

"Go ahead, lie back," says Herman. "Put your feet up. We won't steal your loafers. I promise."

"I'm Paul Madriani." I hold up a business card from the pocket of my robe. "I thought perhaps we could talk for a moment. That is, if you're free."

Menard is still holding on to the two women, their naked backs and buttocks to me. He removes his right hand from the butt of one of them and holds it out.

I step forward and hand him the card.

"Do I know you?"

"No."

He reads the card and says, "What firm are you with?"

"My own," I tell him.

"What do you want?" He holds the women tight, up close to himself like body armor as he uses my business card to scratch the bare buttocks of one of them. Maybe he thinks his wife sent us to shoot him.

One of the other girls comes up behind him jiggling and giggling. She jumps up onto a chair, rubbing her body against him, whispering in his ear loud enough for us to hear. She wants to know what's going on.

"Shhh. Baby, be quiet. Can't you see? I'm talking to the man."

"Sofia Leon worked for me," I tell him.

Instantly I have his attention. He raises his hand off her ass and studies my business card again. "I don't think I know the lady," he says.

"You should. You brokered some pretty fair letters of recommendation from friends on her behalf. Theo Lang, does that ring a bell?"

"Oh, I think I remember now. A young woman I met at one of my companies. I think, if I remember correctly, she said she was interested in finding a job with a law firm. I told her that perhaps I could help her."

"Why would you do that? A perfect stranger," I ask.

"I like to help young people." He smiles at me, tawny skin and a flash of even white teeth.

"Yes, I can see that."

Menard reaches back down with his right hand and squeezes the woman's ass one more time, then slaps it and tells the two women to beat it, go to the bar and grab a few drinks. The second he releases them they spin and skip away, barefooting it toward the bar at the far end of the pool.

The woman behind him, a petite raven-haired beauty, now has free rein. Her arms draped around his neck, she drops her hand, grabs his nipple, and twists it while she sinks her teeth into his shoulder.

"Ayyee! Jeez, Maria. No."

She smiles, then licks the bite mark in his shoulder, the whole time looking at me through flashing eyes, as if I should get in line for some of this.

"What is it you said?" Menard is having a hard time concentrating.

"I didn't say anything."

"Oh, yes, this woman. You say she worked for you. I hope she did a good job."

"What makes you think she's moved on?"

"What do you mean?"

"You said 'did a good job' past tense, as if she were gone."

"Oh, my English is not so good." He smiles.

"I think your English is fine."

"Why don't you go join the others." Menard gets rid of the third woman. He rubs his shoulder. "I'll see you in a few minutes." If his look means anything I'm guessing he'll slap the crap out of her when he does.

She steps off the chair and sashays around him into the open. She is wearing a tiny web of cotton thread looking like fishnet strung between her thighs, with a triangle of black cloth the size of an eye patch at the strategic point. She looks up at me with a devilish grin as she passes by on her way to the bar.

"The two of you should relax and enjoy yourself," he tells us. "Would you like some women?"

"No thanks. I take it you own the place."

"In a manner of speaking. I have a future interest in developing the property," he says. "How about I offer you a drink?"

"Why not?"

"Let's go to the bar," he says.

"Let's have it here. Fewer distractions," I tell him.

"As you like." He calls the waiter over.

I order a Scotch and soda. He orders a beer, one of the local micro-brews. "And some of those little hors d'oeuvres, the ones on the sticks," he tells the waiter.

"What about your man?" He looks at Herman.

"He's working," I tell him. This way if they drop something in my drink, Herman will deal with them.

"Ah. So is mine." He looks at his security man laid out on the chaise longue. "Is so hard to get good help these days."

We sit at one of the tables nearby, Herman standing in the background, filing his fingernails, keeping one eye on the man in the chaise longue.

"How did you find me?" Menard finally asks.

"Seems you're either here, at your house, or in between. When do you find the time to use the polo ponies or the boat?" I ask.

"Sounds like you been doing research. Why would you bother? If you call me I would tell you whatever it is you want to know. I have nothing to hide."

"Everyone has something to hide."

"Not me," he says.

"Perhaps if someone brought your wife and some photographers by here," I tell him.

"Is that what this is about?" He laughs. "She knows about this. She doesn't care. So if you're thinking someone is going to blackmail me, you need not worry. It's not going to happen."

The drinks come. Right behind them is a large platter of appetizers, a variety of items, all of them with wooden toothpicks. The waiter sets the drinks in front of us, lays out two small plates and napkins.

"What was this woman to you, this Sofia, I think you said her name was?"

"You know her name. You made sure your friends put it in all those letters. And there you go again."

He looks at me wide-eyed, taking a swig of beer from the bottle.

"Talking about her in the past tense," I tell him.

"Oh. Sorry," he says. Wipes his lips with the napkin.

"She was my employee," I say.

"There, you see? You did it, too. It's an easy mistake to make. Perhaps I caught it from you, this pass-tens thing. Maybe I should send you someone else."

"So you're the one who sent her to us?"

"No. Did I say that? You must have misunderstood. No, I tol' her to go find a law office. I didn't send her to any one office in specific." He drinks a little more beer.

"Oh, I see. Then she must have found her way to us on her own."

He nods. "I assume so. Here, have one of these." He hands me a toothpick with some cold meat rolled and stuck on the end and takes one for himself. He eats it quickly and takes another. He pries the appetizer off the end with his teeth and licks the toothpick, then lays it on his plate. I watch him do eight or ten of these as we talk around the obvious, that both of us know Sofia is dead, that she's been murdered.

Finally I get up, peering across the large platter to the other side.

"Something I can get for you?"

"I hope you don't mind my boardinghouse reach." I lean over, reach out with my left hand toward one of the toothpicks on the far side. As I do it, I knock the bottle of beer off the table with my right. The glass bottle hits the concrete and explodes. "Aw, I'm sorry," I tell him. "Let me get that."

"No. No," he says. "I'll get the waiter. No problem."

"Be careful. You'll cut your feet up. Get some shoes," I tell him.

"You're right." He steps carefully out of the way, toward the bar.

The second he's gone I grab a clean napkin and sweep the toothpicks from his plate onto it. Then I roll up the napkin and stuff it in the large patch pocket of my robe. I grab another napkin and pretend to blot up the beer from the table as I scan the ground around it. The instant I see what I'm looking for I reach down and grab it, the broken neck of the beer bottle that Menard was drinking from. I wrap it carefully in a couple of napkins and slip it into my pocket. By the time the waiter shows up with a broom and a dustpan there is nothing of any value left.

I make a show of brushing off the two plates over a trash can so that Menard sees this on his way back. He's not only put on a pair of shoes, but shorts. I look at Herman. "Time to go."

He nods, and we both head toward Menard as he comes this way. I shake his hand, tell him we've got to go. We have another appointment.

"Are you sure you don't want to talk some more? As I say, I have nothing to hide," says Menard.

"We'll talk some other time," I tell him.

*   *   *

Ten minutes later we're back in the car, hauling ass downhill toward the airport. "The only other thing I wish I had," I tell Herman, "are photographs of Menard with the women. If the DNA shows him to be the killer, the cops can have him. If not, and it turns out his only crime is fathering Sofia's child and I had photos, I'd turn them over to Joselyn and let her have him. She'd post them online from here to hell and send glossies to his wife. But unfortunately we don't have any."

"Your wish is my command," says Herman.

As I look over, he's holding what looks like a tiny cube of black plastic on the pad of his forefinger.

"What's that?"

"Called a mini camcorder," says Herman.

"You're telling me you took that inside? That we've got pictures?"

"No. I'm telling you we have almost twenty minutes of flesh-tone movies. Two million pixels of high-definition video. You didn't really think I'd be filing my fingernails, did you?"

"Holy shit. How did you get it in there? Where did you hide it?"

"Don't ask. And if you ever tell anybody I'll come looking for you," he says.

It takes me a few seconds before I realize . . . Herman doesn't have any metal in his hip.

THIRTY-SEVEN

wo weeks after our trip to Las Vegas and the Bavarian castle overlooking "Sin City," Herman and I finally have results back from a
private lab. The report shows what the lab believes to be a solid
DNA profile for Ricardo Menard. The problem is, we have nothing
to compare it with. Not for the moment anyway.

We obtained a court order immediately after Sofia's autopsy requir-
ing the state to freeze the embryo taken from her body in order to pre-
serve the evidence. But so far we have been unable to get beyond this. A
subpoena filed in Emma's case earlier this week demanding DNA from
the embryo as well as the microscopic scrapings from under her fingernails ran into problems when prosecutors objected.

They wanted to know the evidentiary basis connecting the two
cases, Sofia's murder and Emma Brauer's manslaughter charge. The only
thing we had was Sofia's telephone trinket found in Emma's backyard,
circumstantial evidence that, if she wasn't murdered there, she at least
arrived at that location before she was killed.

We presented it along with declarations signed under penalty of
perjury: one by Harry attesting to where it was found, and two others by
Joselyn, as well as two of our secretaries, stating that the trinket looked
like the one from Sofia's phone. I filed my own declaration testifying to
the fact that Sofia left my office the day she was murdered intending to
go to Emma's house on an errand for the firm.

Prosecutors argued that this was nothing but a fishing expedition and the court agreed. The judge ruled that without a more definitive showing that the trinket was actually the one that belonged to Sofia, along with forensic evidence demonstrating that she was killed at Emma's house, he had no legal basis to force the state to cough up evidence in an ongoing murder investigation, a case in which we have no client. It's an irony that because we don't represent a defendant in Sofia's murder, we are denied the usual broad rules of discovery that might prove who killed her.

But for the moment we keep our powder dry and look for another opening. Harry and I have been on and off the phone with Tony Pack for the last two days keeping him current. Tony tells us he has another meeting with the police in Oklahoma City regarding his father's murder, some new information that might cause them to take another look. Tony has also found out that the local authorities have a lead as to the possibility identity of the hit-and-run driver who killed Walter Jones. If the information is accurate, it was a killing for hire. I am not surprised. If it proves out, and if it connects to the Blood Flag, it's a major break. Evidence that either one of these was an intentional homicide and tied to the flag would help provide Emma with a defense. If two of the three soldiers involved with the flag have been murdered by someone who wanted it, isn't it probable that the third one who died under similar circumstances was killed for the same reason?

This morning Harry and I are in my office discussing all of this when the door flies open. Brenda, my secretary, is standing there breathless. "Joselyn's on the phone. She wants you to turn on CNN immediately. She says there's something on the news about Brauer's case."

Harry and I head for the conference room, running down the hall behind Brenda. By the time we get there, the entire staff is congregated in front of the large flat-screen mounted on the wall. A running red banner, BREAKING NEWS, flashes by under the image of a reporter on a busy street, what looks like New York.

"According to the story, what happened to Robert Brauer, how he died and why, may not be the only unanswered question in this ongoing riddle regarding what some are now calling the long-lost Hitler Blood Flag. A second homicide, this one involving a young woman in California by the name of"—the reporter looks down to read from her notes— "Sadie Marie Leon, is also believed to be connected to the flag. How is unclear. But according to sources cited in the wire service report, Leon's murder, which occurred five weeks ago, is, and I quote, 'intimately involved' with people who are looking for the flag. That murder remains unsolved, with no arrests and no suspects or persons of interest identified. Efforts to obtain information from the San Diego County Sheriff's Department were met with the response that the investigation remains open and active, but that the department will have no further comment at this time. So far that's all we know. But I'm sure that given the feeding frenzy surrounding the flag and the fact that it apparently exists, we will be hearing more as time goes by."

"Thank you, Barbara." They switch back to the studio. Three talking heads around a table: "What a story. A Hitler Blood Flag, who would have thought? Sort of sends chills up my spine," says one of the women.

"Fascinating," says the guy on the other side of the table. "The fact that dealers in New York are saying it's priceless, the only piece of art, if you could call it that, created personally by Hitler himself, that might be worth really big money . . ."

"Yeah, what did he say?" asks the woman.

"He compared it to a Matisse and then said no; because it's one of a kind and because it's a part of history, even though a dark part, it's probably going to draw higher bids than a long-lost masterpiece. He said the estimates are anywhere from thirty million to one hundred and fifty million dollars. And as they say, that ain't hay." They all laugh. "Especially when you consider that Hitler was a failed artist."

"Well, it's not really a piece of art," says the woman.

"Of course not . . ."

"Try Fox," says Harry.

Somebody hits the remote and flips the channel. A story on politics. They surf the tube and find the story again on one of the business channels. It's making the rounds of all the cable stations. A reporter on Wall Street in front of the stock exchange.

"It's believed that these three soldiers from the 45th Infantry Army Division during World War Two, Robert Brauer, Walter Jones, and Edward Pack, that one or all of them had possession of the flag at one time or another."

"Where is it now?" says a voice in the studio.

"We don't know."

"Is it possible that the dealer, the one quoted in the story, might already have it?"

"If so, he isn't saying," says the reporter. "We talked to his office by phone. They said he was busy. So far he hasn't called us back. What we do know is that, according to the story, the three American soldiers were stationed in Munich, Germany, when the war ended. That's where they found the flag. Scholars and historians confirm that's where it was stored, in the Nazi headquarters known as the Brown House. It's believed that the three GIs took it as a war trophy. Whether they knew what they had when they took it isn't clear. And who actually owns it may be up for grabs. Some are saying it could be the German government. There are other reports that the US Justice Department as well as the Treasury may take an interest. If these men were on duty at the time they took it and they were in occupied territory, which we know they were, then the flag could belong to the federal government. When it was that the soldiers discovered its historic and monetary value isn't known. All we know is that at some point they found out."

"And now one of them, Robert Brauer, has been killed, is that right?"

"Yes, by his daughter, according to the police. Exactly how she fits into all of this we don't know."

"That's why we have cops," says Harry. "To invent shit so they can fill in all the blanks in your knowledge."

"Relax, Harry."

"Listen to the prick," he says. "What he doesn't know could fill an ocean. And he's out there flapping his lips. Emma's just acquired a hundred-and-fifty-million-dollar motive for killing her father because this idiot needs to fill a couple of seconds of dead airtime."

"So there's a lot of unanswered questions," says the studio.

"Exactly."

"Well, we'll be looking for more on it as time goes by. Thanks, Bob, for your report."

"Yeah, thanks, Bob!" says Harry.

"Talk to you later."

"Not if I see you first," says Harry.

The anchor back in the studio says, "One thing is for sure, whoever it is who has this Hitler Blood Flag is going to be doing a whole lot better than most us who are invested in the stock market if today's market reports are any indication."

"Good segue," says Harry. "Maybe next time you can air a lethal injection in between the two."

Somebody taps me on the shoulder. I turn. It's Brenda. "I found this online," she says. She hands me two sheets of printed paper. "It's the Associated Press piece, the one that broke the news on the flag. It appears to be what everyone else is talking about, the principal source. Everything else online refers back to it."

"Thanks." I take it.

"So what do we do now?" says Harry. "You can bet they will come and get Emma. Bump the charges up. Murder for money. She sure as hell would have thought about that in advance."

"I know."

"According to the judge we were unable to connect the dots between Brauer's case and Sofia's murder," says Harry. "It seems the media didn't have any trouble doing it."

"They don't have to produce evidence," I tell him.

"You think the cops fed 'em?"

I shake my head. "I don't know. Anything's possible."

"Maybe they know more than we think," says Harry.

Harry is wondering the same thing I am. Whether the theory from the medical examiner spun to us that day at the crime scene, hovering over Sofia's body, was a fable intended to keep us looking in the wrong direction. Maybe they've known all along that she was killed at Brauer's house. That would explain why they weren't interested in the tiny Eiffel Tower, her cell phone trinket. Maybe they have something that's more compelling.

THIRTY-EIGHT

H arry and I are back in my office. I scan the online news article handed to me by Brenda. According to the story, a dealer by the name of Ivan Rosch, associated with one of the big auction houses in New York, which they name, appears to be one of the sources of their information, along with another, unnamed individual.

I show the article to Harry. He reads it and says: "Call him."

I google the name of the auction house, find the phone number, and call. I punch the speaker on my desk set so Harry can listen in.

"Given the blast in the media, the man's probably hiding in a hole by now," says Harry.

It's answered on the third ring by a woman with a British accent who announces her employer's name and says, "How can we help you?"

"I'm calling for Mr. Ivan Rosch."

"One moment, please."

A few seconds go by. Another woman with a British accent comes on the line. "Mr. Rosch's office, how can I help you?"

"I'm calling for Mr. Rosch."

"So, it seems, is half of the world, at least at the moment," she says. "I'm afraid he's unavailable. May I ask the name of your media outlet?"

"I'm not with the media."

"Well, I'm afraid he's busy right now. If you'll remain on the line I'll have our reception desk take your name and number and either Mr. Rosch or one of his assistants will call you the moment they're free."

"You might tell him I'm a lawyer in California. I represent Emma Brauer, Robert Brauer's daughter."

"Who did you say?"

"Robert Brauer, one of the soldiers who found the Blood Flag."

"Just a moment," she says. "Don't hang up . . ." She doesn't even put me on hold. We can hear her talking in the background, over another line. "Tell him Brauer's lawyer is on the phone. I don't know what he wants. He wants to talk to Ivan. I don't have his name. OK, so I didn't get it. I'll ask him to hold. But get Ivan off the phone. Tell him to hang up . . . I don't care if it's the *New York Times*. Tell him if he wants a shot at the foocking sale, he better get on line one now."

Harry lifts his eyes from the telephone speaker, looks at me, and winks. One thing we know about the Blood Flag that the media doesn't: the New York auction house dealer who's flogging it doesn't have the thing.

In a flash she's back on the line, composed and polite. "I hope I didn't keep you waiting too long. He'll be right with you, I'm sure. I wonder if I could have your name?" she says.

I tell her and give her the city where our office is located.

"May I have your phone number?" she asks. "In case we get cut off."

"Make sure we don't," I tell her. "I'll give it to Mr. Rosch when I speak to him."

"Of course," she says. "I'm sure he'll be right with you." She waits a few seconds and then says, "Give me a moment. Please don't hang up. I'll be right back." This time she puts me on hold. I turn down the volume on the speaker to tone down the music.

"You know what the auction commission is on a sale of, say, a hundred million dollars?" says Harry.

"No. What is it, six percent?"

He shakes his head. "Anywhere from twelve to twenty-five percent of the sales price. Twelve to twenty-five million dollars. British accents come high," says Harry. "I'm guessing she's kicking the crap out of him about now. You wouldn't want to be in Mr. Rosch's pants right now. Caught between us and the *New York Times*."

Before Harry can finish the thought she's back on the line. "Mr. Rosch will take your call now."

A second later a melodious voice comes over the speaker. This one sounds like it's from the Bronx. "Ivan Rosch here. Who am I speaking to?"

"Mr. Rosch, my name is Paul Madriani. We're on a speakerphone. My partner Harry Hinds is with me. We are criminal defense attorneys here in California. We represent Emma Brauer. I think you know the name."

"I do indeed."

"I read with interest today's news article off the wire service in which you were quoted several times."

"Yes. It's all over the media," he says. "It's going to be quite a sale. Your client is going to make a great deal of money. I assume she is the holder of the item in question? I can assure you we will get top dollar. Of course, there will be costs, authentication, marketing . . ."

"At the moment her principal concern is the potential of a long stretch in the state penitentiary. Where did you get your information connecting Robert Brauer's death with the Blood Flag and who told you that Sofia Leon's murder was in any way connected?"

There's a long silence at the other end, followed by Ivan clearing his throat. "I'm afraid those are confidences I can't disclose," he says.

"I'm afraid you're not going to have a lot of choice when the police come visiting."

"What do you mean?"

"I'm sure that homicide detectives Owen and Noland are going to want to question you, to find out exactly how much you know and where you got your information. The same reason I'm going to have to hit you with a summons to appear at trial as a witness."

"You don't want to do that. It would be a waste of time. And expense," he says. "I don't know anything. Really."

"It certainly doesn't sound that way based on the news article."

"I didn't write it. All I did was answer a few of the man's questions."

"What man?"

"The reporter," he says. "The one from the wire service."

I look at the byline on the wire services piece and run the name by him, to which Rosch says, "Yeah, that's him. That's the man. It's been rumored for months that the Blood Flag was coming on the market. All of the dealers have been getting calls. Wealthy collectors from Asia and Europe. The word is out. Apparently from what I gather, the reporter heard about it as well. Trust me, I don't deal in this stuff on a regular basis."

"What stuff?"

"Nazi memorabilia. It's a narrow-niche market, creepy people, low end, and no real profit. Ordinarily our house wouldn't touch it. But this is different. It's unique. It's a part of history. It has provenance. If you've done your research you know that. Like it or not, there are collectors who will pay huge amounts for something like this. Mostly over the phone. That's where the big money will come from. The buyer and the people bidding against him in the final round will be long-distance over the phone. They will want to remain anonymous. That's what the reporter wanted to know. How much was it worth? What was it likely to go for on the auction block? He asked me to give him a range of values, so I did."

"And of course it helps to flog a sale," I tell him. "All that publicity."

"Yes. If we can get it. It's part of the marketing."

"So that's why you went to the reporter?" says Harry.

"I didn't go to him," says Rosch. "He came to me."

"What?"

"I didn't search the man out. He showed up here. He already knew everything."

"What do you mean?"

"He knew about the flag and all of the details. He had the soldiers' names. He knew about the Brauer murder, about Brauer's daughter, and about the other woman."

"You mean Ms. Leon," I say.

"Yes. And he had my name," says Rosch. "He was told to come here. That I could help him out as to a valuation."

"Where did he get the information?" I ask.

"A source he said he talked to over the phone. This person gave him all the details. The reporter said he didn't believe the man at first. He thought he was crazy until they started checking it out. That's when everything squared, the history of the flag, the soldiers' names, where they were stationed during the war, the fact that two people had been murdered and one of them was associated directly with the flag. All of it checked out."

"What about the woman? Ms. Leon, the one who was killed?"

"The reporter said there was specific information connecting her, tying her in, but he didn't say what it was. He said they checked it out and confirmed that the information was accurate. It's why they ran with the story. Every detail he gave them was confirmed."

"Who was the man on the phone?" I ask.

"It was an anonymous call. According to the reporter, the man didn't give his name."

THIRTY-NINE

Tony has told me so much about the two of you that I feel I know you." Lillian Pack is a petite brunette with short pixie hair, full of energy and smiles. The mother of two teenage daughters, she dashes about between the kitchen and dining room of the Packs' stately old brick home with the enthusiastic electricity of Tinker Bell. "Do the two of you have children?"

"Paul has a daughter by a prior marriage. She's grown," says Joselyn. "Sarah lives up near Los Angeles at present, but . . ." She looks at me. "We are both hoping that in time she'll move south again to be closer."

"Yes, family is everything." Lillian smiles at her. She finally sits, takes a deep breath, looks over the bounty spread out on the table in the spacious dining room, and says, "I don't think I've forgotten anything." Then she looks at us. "Well," she says, "don't stand on ceremony, dig in. Help yourselves."

After the media blast, Tony and I were on and off the phone so much we decided it was time for another meeting. Joselyn and I caught a Saturday flight from San Diego to Dallas and on to Oklahoma City. By seven this evening we are seated here with our feet under their table. Tony picked us up at the airport. They want us to stay at the house. We reminded him that he wouldn't stay at our house when he was out to the coast, and he promised that next time he would.

"Lill is famous for her roast beef," says Tony. "Try some of her gravy."

"Au jus," she corrects him.

"Call it what you want," he says. "It's delicious." Tony is already loading up his plate.

"It's probably the only reason he married me," she says. "Tony likes to eat."

"I can see that." Joselyn smiles. "The way to a man's heart."

"Listen to them," says Tony to me. "I don't know about you, but I'd be living somewhere in a ditch under cardboard if I didn't have Lill. Don't know what I'd do." He puts his plate on the table, leans over, scrunches himself down a little so he can reach, and kisses her on the cheek.

She smiles.

"Hear! Hear!" I say, and raise my glass. The four of us salute our good fortune with a sip of wine, a fine Merlot that Tony poured.

Tony's size is subtle. You don't realize how big he is until you see him sitting as he is here, next to his tiny, diminutive thimble of a wife. He is a big man, tall and rangy with hands like an NFL receiver.

"Girls, don't wait," Lillian tells the teenagers. "Hailey, where are your manners? Pass Mr. Madriani the rolls."

The youngest of the two daughters lifts the checkered red and white cloth, takes one of the steaming rolls, and hands the basket to me. Hailey is the image of her mother, tiny with an infectious smile. She flashes it at me and says, "Would you like some butter?"

"Sure."

The older girl is more like her dad, tall, with a more devious look. She studies Joselyn and me from the other side of the table with occasional stolen glances. She is in the grip of those teenage years of insecurity. I recognize this. As difficult as they sometimes were, it was one of the happiest times of my life. Sarah and I were together.

"You shouldn't have gone to all this trouble," says Joss. "It's too much. Especially on such short notice."

"Nonsense," says Tony.

"And there's no need to stay in a hotel," says Lillian. "Not with the empty rooms we have upstairs."

"They already agreed to stay," says Tony. "Let's not belabor it."

Tony and his family are living in his father's old house, one of the stately brick mansions in an area known as Heritage Hills. By the time we pulled into their driveway Joselyn was getting whiplash trying to take in all the elegant homes and gardens along the way. Tony said he'd take us on a tour in the morning, walking the neighborhood. But he warned us not to become too impressed. According to Tony, the real estate dollar goes a lot farther here than it does in California.

By the time we're finished with dinner the two women have bonded. They take their coffees and retreat to the kitchen. The kids have gone upstairs. Tony and I are alone at the dining room table talking in half whispers.

"If you had to just take a stab in the dark," he says, "where do you think the information came from? The voice on the phone, the source the dealer told you about?" Tony is talking about the revelations in the wire service story, all the details that played out in the media about the Blood Flag and the three soldiers.

"I've been asking myself the same question for the last two days," I tell him. "And I still don't have an answer."

"The only ones who had that kind of information are you, me, and some of the people in your office?" He looks at me with eyes like a question mark.

"No. You can forget that," I tell him. "Harry and I have been together forever. At the moment we both have more money than God. As for Herman, I'd trust him with my life. In fact I have on more than one occasion. When it comes to confidential information he's tighter than a drum."

"What about the people he hired?" says Tony.

"The other investigators?"

"Yeah."

I shake my head. "I checked with Herman just to be sure, before I left. He assured me they don't know anything. If they do, it didn't come out of our office. He's told none of them any details. According to Herman, they work on the clock, doing whatever they're told, and that's it."

"I hadn't even told Lillian," says Tony. "She thought I was following up on Dad's death because somebody at the VA killed him or else they screwed up. She thinks that's why I'm seeing you. I told her your firm specializes in elder care litigation."

"Why didn't you tell her?"

"I was afraid the more she knew, the more danger she'd be in. Lillian is a headstrong woman," says Tony. "If I told her what was happening she'd he out there on her own, turning over every rock. Especially if she thought there was something happening that was putting her family in jeopardy. You don't know her," says Tony. "Don't let her size fool you."

"I understand."

"The problem now is that she's asking questions ever since the news broke. She's talking to her friends. They've all seen it on TV, Dad's name being mentioned. Then she got a hold of the local newspaper. They made a big front-page splash out of it because of the connection with Fort Sill, the history of the 45th Infantry. She read it and wanted to know if I knew anything."

"What did you tell her?"

"I lied. I told her no. I don't want to worry her. Do you understand?"

I nod.

"You don't think Joselyn will say anything, do you?"

"I wish I'd known. I think they're probably talking about other things. The second I get her alone I'll ask her not to discuss it."

"Thanks," he says. "I told Lill the only thing I knew is what I read in the paper and the stories on TV. I downplayed it as much as I could. I told her I was sure it was all nonsense. When the newspaper called me I told them I didn't know a thing. And I told them they could quote me. But I'm worried," he says. "I'm thinking about whoever it was, the voice on the phone, the one you say called the reporter. If it's not you, and it's not me, and it's not the people in your office, then there's only one other possible source. Whoever it is who killed them all."

Tony has come to the same conclusion I have. "But why would he do it?"

Tony shakes his head. "I don't know. It would seem to make things worse for him. But then again, not necessarily."

"What do you mean?"

"I told you I had another meeting with the police on my dad's case?"

"Yes."

"The publicity, the stories, the fact that the source told the reporter that my dad was murdered didn't make a dent on the local cops. They're still insisting that he died of natural causes. They told me that until they find new evidence to the contrary, that's their official position."

"That doesn't surprise me," I tell him. "In fact, if you look at the story there's nothing there that you and I didn't already know."

"And the killer," says Tony. "Don't forget the killer."

"Yes. Maybe he's trying to turn up the heat."

"How do you mean?"

"To force the flag out into the open. Maybe he thinks by doing this, whoever has access to the flag will use it, and then he can make his move."

"That's possible," says Tony. "But you're the only one with a key."

"So you still haven't found your dad's yet?"

"No." He shakes his head. "Let's go in my father's study. We can talk better there."

FORTY

The house is large, rambling, with hardwood floors and old mahogany everywhere. Tony tells me that it was built at the turn of the last century, early 1900s, by one of the oil barons. The area went through a period of decline during and after the Depression in the 1930s, but it came back after the war and experienced a renaissance since. For a while Heritage Hills was known as "Doctor's Row" because so many of them had moved in. They bought the old homes and fixed them up. Today it's a gentrified historic area close to downtown. Ed Pack and his wife bought the house in the late fifties. Tony has fond memories not only of growing up in the home but of roaming the neighborhood around it.

We do small talk as we walk toward the study. I ask him how business is going at the bank.

"So-so," he says. To listen to Tony, small-time banks have become a tough business. He tells me he's spending increasing amount of his time fending off takeover bids from larger banks.

"That's good. That means you must be making money."

"That's the problem," he says. "If you don't generate enough revenue, you go broke. Make too much and you start showing up on the predator's radar screens. The bigger banks will come in and swallow you whole. They will buy you up, shut you down, and open one of their branches at your location. To survive and remain independent you have to keep your earnings in the Goldilocks zone," says Tony. "Not too much. Not too little. Banking, whether it's retail or commercial, has a natural evolution toward monopoly. We're going to wake up one day and discover that the country has one big bank, and they're in business with the federal government and the politicians who run it."

"Sounds like life on a tightrope."

"It is," he says.

"What happens if they buy you out?"

"I don't . . . I don't want to find out," he says.

My gaze is fixed on a small glass display case hanging on the far wall. "I see your dad had one of those as well."

"What's that?"

"The arm patch. The swastika," I tell him.

"Oh, yeah. You know about that?"

"Robert Brauer had one just like it hanging on the wall in his home office."

"I suspect they all did at one time or another," says Tony. "I'm sure you can't buy them anymore. Not the originals anyway. They're probably worth some money, but I wouldn't sell it. My dad used to smile every time he talked about it. He said he always wanted to be a fly on the wall at the War Department the day they geared up to go visit Hitler and discovered they had an entire US Army division wearing swastikas on their uniforms."

I laugh. "Your dad had a sense of humor."

"He didn't suffer fools. He did a lot of after-hours work in this room," says Tony. "Mostly research and reading. Sometimes he'd dictate notes. He worked from the table over there."

I turn. There is an antique oak dining table, rectangular, about eight feet long in the center of the room. Behind it is an old wooden swivel chair. On this side are two simple ladder-back chairs. On top of the table is a lamp, what looks like brass in the form of a human pelvis and a flexible spine so that the user can bend the light to his work. The lamp is on and there are piles of papers and stacks of books strewn across the top of the table, as if Edward Pack might have just stepped out for a moment.

The walls are lined with shelves, stacked with what appear to be medical books and old journals. There is an ancient poster of the periodic table with tattered edges hanging on the back wall. In the far corner there is what appears to be a full human skeleton hanging from a rolling metal frame.

Tony sees me looking at it and says, "That's Hubert. Dad brought him home from the office when he retired. I don't know if he's real or not. I never asked him. I don't mean Hubert. I mean Dad. But it doesn't matter either way, the girls have a good time using him out on the front porch on Halloween. It's a wonder he's still in one piece. At least I think he is. I haven't counted his fingers or toes lately.

"On occasion Dad would see patients here, usually old friends or people from the neighborhood. He had a small examining room across the hall. Lillian wants to turn that into a downstairs powder room for guests. I suppose I'll let her do it."

"I can see why you're having a hard time finding the key," I tell him.

He looks at me, wrinkles an eyebrow, and nods. "You can see the clutter. And this is just one room. You haven't seen the upstairs yet. It's a rabbit warren. And then we have the attic, which is full of stuff including old filing cabinets and boxes, and then there's the basement. Are you sure you guys can't stick around a few more days to help me look?" he says. "There's a million places Pop could have hidden it, assuming he didn't throw it out."

"I'd love to, but we can't. I have to get back to the office," I tell him. "I've got a hearing Monday morning. We can stay the one night and that's it."

"I understand," he says. "Let's sit down for a minute. We need to talk."

We take the two ladder-back chairs facing each other. I want to lean my elbow on the wood of the table but I can't. It's covered with papers and books right to edge, some of it printed items from sites on the Internet.

"I wanted to fill you in on what I found out from the local police," says Tony. "There is something new."

My eyes scan the decoupage of printed material as we talk. I'm interested in what the old man was into. It's an eclectic lot. "What did you find out?" I ask.

There is a pile of history books on the war, a few by Stephen Am-

brose and several others. All of them seem to be on the European Theater of the war. Some of them I've read. Others I haven't.

"In terms of my dad, as I said, nothing's changed," says Tony. "No
movement."

There's a printed article on tropical diseases. I can see only the top
layer of paper. And a large blue picture, what looks like a photographic
print from an electron microscope, a vastly magnified spiraling helix,
under it the words "Evidence Ends the 126-Year-Old Mystery." I can't
see the rest of it.

"The cops are still insisting that he died of natural causes," says
Tony.

There's a treatise on hemophilia, an article on fabrics, silks, and the
ancient art of Eastern dyes.

"Is there something on the table that interests you?" he says.

"Oh, no. I'm sorry. I take it this is all stuff that was left over from
your dad?"

"Yeah. You can tell I'm not very good at organization. I go through
his papers and I can't decide what to throw out and what to keep. And if
I decide to keep it, why, and how to file it. Lill says I suffer from decision
disorder. She's probably right. In fact, I know she is."

"Go on," I tell him. "You said there was something new?"

"It regards Walter Jones," he says. "There's a woman I know who
works at the police department. I can't give you her name because she
could get in serious trouble. But she told me that the investigation into
Jones's death has opened up. Remember I told you that they had a lead
as to the hit-and-run driver they suspect may have run Jones down?"

"Yes, I remember."

"It's more than that," says Tony. "According to this woman the cops
found a witness who says the driver was hired. He was paid. It was a
contract killing to get rid of Jones. She said the cops were still looking
for a motive. They didn't know why."

"If they read the newspapers or watch the news they know now,"
I tell.

"Exactly," says Tony. "According to the woman I talked to, the witness who talked to the police identified the driver. The man has a long
rap sheet. He's done time in prison. If the police can find him, and the

woman tells me they think they can, there's a good chance they can get him to talk. She said something about trading up."

"They'll want the man who hired him," I tell him. "They'll offer the driver a deal in return for his testimony."

"That's what I thought. If so, whoever hired him killed my father, Robert Brauer, and probably the girl mentioned in the story."

"Sofia," I say.

FORTY-ONE

Joselyn has that mark of every intelligent person, a highly tuned and adept talent for listening. In this case it is fortunate, not only for Joselyn and me, but for Tony. During her time in the kitchen with Lillian, Joselyn picked up on the fact that the woman was in the dark regarding Tony, his father, the Blood Flag and what was going on, and the fact that Tony was leading her astray. Joselyn didn't say anything to Lillian, but she listened.

On the flight back from Oklahoma City we compare notes and I explain to her what had happened.

"I hope you didn't encourage him in this deception," she tells me.

"I didn't."

"Good," she says.

"But I told him I understood."

She looks at me and I know instantly that I'm in trouble. "If you ever do that to me," she says, "I will leave you, but not until I kill you first. Tony made his wife look like a fool. I trust you can understand that?"

"He was trying to protect her."

Joselyn turns in her chair and amps up her cold stare. "Do you understand?"

"I understand what you're saying."

"Good. Because men who believe that grown women should be deceived from time to time, even for their own benefit, are only deceiving themselves," she says. "Women are adults, not children. If you can't trust them with the truth, then you shouldn't marry them, or live with them for that matter."

If her tongue were a rapier, its sharp, pointed tip would be coming out of my back about now.

"It's not our place to interfere in their marriage," I tell her.

"Of course not. That's the reason I didn't say anything," she says. "I'm telling you."

"Point taken."

"Good." She waits a few moments for the roar of the jet engines to melt the ice, and then says, "What did you guys talk about?"

I tell her about the hit-and-run driver and Walter Jones, the fact that the police believe it was a killing for hire and that they may be closing in on the man behind the wheel. I also tell her about the things I saw on Edward Pack's desk, the books and the papers on tropical diseases, diseases of the blood, and the photograph of the blue helix, something about solving a 126-year-old mystery, and the swastika on the wall.

"But I take it he hasn't found the key," says Joselyn.

"No, not yet. But he's still looking."

"This man, Jones, if they find whoever hired the driver, do you think that person murdered Sofia?"

"It's possible. We'll know if and when they catch him."

"How?"

"The DNA under her fingernails. Whoever it was left his calling card." I begin to wonder if Ricardo Menard has ever been to Oklahoma City.

When we get off the plane I turn on my cell phone and there's a message from Herman. Sunday afternoon, the office is closed. I wonder what he wants. He says I should call him. It doesn't matter what time. So I do.

His cell rings a couple of times and then he answers.

"You're back in town?" says Herman.

"We just got in. I got your message. What's going on?"

"It's that car," says Herman. "Remember? The rusted-out heap the neighbors saw out in front of Brauer's house?"

"What about it?"

"We think we found it. At least we found the license number. It's California 5QPU783," says Herman.

"Who does it belong to?"

"We don't know."

"If you've got the plate number . . ."

"We can't find a registered owner," says Herman.

"Then it must be stolen."

"Possibly," says Herman. Then he explains. One of his people found a record of a stop by the police out in the east county, in a small town. According to the police department computer the plates were on a 1977 Chevy Chevelle.

"Apparently the rear plate had a current-year tag, because the box on the ticket form was checked," says Herman.

"If there was a current tag, then it has to be registered to somebody," I say.

"You would think so," he says. "But it's not. We checked. The cop pulled the car over for a broken taillight. According to the single note on the ticket, the vehicle appeared to be in bad shape. The cop was getting ready to write a 'fix-it' ticket, but then for some reason he stopped."

"Why?"

"We don't know," says Herman. "All we know is that the cop crossed out the ticket and canceled it in his book. The information from the canceled citation showed up in their computer because the ticket forms are numbered in series. They have to account for each one, to make sure the cops don't go into business for themselves, taking cash on the roadside and tearing up tickets. There's a box, a field in the computer for a written explanation, but this one was blank. We're checking to see if we can get more information. We have the officer's name."

"It could be he got an emergency call," I tell him.

"I thought about it. That's possible."

"And he forgot to enter it in the computer. Or the driver talked his way out of it."

"I doubt that," says Herman.

"Why?"

"Remember what the neighbor said? The driver had gang graffiti tattooed on his neck and face and a piercing in his lip."

"Maybe it's a different car?"

"No. It's the right car," says Herman. "When my guy looked at the color of the vehicle in the computer, all it said was 'Rust.' "

FORTY-TWO

Four days after arriving home from Oklahoma City, I open my e-mail on the computer in the office and among the messages is one from Tony Pack. The subject line reads: "Eureka—I found it!"

I open the message.

Paul:

Early this morning rummaging through a file cabinet in the attic I found the safe-deposit key. It's the one sent to my father by the lawyer, Mr. Fish. The key was still in the same box that I picked up that day at the post office. I recognized it. The box looked the same as the one you showed me in your office. To me the key looks a little different than the one you had. It is straight-sided, no grooves, brass the same as yours. The part you grip with your finger to turn the key, I think it's called the bow, is square, not round like yours. Perhaps that's why it looks different to me. I can't be sure and we won't know for certain until we compare them. As I told you, the wrapper and whatever papers were inside the box were burned by my dad in his office the day the box arrived. And there's one more thing. In the same cabinet drawer where I found the box, I found a file. It was labeled "B.F. Instructions." Inside was a small plastic sandwich bag containing a computer thumb drive. I tried to open it in my PC but I couldn't. It looks like whatever is on the drive may be encrypted. I didn't want to mess with it and take a chance on losing whatever is written on it so I took it out and put it back in the bag. I'm sorry we need to meet again but it's the only way I can think to do this. I know you're probably tired. I'm exhausted. I've been up all night.

I look at the time on his e-mail. It arrived in the middle of the night, 1:10 A.M. my time, 3:10 in the morning, Oklahoma City time.

"Maybe we can find someplace in between here and there to meet so that we can do it quickly. Call me when you have time."

I grab my cell phone and check the numbers, his office at the bank or the house. I'm thinking that if he was up all night there's a good chance he's home. I call. Lillian answers the phone.

"Lillian, it's Paul Madriani."

"How are you?"

"Good, thanks. Is Tony there?"

"He is, but he's sleeping."

"I thought as much. I got an e-mail from him this morning. He and I need to talk."

"Is it important?"

"It might be."

"I hate to wake him," she says. "He's only been down about two hours. He's been up all night going through his dad's stuff. Sometimes he gets so wound up."

"Listen, that's fine. Let him sleep. When he wakes up, could you please ask him to call me?"

Tony has my cell number, but I give it to her anyway. "Also, tell him I am sending him an e-mail in response to his. Tell him to read it and not to do anything more until he and I talk."

"What's going on?"

"Nothing important. It's just business," I tell her.

"How's Joselyn?"

"She's fine," I tell her, except she would kill me if she knew I just blew Lillian off. "Listen, I've got to run."

"I understand. Thanks for calling. I'll give him the message when he wakes. Bye." And we hang up.

I punch the intercom for Harry. When he answers, I tell him what's happening and ten seconds later he's in my office. I tell him about Tony's key, the file labeled "B.F. Instructions," and the encrypted thumb drive. I print out a copy of Tony's e-mail and hand it to him.

Harry studies it for a couple of minutes while I study maps on the computer, a place where Tony and I might meet that would cut down traveling time and distance for both of us.

"It's not hard to figure out what the instructions are," says Harry. "Not the content. That's hidden behind the encryption, but the purpose," he says. "Assuming three soldiers find something in Europe and bring it home. Years later they discover its value and suddenly they need help. They aren't sure precisely what it's worth and they want to avoid a dispute, probably between themselves."

"Or maybe they can't be sure if they own it."

"That too," says Harry. "So they'd want to know what their rights are under the law. They'd go to a lawyer."

"Fish."

Harry and I are on the same wavelength. Fish probably advised them as to their ownership if others came forward and laid claim to the flag.

"It could be that that's why it's remained subterranean, undercover all these years," says Harry. "Maybe there's a statute of limitations and Fish told them to wait until it lapsed. That might cut off other claims, say the German government, Hitler heirs, assuming there are any, anyone else coming forward."

"That would explain why they waited. But why were they scared?"

"I don't know," says Harry. "But I'm guessing that if Fish is any kind of a lawyer, and it sounds like he is, he would have had the three men sign off on the instructions to avoid any later disputes among themselves."

"You mean an agreement." I look at him.

"Absolutely. I'm assuming Fish isn't a fool. If he were to write instructions on his own without their mutual consent, Pack, Jones, and Brauer, any one of them, or their heirs could sue him later for damages if somehow they were frozen out. But not if the men agreed. Especially if each of them had the agreement reviewed by independent counsel before they signed it. I have a feeling when we see this thing, assuming that we do, we're going to see signatures all over it. Clients and their lawyers," says Harry. "Assuming that's what's on this thumb drive, do you think we can crack the encryption?"

"You and I can't."

"I meant someone who knows what they're doing."

"Maybe, I don't know. Give me a hand here. I have to find a place to get together with Tony, so we can compare keys and talk about the thumb drive. I want to make sure he doesn't put it back in his machine. If he tries to open it with the wrong software he might erase it or destroy it."

I make a note to tell him in my e-mail to hang on to it, not to do anything more until we meet. Harry and I look at the map, Google Earth, and try to plot a point somewhere easy for both of us to reach.

"What about Denver? Denver's a possibility," I say.

"Yeah, if you both want to go north out of your way, and the weather this time of year can be nasty," says Harry. "Here's another option." He points with his finger. "It's closer for you and farther for him." He checks the flight schedules on his phone. "There is a nonstop out of Oklahoma City on Southwest."

"To where?"

"Where you just went," says Harry. "Las Vegas."

I make a note. I check the flights and write them down. Given the fact that I'll be asking Tony for a favor, I'll let him pick the meeting site. What I want is to borrow his encrypted thumb drive, or at least steer it to the right computer lab, and do it quickly.

"What do you think happened to Brauer's copy?" says Harry.

"What?"

"The thumb drive," he says. "Assuming it's in the nature of an agreement, Fish would have given each of them a copy. The original is probably in the lawyer's safe. In which case I'm assuming he would have given each man a copy on an encrypted thumb drive."

"I hadn't thought about it," I tell him.

"It's possible the police snagged it," says Harry. "When they did their search at Emma's house the day they arrested her. I didn't notice it on the list of items they took. But then I wasn't looking for it."

"You're full of all kinds of positive thoughts," I tell him. But he's right. If Brauer had a thumb drive and the police found it, they know more than we do at this point. They would know about the flag and its speculative value from the news stories. If they got curious and cracked the encryption on the thumb drive, they might know where it was and, more to the point, who has a claim to it, which sets off another alarm. "You know more about this stuff than I do."

"What's that?" says Harry.

"Do you think this agreement, assuming there is one, might have addressed questions of succession as to ownership in the event that any or all of three men died?"

Harry looks at me. "Why do you ask?"

"Would it?"

"It's entirely possible. Why?" says Harry.

"Fish's statement to me on the phone, and the way he said it. At the time it didn't seem important, at least not to me. But it did to him. That Brauer was the last of them to die."

FORTY-THREE

Nino leaned back in the chair and put his stockinged feet on top of the open drawer of the desk in his hotel room. He read with interest the latest missive on his laptop. The two of them finally agreed. It was about time. These guys were worse than politicians. It took them forever to make a decision. Nonetheless, Nino was happy with their choice. He hadn't been to Vegas in years, so a trip there was just what the doctor ordered.

What he couldn't figure out from reading all their e-mails was the stuff about the two keys. Still, he knew he'd find out soon enough.

For the most part Nino already knew everything they knew. More, in fact. Ari had accused Nino of trashing Brauer's house for no reason and faulted him for not taking anything when he left. Just because he didn't share it with Ari and his Israeli employers didn't mean that Nino came out empty-handed. People always seemed to misjudge him.

The fact was, Nino already had a deciphered set of Fish's written instructions, the agreement he wrote up between the three soldiers and which they signed. He had found them already printed out, in Robert Brauer's home office, when he tossed the place. This was something Pack and his new friend, the lawyer from Coronado, were still trying to figure out.

This was how Nino found Pack. Edward Pack's home address was listed in the agreement, as were the home addresses of the other two platoon members. With the written instructions and knowing where they lived, it didn't take Nino long to figure out what he had to do. He went to Oklahoma City to check things out.

He started with the lawyer, Elliott Fish, observed his office, and followed him until he found out where he lived. Nino kept his distance. He didn't want to get into a situation where he had to kill the man, because he knew he needed him. Fish's signature would be required to gain entry to the bank vault where the flag was locked away, along with what Nino understood to be a single safe-deposit key. Now he had to wonder if perhaps there was more than one key.

Nino had been tapped into Anthony Pack's e-mails through the man's home server. This was accomplished well before Pack hooked up with the lawyer in Coronado, and well in advance of the media buzz over the flag, which seemed to set them off and fired up the frequency of their e-mails. Nino chuckled at his good fortune. The banker was the weak link. His server was wide open. It took Nino and an underground hacker parked in a van outside Pack's house in Oklahoma City less than an hour to get past the simple password on the home's wireless router. Ten minutes later they discovered that Tony Pack had foolishly used the same weak Wi-Fi password to secure the server.

Once they had root access to the server the hacker set up a "back door" that provided Nino with all the tools required to read all incoming and outgoing mail from Tony's system. The server was configured to drop a copy of each message into a disposable e-mail account that Nino could access anytime he wanted without being noticed or leaving a footprint. He could do it remotely from anywhere in the world. Nino didn't bother to hack the man's work e-mail at the bank. He suspected that this would be more highly regulated, and for that reason, the banker and the lawyer were not likely to use that system for this type of private communication. Increasingly whenever Pack and the lawyer named Paul Madriani wrote, the subject turned to the Blood Flag. They used the code initials BF, but of course Nino knew what they meant. He would sit there looking at his computer screen as if it were a crystal ball, reading their minds.

The thread of e-mails back and forth over the last two days ballooned out to seven before the two men nailed everything down. Nino knew their flight itineraries, the airlines, flight numbers, departure times, exactly when they were to arrive and where. They were both taking nonstop flights. Nino knew how long they'd be in the air and where they were planning on meeting. Madriani wanted to meet in a restaurant at the airport. He was planning on catching an early evening flight back to San Diego.

Pack wrote back and told Madriani that he was tired. He wanted to spend the night and fly back to Oklahoma City the next morning. He was staying at one of the big casino hotels on the Strip because he got a good rate. He suggested they meet at a small restaurant about a mile from the airport, halfway between the airport and the Strip. The restaurant would be a good place to meet, he said, because it had large private booths. It was suggested by a friend of Pack's who knew Las Vegas well and who told him it was a perfect meeting location because they could talk and do their business without being disturbed. Madriani agreed, and it was done.

Nino worked backward in terms of planning. Each of them would be carrying a key. They were hoping to compare them. Anthony Pack would also be carrying the encrypted thumb drive. It was probably nothing Nino needed since he already had a copy of the lawyer's instructions. Still, it might be important. Maybe there was something else on the drive. Something he didn't know about. And since he was taking the key anyway, why not get the drive at the same time? Besides, why allow someone else to get their hands on it? They might beat him to the prize.

Pack was flying out early. He was covering the longer distance, but according to the itinerary he would land first, almost an hour ahead of Madriani, assuming their flights were on time. It presented Nino with the perfect opening.

The beauty of the e-mail hack was that it gave Nino everything he needed. He had both men's e-mail addresses from their messages. It would be an easy thing to step between them and shoot one of them a "ghost message." By spoofing the "From" line on an e-mail to Pack, Nino could make it look as if it came from Madriani. If he could change the location of their meeting in Las Vegas and direct Pack a new location where there was no one around, he could pick him off. A last-minute e-mail sent by Madriani as he was boarding his flight in San Diego couldn't be checked or confirmed by Pack using his cell phone, not once the lawyer was in flight. The timing would be critical, but apart from that it would be easy to do.

Once Pack was on the ground in Las Vegas, confronted with the change of plans, he would have to make a decision. The question was, what would he do? If he called Madriani on his cell he would get no answer. He might just go to the new meeting site, in which case Nino would have him. Or he might decide to be cautious. He might choose to wait at the airport for the lawyer to arrive. After all, he had Madriani's itinerary. He would know what airline he was coming in on and when. Pack struck him as the cautious type.

Nino decided he needed something more. He glanced at the open attaché case on the bed, the loose business cards inside on the bottom, Nino's various personas, and racked his brain for variations on the theme.

FORTY-FOUR

Evening at home with Joselyn and I am worried about Emma, her case, and where it may be headed. Harry and I grilled her in the office this afternoon, making sure she has told us everything she knows. Our growing fear is that there may be elements, facets of the case we can't see. We don't want to stir up the cops because of concerns they may bump up the charges and rearrest her, but Harry was compelled to burnish his motions for discovery in hopes of finding anything that prosecutors may have withheld.

We braced Emma about the Blood Flag, and not for the first time. She has told us before that she knows nothing about it. She's never heard of it. She said her father never mentioned it. When we told her about the history she seemed legitimately surprised. I asked her today whether she had ever seen her father in possession of a thumb drive. She didn't know what one was. When we showed her one from my desk drawer, she looked at it and simply shook her head.

The question here is what she knew and when she knew it. If the agreement between the soldiers, the instructions crafted by the lawyer Fish, dealt with the issue of ownership following death among the platoon members, Harry and I have to know what the terms are. If, as a result, ownership of the flag devolved upon heirs who might include Emma, and if there was some limitation on this, cutting off claims, say after a period of time or on a certain date specified in the agreement, it could be a problem. The police already know that she receives title to the house and whatever money Robert Brauer had in the bank. These she would have inherited in any event, regardless of when he died.

In a capital case for murder, prosecutors have no formal obligation to prove motive. But if they're smart they'll dig one up and try to tag it on the defendant anyway. Otherwise jurors will always wonder, even if the judge instructs them not to, Why did the accused do it?

If Emma was running up against a contractual deadline to lodge a claim as to ownership of the flag, and she knew about it, that would answer the question. It could provide a wicked motive for hastening the death of her father. And the intrigue wouldn't be lost on a jury, not given the abundance of publicity surrounding the Blood Flag, and the speculation as to its value.

I wouldn't even be thinking about this except for the words of Elliott Fish on the phone the day I talked to him, that Robert Brauer was the last to survive. Whether this had some significance beyond the simple statement, I don't know. But we have to find out.

It's for this reason the thumb drive held by Tony may be far more important at the moment than the brass key sent to his father. Whatever else I accomplish during our meeting tomorrow in Las Vegas, I have to convince Tony to trust me with the thumb drive.

"There is one common element to all of this that seems to surface no matter how you look at it," says Joselyn. She is working at the computer, a desktop situated on a table against the wall in our living room, her back to me.

"What's that?"

"DNA," she says. "It's at the root of everything."

"You mean as to Sofia? The paternity of the embryo and the tissue under her fingernails?"

"No, I mean as to everything," she says.

She's talking macroscience, as in the fundamental building blocks of life. "You're waxing philosophic," I tell her.

"No, more to the point," she says, turning in the chair to look at me, "doesn't it strike you as odd that this flag, according to every source I can find, disappeared at the end of the war—that was what, seven decades ago?—and it picks this point in time to suddenly surface?"

"Harry and I talked about that. We're guessing that they probably didn't know precisely what they had until very recently. We're thinking two, maybe three years at most. Fish, when I talked to him on the phone, tried to lead me into the weeds. He said he had been retained some years earlier, but he didn't say exactly how many. We'll know more when we see the date on his instructions," I tell her.

I am guessing that Fish was being cagey, unwilling to give up anything, especially if the information could be connected to the flag, what they knew, how they discovered it, and when.

"How do you think they found out?" she says.

"You mean that it was the Blood Flag? I don't know. It's possible someone told them."

"Who?"

"You got me."

"Anyone who had firsthand knowledge with access to the flag to make them sufficiently familiar to recognize it on sight would have to be ninety years old, or very close to it. Grimminger, who was the regular flag bearer, the man most familiar with it, died back in the sixties. And even if they found someone who was still alive, that person wouldn't have seen the thing for seventy years."

"What's your point?" I say.

"Every flag, even the Nazi flag, looks like every other Nazi flag, unless you have some way of identifying it. How would the former GIs who had this one be able to identify it? More to the point, how would they prove to others that it was the authentic article when they went to sell it?"

"You mean provenance?"

"Exactly," she says.

"The dealer mentioned it when I talked to him on the phone, that no high-end bidder would play unless there was evidence establishing the flag's authenticity."

"Did he say how they would do this?"

"I didn't ask."

"Shame on you," she says. "But let's say they had it back in the fifties and sixties and they had reason to believe it was the Blood Flag. How would they go about proving it then?"

"I don't know. Maybe by the pattern of the bloodstains that were on it? It's possible. Ask me when I see it."

"Unless you had highly detailed photographs of the original stain pattern, before the flag disappeared, you'd have nothing to compare it with. There are photos of the flag, but none that are that detailed. Most of them show the flag hanging down from its standard, with folds so that you can't even see the swastika," says Joselyn.

"Back then I suppose you could ask Grimminger," I tell her.

"If you could find him, and assuming a buyer was willing to pay hard cash and lots of it, based solely on his word, with nothing more. Don't you see? That's the problem," she says. "You couldn't establish the authenticity, not with certainty, until 1985, when the first practical protocol for DNA profiling came into use. We know whose blood it is on the flag." She turns around and fishes through a stack of papers on the table. "Here it is. Andreas Bauriedl was his name. I think I'm pronouncing it correctly. He was one of the men who marched with Hitler during the Beer Hall Putsch in 1923. Bauriedl was shot by the Munich police during the march. He fell on the flag and bled out. It's all documented."

"Yeah, I remember the name, Harry telling me at one point. What you're saying is that the blood on the flag establishes its provenance."

"If you connect it to this guy Andreas, it does."

That involves some major assumptions. First, that this Andreas character has living descendants, at least one who can provide a DNA sample for comparison, and two, that you can find a sufficient amount of cellular material, white blood cells, on the flag to extract DNA in the first place. The blood on the flag, assuming there is any, is not seventy years old. It's more than ninety years old.

"I know," says Joselyn. "But haven't they extracted DNA from dinosaur fossils much older than that?"

"Yes, they can get dinosaur DNA, but it's because they're taking it from bones, inside near the marrow. And the bones have been buried underground." I have been through all of this with DNA experts on the stand. Read tomes on the subject in an effort to avoid having my ass kicked in the courtroom.

"With DNA," I tell her, "it's all about how the materials are stored or preserved by natural conditions. Whether they were protected from UV radiation, heat, and water. Two things that will destroy DNA faster than anything else are sunlight and rain. Here you're talking a flag that was taken outside in the weather for ceremonies on a regular basis. And we don't know the conditions under which it was stored. You're talking a real long shot."

"Apparently Dr. Pack didn't think so."

"Why do you say that?"

"Because he had information on a similar case in which DNA from blood was taken, and it was older than this. By about thirty years."

"What are you talking about?"

"It was something you said on the plane the other day on the way home from Tony's. You said there was an article on his dad's desk, a photograph. I think you said it was blue, of a helix, an article from the Internet. Something about a hundred-and-twenty-six-year-old mystery that was solved. When I started looking at this stuff, it got me thinking. So I googled what you described. And guess what I found."

I shake my head.

She swivels back to the table, fishes through a stack of paper, and when she turns back again she's holding it up. It's the article I saw on Edward Pack's desk. Even from across the room I recognize the baby blue photograph of nature's spiral staircase, the DNA helix. I get out of my chair and start to walk across the room.

"I had to wade through an ocean of articles on the browser to find the right one," she says. "There's a ton of material on it, and a lot of controversy. Trust me. Some say yes, it's valid, and others say no. As far as we're concerned, it may or may not matter. I'm still trying to sort that out. Mostly what I wanted was to find the article you saw, the one with the picture of the helix, so that we would know exactly what it was that Dr. Pack was reading about. It was Jack the Ripper," says Joselyn.

FORTY-FIVE

Before Tony even stepped off the plane in Las Vegas he was on edge. Taxiing to the jetway he had turned on his cell phone and found an e-mail message from Paul Madriani. Paul apologized but said he couldn't make it to their meeting. Madriani had gotten hung up in court, a last-minute appearance in the judge's chambers on Emma Brauer's case. It was something the lawyer couldn't avoid. He explained in his e-mail that he wanted to call but he knew Tony would already be in flight and he wanted Tony to have the message as soon as he landed.

According to the e-mail, Paul had dispatched an investigator to meet Tony in Las Vegas. He was one of the people employed by the firm. The man's name was Victor Palma. Madriani told him that Palma would be carrying the key held by Madriani so that Tony could compare it with the one he had found.

Tony wondered why Madriani didn't mention the encrypted thumb drive. It had been a hot item in their exchange of e-mails earlier. It seemed now that he'd forgotten about it. Tony looked down at the message on his phone.

There was more disturbing news. The investigator was already on the ground waiting for him in Las Vegas. The reason Palma had gotten there early was that he had a previously scheduled meeting in Las Vegas earlier in the day with another client. For that reason he took an earlier flight. And one final change: they were no longer meeting at the restaurant between the airport and the Vegas Strip, the place Tony had picked.

Instead the e-mail instructed Tony to take a taxi to an address. It was described as an industrial area where Palma had his earlier meeting. The e-mail explained that the investigator would probably be finished with that meeting by the time Tony arrived, in which case Palma would simply wait for him. On the other hand, if the meeting went long, he and Tony wouldn't run the risk of missing each other.

It made sense. But still, Tony didn't like all the last-minute changes. It knocked him off his stride and made him wary. He considered for a moment, thought about it, wondered, and then said to himself no. Madriani wouldn't set him up. He had a sense for the man. He'd met Joselyn, Harry, and Herman, their lead investigator. Tony had the feeling that he knew them all. Most of all, he trusted Paul. At the moment, what he wanted was to get to the meeting and get it over with.

Besides, what else could he do? It would have been good if Paul had given him the investigator's cell number. But he didn't. At least then he could have called the man, checked with him to see exactly what was going on. Tony thought about calling Madriani. He looked at his watch. Chances were he was still in court. And even if he wasn't, what could he do from San Diego? The other man had the key, and he was here. The only thing for Tony to do was to go and deal with the investigator.

It was less than ten minutes from the time Tony stepped into the taxi in front of the airport to when it stopped at the curb on the empty street in front of the faded white concrete building. The message was right. The area was a small industrial zone about a mile east of the end of the airport runway. At least it was close.

The driver asked Tony if he was sure he had the correct address. The building looked deserted. The exterior walls were cinder block, painted white, apparently some time ago. The paint was cracked and peeling in places. There was a single row of horizontal windows high on the walls. Two of them were broken. The building had a steel roof. From what Tony could see, it looked like a warehouse.

He checked the address on the e-mail from Paul and then looked at the street number painted on the side of the building.

"It's the right address," he told the driver.

"Do you want me to wait?"

Tony thought about it for a second and said, "No. The airport's pretty close. I'll just call when I need a ride."

The driver held out a card with his cell number and told Tony to give him a call. He'd come back.

Tony thanked the man, paid him, gave him a nice tip, and took the card. He stepped out onto the sidewalk and into the hot sun. The taxi did a quick U-turn and headed down the deserted street. It turned right at the first intersection and disappeared.

Tony was left standing alone, squinting in the bright sunlight and the glare off the stark white walls of the building. He turned, shaded his eyes with his hand, scanned across the front of the building, and saw a door about forty feet away. It was the only opening in the otherwise solid wall.

He started walking. When he got to the door it was locked. He looked to see if there was a button for a buzzer or a bell anywhere around the door, but there was none. He was beginning to wonder if he'd been stood up.

He stepped away, back out onto the sidewalk and from there out into the street to get a better look at the building. About fifty yards away in the other direction was a chain-link fence with a rolling gate, what looked like a vehicle entrance. From what he could see, it appeared that the gate was open. Palma must be down there waiting for me, he thought. He started walking.

By the time he got to the open gate, sweat was running down the back of Tony's neck. The dress shirt under his suit coat felt as if he had been swimming and his feet were beginning to hurt. Tony was wishing he'd worn casual slacks, a polo shirt, and running shoes. Being a banker had its limitations. People always expected you to dress.

He walked through the open gate. Inside was a large paved area with a loading dock on the shaded end of the building. The area was fenced all around with chain link, topped by rusted barbed wire. Two of the strands were broken. They dangled down and meshed with the chain link like prickly vines on a berry bush.

Sharp edges of rusted scrap metal poked out of the top of a large rectangular steel container that was up against the fence on one side.

Scattered around on the paved yard were discarded pieces of old pipe, various sizes, odds and ends along with rusted parts from machinery. One of them, a housing of some kind with a rusted set of gears, was the size of a pickup truck. The place had the look about it as if some giant had picked through whatever was here, took what he wanted, and left the rest where it fell.

The only thing of any color was a small red SUV, shiny and new, parked near the loading dock. It looked like a rental car. Probably the one picked up by Madriani's investigator at the airport. Tony was beginning to relax. Given his initial concerns, things were starting to look up. The location was conveniently close to the airport and best of all, it was private, certainly better than the restaurant.

He climbed the stairs onto the loading dock and headed for the large overhead door that was rolled back and open.

"Hello? Anybody there?" Tony waited and listened. He could hear the vibration of his own voice as it echoed off the walls inside the cavernous building. But there was no reply. He called out again and listened. Nothing. He wondered if there was an office at the other end of the building. Maybe the guy was still tied up in his meetings.

Tony stepped into the building and took five full strides before he put his hands out in front of his face and stopped. The inside of the building was a black hole. Two feet past the open door and every hint of light from the outside seemed to be swallowed up. Tony didn't know what caused it. All he knew was he couldn't see a thing. It must have been human radar, the prickly hairs on his face and neck that stood out, to warn him. There was something directly in front of him. Something big.

As Tony stood there perfectly still, he could just barely make out the dark edges of its gigantic form. He waited for thirty seconds, then a minute for the cones in his eyes to adjust to the darkness. Whatever it was it was massive, at least fifteen feet tall, and five or six feet across at what might be its shoulders, and still. It didn't move, but in the darkness it looked as if it were alive. It had black shimmering hair. Tony's eyes slowly adjusted. He could now see tiny glints of quiet blue light as they reflected off the outer coat of the frozen beast. He reached out and touched it.

The hair came off on his fingertips. Magnetized metal filings, millions of them, black as crude oil and smooth as baby powder. Unless, of course, you got them in your eyes or your lungs.

It was part of the reason the building was so dark. The black filings adhered to the walls and swallowed up any particles of light that wandered in.

As Tony slowly regained his vision, even in the faint light he realized that the tiny shavings coated everything inside the building, including the massive beast that stood in front of him. It was a drop-forge hammer. This one was big. They were used in tool-and-die work to hammer and shape metal parts. Tony had seen one before in a small factory in Ohio that was looking for a loan from his bank.

This one was much more powerful and the elevated tempered steel hammer looked as if it was primed and ready to be tripped. Whoever left it in that position should have had their head examined. The hammer if dropped probably would have produced close to two tons of kinetic energy, enough force to crush a granite bolder the size of a watermelon and turn it into sand.

"I thought I heard somebody down here."

Tony turned and looked. There was a man, tall, dark-haired in a sport coat and slacks just stepping out of the shadows off to his right.

"You must be Tony Pack."

"I called out several times. Nobody answered," said Tony.

"Yeah, I was upstairs." The guy held out his hand. "Vic Palma from Paul Madriani's office."

Tony took his hand and they shook.

Nino Toselli sized him up as if Pack were a customer being fitted for a coffin. Tony had a firm grip, perhaps a little more fit than Nino had thought. But surprise was the thing, that and the fact that Nino had a sharp blade ready for him and waiting, spring-loaded under the sleeve of his jacket on his right arm. Two more steps in the dark by Pack and he wouldn't have needed it. Nino would have pulled the hundred-pound-test monofilament line releasing the trip on the hammer and Tony Pack would have lost both arms up to his shoulders. Nino could have finished him on the floor, cleaned out his pockets for the key, and the thumb drive and would have been gone in three minutes.

"Paul said you would be coming by. I was just getting ready to lock up. I was going to wait for you in the car out in front. But as long as we're here . . ." Nino fished in his jacket pocket with his left hand and came up with a brass key. It was, in fact, a safe-deposit key. As far as Nino was concerned they all looked alike. He held it out at arm's length in the open palm of his left hand, the bright sparkle intended to divert Tony's attention.

Pack reached out with one hand. Just as he started to lean into the man he realized something was wrong. Even in the dim light he could tell that the bow on the key in Palma's hand was elliptical. It was a different key. Not the one Paul showed him. But it was too late.

Nino's thumb pressed the button on the spring-loaded blade as he jammed it into Tony's back. The needle-sharp point skidded off the bottom rib and out through Pack's side, piercing him like a giant safety pin.

Tony tried to fling him around, but Nino rode him like a bronco. He wasn't going anywhere. All the while he worked the blade in Tony's side, pushing and pulling, gouging flesh.

Tony reached over his shoulder and clawed Nino's face with his fingers. He tried for an eye and missed. On the way down his finger caught on the inside pocket of Nino's jacket. He ripped the pocket and Nino's wallet and keys to the rental car went flying. Tony pulled and shredded the lining of the jacket.

Toselli went wild. He was furious. He reached around with his left hand, caught Tony under his eye, and clawed his face. At the same time he bit into Tony's neck from behind, sinking his teeth like a vampire. Nino felt Tony going down under his weight. Toselli could sense the end coming. He dropped his feet to the floor and steered the taller man toward the anvil on the drop hammer.

Tony reached back with his last ounce of strength. He twirled them both around, two figures dancing in the shadows in a death waltz. He lashed out wildly and spun his body, picking up speed like a bronco trying to dislodge the man from his back.

A hand went up in the darkness, head down on the anvil, fingers gripped the trigger pull. The two tons of brute force stored in the massive hammer dropped. The collision of tempered steel shook the walls of the building. A cloud of metallic dust filled the air and fused with the red mist of blood.

Vibrations from the corrugated metal roof and the walls resounded for several seconds and slowly ebbed. Finally there was nothing to fill the silence but the wheezing breath of the silhouetted man, standing, stooped over, hands on his knees, panting in the darkness, trying to recover his strength and catch his breath. It took more than half a minute before he composed himself enough to reach down and pluck the wallet and the keys from the floor. Then the shadowed figure rose up, turned, and walked toward the loading dock and the car parked outside.

FORTY-SIX

When I finally get to the restaurant in Las Vegas I am running late, about twenty minutes. I fully expect to see Tony sitting there waiting for me, but he's not. Assuming it was on time, his flight should have landed an hour ahead of mine. I look around the restaurant to see if there might be another room. Someplace where he might be seated where I can't see him. But there isn't. I sit down in one of the spacious booths and order coffee. I wait and watch the door as I drink. Each time it opens I look up expecting to see his smiling face, but I don't.

By the time I'm working on my third cup I am starting to get the jitters. I'm thinking Tony's flight must have been delayed, or else it was canceled.

I check the flight status using 4G from my iPhone. According to the airline site, Tony's plane landed on time, almost two and a half hours ago. I wonder if perhaps he got to the restaurant early, got tired of waiting and left. I was less than twenty minutes late.

I tried to connect with his cell phone on the way in, to tell him I was running late, but there was no answer. The second it started to ring, it rolled over immediately to voicemail. I try it again sitting in the booth and I get the same result. Either his battery is dead—it happens fast on flights if you forget to put it on airplane mode or to turn it off—or his phone was off. Perhaps Tony forgot to turn it back on after landing.

I have done that more than once without realizing it. But it still didn't answer the question, why wasn't he here?

I check my voicemail, e-mail, and texts, thinking he might have left a message. But there are none. I call the office and talk to Sally at reception and Brenda to see if he called there. They haven't heard from him. I am beginning to worry.

He might have missed his flight, but if so, I am sure he would have called. There was one other possibility. He might have gone to his hotel room to check in. Tony said he was tired, the reason he was holding over. If he was that bushed he might have fallen asleep in his room. The problem is, I have no idea where he's staying. All he said was that he got a good deal. It was one of the big resorts along the Strip. That would narrow it down to a couple dozen places.

I'm thinking the only one who might know for sure is Lillian, Tony's wife. But I don't want to call her. She might know the name of the hotel, but the minute we hang up she would call it, and if Tony wasn't there she'd start to worry. Lillian struck me as being tightly wound, especially when it came to Tony and the kids. Her life seemed to revolve almost entirely around them.

I wait a few more minutes. Then I call Tony's number again and get his voicemail once more. This time I leave a message. If his phone is turned off, at least when he turns it back on he'll see my message and call.

The waitress comes by to fill my cup again. I put my hand over it to stop her. Before she can leave, I tell her I'm waiting for someone. I describe Tony and ask her if she's seen anyone matching the description.

She says no. She has been working here all morning.

The restaurant is out of the way and it's not exactly Grand Central. In the time I've been here there have been fewer than ten customers. If Tony had come through the door, the waitress would have remembered him. It was possible he could have been involved in an accident coming in from the airport.

I hit the button and look at my phone again. I am running out of options. I punch up my "Favorites" and look at the list. As soon as I see it, I touch Herman's name. When all else fails.

On the second ring he answers: "Yeah, what's up? They told me you were back in Vegas."

"I am."

"Don't tell me you're going to see Menard," says Herman. "Not alone, at least."

"No."

"Good." Herman sounds relieved. "You don't want to be goin' near that place. Cuz if Ricardo doesn't get you, Joselyn will," he says.

"Stow it," I tell him. "I've got a problem."

"What else is new?"

"I was supposed to meet Tony Pack at a restaurant here in Vegas today. He never showed. His flight arrived on time. He should have been here ahead of me, but I haven't seen him. And his phone is not answering. I've tried to call it several times for more than an hour. It goes immediately to voicemail."

"You mean . . ."

"I mean immediately. Almost before it rings."

"That ain't good."

"I know." I tell him it's possible Tony could be at his hotel, but I don't know which one, and I don't want to call his wife. I ask him if he has any ideas. "It's also possible he might have been in an accident."

Herman thinks for a moment. "You got his cell number?"

"Yeah."

"Give it to me," he says.

I do it.

He tells me to hang up and sit tight. He'll call me back in a few minutes.

Twelve minutes go by before my phone rings. I punch the button and lift it to my ear.

"Paul."

"Yeah."

"Pack's cell phone is down."

"What do you mean 'down'?"

"No power," says Herman. "Either the battery is dead, or someone has removed it. Or . . ."

"Or what?"

"Or the phone's been destroyed."

"How do you know?"

"The carrier pinged the phone. Nothing came back. No signal. No data."

I would ask Herman how he got them to do this, but I'm afraid to.

"Maybe he just turned it off," I tell him.

"If that's the case, it's been off for hours," says Herman. "The last time the carrier had any record of a signal from the phone was a little over two hours ago."

"Do they have any record as to location, a tower?"

Herman says: "No. That's more than I can get, especially on short notice."

FORTY-SEVEN

For the next six days following my return from Las Vegas I am on and off the phone constantly, several times each day with Lillian Pack. She is holding up better than I thought. Probably because she is busy, desperately trying to find out what happened to Tony. Lillian has convinced herself that he probably had an accident. She's even gone so far as to suggest that he might be suffering from amnesia, wandering around somewhere, lost. But no matter what she hears, she refuses to accept the possibility that he is dead.

She has been calling every hospital and clinic in the Las Vegas area trying to find him, her own one-woman missing persons bureau. In the meantime I had Herman dispatch two of his investigators back to Sin City in an effort to smoke out leads, starting at the airport, talking to anyone who might have seen Tony coming off the plane, getting into a car or a taxi. Herman has been working the Vegas police long-distance by phone. He had one of his investigators from the airport file a missing persons report and check with the Clark County coroner's office, the morgue. So far we have turned up nothing.

If I didn't know better I might think that Tony Pack had wandered out to Area 51 or off to Roswell and gotten himself beamed up to a mother ship by aliens.

I called Lillian from Las Vegas before I left, and asked her if she knew where Tony was staying, the name of the hotel he had booked.

She told me that she didn't know. According to Lillian, Tony traveled frequently on business. There were times when he didn't tell her where he was going or what hotel he might be staying in. Not because he was secretive, at least according to Lillian, but because they were busy, like two ships passing in the night. His mind was on a lot of things. According to Lillian he was under constant pressure at the bank. It was part of the reason he was so tired. She said she never questioned him on trivial matters like travel arrangements, or for that matter about his work. She trusted him implicitly, and besides, she was often busy with the girls. Tony would tell her how long he would be away and when to expect him home. It was all the information she needed.

I asked her if she knew who made Tony's travel arrangements, whether it was done by one of the secretaries at the bank, by a travel agency, or if Tony made the arrangements himself on a computer. She didn't know.

I asked her if she had access to Tony's computer. She said no. They each had separate laptops. Tony had another desktop at the bank. She said the girls shared a separate computer in a room upstairs. She told me that access to Tony's computer, the laptop at home, was locked behind a password. Lillian didn't know what it was.

I asked her if she ever worried about him when Tony was on the road. She said no. Whether he was home or away, whenever it was necessary to get a hold of him, Lillian said, she could always reach Tony on his cell phone. If he didn't answer she could leave a message or text him, and he would always get back to her, usually within minutes. Whenever he was out of town on business he would invariably call home in the evening, before the girls went to bed. He would talk to each of them and say good night. It was a habit, part of their family culture. Tony had done it since the girls were little. Lillian said she had visions of him on the phone even when the girls were married and with children of their own, of him calling them at night to tuck them in.

It was then that she went silent on the phone for a long moment. I could hear sniffling at the other end, and I knew that she was crying. She could put a brave face on it, but reality was beginning to close in on Lillian Pack. According to Herman there has been no signal from Tony's cell phone through his carrier since shortly after his arrival in Las Vegas.

*   *   *

At the moment Zeb Thorpe had his hands full. This wasn't unusual. It came with the turf. Anyone with the title Executive Director for the National Security Branch of the FBI should expect to have his ass in the flames of a crisis at least half the time. Right now Thorpe seemed to be exceeding the quota.

There were at least forty cases of suspected lone wolves, active files of potential terrorists, some of them under surveillance, others being periodically monitored. There were three cases for which arrest warrants had already been issued under sealed grand jury indictments. These were people being tracked by Thorpe's agents, US marshals, and local authorities, usually working in tandem through multijurisdictional task forces. Their job was to apprehend these people before they could detonate explosive devices in a crowd, poison a reservoir, set fire to a chemical plant, or wreak havoc on any one of the thousands of soft targets that make up America's infrastructure. The challenge was to do it safely, quickly, and quietly, without causing public panic or igniting a media frenzy. It wasn't just a tall order; over time it was an impossible one.

So far Thorpe and his people had been fortunate. They were blessed by a civilian and military intelligence apparatus, armed with technology that was second to none. But as time went by, this was becoming increasingly fragile. The further removed the American public got from the last great trauma of terror, the more complacent they became. Politicians and lawyers started picking at the delicate web of data collection and information sifting that to this point had managed to keep the nation safe. Sooner or later they would rip a hole in it and there would be hell to pay.

America was already missing having feet on the ground, the military intelligence resources that provided eyes and ears in various trouble spots of the Middle East. Many of its assets, mostly foreign nationals sympathetic to the Western democracies, were either dead or on the run. Hundreds if not thousands had been forced into exile by ISIL and other radical groups claiming a new caliphate, with its eyes already shifting from Africa to the soft underbelly of Europe.

Thorpe settled into the chair at the head of the conference table and said, "OK, what have we got?"

"Two items." The agent to the right of Thorpe started the briefing. "You asked that we keep you posted as to any progress regarding the investigation in Los Angeles. The matter of the Israeli consul's office, whether the Israelis had an active ongoing intelligence operation out of the consulate."

"I remember. The attaché with the cell phone SIM cards," said Thorpe. "Don't tell me you found something." He didn't want to hear it. It was the kind of message filled with political toxin that you never wanted to have to carry up the chain. One of those thankless tasks where political types usually shoot the messenger.

"Not exactly," said the agent. "We're not sure. It seems the attaché is dead."

"What?"

"The man's name was Ari Hadad. He was found stabbed to death in an open outdoor market near downtown Los Angeles about ten days ago."

"Why are we only hearing about this now? What's the State Department saying?"

"It seems they only found out about it two days ago."

"What?"

"I know, it doesn't make any sense," said the agent. "You would think the Israeli government would be climbing up into the rafters, and screaming."

"Let me see that."

The agent handed the file jacket with the report to Thorpe.

He scanned it quickly. One of their nationals gutted like a fish in a public market in broad daylight, an attaché attached to their diplomatic mission no less. He read the public statement issued by the Israeli consul general. The printed half-page item was sanitized so well that if you didn't read it carefully you might conclude that Ari Hadad died of old age. Thorpe looked up and asked, "Who killed him? Do they know?"

"Apparently a woman," said the agent. "LAPD has some security video, but from what we understand it's unlikely they'll be able to make the suspect from any of the video. Her face was pretty well covered."

"Do they have any theories?"

"Well, they don't think it was a jealous lover," said the agent. "I'm told you'd have to see a print of her backside to get the full picture, but according to one of the homicide detectives it didn't look from the video as if the two of them knew each other. He didn't seem to want to have anything to do with her."

"I can understand that," said Thorpe. "Woman with a knife. What else do they have?"

"That's it."

"Have we turned up anything on the ground here involving an Israeli intelligence op?"

The agent shook his head. "Not yet. But we're still looking."

"That's what I'm afraid of," said Thorpe. "So what are we supposed to make of all this?"

"All what?" said the agent.

"Mata Hari stepping up out of nowhere and stabbing a perfect stranger who just happens to be a foreign diplomat while the unlucky man is having his lunch? And the Israeli consul who seems to want to sleep through the aftermath."

"Pretty obvious," said the agent. "They're covering something they don't want us to know about."

"In time, if you last long enough, you'll learn not to be so cynical," said Thorpe. "If the Mata Hari theory makes the rest of whatever it is all go away, I'm prepared to buy it."

The agents sitting on each side of the table looked at one another.

"Let me suggest this," said Thorpe. "Why don't we have the agent in charge of the L.A. office go over and have a chitchat with the consul general, or if he's not available, one of his legal attachés. Convey our sympathies for the passing of Mr. Hadad and suggest to them that maybe they should take whatever games they're playing home. Otherwise we're going to have to open a very detailed and public investigation of the untimely death of their fallen comrade, an investigation that might end up inconveniencing and embarrassing a lot of important people—which, unless they want to force the issue, would be entirely unnecessarily. Given the wisdom of Solomon I think they'll understand."

"Should we coordinate with the State Department?" asked the agent.

"Leave the Foggy Bottoms alone," said Thorpe. "Why bother them? They've got enough problems trying to figure out which American ally to alienate next. Just do it. OK, what else is there? You said there were two items."

"The other matter relates to James Arnold Pepper." This time the arrow came from the agent on the left side of the table.

"I remember the name; refresh my recollection."

"Mr. Pepper was a former chief naval petty officer involved in a highly classified DARPA project having to do with subsurface drones, antisubmarine warfare."

"I remember," said Thorpe. "As I recall, didn't he have some connection with the last item. The Israeli attaché?"

"We're not sure," said the agent. "It's possible. But there's some new developments."

"Pray tell," said Thorpe.

"Police in Las Vegas found an unidentified body, badly mangled at an abandoned industrial site not far from the airport, a little less than a week ago. There was nothing in the man's pockets, no identification, no phone, no wallet. The head was pretty much gone. There was a lot of blood splatter, but the site was heavily contaminated by metal fragments and filings, caustic chemicals and the like. So getting any useful DNA from around the site is almost impossible. We can get it from the body. But that's it. According to the initial forensics, the death was not an accident, it was a homicide. They found tissue scrapings and blood under the victim's fingernails. And the piece of equipment used to kill him, a large industrial press of some kind, showed signs of having been prepared and primed in advance."

"What does this have to do with Pepper?"

"Investigators found a US Navy ID card on the floor buried under some of the metal shavings near the press where they found the body. The name on the card was James Pepper. The minute we found out Pepper was involved, FBI in Las Vegas moved in and took over the investigation. They saw the BOLO we had out for him. They took charge of the body and sent it to Dover and had the military do the autopsy. They expedited the lab work, including the DNA."

"Correct me if I'm wrong, but I thought Pepper died in a tallow plant somewhere," said Thorpe.

"We're pretty sure he did," said the agent. "We think whoever killed him took his identity."

"Meaning the headless body," said Thorpe.

"Either that, or whoever set up the press and killed him. Now here's the interesting part," said the agent. "You're gonna love this. We took prints from the headless body and we ran them. We got no hits. And Pepper's prints are on file from the navy. So we know it's not him. They took the scrapings from under the victim's fingernails, tissue and blood from whoever laid him out on the industrial press. The got a DNA profile. They ran it, and they got a hit."

"Go on," said Thorpe.

"It's an unsolved homicide in Southern California, San Diego County, a young woman by the name of Sadie Marie Leon, aka Sofia Leon. The DNA was a match with scrapings from under her fingernails. Whoever killed the man in Las Vegas also killed her."

"But's that's not all," said the agent. He reached into a file and pulled out a copy of a newspaper article. He handed it to Thorpe.

The headline read:

HISTORIC BLOOD FLAG CONNECTED TO
TWO SOUTHERN CALIFORNIA MURDERS

FORTY-EIGHT

Took us a while, but we finally nailed it all down. Turns out you were right," says Herman. He sits in the client chair on the other side of my desk, dark, brooding eyes looking at his notes. Herman and his crew have dug up some interesting details. As he talks, I look through the file he has handed me.

"Andreas Bauriedl was forty-four years old when he died on November ninth, 1923. The Beer Hall Putsch, as you know," says Herman. "Given the fact that he followed Hitler to an early grave he may have been the original 'mad hatter.' That was the man's occupation. He made hats.

"Bauriedl was shot in the abdomen by the Munich police during the march. He was walking directly next to the flag bearer at the time of the shooting, a man named Heinrich Trambrauer. This was before Grimminger took over the duty. When the police opened fire, both Trambrauer and Bauriedl were hit. Trambrauer survived his wounds but died a few years later after a brawl with some communists. Bauriedl fell on top of the flag mortally wounded and bled out. There is no question, according to everything we could find, that it is in fact Bauriedl's blood on the flag. Every source confirms this. There is no dispute. The reason they know," says Herman, "is that at some point after the shooting stopped, Trambrauer, the flag bearer, was able to grab the flag and escape. He transferred it to comrades who removed the flag from its original staff and hid it. Shortly after this it was handed off to a man named Karl Eggers. Eggers hid the flag in Munich until shortly after December twentieth, 1924, when Hitler was released from Landsberg Prison.

"Hitler had finished a nine-month stretch for a conviction on charges of treason for his part in leading the putsch in an attempt to overthrow the Bavarian government. At that point Eggers transferred the flag back to Hitler, who made an icon out of it. He had it attached to a new staff, capped by a finial, and he put a silver dedication sleeve around the top of the pole engraved with the names of the sixteen men who died during the march. After Hitler took power in '33 he had the dead martyrs dug up and reburied in a special temple. He consecrated the place and had them declared patron saints. By then there were very few survivors of the early Beer Hall days still living. Any of those who made it through the march and who might have been positioned to challenge Hitler for power in the party were assassinated. The few who remained were followers who quickly got the message and fell into line," says Herman. "Honoring the old dead martyrs was the fastest way of elevating himself to a kind of godhead who was beyond question.

"In 1926, before he took power, Hitler assigned the SS to provide an honor guard for the flag. Seems a contradiction in terms," says Herman, "but then this was three years before Himmler came along and turned the SS into the fully fledged product of a diseased mind. The SS stored the flag in a special display at the old Nazi headquarters in the Brown House in Munich. The rest you know. So much for the chain of custody," says Herman.

"Now as to the other matters. The continuing saga of Dr. Ed, Tony's dad. We did some checking. I don't want to bust your bubble, but it turns out Joselyn was right on both counts. Female intuition. You never want to discount it," says Herman.

"What did you find out?"

"We hired a professional genealogist to climb the branches of Bauriedl's family tree, and the man does indeed have descendants. Several in Europe and three that we could find living on the East Coast."

"In the US?" I say.

Herman nods. "Descendants of an Andreas sibling, but close enough for a DNA match. And as to Joselyn's second point, you can tell her for me that she was right again. It was Edward Pack who figured out how to go about establishing the authenticity of the flag, the issue of provenance."

"How do you know?"

"We found one of the Bauriedl descendants, different surname, a male, thirty-five years old, living in Florida. He was approached by Dr. Pack almost two years ago."

I am all ears.

"It's all there in the report. Take a look under the last tab," says Herman.

I flip to the page.

"Bauriedl's heir is a wannabe rock star, over the hill, and probably about as good on the guitar as Andreas was at dodging bullets. From what he told us the recording studios weren't knocking down his door when Dr. Pack came calling. It's too bad the doc was such a bad judge of character, cuz he could have saved himself a lot of money and a long story. Pack used his doctor's license and told this guy that his medical records showed that the fellow had a unique enzyme in his blood that was needed to save the life of a young woman, one of Pack's patients. He told him the woman's family was rich and he offered the guy five hundred bucks."

"And the man believed this?"

"He believed the five hundred bucks," says Herman. "Pack took a couple of swabs from the man's mouth and the rest is in the report."

I read it, look up at Herman, and say: "Then what you're telling me, according to this, is that . . ."

"Yep. You can tell Joselyn that two out of three ain't bad."

FORTY-NINE

Thorpe read everything he could find on the Blood Flag, especially current news items. For the most part they all said the same thing. He sent agents out to question the auction house dealer quoted in the main story. The man claimed to know nothing, and then told them about the reporter and the anonymous phone call.

When the FBI approached the reporter the man saw the opportunity to do a little jail time for contempt and become a national news folk hero.

He challenged the agents to drag him into court and claimed a journalist's duty to protect his sources. He cited a press shield law that the courts had slapped around like a hockey puck until it went over the glass and out of the courtroom. When the agents told him he had already waived any privilege by telling the broker that the information came from an anonymous call, the guy folded his tent. He told them everything he knew, which was nothing other than what had appeared in the original story. Whoever fed the man the story knew what he was doing. The FBI was chasing its tail. Thorpe was back to square one, except for two things.

There were three names mentioned in the news story on the Blood Flag, the three soldiers who presumably found it in Germany after the war. According to the wire story as well as information from his field agents in Oklahoma City and San Diego, all three of the men were dead. But there was fresh information on one of them that crossed Thorpe's desk that morning. Walter Jones, one of the three, had been killed in a hit-and-run accident in Oklahoma City some months earlier. According to investigative reports there was reason to believe that the accident was, in fact, a murder and that Jones was the target of a hired hit. Police had been looking for the driver of the car. They had a lead as to his identity. They were hoping they could roll him and convince him to turn state's evidence against the person who hired him. This morning's report indicated that they found the driver—dead. He had been stabbed and his throat cut in a skid row hotel room in the downtown area. Thorpe had a sense, a feeling, call it Bureau intuition, that the hand that wielded the blade was probably the same one that held the phone on the anonymous call to the reporter at the wire service. There was too much symmetry for it to be anything other than a plan. Someone was tying up loose ends.

Just when he thought he was about to crawl off the griddle over the Israeli spy controversy, Thorpe now found himself roasting in the flames rising out of the Blood Flag. The news of the flag's existence had politicians in Washington groping, looking for someone, anyone in the bureaucracy who was in charge of such matters. They wanted the thing found, seized, and made to go away. Members of Congress with large Jewish constituencies were particularly offended.

They were demanding that lawyers at the Justice Department hatch an argument that if the flag was found on US soil, it belonged to the United States government. The theory was that the soldiers who took it were agents of the United States at the time, occupying foreign soil in Germany. Part of the argument was obvious. Whoever had it, assuming it was in the United States, would be well advised to take it somewhere else, at which point it would become the problem of some other government.

If it was found here, those in power in Washington wanted it immediately destroyed as a symbolic gesture if nothing else, and to prevent it from becoming an icon of continued racial and sectarian violence.

There were cases on point involving stolen artworks and other valuables. Except that in those cases the property was restored to its prior owner or their heirs. The prior owner in this case was Hitler, and he was dead. No one was even jokingly suggesting that the flag be returned to his heirs. It was out of the question. As far as Thorpe was concerned, if they wanted it burned, he was willing to strike the match.

But lawyers at the Justice Department told Congress that if the government asserted control and took the flag it could not be destroyed until there was a final determination by the courts as to its ownership. Thorpe had visions of every skinhead in the world lined up with his own lawyer trying to lay claim, probably along with ISIL and their attorneys, and lawyers for the heirs of the soldiers who found it. It would be a judicial circus.

Members of Congress turned their wrath on the Justice Department. To this point the FBI had managed to stay off the radar. That was before an unnamed source passed a rumor to the *Los Angeles Times* that the recent murder of an Israeli diplomatic attaché in that city was connected to the flag. It was the second lead that got Thorpe's attention, word that the FBI had the attaché under surveillance and had botched it. Thorpe saw the fiery finger of God writing on the wall and recognized the slant as belonging to the wily consul general from Israel. Thorpe's agent in charge in L.A. delivered his message the day before. The Israelis had shipped the body of their agent home and now they were ready for war. Suddenly the entire world was pointing at Thorpe. They were taking straw polls in Congress to see which committee would be calling him to testify first.

Thorpe's tribulations over James Pepper, DARPA, and an espionage plot to steal naval plans for an underwater drone, an Israeli intelligence op that never existed, suddenly seemed trivial.

He had only one more string to pull, and if that failed, Zeb Thorpe was in trouble. The problems he faced now were a career capper and he knew it.

A familiar name had crept into the case involving the Blood Flag. It was a San Diego lawyer named Paul Madriani. A few years earlier Madriani had gotten sideways with a Mexican cartel killer known as Liquida. He had landed on some of the Mexican's ill-gotten assets and earned his anger. As a consequence Madriani, his family, and half of his firm ended up in federal protection and, as a result, under Thorpe's thumb. They had developed a warm relationship, though Thorpe was not entirely certain if the two lawyers, Paul and his partner, Harry, saw it the same way. At the moment Thorpe didn't have a lot of options.

He picked up the phone and dialed.

FIFTY

've got a problem. I was hoping maybe you could help me out."

As I listen to his voice I'm thinking that it must be something personal. I haven't talked to Zeb Thorpe in a while, but his voice seems restrained, out of character for the man Harry calls Jughead, the Mad Marine. Not to his face, of course. I'm wondering if he's sick.

"If I can. What is it?"

"It seems you're sitting on something that's in the middle of my career at the moment. I need information."

"What does it regard?"

"The Blood Flag," he says.

"You've been reading the newspapers."

"Among other things," he tells me. "I understand that you represent a client, Emma Brauer, the daughter of one of the soldiers involved with the flag."

"She's my client. As for the rest of it, Robert Brauer's involvement with the flag, you may know more than I do." I feel him out.

"I doubt that," he says. "Let me come directly to the point. Does the flag exist? Do you know?"

There is a long silence from my end for the reason that there are things that I know that I can't tell him. "The difficulty here is that all of this, the information you're seeking, is bound up in the theory of our defense. What I know is confidential, attorney work product, the re-

sult of our investigations and lawyer-client communications. You know
I can't discuss any of that."

"Do you know where the flag is?"

"Why are you asking?"

"I'm not talking to the state prosecutors, if that's what you're thinking. Nor are any of my people. Our interest in this is purely federal. We
want to know where the flag is because it presents some real problems."

"Ah. I've been watching the news," I tell him. "Washington is worried about the political fallout. What else is new?"

"They are planning on having an auto-da-fé, meeting for me with
the grand inquisitor," says Thorpe. "They want to tie me to the stake and
set the brush under my feet on fire."

"How did you get yourself in that situation?"

"It's a long story," he says.

"I have the time."

"Unfortunately, I don't. Do you know where it is?"

"If you're asking me whether I have it, the answer is no."

"Do you know where it can be found?"

"I can't answer that."

"Then I take it you do," says Thorpe. "Tell me."

"I've told you already. I don't have it and that's the truth. I can't
go beyond that for the reasons I've stated." The fact is that everything
I know about the Blood Flag, the key, the box, the stuff on Grimminger,
is all we have to keep the jury off Emma's back. The theory that someone else killed her father, Walter Jones, and probably Edward Pack to get
to the flag is our only defense. How much of it I can get into evidence is
at this point the big question. I was counting on the encrypted materials, the instructions from the attorney Elliott Fish to tie it all together,
in order to bolster our case. But the thumb drive with the instructions
disappeared with Tony Pack.

"Have they told you yet who murdered your employee?" he says.

"What?"

"Sadie Marie Leon."

"Sofia."

"Was that her name?"

"What do you mean, have they told me yet? What do you know?"

"Tit for tat," says Thorpe. "An exchange of information."

"Come on," I tell him. "She was a friend. She was my assistant."

"*We're* friends," he says.

"I know, but there are limits."

"You said it, not me," says Thorpe.

"You know I can't."

"During the course of your investigation did you ever run across the name Ari Hadad?" he says.

"How do you spell it?" I ask.

He spells it for me. I write it down.

I look at it. "It doesn't ring any bells."

"What about James Pepper? Do you want me to spell it?"

"You said Pepper, right?"

"Yes."

"I don't recognize it. Who are they?"

"Hadad was an attaché to the Israeli consul general in Los Angeles. He was murdered last week. We believe he had been assigned by his government to hunt for the flag. The Israelis want it, as you can imagine. The story was in the newspaper in L.A. yesterday morning."

"I haven't seen it. Did it mention the flag?"

"Yes."

"Then the clipping service should find it. Or our investigators will file it for review. Who killed the man, do you know? Do you have a name?"

"No. They say it was a woman. But I'm not so sure," says Thorpe. "See, we're exchanging information. At least I am."

"You're asking for information I can't disclose."

"You're playing with fire," he tells me. "You're out of your league. The Israelis are not the only ones looking. You're up against neo-Nazi groups. Do you understand?"

"I'm aware."

"Have they visited you?"

"Not that I'm aware of."

"How's Joselyn?" he says. Thorpe is playing every angle.

"She's fine."

"Let's hope she stays that way. We can provide you with protection."

"We don't need it."

"Are you sure? How can you be sure? Your assistant could have used some."

"That's below the belt," I tell him.

"Help me out," he says.

"I wish I could."

"I do, too," he says.

"What do you know about Sofia? Who killed her?"

"Ah. Something you want to know," he says. This is the old Thorpe I know.

I could throw him Fish's name and let the FBI descend on his office. They might find a copy of the written instructions for the Blood Flag, perhaps even the flag itself. The question is if they do, would they share any of it with us? Probably not. Even if Thorpe promised. On an issue of high profile involving other nations, Israel and probably Germany, it's a promise he would never be able to keep. Governments, I have learned from long experience, take care of themselves and their own lofty interests first. This is true in particular if it involves the political class, for whom there are always special rules. I can be sure that if they landed on Fish and found what they wanted, it would probably disappear, all of it into some dark hole labeled "Classified."

"I'm waiting. What do you have to offer?" he says.

He listens to the silence coming over the phone and then says, "Just give me a hint as to where I can find it. That's all I'm asking."

"I can't."

"But you know where it is?"

"Actually I don't."

"But you have an educated guess. I can hear it in your voice. What are you afraid of?"

"That it disappears," I tell him. "I need it, not because I want it. My client requires what I know for her defense. Can't you understand?"

"We can work together." When he says this, he sounds like the devil.

"Don't make promises you can't keep."

"I'm not," he says.

I can hear the desperation in his voice. For a man like Thorpe, who is always in control, in almost every situation, it's not something I've ever heard before.

"I can't discuss it. My lips are sealed," I tell him. "I wish I could."

"Then I guess it's goodbye," he says. "Until next time. Let's hope it's under better circumstances."

"Zeb, listen." I hear the click on the other end of the line as he hangs up. I sit there looking at the receiver. He's gone.

FIFTY-ONE

So how is Jughead?" says Harry.

I catch him in his office as I'm headed for the door on my way home. It's almost seven in the evening.

"How should I characterize it?" It's the first time we've had a chance to talk since my telephone conversation with Zeb Thorpe yesterday morning. "He was disappointed. He was looking for information but I couldn't help him."

Harry is at his desk, his nose in a file as I stand in the open doorway to his office. "He wanted to know if I could tell him where to find the Blood Flag," I tell him.

Harry lifts his eyes and looks at me.

"Apparently he's in some difficulty," I say. "He was thinking I could help him out."

"He's been reading the newspapers," says Harry. "That the firm wasn't mentioned in the stories, even as to Sofia's murder, the fact that she worked for us wouldn't slow Thorpe down," says Harry. "His agents would have sniffed that tidbit out before the ink was dry on the newsprint. What did you tell him?"

"I told him you had it."

Harry gives me a quizzical look, smiles, and says, "Come on, the truth. What did you two really talk about?" His eyes go back to the open file on his desk.

"I told you. The Blood Flag."

He looks back at me.

"I told him I couldn't help him."

"You're serious?"

I nod.

"That must have made him happy," says Harry.

"Like I said, he was disappointed."

"As I recall, the last time we disappointed him we ended up in isolation scratching our asses in a flea-bitten tenement the man called a 'safe house.' Safe from what, I'm not sure," he says. "It took me a year to get the bedbugs out of my creases."

"He offered to do it again, but I told him we weren't interested."

"Why would we need federal protection?" says Harry.

"Thorpe claims there's some nasty people looking for the flag."

"Yeah. He's one of 'em," says Harry. "What the hell would he want with the flag?"

"I'm not sure. But I don't think he plans to run it up the pole out in front of FBI headquarters, if that's what you're thinking. I got the sense he was being motivated by outside forces."

"You mean the dark side?" This is Harry's term for politics and the people who practice the shady art. "Maybe they should fly the thing up top of the Capitol Building, put a hex on the people inside."

"I'm only guessing, of course. Zeb didn't identify the precise source of this inspiration. But he was adamant nonetheless. He wanted it, and in no uncertain terms. He offered to trade some information."

"What?" says Harry.

"The identity of Sofia's killer."

He looks at me with large, round eyes. "What did you tell him?"

"What could I say? The only thing he wanted was information on the flag, the heart of our defense, Emma's dilemma," I tell him. "I pleaded with him and he said no. He threw me a couple of names." I cross over to his desk and lay a handwritten note in front of Harry with the name of the murdered attaché and a news story out of L.A. that I found online.

"You think he actually knows?"

"Unless he's lying."

"Which is entirely possible, knowing Thorpe," says Harry. "Especially if he's desperate."

"Are you working late tonight?" I ask.

"I'm waiting for a phone call."

"I take it you and Gwyn are doing a late dinner."

He looks at me. "Go ahead, put it on the social network."

I smile. "Have a good evening. See you in the morning," I head for the door.

It's a moonless night, and dark in the parking area behind the office. A single streetlamp lights part of the alley that runs behind the office bungalows. I can hear the salsa music coming from Miguel's Cocina as I slide behind the wheel of my old Jeep, buckle up, and close the door. I start the engine, back out into the alley, and head for home.

I turn right onto Adella and as soon as I do, I see the old-model muscle car, all rusted out, parked along the curb. You can't miss it. The rust is palpable, the texture of barnacles growing on a pier. The second I pass it the twin headlights of the old Chevelle flash on behind me and the car pulls away from the curb.

I stop for the light at the intersection and it pulls right up behind me. I lock my doors and glance at the car in my rearview mirror. It stays just far enough back so that the bright beams from the old muscle car blind me. I can't see the face of the driver or whether he's carrying any passengers.

The light at the intersection changes. I turn north onto Orange and punch the gas just long enough to put some distance between us. I can't see facial features, but I can now make out two silhouettes in the front seat. The second I ease off the accelerator they close the distance.

I certainly don't want to lead them home, not with Joselyn sitting there alone. Whoever it is, they aren't being subtle. At the moment I'd feel a lot safer if I had a pistol.

The best I can do is a cell phone. Harry is the closest, but in a situation like this, the go-to guy is Herman. I light up the phone, find his name, and punch it. I hold my speed down and hit the speaker button.

Herman's usual answer. "What's up, Paul?"

"I've got a problem. Remember the muscle car, the one with the missing plates?"

"You mean the rusted-out Chevelle? What about it?"

"I'm traveling north on Orange just past the Del and at the moment it's right behind me. Two guys in the front seat. They picked me up when I left the office."

"Where are you headed?"

"I was headed home, but not with them on my tail."

He thinks for a moment, then says, "Lead 'em to the PD. It's only a few blocks north."

Herman is thinking that if I can make it to the Coronado Police Department the driver of the Chevelle will cut and run. The problem is, he's not seeing what I am.

"Nice thought, but I don't think it'll work. Whoever they are, they're not shy. Looks like they want to play bumper cars," I tell him. "If I stop or even slow down I get the feeling they're gonna grab me."

"Give me a second." Herman goes offline.

"Damn it!" I look down at the phone in my lap thinking he's dropped the call. But he's still there. A few seconds later he comes back on the line. "You there?"

"Yes."

"You know where I live. Do you got enough gas to make it over here, across the bridge to my house?"

I look at the gauge. "Plenty," I tell him.

"Good. Listen, don't try to outrun 'em," says Herman. "Just keep a constant speed and stay out ahead of them. Pretend you don't see them and come directly here. When you get here, pull into the driveway. There'll be plenty of support. Let 'em look down the business end of a couple of twelve-gauge pumps and we'll see if that changes their minds. Get over here quick, but don't race."

"Got it."

He hangs up.

I slip the phone back in my pocket, put both hands on the wheel, and head for the Coronado Bridge. The second I hit the gas they fall into line behind me. Through town, up onto the bridge, and over it they maintain an even distance until we reach the other side. As soon as I clear the bridge on the San Diego side, I look in the mirror and suddenly they're gone. I take a deep breath until I look to my left and see them next to me. Two skinheads, tattooed and pierced; the guy in the passenger seat is holding a pistol-gripped sawed-off shotgun. He motions for me to take the next exit. I see the sign and hold my ground. He points the gun at me. I wait until the last second.

They bump the side of my car. I try to fight them off, but the Jeep is no match for the heavier Chevelle. If they get underneath me they'll flip the Jeep. We ride side to side over the gore point headed for the V-shaped steel railing that separates National Avenue from the downtown freeway. At the last second I veer to the right and take the off-ramp. I hit the gas, slide into the far right lane, and take the corkscrew turn all the way down onto the surface street below.

When I reach the cross traffic at National Avenue I don't even slow down. Instead I steal a quick glance to my left, rocket past the stop sign and out into the intersection, then hang a left. When I glance in my mirror I don't see their headlights. I head south on National and take a quick right at the next intersection. Immediately I turn off my lights, pull in between two cars, and park at the curb. I take a good look in the mirrors. When I do, the twin headlights of the Chevelle are gone. I watch to see if the rusted-out hulk drives past the intersection behind cruising by on National. But I don't see them. Somehow I've lost them.

I'm in an area of low-income apartments, light industry, and small warehouses. Behind me, elevated overhead, is I-5 running north and south. To my right a block away are the highway spans connecting the freeway to the Coronado Bridge. I reach for my phone and call Herman.

Two rings and he answers. "Where are ya?"

"Somewhere off National Avenue, just south of the bridge access. I can see it overhead. They forced me off. But I think I lost them."

"Stay there, we'll come to you," says Herman.

"I think it's all right." Just as I say the words I look up and see the bounding twin headlights of the Chevelle as it turns through an intersection across a deep swale two blocks ahead. They're coming straight at me. "I was wrong. They're back," I tell him. I duck down below the window and pray they'll drive by without noticing the Jeep. "If you're gonna come you better get here fast because I'm trapped."

"We're coming," says Herman. "Don't hang up. I need to know where you are."

"I'll try." I leave the keys in the ignition and slide across the seat toward the passenger side, keeping low beneath the windows. I un-latch the door on that side and open it a crack in case I have to jump out and run. Once they pass by, even if they should turn and see the Jeep, if I move fast enough I could start the engine and pull out. By the time they turned around I might be able to lose myself again in the rabbit warren of streets under the intersecting highways. If I have to run I don't know the area, and if I stay to the streets they'll hunt me down with the car.

I see the glare of the bright headlights hitting my windshield and flashing overhead as the Chevelle crosses the intersection a hundred feet away. They're moving slowly, I can tell. Looking for my car. My knuckles turn white as I grip the worn upholstery on the passenger seat. As they come closer I can hear their tires gripping the asphalt as they pull slowly forward. I expect them to cruise on past. Instead they're slowing down. It's as if they know where I am.

"Paul, can you hear me?"

It's Herman on the phone. I hang up and pray he doesn't call back. I hit the two buttons and try to power it down. Just as I do the lights from the Chevelle pull even with my driver's-side window. My phone rings, the blaring sound of an old car horn. The skinheads hit the brakes. The Jeep is blocked. I raise my head a few inches to sneak a peek. When I do I see them both sitting there looking at me with sinister smiles.

I push the door open, jump out, and run toward the front of the Jeep, west toward the bay. The second I do it, I can hear screeching tires as the driver throws the Chevy into reverse and guns it. The smell of burning rubber fills the night air as the car hesitates, building inertia, and suddenly begins to peel backward.

I run as fast as my feet can carry me toward the intersection. I know I'll never make it. Then I see something, the entrance to a narrow alley twenty feet ahead. I race for it, turn, and run into the alley. Suddenly I'm hemmed in by buildings on both sides, high fences and cars parked along the sides with only enough room for a single vehicle to pass.

I want to stop and turn to look, but there is no need. I see the glare and feel the heat of their headlights on my back, like glowing coals as they bear down on me.

FIFTY-TWO

arry turned off the lights and locked the front door to the of-fice as he chatted on the phone. "Where do you want to do dinner?"

Gwyn gave him a choice of three restaurants as Harry walked down the path toward the lot where his car was parked.

"Why don't you make the pick," said Harry. "You know I'm not good at decisions. That's your turf."

"You do this every time," she told him.

"I picked the last time," said Harry.

"No, you didn't."

"Yeah, I did, and you didn't care for it, remember? The place with the Thai name, the one over by Old Town."

"That didn't count," said Riggins.

"Why not?" Harry reached the car, set his briefcase on the ground, and fished in his pocket for his keys.

"What do you expect from a Thai restaurant serving Mexican food?" said Riggins. She sat in her well-lighted courtroom chambers on the other side of the bay, and smiled as she rocked just a little in her executive leather-tufted swivel chair. It was one of her growing joys: Harry on the phone after work.

"I'm tired," said Harry. "The little gray cells are all burned out."

"If you're that tired maybe we should just do the drive-through at

McDonald's. And we can get you some Viagra on the way home. Or perhaps it would be best if we pitched it in, went our separate ways, and got some sleep tonight."

"I didn't say I was dead," said Harry. "I'm just suffering from a decision disorder. You pick the restaurant, and that way it's my turn to complain."

"Sounds like someone's definition of the perfect division of labor," said Gwyn. "I get to decide. You get to complain."

"Anybody I know?" said Harry.

She laughed.

"You know this is serious stuff," said Harry. "If we're gonna make this thing work, you and I, we need to understand where our natural talents lie. You're a world-class decision maker. And I respect you for that. I'm an Olympian complainer. I come from a long line of complainers. All the Hindses were great complainers. We're proud of our complaining. If we don't have something to complain about, we invent it. It's what we're good at," said Harry. "That's why we have diversity. You're a liberal. You can understand that. I'm a conservative and I can't. But that's OK because I can complain about it. And as long as I can complain, everything's fine."

She giggled and said, "Yes, but do I have to listen to it?"

"No. You can buy earmuffs or headsets, drown it out with music if you like; that's allowed. I don't know about those little buds the kids stick in their ears. But we can talk about it. Some things are negotiable," said Harry.

"OK, fine. You wore me down. You're the only lawyer I know who can argue me into a hole. Just remember you're barred from bringing a case in front of me—for life." She waited for him to pick up on it, to say something like "that's a long commitment," but he didn't. One of those awkward social lapses. Maybe she shouldn't have said it. "OK, so you must be tired. I'll pick the restaurant. Why don't we do the Red Sails? I know we both like that. Would you like me to meet you on Shelter Island or do you want to come by and pick me up? Or do I have to make that decision, too?" She waited for him to answer.

He didn't say anything.

"Harry, I didn't hurt your feelings, did I? . . . Hello? Harry, are you there?" Gwyn looked at her cell phone. It was a wonderful device, a great convenience, except when it dropped calls. She hit "Favorites" and touched Harry's name on the screen again.

This time she heard half a ring before her call rolled immediately to voicemail.

FIFTY-THREE

I am on my knees, hands on top of my head, looking down the double barrels of the sawed-off shotgun. This after they used the car to run me into a row of trash cans that sent me tumbling onto the concrete.

The man, if you could call him that, holding the gun looks like something out of a sci-fi film, *Reptoids from Folsom*. He glares at me through sunken eyes. His long, graying hair, caught up in a ponytail, runs down the back of his studded leather jacket. The open collar in front reveals a tattoo crawling up his neck. It reads "Snake" with two blue-red fangs emerging from the top fork of the letter *k* just under his jaw. He's the kind of man your daughter might bring home if an evil prince turned her into a frog.

He holds me under the gun as the driver goes through my wallet, looking at my driver's license and a business card, then closes the wallet and puts it in his pocket. He asks me for the keys to my car.

I tell him they are in the ignition. "You want the car, take it."

The guy looks at me and grins, a manifestation of evil made more sinister by the set of rings piercing his lower lip. "Why would we want that piece of crap?" he says.

"And here I was thinking it was a valuable relic," I tell him.

"How did you make us?" he asks.

"High beams burning the back of my neck. You weren't exactly elusive," I tell him.

"Don't get cute," he says. "You looked right at us when you drove by. Was it the car?"

When I don't answer, the guy with the gun says, "We can make this very painful if that's what you want. I'd suggest you cooperate."

"Serpents having a forked tongue, I halfway expected to hear a lisp," I tell him. "Instead you sound like a college professor."

"Diction can be deceiving," he says. "Perhaps a little pain will dull your sense of humor."

It's better to throw them something than end up with broken ribs. "A witness saw your vehicle loitering near a house out on Winona a couple of months back," I tell him. "We got a partial plate and we ran it."

"You're lying," says the driver. "The plate's not registered, so how could you find it?"

"You got stopped on a fix-it ticket in East County," I tell him. "Your license number turned up in their computer. From that we got the description of the car."

The Snake looks at his friend and says, "I told you. We should have changed our wheels two months ago."

"You were right, what can I say? So we'll have to do it now. Get up!" The pierced one grabs me by the arm and hoists me onto my feet. The guy is stronger than he looks. "I hate goddamned lawyers," he says, "so all you have to do is gimme an excuse." He spins me around and pushes me from behind toward one of the trash cans against the fence. He bends me over the can and frisks me, feeling my pockets. He finds my cell phone and takes it. Then he feels down both legs all the way to my shoes. "You got a knife, a gun, any weapons?"

"If I had a gun, don't you think I would have used it by now?"

"Anything in your car?" he says

"No."

"Is your phone locked?"

"Yes."

"What's the code? The pin number," he says.

I give it to him. "If you want money I can get it for you," I tell him.

"Really? How much?"

"Whatever you want."

"This guy must be loaded," says the driver.

"Yeah, but even lawyers have a daily limit on their ATM," says the Snake. "Looking at his car I'd say his isn't very high."

"Shut up," says the driver.

"If it's not money, then what are you after?" I ask.

"Relax," says the driver. "Nobody's gonna get hurt. My man here likes to play games sometimes."

"Ssszz!" The guy with the shotgun is in my ear hissing like a snake.

The longer I can remain here and stay out of their car, or keep from being shot, the greater the chance that Herman and his people will find me. The directions I gave him on the phone weren't great. But the skinhead has just solved that problem.

The four cell phones on our network, Harry's and Herman's, Joselyn's and mine, are primed through the cloud for tracking, in case they are lost or stolen. The second that ring-lip turned mine on, he enabled the tracking app. As long as we stay here with my phone on, Herman and his guys can find us on the map in Herman's phone. My biggest fear now is that the skinhead tosses my cell in the trash, throws me in the trunk of their car, and I disappear.

I'm bent over the can looking back at the phone in his hand when he catches my eye and says, "Does this thing have a tracking app?"

"I don't think so. That's an old phone," I tell him.

"Listen to him. Damn lawyer and he can't even lie straight," says the driver. "He's got a brand-new phone here and he's tryin' to bullshit us. Look at all the apps on this thing." He shows it to his buddy. "I wish I had a phone like this."

"Keep it," I tell him. "It's yours."

"Gee, thanks. You mean it?"

"Sure."

"How long before you think your friend's gonna show up?" he asks.

"What friend?"

"What's his name, Herman?"

I don't say anything.

"What's wrong, cat got your tongue? I wouldn't want you to be too disappointed, but from what I understand, Herman and his friends won't be joining us tonight. Seems they had a previous engagement."

"Yeah, it was kind of a last-minute surprise," says the Snake. "Let's hope he enjoyed it," he says and laughs.

The driver grabs me from behind by the collar of my suit jacket, stands me up straight, and says, "Mr. Madriani, put your hands behind your back. You can lower the gun," he tells the Snake. "I'd show you my shield, but safety requirements don't allow us to carry them when we're working undercover. It's considered hazardous." He slaps a pair of handcuffs on my wrists, ratchets them closed until they're tight, and then tugs me by the elbow and turns me around. When I look up I see the flashing overhead light bar of a patrol car racing this way, down the alley toward us.

"What the hell's goin' on?" I say. "Who the hell are you? Am I under arrest?"

"Just be quiet. Don't give us any trouble," he says.

FIFTY-FOUR

Whoever said that the law is a jealous mistress knew the reality. Joselyn looked at the time. It was almost eight o'clock. Paul was late again. Increasingly this was becoming the norm. But she understood. It was the price paid for rebuilding a law practice that had withered for two years through no fault of the partners. Joselyn felt she had no right to complain.

She and Paul both understood what they were buying into when they became involved with each other. And after all, her own position with the foundation had her traveling regularly. There were periods when Joselyn was away for weeks at a time. It was the price they paid for her career and Paul didn't complain. Joselyn felt she owed him the same.

She fought off the urge to call him and turned her attention instead back to the online research sites and the piles of paper on her desk. For Joselyn, this was not work. It was a quest for answers, for the cold, hard truth. She struggled to understand the meaning behind Sofia's death, not in the metaphysical sense, but in terms of motive and reason: who was induced to kill the girl and why.

Joselyn had yet to give up on the theory of the threatened Latin lover. One of the stacks of paper on her desk related to Ricardo Menard, his wealthy wife, and the sham that was their marriage. Joselyn had difficulty imagining someone as bright as Sofia being taken in by the likes of Menard. But if so, she wasn't alone.

Paige Proctor had married the man. When it came to smarts,

Mrs. Menard was no slacker. Paige held two advanced degrees at the time. She was older than Sofia and far more experienced with men. She had been involved in several relationships before she met Menard and had the benefit of her father's private intelligence gathering. According to the social sheets, this included two investigative reports exposing Ricardo's world-class womanizing. And still the Latin Lothario took her over the falls. It was possible she was just rebelling against her father. But to Joselyn, marrying Menard under those circumstances seemed an excessive way of acting out. What was more likely was that Ricardo was well practiced in the ways of deceiving women, even those who were more mature and informed.

It was clear that Menard could not afford a public scandal. Paige Menard might pretend to be blind and deaf, but only on condition that Ricardo's volcanic appetite for a continuing stream of young women remained subterranean, confined to the farthest, darkest recesses of the deepest hole he could fine. If any of it erupted in public, Menard knew that his ride on the money train was over. Joselyn didn't know the precise terms of the prenuptial agreement crafted by Paige's father, Henry Proctor, and his lawyers. But she didn't need the powers of a psychic to make a pretty good guess.

Menard possessed the bargaining leverage of a beggar when he entered the marriage. Paige's father detested him and made no secret of it. The social columns were full of it. He did everything he could to publicly insult and humiliate Menard, up to and including libel. In an earlier age, honor would have dictated a duel between the two men, in which case, if Joselyn's judgment of Ricardo was accurate, the man would have beat a hasty retreat home, his tail between his legs. Based on her research, money wasn't the only thing lacking from Menard's balance sheet.

Joselyn discovered things about Menard that Paul didn't know. She read Spanish. Paul didn't. Small news items off the Costa Rican Internet revealed that Menard had been pounded into the sand on three earlier occasions, twice by jealous Costa Rican husbands and once by another Tico who horned in on Menard's date for the night. If anger was the product of hot Latin blood, it didn't seem to flow through Ricardo's veins. That he kept putting his manhood at risk seemed to be more of a testament to testosterone than anything else.

Had he screwed with Henry Proctor in a duel, the old man would have dispensed with the need for seconds, pulled a pistol, and dropped him on the spot. Proctor was the ultimate indignant father, and rich. His lawyers would have defended on grounds that it's not homicide to shoot vermin. Joselyn, had she been on the jury, would have voted to acquit.

But that didn't make Menard a killer. On the contrary, he displayed every aspect of the coward.

There was no doubt that a lawsuit by Sofia over the question of paternity would have pushed Ricardo's infidelity out into the sunlight, center court, for all of Paige's social set to see. Even an attempted hushed-up settlement would have been one peccadillo too far. While Ricardo's DNA was still languishing, Joselyn harbored little doubt that he was the father of Sofia's budding child. And if so, there was no question the man had a clear motive for murder. The only issue was whether he possessed the brass either to do it himself or hire it done. And as to either option, Joselyn was having serious doubts.

The second stack of papers on her desk was even more confounding. It was topped by the article on Jack the Ripper, the one that Joselyn found online, the same article that Paul had seen on Edward Pack's desk during their visit to Tony and Lillian in Oklahoma City.

A researcher had used DNA extracted from a bloody shawl found at one of the Ripper's crime scenes. Originally the shawl was believed to belong to the victim, Catherine Eddowes. But the researcher reasoned that it was too fine a garment to belong to the impoverished Eddowes, and instead theorized that it belonged to "Jack" and that he had left it behind after he killed Eddowes. Experts scanned the garment and discovered several different strains of DNA. Some were believed to derive from human semen, others from cellular material from human organ systems. The Ripper was known to dissect his victims. Working on this supposition, a lab extracted DNA from the various strains sufficient to establish a profile. According to their report, they matched it to an immigrant on a short list of suspects in the Ripper murders, a man named Aaron Kosminski, a Jewish itinerant from what was then the Polish area of Russia.

The findings sparked immediate and intense controversy, with a good number of experts questioning both the methods employed and the conclusions drawn. None had any particular relevance for the Blood Flag, except for one thing—the age of the bloody shawl and the flag.

Joselyn couldn't help but be struck by the similarity. It was obvious why Edward Pack was interested in the article. The Eddowes shawl and the crime scene from which it was taken were estimated to be 126 years old. The Blood Flag, assuming its origin dated from the attempted Beer Hall Putsch, was more than ninety years old.

The key finding in all this was the conclusion by all experts, those who agreed with the Ripper analysis and those who did not, that blood alone, without other cellular material, given current methods, would not be sufficient to establish a reliable DNA profile, not when the blood was that old and the fabric that was the medium had been subjected to variations in heat, moisture, and other degrading conditions. Paul was right.

Joselyn had argued as to three points: First, that Edward Pack as a physician would clearly have seen the potential for DNA as the best and perhaps only sure method to establish the provenance of the Blood Flag. Second, that Andreas Bauriedl, the man who was shot and whose blood was on the flag, might well have genetic descendants who could provide a DNA profile to authenticate the flag. She was right on both points. It was what Herman meant when he told Paul that "two out of three ain't bad."

It was the third issue that was most telling. Paul had argued that it would be almost impossible to extract DNA from the blood on the flag after all these years, and on this score he was right, because the flag was a fraud. And Herman had the evidence.

FIFTY-FIVE

The ride in the back of the squad car, hands cuffed behind my back, my body seat-belted in, is not intended for comfort. The two uniforms in the front seat treat me like freight, ignoring my questions. These are generally confined to why I am here and what I'm being charged with. It's the usual guff from a furious lawyer who has been driven off the road and Shanghaied by two covert cops pretending to be monks from the universal church of white supremacy.

I stop with the interrogatories the second I realize this is no regular ride. The minute we hit the freeway the overhead lights on the squad car come on. The driver does a beeline for the fast lane, stomping on the accelerator as the g-force pushes my body into the back of the seat. My hands are crushed behind me as if somebody flipped on an afterburner. Before I know it, we're tripping the meter at close to a hundred miles an hour, passing slower cars like pickets on a fence.

As we shoot by all the off-ramps, I realize they're not taking me downtown. It's strange how fast you can get somewhere when you're doing hyperspeed and clearing traffic with your own laser light show. A few miles north of downtown he takes Highway 8 east and quickly jumps onto the 805.

When he pulls off on Miramar Mesa Boulevard, suddenly all of my questions are answered. I know who is behind this because I've been here before. It's an FBI building not far from the Miramar Naval Air Station. It's one of the West Coast haunts for Zeb Thorpe whenever the federal vampire is in town looking to sink his fangs into somebody for information. Son of a bitch! Harry was right. We had good reason to be wary of Thorpe.

Inside the building I am transferred to two agents who take me upstairs. They lead me past two interrogation rooms, one on each side of the hall, where they make sure that I get a quick glimpse through the glass. Inside Harry and Herman are seated in chairs, each being questioned separately. They want us to know that we're all here, but they don't want us to know what the other is saying. I am guessing, knowing Harry and Herman, that they've already demanded to see their lawyer—me.

Before I'm even settled into the hard metal chair in the little room, Thorpe is through the door, smiling, energetic as ever, his old self. "Hi, Paul. Good to see you. You can take the cuffs off," he tells the agent.

The guy does it.

I bring my hands around to the front, rub my shoulders and wrists.

"It's too bad we couldn't have resolved this on the phone," says Thorpe. "Would have saved both of us a lot of trouble."

"I told you. Whatever I know is privileged."

"I realize that," says Thorpe. "That's your job. This is mine. And work is work. By now you probably figured out about the two Aryans, the ones who picked you up. Part of a joint state and federal task force working on leads out of some of the prisons. We have intelligence that white supremacist gangs are on a crusade looking for the Blood Flag. We'd like to get it before they do. Besides, the thing is an embarrassment. You of all people should realize that. Why don't we work together? Save ourselves a lot of trouble. I'll do what I can for your client. In the event of any adverse fallout I'll tell the court what happened. What do you say?"

"I want to see my lawyer."

"Don't tell me. Let me guess," says Thorpe. "Harry Hinds. You know, Harry's an incredible guy. Man's got one hell of a temper."

"You don't know the worst of it," I tell him.

"You'd think he'd be doing the same as you, calling for his lawyer. But he's not. Instead he keeps telling me I'm gonna rue the day, blabbering on about somebody named Gwyn. I didn't know Harry was married."

"He's not. But if I were you I'd get a quick return ticket to D.C., take one of those two-seat fighters out of Miramar, and get out of Dodge before Judge Riggins finds you."

"Who's Judge Riggins?"

"You'll know when you see her," I tell him. "Touch a hair on Harry's head, she'll give you a lifetime term for contempt and make arrangements with her counterpart in Tijuana so you can do your time down there."

"I wouldn't hurt Harry. You know me better than that. Still, it sounds like love. When this is over we'll have to meet the lady. I'll send a wedding gift," he says. "But right now we've got some things to discuss. So why don't we get down to it. I'm dealing with some loose ends," says Thorpe. "Let's see if you can tie them up for me. Local authorities found a body in Las Vegas. Because of some federal issues, the Bureau took possession of the remains, but we had difficulty identifying the man."

"Why is that?"

"His head was crushed. The victim got caught in an industrial press of some kind. Trust me, you don't want to see the pictures," says Thorpe.

When he tells me the date and the approximate time that this all happened, there is no question. It's Tony Pack. It's the reason Tony never showed up at the restaurant, why I couldn't reach him on the phone, and why he hasn't called Lillian or the kids. He was murdered before we could meet up.

Thorpe tells me about a man named James Pepper. It's one of the names he mentioned on the phone, the fact that the FBI had been looking for him, that they believed his identity had been stolen, and that Pepper was probably already dead.

"The problem is we found Pepper's ID in Las Vegas near the body of the unidentified man. But the victim is not Pepper. We know that because we have Pepper's prints on file. We suspect that either the killer or the unidentified victim is the one who stole Pepper's identity and was using it.

"Now here's the part that should interest you," says Thorpe. "The man who was killed in Vegas fought off his assailant at least long enough to give us a clue. Under his fingernails we took some scrapings, found tissue, and did a DNA profile. We were unable to match it to any known individual in the database. But we did get a hit, an unsolved case out here on the coast. It was the murder of your assistant, Sadie Leon."

"Sofia?"

He nods. "It was a tissue match to the DNA taken from under her fingernails. Whoever killed the man in Las Vegas also killed her. We were hoping that you might be able to help us. That you might have a clue as to who the other man was, because we finally discovered the identity of the headless victim," says Thorpe. "His name was Nino Toselli."

FIFTY-SIX

t wasn't the first time that a Hitler relic had been faked. Some time in the 1970s a German named Konrad Kujau, a man who had some minor experience forging counterfeit deutsche marks, turned his limited talents to a more ambitious task.

Kujau tried to create sixty volumes, journals that he later passed off as the handwritten diaries of Adolf Hitler, the dictator's personal memoirs of the World War II years. When news of the long-lost journals broke, the discovery was considered one of the major finds of the latter half of the twentieth century. Publishers lined up to purchase the rights, offering vast amounts, knowing that the diaries would be the subject of worldwide publicity followed by mammoth sales.

Joselyn was aware of the story. She remembered reading about it in school now that she sat there this evening in her study browsing the subject on the computer. It refreshed her recollection.

The Hitler Diaries was a stunning scandal. The German magazine *Stern* had paid almost $4 million, an even more significant sum at that time, for exclusive serial rights to the journals.

World War II was one of the watershed periods of modern history. Hitler was perhaps its most enigmatic figure. It was his mesmerizing power over the German people and his charisma in front of huge crowds that paved the road to war. When he died, the man who had capital-ized the *D* in *Demagogue* and voiced full-throated, rash, and often vile judgments on every subject was gone. When he disappeared into his bunker and took his own life, the sudden silence left the world with an unquenchable hunger for answers.

More than fifty million people lost their lives in the war. Nations were destroyed, their names wiped from the map. The world had been catapulted into the nuclear age. The Cold War divided the planet in two, with all of humanity now living under the threat of radiation from the feared cloud, and no one knew why. It was difficult to comprehend how all of this could have occurred as the result of the intemperate and often illogical rants of a failed itinerant artist, vagabond, and political malcontent.

It was only natural that the world might want to look for the answer in Hitler's own words. It was the reason why the poorly crafted fraud took so long to expose. The journals' forged handwriting bore almost no similarity to Hitler's own except for a feeble attempt to mimic the slant. The sixty volumes were so miserably generated that the journal covers themselves displayed the initials "FH" instead of "AH." The forger had difficulty discerning the arcane lettering of the Old English font and picked the wrong letter.

None of this slowed the bidders or their insatiable quest for the diaries. When questions were raised as to authenticity, some of them doubled down. People wanted to believe the journals were real. Publishers wanted to make money. And the world wanted answers. When the scandal finally hit the fan there was plenty of egg to go around. Everyone seemed to wear at least some. Much of the money paid by *Stern* disappeared. A few executives involved in negotiations for publishing rights lost their jobs. The three principal perpetrators ended up doing a brief stretch in prison. As for Kujau, he returned to his old trade, selling forged artworks of famous artists signed in his own name. His last brush with the law came shortly before his death when he was arrested and charged with forging driver's licenses. The judge levied a modest fine. Kujau paid it and disappeared into history.

Joselyn was intrigued by something she saw in one of the articles. Included among his many activities over the years, Kujau was active in forging letters and artworks presumably written and painted by Hitler. He made a steady income off this and maintained a collection of what he claimed to be "Nazi memorabilia," which he sold to collectors from time to time. According to the articles it was believed that virtually all of the items in Kujau's collection were counterfeit, including a pistol claimed to have been used by Hitler to commit suicide, and "a flag identified as the Blutfahne ('Blood Flag'), carried in Hitler's failed Munich Beer Hall Putsch of 1923, and stained by the blood of Nazis shot by police."

There was a footnote as to the source. Joselyn checked it. The information came from the noted author Robert Harris, one of her favorite writers, the man who had written historical novels about ancient Rome as well as about Hitler. When it came to research, Harris did his homework. He had authored what was believed to be the seminal nonfiction work on the Hitler Diaries.

She wondered if Edward Pack might have seen the article online or whether he had read the Harris book. Perhaps it was this that was the inspiration for his plan. No one would ever know for sure.

It was Herman and his investigators who rooted it out when they found the aspiring rock artist, the man whose genetic code linked him to the Bavarian hatmaker Andreas Bauriedl. Ed Pack had paid the man five hundred dollars to swab his mouth for DNA. But according to Bauriedl's heir, the doctor also took two pints of blood.

Dr. Pack wouldn't have needed blood if he was merely taking a DNA sample to do a match against the profile of the blood already on the flag. He would need blood only if he was creating his own flag. He no doubt already had his eye on another of Bauriedl's descendants for use later to show a match with the flag that he had fabricated. In that way the two profiles would not be a 100 percent match. Such a finding would reveal the fraud. Ninety-nine and some fraction more was all that would be required.

Joselyn and Paul had theorized that Pack probably had an old Nazi flag, perhaps a war trophy; either that or he had purchased one. No doubt he would have taken care to ensure that the design and materials conformed to the period, the early twenties. He would have applied the blood to the fabric and then probably tried to age it without destroying the available DNA, whatever was deposited from the white blood cells. When it was finished, they assumed, he stored it away in the safe-deposit box. Joselyn and Paul had no idea how long it might have been there waiting for Pack to spring it on the world.

But before he could do that, he had to gain the cooperation of the last two survivors who had been with him in Munich.

How much of the original plan was known by Robert Brauer and Walter Jones or the lawyer Elliott Fish, no one could know. Not unless Fish was in on the plan and confessed, which wasn't likely.

As for Brauer and Jones, Pack required their cooperation. Otherwise he ran the risk that they would denounce him when he went public. They might tell the world that they had no recollection of anyone in the platoon ever having found such a flag, not in Munich, and not near the ruins of the bombed-out Brown House, where the flag was stored.

It was possible that Pack told them that he found the flag when in Munich after the war, but never mentioned it before because he didn't realize its significance until more recently. Regardless, by including them in his plan and gaining their assent by written agreement, he gained their cooperation or at least their silence.

It may have been the reason why Robert Brauer was afraid. He would have found it hard to say no to his old buddy, the army medic. Once having signed on, Brauer, who was old and failing, probably had second thoughts, especially when he learned that Ed Pack, the man who was behind it all, was dead. When the box with the key arrived, Brauer probably didn't know what to do. He just wanted it to go away. When the house was burgled he panicked.

But before that, before he died, Ed Pack ran into a problem. The Ripper article made clear that his plan would never work. He would need tissue or bone in addition to blood for anything that was ninety years old. This was true especially if it had been exposed to the weather, UV radiation from the sun, and variations in heat where it had been stored. These were the conditions that affected the real Blood Flag.

Joselyn and Paul theorized that the doctor was probably about to give it up, abandon the entire scheme, when he was murdered. Paul suspected that Ed Pack probably didn't have time to tell anyone what he had discovered, the limitations of DNA, and that the flag wouldn't work. Whoever killed him wanted it. This was the person Tony Pack was after when he disappeared. The reason he kept pushing the Oklahoma City police to get involved.

The only thing that didn't make sense was why Edward Pack himself was so frightened. According to Tony, his father was terrified. And yet Ed Pack knew what was happening because he was behind it. The flag was a beast of his own making. All he had to do was quietly walk away and no one would ever be the wiser. Unless someone he was afraid of was trying to get his hands on it.

As Joselyn sat there staring at the screen, thinking, the doorbell rang. It couldn't be Paul. He had a key. She looked at the clock. It was almost nine thirty. Where was he? Joselyn got up, walked out of the study, down the hall, and across the living room to the front door, and opened it.

FIFTY-SEVEN

The man Toselli held a passport, owned a residence, and had several bank accounts on the island of Curaçao," says Thorpe. "For those who don't know, that's way south in the Caribbean, very end of the Antilles . . ."

"I know where it is. I've been there."

"Bully for you," he says. "See, the man can talk." Thorpe turns and smiles at the other two agents standing in the room. "The island is a constituent entity of the Netherlands, which retains some jurisdiction. Lucky for us the man's prints were on file in The Hague. We got a hit on them from Interpol. They got them from Europol. That's the reason it took so long for us to get a fix on the man, but then, he didn't have a head, so a photo was out of the question. Do you follow me so far?"

"I'm spellbound," I tell him.

"Are you sure you don't want to tell me what's happening here?"

"You're doing fine. Keep going," I say.

"I could use a little help."

"You're not gonna get it from me."

"Fine. The timeline for the man's death in Las Vegas is too much of a coincidence to ignore. We know you were in town that day. We checked with the airlines."

"You think I killed him?"

"Did you?"

"Don't be foolish," I tell him.

"What were you doing there?"

"I had a meeting."

"With who?"

"It relates to attorney work product," I tell him.

"Did your meeting come off OK?" He looks at me, waits for an answer, and when I don't, he says, "OK, if you want, we'll come back to that later. Did this meeting have anything to do with Ricardo Menard?"

I look at him. He smiles. "We know you met with the man. We have pictures."

"How lewd. That must have knocked the intel sats out of orbit."

"Is Menard involved with the Blood Flag?" asks Thorpe.

"What is this, Twenty Questions?"

"Who's counting?" he says.

"You keep coming back to the flag."

"It's why I'm here," he says. "My reason for existence at the moment. Is he involved?"

"A fair question," I tell him. "I don't think so."

"But you're not sure."

"He never raised the issue when we talked."

"No, he didn't, did he," says Thorpe.

"How would you know?"

He offers me a sage smile.

"You wouldn't need a wire to figure that one out. And if you were reading his lips you were monitoring the wrong body part."

"How's that?"

"Menard's not interested in the flag."

"How do you know?"

"Tell your analysts to study their photographs more carefully. If they take a closer look they'll discover he has his hands full with other things."

"So then we agree," says Thorpe. "We can cross Menard off the list?"

"What list?"

"The list of prospective killers and the people involved with the flag," he says.

"I didn't say that."

"You said he wasn't after the flag."

"Yeah, but I never said he didn't kill anybody."

"So you think he killed your assistant?"

"I don't know, but I'm not ready to give him a pass."

"Did he or didn't he?"

"I don't know. You tell me."

"OK, I will," says Thorpe. "The sheriff wasn't anxious to do your little experiment in DNA, but we did. The results came back this morning. Ricardo Menard is the father, or was, of the unborn fetus being carried by your assistant, Sofia. Don't say I never give you anything. I just did. And you don't have to thank me."

"I won't."

"But just so that you know. We don't think that Menard killed her."

"Why not?"

"For one thing, he was out of the country on the day she was murdered. He left for Costa Rica the previous Wednesday and didn't return until the following week. We checked."

"He could have hired somebody to do it," I tell him.

"Who, Toselli?"

"No," I say.

"Nino may have lost his head," says Thorpe, "but he has an alibi even better than Ricardo's. He was carrying the DNA of Sofia's killer under his fingernails, which means he didn't do it. So who else is there?" says Thorpe. "We're running out of suspects."

"It could be anybody," I tell him.

"Or it could be somebody you know. Who were you going to meet in Las Vegas?" he says.

I have been playing mind games with myself for the last twenty minutes, ever since Thorpe told me about the unidentified headless body. I immediately leapt to the conclusion that it had to be Tony, until Thorpe told me about the fingerprints and Toselli. Why was I thinking that Tony was involved at all? I wasn't sure. There was no reason except for the fact that he was missing. The growing realization that he might be dead is difficult enough. How could I possibly get my head around the obscene concept that he might have killed Sofia? I couldn't. We had broken bread with the man in his house. I can see images of the gathering around the table that night. Lillian and the two girls, Joselyn, myself, and Tony, sitting at the head of the table laughing, telling stories, sampling wines. It's not possible, beyond comprehension. At least it is for me.

It will be a relief when they find his body, painful as that might be. Thorpe can do the DNA, exclude him as a suspect, and Tony can rest in peace.

"There's a phone call for the lawyer."

I look up. There's an agent standing in the doorway. He has my cell phone in his hand.

"Who is it?" says Thorpe.

"A woman, says her name is Joselyn."

Thorpe smiles. He knows her. "Go ahead, give him the phone. Apologize for me and tell her you'll be home shortly."

"You letting us go?"

"What else can I do?"

I take the phone, put it to my ear, and say, "Hello."

"Where are you?" she says. Joselyn is upset. I can't blame her. I look at my watch. It's almost ten o'clock.

"I'm sorry. I got tied up," I tell her.

Thorpe smiles. One of the agents sniggers.

"Who was that who answered your phone?"

"I'll tell you about it when I get home."

"Well, hurry up because we have company for dinner."

"Who?"

"It's a surprise," she says. "You'll never guess."

I already have. "Tony's there."

"How did you know?"

"I guess he was on my mind," I tell her.

"That's amazing," she says. "I'll have to tell him."

"No. Don't!"

"Why not?"

"Never mind," I tell her.

"Is something wrong?"

"No, nothing. Everything's fine. Where is Tony right now?"

"He's out in the living room."

"Where are you?"

"I'm in the kitchen."

"Where's your car?"

"It's in the garage. Why?"

"Listen to me. This is what I want you to do. Grab your keys. Go out the back door. Don't say a word. Get in the car, start the motor, and once you start to back up, don't stop."

"What? What are you talking about . . . Oh, hi, Tony. Can I get you something to drink?"

I hear Tony's voice, "Nah, I'm fine. Can I help you with dinner?"

"No, no. I've got it. Paul's on the phone. Here, why don't you talk to him?"

"Hey, Paul, where are you?"

"I'm working late. Sorry I missed you," I tell him.

"Jeez, it's ten o'clock. I guess so. Listen, I'm sorry about Vegas," he says.

"Not a problem."

"No, but I need to tell you what happened."

"No need to explain. I understand."

"Understand what?" he says.

"I assumed you must have had a problem of some kind."

"You mean Joselyn didn't tell you?"

"No."

"Well, then I need to explain. I had an accident. Got in a wreck with the rental car. Ended up in the hospital. That's why I couldn't call," he says.

"Nothing too serious, I hope."

"No, no. Nothin' like that. It's gonna be fine. When are you coming home?" he says. "I've got that stuff to show you. You remember, the key and the thumb drive?"

"I remember. I'll be there shortly," I tell him.

"Where is your key?" he says. "Is it here at the house?"

"No, no, it's not there. It's locked in a safe at the office." I lie to him. It's in the center drawer of my desk at the house.

All Tony wants is the key. I can tell by his voice. The minute he has it he'll kill whoever is around and disappear.

"I thought you were at the office."

"No. No. I'm across town at another law office in a library meeting with some other people. But I'll be home shortly. Can you put Joselyn back on the phone?"

"Sure. Listen, can you do me a favor? Can you go to your office, get the key, and bring it home with you? I really would like to compare it with the one I have, and do it tonight."

"I can try to do that, sure. Let me talk to Joselyn."

"She's right here. He wants to talk to you. I gotta get something out of my car. I'll be right back."

I hear the phone being handed off.

Thorpe is looking at me. He realizes something is wrong.

"Joselyn, listen, do me a favor. Is he gone?"

"Who?"

"Tony."

"Yeah. He just went outside."

"Listen. You haven't said anything to Tony about what we discussed last night, have you?"

"What's what?"

"About the flag, what Herman found out."

With mention of the flag Thorpe reaches out and taps one of the other agents. He motions for him to get some help.

"Oh, you mean about the fact that it's—"

"Don't say anything!" I tell her.

"Why not? What's wrong?"

"We'll talk when I get home. In the meantime, don't say a word to Tony. Promise me."

"OK," she says. "If you say so."

"I do. I'll take care of it when I get there. Let me do it."

"What's the problem? Why don't you tell me what's going on?"

"I can't. Trust me. Please. I'll be there as fast as I can. Promise me you won't say anything."

"I said I wouldn't and I won't. Either just tell me what's happening or come home." Joselyn is getting her back up. Start an argument and Tony will hear it. If I tell her what's happening it may set her on edge. If he senses that something's wrong, he'll kill her. I know it.

"I'll be there quick as I can. Just hang on."

"Well, hurry up, cuz it's after ten and dinner's going to get cold. You'd think we were living in Spain," she says, and hangs up.

"What's wrong?" says Thorpe.

"Joselyn's in trouble. A man just came back from the grave," I tell him.

FIFTY-EIGHT

Thorpe has assembled a caravan of FBI vehicles streaming south at high speed on the 805, racing toward the bridge to Coronado. He and I sit in the backseat of one of the big black SUVs screaming along the freeway as I fill him in on everything that's happened.

I explain the relationship between Edward Pack, the father, and Tony, his son. It is clear to me now that Tony has killed them all—his father, Walter Jones, and Robert Brauer—in order to gain access to the key.

There is and always has been but a single client key to the safe-deposit box containing the vaunted Blood Flag, the replica manufactured by Edward Pack. The sole key is the one in the center drawer of my desk at home. If Tony knew it was there, I am convinced he would take it, kill Joselyn, and head to Fish's office and from there to the bank to get the flag. The key was sent to Robert Brauer because, as Fish stated to me on the phone, Brauer was the last survivor. The lawyer's instructions, when we get them, will give us the answer. I suspect that Fish was to maintain possession of the key as long as two or more of the former army comrades remained alive. The moment their number was reduced to one, the agreement they signed and the instructions probably required Fish to send the key to the sole survivor.

It must have burned in Tony's hand that day at the office when I handed Brauer's key to him and he had to give it back. There were too many people in the conference room for him to do anything else.

The other key, the one invented by Tony, and possibly the encrypted thumb drive, was a ploy. They were intended to lure me into the open along with Brauer's key, presumably for comparison. Fortune, through the intercession of Nino Toselli, spared me. How and why, I don't know. But one thing is clear: just as the fates had taken the life of Sofia, they saved mine.

As for Sofia's murder, it has become obvious that her death, like the fate of her unborn child, was the product of misfortune. Tony never planned to kill her. The discarded and torn V-belt, a weapon of ultimate chance found on the floor in the cellar by Harry, is evidence of the fact. She was in the wrong place at the wrong time. Tony was busy searching Brauer's house for the key when Sofia showed up looking for the dog. Somehow she stumbled onto him. For Tony there was only one thing to do. He had already killed three people.

My greatest fear now is that Joselyn says something that sets him off before we can reach the house. If she lets slip with some sliver of information that reveals to Tony how exposed he is, he will disappear forever, but not before killing Joselyn.

"It's the reason I didn't want her to tell him that the flag is a fake."

"You don't think he already knows?" says Thorpe.

"No. If he did he wouldn't be doing this. He'd already be on the run. If you killed four people, five including Toselli, and you knew you had an item you couldn't sell because it wouldn't pass muster on inspection, would you stick around?"

Thorpe looks at me, shakes his head, and says, "Probably not. But that still doesn't answer the question, why didn't the old man tell him?"

"Any one of a number of reasons. But if I had to pick one, I'd say it was that Ed Pack was a stand-up guy and a good father."

"What are you talking about? You mean the fraudster?"

"Think what you want, but you asked me for an answer. Life's complicated. People have facets, sometimes too many of them. Everything I saw, read, and heard about Edward Pack confirmed one thing. He was a good man, cared about people, treated them for free, some of them for years. True, some of the information came from Tony, the son who killed him. But that doesn't diminish the stature of the man. If he failed to tell Tony that the flag wasn't real, it was for a simple reason, the most fundamental instinct of any parent, that he wanted to protect his son.

He didn't want to involve Tony in the fraud. The fear that if things went south during the attempted sale they'd all end up in jail. So, thinking that ignorance was innocence, he kept Tony in the dark."

"And the kid killed him," says Thorpe.

"Along with four other people that we know of. Ed Pack didn't know it, but he left a ticking time bomb in that safe-deposit vault. He probably would have warned the kid on his deathbed even as Tony was killing him if he had had the time and the presence of mind. But Tony, true to form, probably pumped him full of enough insulin to kill a cow."

"Are you sure you want to do this?"

I nod. "What other choice is there?"

"We could surround the house and call him out," says Thorpe.

"In which case he takes Joselyn hostage, and if things go badly, he kills her."

"We could try to get her out before he knows we're there."

"If we had more time, perhaps. But we don't. If I don't get there soon Tony's gonna know that something's wrong. If that happens, Joselyn's life won't be worth spit. If there was some other way, believe me, I'd do it. But there isn't," I tell him.

"It's against my better judgment," says Thorpe, "but maybe you're right. I wouldn't want to be the one responsible for losing her."

"Think of it as gaining a good woman and losing a lawyer."

"Leave it to you to find the silver lining," says Thorpe. "Before you go in you gotta sign this."

"What is it?"

He hands me a waiver form. I reach for the pen in my shirt pocket.

"Not that one," he says. "Here, use mine."

"What do I do if he asks to borrow my pen?"

"Give it to him," says Thorpe. "It writes. It's got a small cartridge. But if it starts to skip, whatever you do, don't let him try to take it apart. Just make sure you get it back, and when you do, put it in your pocket the same way with the clip facing out. You don't have to worry about turning it on or off. We'll take care of that. And whatever you do, don't give him the pen in your coat pocket."

"I know, that's the pepper spray."

"Get 'em mixed up, you're gonna end up writing a tearjerker," he says.

Thorpe has me wired seven ways from Sunday. I'm a walking television studio with tiny minicam lenses and mics in every crevice and opening. If I belch or pass wind I'm hoping it results in an Emmy.

I look at the waiver form and put it on top of the slick new attaché case on my lap, the one given to me by Thorpe with the twin canisters of pepper spray inside and the nifty little nozzles, one pointed in each direction. There's a trigger in the handle so that if I turn my face away, cough and pull it, and it's aimed at Tony, it may incapacitate him long enough so the cops can get in and cuff him.

Under the terms of the waiver I assume all risk, waive all claims as to liability, and agree to hold the government harmless in the event that I am injured or killed. It's similar to the boilerplate signed by lawyers visiting clients in high-security prisons. Tonight it's the price I pay to get into my own home.

"Don't waste your time reading it," says Thorpe; "it's ironclad. Put together by the best minds at Justice."

"Just want to make sure it only covers me," I tell him. "That way if anything happens, Joselyn can sue the shit out of you."

"That's what I love about you. You're always thinking of others."

"I figure she'll hire Harry and me, so we ought to be able to at least get a third."

He laughs. "What am I gonna do without you?"

"Let's hope it doesn't come to that," I tell him.

"Which reminds me. One last item," says Thorpe. "Do you want a firearm?"

"I don't know."

"Do you know how to use one?"

"I've been to the range a few times. I wouldn't call myself an expert."

"We could strap it on your ankle," he says. "Just in case. You have to figure he's probably armed. He's been on the lam for what, a week now?"

"Almost."

"We could outfit you with a small Glock or a SIG Sauer, in which case you're gonna want to chamber a round before you go in. On the SIG you gotta deal with the issue of the safety, whether you want it on or off. You can shoot yourself in the foot if you're not careful. My advice," says Thorpe "I'd use a thirty-eight special, a small snub-nose revolver, two-inch barrel. At close range it'll get the job done and it's pretty much idiot-proof."

"Thanks for the confidence," I tell him.

"Just because we're here to serve and protect doesn't mean we want to get shot in the process by some dumb-ass citizen," he says.

"Touché."

"How about it? Do you want a gun?"

"What if he sees it?"

"That's the downside," he says. "I can't advise you on this. Once you're inside, it could go either way. If he's edgy and he sees or even suspects that you're carrying, it could send him off the rails. The only place I'd suggest is on your ankle. But if he's nervous and he sees the bulge, well, it's a long way down to get to it. In all candor, you'd be better off throwing something at him. The gun's good if you can grab Joselyn and barricade yourselves in a room. Use the pistol if you need to, to hold him off, until the cavalry arrives. And you can trust me, it won't take long."

"But that's not the plan," I tell him.

"No, it isn't. But then, plans sometimes don't work out."

"If it's all the same, I think I'll leave the gun."

"That's your decision."

"If I can talk him out, get him into the front yard, I'll step away and your guys can take him down. I don't mean kill him. I'm hoping that with a sufficient show of force he'll give himself up."

Thorpe looks at me. "Hope is what gets people killed. It causes them to hesitate. In the time it takes to think the word, a bullet can travel a thousand yards. Do you want some more advice?"

"Yes. Go ahead."

"When you enter the house tonight, park your emotions outside with the car. Emotions cloud judgment. They're a luxury you can't afford when you're trying to stay alive. You do want to stay alive—keep Joselyn alive, right?"

"Of course."

"Then reduce everything to a simple, fundamental formula," says Thorpe. "It's either you or him. There is no middle ground. The man has killed five times that we know of. If you can get him outside, we'll take him down. We'll use reasonable efforts to take him alive. But if he is armed, and I assume he is, and if he makes a move, we will shoot to kill. Chances are he'll die. My people don't miss. Do yourself a favor and don't get in the way. You can't negotiate with a speeding bullet, and trust me, it doesn't understand the meaning of hope."

FIFTY-NINE

Thorpe's driver delivered me to a government parking area on the San Diego side of the Coronado Bridge, where I picked up my Jeep and headed home. It took me ten minutes to make it across the bridge, through town, and home. On the way I passed a large vehicle that looked like an RV parked at the curb on the other side of the street about half a block north from my driveway. It was the FBI command vehicle. Thorpe called it to my attention earlier when we were leaving the area around Miramar.

I pull into the driveway, turn off my headlights and the engine, and take a deep breath. I take a casual glance around. If there are snipers set up around the house I can't see them. But then, I suppose that's the point. If I could see them they wouldn't be doing their job. I grab the attaché case, step out of the Jeep, and head across the lawn toward the front door.

Before I can get up onto the porch the door opens and Tony is standing there looking at me, smiling, something sinister, or perhaps it's just me, the fact that I know.

"It took you a while," he says. "How come you're running so late?"

"I'm busy. Business is booming. What can I say?" I beam back at him and shake his hand. "I hope you guys waited dinner for me."

"Of course we did. Joselyn told you on the phone."

"Yeah, I guess she did."

"Here, lemme take that." He reaches out to take the attaché case.

"No, no. That's OK. I got it." I lean into him with my right shoulder so he can't reach across my body to my left hand to grab the case. If he feels the weight he's going to know that there's something inside it beside papers. The case has a combination lock so it can't be opened.

"Did you manage to pick up the key?" he asks.

I'm not even in the house and he's asking. Tony must be in a hurry to kill us.

"Oh, jeez, I forgot. Tell you what, why don't you and I go get it?"

"You mean now?"

"Sure, why not?"

"Fine with me," he says.

"It's about time you got home," she says. I see Joselyn coming across the living room behind him. "Where have you been?"

"I'll tell you about it later. Why don't we eat?"

Tony does a double take like he's confused and says, "I thought . . ."

"Right after dinner," I whisper out of the side of my mouth. "Otherwise she's gonna kill us both."

"How are you, sweetheart?" I turn away from Tony and give her a kiss.

Not even through the door and I'm already in trouble. If I say anything in front of Joselyn about going to the office to get the key, the first thing she's gonna do is remind me that it's in my desk and then ask me why I'd bother with the key since the flag is a fake.

It's like walking on thin ice. Until I can get her alone in a room somewhere away from Tony and tell her what's going on, I have to tread carefully.

"Where did you get that?" Joselyn is looking at my new briefcase.

"Oh, I should have told you, I suppose. I saw it in a shop window this afternoon so I bought it. Looks nice, doesn't it?"

"Yes. Very nice," she says. "What's the inside look like? Does it have a lot of pocket space for files? I've been looking for something like that. Can I see?"

"Later," I tell her. "Why don't we eat first? I'm famished." I sneak a glance at Tony.

He's eyeing the leather attaché case, studying it with suspicion, then lifts his gaze to look at me.

I smile at him and say, "Let's go eat." The second Tony turns his back I take the opportunity to ditch the case under a narrow library table against the wall in the entry. Before he can turn around again I come up behind him and put my arm around his shoulder. "It's good to see you again."

"Same here," he says.

He is wearing a loose cardigan sweater, buttons down the front. It looks about two sizes too big for him. I'm tempted to pat him down to see if he's packing any lumpy pieces of steel underneath it, but I don't dare.

In the mental search for small talk I keep running into items that are off-limits. I would ask him about the wife and kids, but that's a taboo subject. I wonder if Joselyn has broached it and, if so, what lie he may have told her.

The more I learn about Tony the more convinced I am that he's the original mystery man. Besides his being a closet killer I'm beginning to think he has a secret life, maybe more than one. After I found out that Tony was waiting for me at home, I called Lillian in Oklahoma City from Thorpe's digs at the FBI office. I asked her how she was doing and nosed around to see if she'd heard from Tony. She referred to her situation as a continuing struggle and said nothing about her missing husband. Finally I asked if she'd heard from him. She said no, but she still had hope. I should have introduced her to Thorpe. Being the romantic that he was, he would have told her that hope might heal the human heart, but it wouldn't stop a bullet. And that anyone married to Tony might want to think about buying a Kevlar overcoat.

I asked her if he'd ever done anything like this before, disappeared for periods of time. She broke down on the phone and started crying. It seemed I finally pierced the veil. She told me that Tony disappeared several times previously. Once for more than a month, and often for more than three or four days. The one time she filed a missing persons report, the police brought him home. But they refused to tell her where they found him. Lillian assumed it was another woman. If so, my question is, was she alive?

Lillian told me that Tony was so angry that he beat her. Whenever he disappeared after that, she never called the police again. She told me that Tony had a violent temper, but that she still loved him. She was certain that sooner or later he would come home.

I didn't tell her what was happening. I was afraid that if Tony decided to call home or connected with Lillian by text, she might warn him. Battered women are often protective.

Inside the kitchen, Joselyn and I are doing the final prep for dinner. The entire time Tony hovers over us. Joselyn tells me she's amazed that he is doing as well as he is given everything he's been through, the accident with the rental car, and the time he spent in the hospital. She tells me that according to Tony, Lillian wanted to fly out with him for the visit, but she was too busy with the girls in school.

I uncork the wine and hand the bottle to Tony. "Would you mind putting that out on the dining room table? Also there's some wineglasses on the shelf. You'll see them out there. Put one for each of us on the table. Thanks, Tony."

"No problem." He takes the bottle and pushes his way through the kitchen's double swinging door.

The second it slaps closed behind him I skate across the kitchen to Joselyn at the sink. I grab her by the arm.

She turns. "What's the matter?"

"Tony's the killer," I tell her.

"What are you talking about?"

"I've been with the FBI all evening. They're outside the house. He killed his father, Bob Brauer, and Sofia." I don't even have time to mention Walt Jones or the headless body in Las Vegas. Tony is racking up bodies, and I'm concerned that ours may be added to the growing list.

I hear him coming this way, footfalls across the hardwood floor in the dining room. By the time he gets to the kitchen door I'm back at the island getting ready to slice the French bread. I see him looking into the kitchen through the little square window in the door. Joselyn is still standing at the sink sideways, looking off into the distance as if she's stunned or getting ready to sleepwalk.

He comes through the door a second later and says, "Can I help with anything else?"

"Yeah, you can take the hot water kettle and plug it in out by the table. We'll have some tea later with dessert."

He listens to me, but he's looking at Joselyn. Something is wrong and Tony can smell it.

"When you're done with that you can take the bread out. Why don't you grab one of those baskets?" I point to the top shelf in the hutch against the wall.

Slowly Tony turns, walks to the hutch, and grabs one of the baskets. He brings it to me. The entire time he's looking at Joselyn, who's standing sideways, leaning with her hip against the sink, a paring knife in her right hand dripping water onto the tile at her feet. "What's wrong with her?"

"What's that?"

"Joselyn. She doesn't look well."

"Oh, I think she's OK. She has a headache. I think I delayed dinner too long. If we hurry up and eat she'll be fine. She's has a touch of hypoglycemia."

"Really."

I unplug the electric water kettle and hand it to him. I tell him to put it out on the table and plug it in. I've never done this before. In fact I'm not even sure if there's an outlet close enough to reach. I'm hoping it will take Tony a while to find out.

He takes the kettle and walks slowly and reluctantly toward the door. He looks at Joselyn standing at the sink like a statue and then flashes a quick glance at me.

I pretend not to notice as I play with the French bread that's already sliced in the basket. When the swinging door closes I wait a couple of seconds before I creep over and take a peek through the square window to make sure he's gone into the dining room. As soon as I'm satisfied I race over to Joselyn at the sink, take the knife from her hand, and splash some drops of cold water on her face. Finally she shakes her head and looks at me.

"Snap out of it," I tell her. "We have to keep it together. I think he's armed, but I'm not sure."

"How did you find out?"

"Zeb Thorpe," I tell her.

"Is Zeb here?"

"Outside somewhere. Listen, sweetheart, do something. Stand at the sink, wash your hands, but try to look busy. I'm gonna try to get you out of here."

"Not without you. Not unless we go together," she says.

"All right." There is no sense arguing with her. There isn't time.

I'm hoping that all the electronics are working and that Thorpe and his people are listening. As I turn my head to the right and glance over my shoulder I see Tony standing there, peering through the window in the door. He's smiling like some mad entomologist busy studying two bugs under glass. I wonder how long he's been there.

He pushes his way through the door, stands there, and says, "She's lookin' much better. It must have been something you said. Maybe you wouldn't mind sharing the secret with me?"

Obviously long enough. The buttons on his cardigan sweater are open halfway down his chest. His right hand is inside gripping something I can't see. But it's not hard to imagine.

"Well," says Tony, " you went to a lot of trouble, so we may as well sit down and eat. Be a shame to waste a good meal like that. And besides, you can tell me all about it over dinner."

SIXTY

ony arranges everything as we sit down to eat. His own version of the Last Supper. Our dining table is rectangular, solid oak, and almost eight feet long. Tony takes the seat at the head with his back to a solid wall. He's a careful man.

He places a large blued revolver on top of the linen napkin next to his right hand. It looks like an old .44 Magnum. It has a long vented barrel, seven or eight inches if I had to guess. There is some wear on the bluing, so it's not new. Whatever the make, from the look of the bore of the barrel and the size of the chambers in the oversize cylinder, the piece is big enough to do the job, even if your sport happens to be shooting locomotives.

Tony tells me to sit in the chair next to him, on his left. This arrangement places the two of us seated on the angle at the corner of the table, ninety degrees of separation. It places the pistol well beyond my reach. Tony's entire body is between me and the ten-pound hand cannon resting on the napkin. And yet it's close enough so that if I give him any trouble, Tony can't miss. He could hold me off with one hand while he put holes in me with the other. At least that's the theory. This is a whole new side of the man, one I've never seen before. The careful, plotting killer whose choreography of murder demands a well-designed and engineered edge.

On the other side from me, just to the right of Tony's chair, the gurgle of the electric kettle plays background to the drama he is directing at the table. It seems he found a place for it, plugged into a wall outlet right behind where he's sitting.

The fact that Tony hasn't patted me down for weapons causes me to regret that I didn't take Thorpe up on his offer of the ankle holster and the snubbed-up .38. With that, and seated up close to him as I am here, I would have had a fair chance of turning Tony into a gelding from underneath the table.

"Joselyn, why don't you take that chair right down there." He gestures toward the seat about four feet away from me on my side of the table. "That way you can serve all of us. You don't mind, do you? Of course you don't. You've got a good woman there, Paul." He gives her a lusty look. To Tony, this is woman's work, serving food.

Of course, he couldn't possibly grasp Joselyn's full measure, the depth of her passion and the flavor of her fury, unless she gets up behind him with something sharp in her hand. Joselyn doesn't say anything but the look in her eye, the burning resentment and the boiling anger for what Tony did to Sofia, could melt the steel on the pistol next to his hand. I can feel the heat of her anger register on the surface of my skin. But Tony can't sense this. To him women are interchangeable widgets. He thinks Joselyn is Lillian. She might be, but only if you mistake a cobra for a garter snake.

Tony is a fool if he thinks he can safely allow Joselyn to move freely around the room while she serves him. She doesn't know the plan and hasn't talked to Thorpe. The first chance she gets she'll try to stick a fork in Tony's eye.

"Do a lot of shooting, do you?" I look at Tony.

"Some," he says. "Do you like the gun?"

"How long have you had it?"

"I bought it yesterday. Why?"

"Just wondering."

It's what I thought. I know nothing of Tony's marksmanship. But if had to bet, I'd take wagers that he'd have trouble trying to hit the wall on the other side of the room with the bazooka that's on the table. It's a foolish piece, often purchased by foolish people, trying to overcompensate for things they don't have. They've seen too many movies.

The kinetic energy of a single round from a .44 Magnum would no doubt be lethal even if it impacted only your big toe. But if Tony happened to miss on the first shot, then it's a whole new game. If the recoil from the initial round didn't take his head off, the punishment he's going to absorb from behind the sights on each successive shot is going to play havoc on his aim. He could put a lot of big holes in the walls of our house before he was lucky enough to hit anything he aimed at.

If Joselyn and I could move fast enough after the first well-aimed shot, Tony would get only five more, all of them rattle-bangers, before the FBI moved in and waxed him.

It's clear that he has no idea what he's dealing with. Otherwise he wouldn't be sitting here calmly preparing to dine while FBI snipers are measuring the distance from his hairline to his chin. I suspect that Tony assumes I came home alone without a police escort because he was here with Joselyn and whatever suspicions I might have were sketchy at best, based only on the fact that he showed up on our doorstep so unexpectedly.

"Tony, listen, why don't you give it up? It's over."

"What are you talking about?"

"The Blood Flag. It's done."

"How much do you know?"

"Not much."

"Where's the key?"

"I told you, it's at the office. Let's you and I go get it."

"What, and leave Joselyn here alone? You must think I'm stupid."

"I don't understand. We were just sitting down to have a friendly dinner and you pull out a gun. What the hell's happened to you?"

He looks at me like he's confused, as if perhaps he might have misjudged the situation. His problem is, how to do you pick up Big Bertha from the table put it back in its holster and say "never mind"?

"Why don't you and I just go get the key?" I try again.

"No. There's too many of us."

Suddenly I understand his dilemma. Joselyn is in the way. I have access to the office safe, where Tony thinks the key is located. He needs me, at least for the moment. But Joselyn is excess baggage. Tony plans to leave a body behind. I'm praying that Thorpe is listening to this and that he has arrived at the same conclusion.

*   *   *

Thorpe watched on the screen inside the command vehicle half a block away, live video from the tiny pen lens in Paul's shirt pocket. He got fleeting images of the side of Pack's body, his head from time to time, and a couple of still images his technicians snapped of the handgun on the table. They knew now what they were dealing with, assuming there weren't any other surprises.

He listened to the calm chatter on his headset, the three teams of snipers surrounding the house as well as the increasingly sparse conversation from inside on the other channel. He could sense that things weren't going well. That it hadn't turned into an outright hostage situation with lights out and barricaded furniture was simply because Pack didn't realize how much they knew. Toselli's headless body and the DNA under his fingernails had brought the FBI and local authorities to Madriani's doorstep.

One of the sniper teams was perched on the back side of the roof on the house next door with the heavy-barreled Remington resting on a sandbag right at the ridge of the roof. Authorities had quietly evacuated the houses surrounding Paul's home.

From what Thorpe could hear, the man on the roof next door had the best angle for a shot. But he couldn't get a clear bead on a head or center-chest shot because of where Tony was seated. He got occasional glimpses of the assailant's hand near the handgun and his other arm near the hostage, the lawyer sitting next to him. The image came through a sliding glass door. If he could get him to stand, there was a high set of windows through which the sniper might get a perfect shot. If all he did was wound the man, the suspect would push back against the wall and take out his wrath with the handgun on the two hostages.

Thorpe told the man he had a green light to take the shot the second he got a clear target.

The sniper came back on the channel saying, "I won't have a target unless we can get him up out of that chair."

"Darlin', we're waiting. Why don't you serve up the food?" The way Tony looks at her, I can't tell if he wants to eat or if the moment has come. I know that if he makes his move to kill her and thin out the crowd, it will happen with lightning speed. Tony isn't a talker. The fact that he's killed so many people and has done so with such efficiency tells me that. The instant Joselyn gets out of her seat and reaches for the plate of pasta I begin to sweat.

Half a beat later, the phone on the table in the living room rings. Joselyn and I look at each other.

Tony says, "Who could that be at this hour?"

Joselyn replies, "We won't know until I answer it."

It rings again. Tony looks at her. He has a problem. If he allows it to go unanswered and it's a relative or a friend who knows we're home, it might cause them to check on us. He looks at me, tries to read my mind, and before I can say anything the phone stops ringing. It rolls over to voicemail. It's an old system, the kind where you can hear messages and screen calls. But whoever is calling doesn't leave a message.

Tony starts to relax and the second he does, it rings again. Whoever it is knows we're home. He has no choice. "Go ahead and answer it." He pushes his chair back, starts to get up, and then stops. "Is there any way to turn the speaker on so we can listen in?"

"I think so, I'll have to look," says Joselyn.

"Do it," he says.

She walks to the phone and picks up the receiver.

"Hello?" She fumbled around as if she was having trouble finding the speaker button.

"Joselyn, it's Zeb Thorpe here. You've got to get him up and standing. Out of that chair."

The sniper on the roof watched as he got the first glimpse of the target rising from the chair. The crown of his head came up like the sliver of the moon at the bottom frame of the glass in the window.

"Sorry, you must have the wrong number," and Joselyn hung up.

The rising target disappeared from the glass. If she had kept the conversation going for two more seconds, Pack would have been dead.

"Who was it?" asks Tony. He has his hand on the gun.

"Somebody looking for Madelyn. He sounded drunk." She looks at me.

Madelyn was the code name given to Joselyn by Thorpe when we were hiding out from the cartel man Liquida. Thorpe has given her a message. The problem is, I don't know what it is.

Tony settles back down. "It's gettin' late, let's hurry up and eat." He picks up the pistol and points to the pasta bowl.

Suddenly he has the gun in his hand. If he wanted to eat, he would have picked up his fork.

Joselyn heads back to the table and grabs the bowl again. She turns and starts to walk toward me to go behind my chair and Tony stops her.

"Other way," he says. Tony doesn't want her approaching from this side of the table, getting between us, providing me with a diversion.

Joselyn looks at me. She knows something is coming. He's positioning her for a clear, close shot, in tight where even he couldn't miss. She turns and heads away, around the other end of the table, and starts walking toward him.

He watches her every step of the way. She has his undivided attention. My right hand, a finger at a time, creeps over the edge of the table toward my fork on top of the napkin. Tony doesn't see it. He's fixated on Joselyn. As she draws closer he doesn't move the muzzle of the gun. Instead he leaves it where it is. Why cause a panic? Just like a professional, he waits. He wants her right up next to him. Then he'll move like lightning and put a bullet in her head.

She gets there. She knows it's coming. There's nothing she can do until she says, "Why do you want the key? Don't you understand that your father's Blood Flag is a fake?"

The expression on Tony's face is one of bewilderment. He sits there looking at her, certain that what she's saying can't be true. He turns to look at me.

"You wondered what we were talking about in the kitchen. Now you know."

"You're lying," he says.

"No. It's the truth," says Joselyn. "We couldn't figure out how to explain it to you, the fact that Dr. Edward Pack never thought enough of his own son to share the secret with him."

The look in his eye as he turns the muzzle of the gun toward Joselyn says everything. All of his fury is suddenly focused the other way, turned on her. I lift the fork above my head and plunge it with all of my strength into the back of Tony's left hand. But for the hardness of the oak table I would have nailed it to the surface.

Tony howls like an anguished wolf. Fork still protruding, he draws the wounded hand toward his chest, turns in his chair, and instantly brings the gun toward me. Tony cocks the hammer, preparing to annihilate this newest source of pain.

The pistol's huge bore, like a dark tunnel to the afterlife, just comes into focus as a flash of motion at the other side of the table shifts my vision. Joselyn, with fire in her eyes, catches the electric kettle with the lightning sweep of her arm. She dumps the scalding hot water into Tony's lap.

Like a wounded animal caught between two predators he shoots out of his chair. His face is a map of pain. Instinctively he clutches with his forked hand toward the steam rising from his midsection. The impact of the sniper's supersonic bullet erases all expression from Tony's face. It leaves him standing, for an instant, suspended in space, and trails in its wake a shower of glass and a cloud of fine red mist that settles on Joselyn and me.

SIXTY-ONE

L ess than a week had passed following Tony's timely death when Joselyn and I traveled north to visit with Frank and Ida Leon, Sofia's parents. We wanted to tell them what had happened, how their daughter had died at the hands of fate. The only sliver of justice in any of it was that her killer was now dead.

He left in his wake a trail of innocents, including his own children, who are traumatized, and a bewildered wife who now realizes that the man she married, Tony Pack, was a stranger she never really knew.

Part of what we were told by Tony was fact, and part of it was lies. We suspect that Dr. Pack was not fearful regarding anything he received from Fish or anyone else. He was, after all, propelling the fraud to invent the flag. The fear on his part was a fiction invented by Tony, to conform to what we already knew about Robert Brauer. Brauer was in fact afraid. Perhaps it was because he didn't want to participate but couldn't say no to his old buddies. He knew if they got caught they were looking at prison time. He certainly didn't want to have his daughter involved. There were other reasons for fear as well. His house had been burglarized. He knew what they were looking for. He may have also realized that Ed Pack's death and the accident that killed Walter Jones were the result of homicide and that he was on the hit list. He had reason to fear.

We debated whether to tell the Leons about Sofia's condition at the time of her death, the grandchild that was never to be. In the end, Joselyn handled it as delicately as she could, and for reasons of her own. She told them how it happened. She did not provide them with a name. With all the senseless violence that had already occurred, the last thing she wanted was to inspire a blunt act of reprisal by Frank Leon on behalf of his dead daughter. Instead she assured him that justice would be done.

For that, Joselyn had her own plans, a form of social castration that would be relentless and far more painful. She leaned on Thorpe and got him to hand over the raw data on the DNA from the FBI lab, the DNA profile from Sofia's soon-to-be child as well as that of Ricardo Menard, showing him to be the father. Thorpe never told her where the DNA from Menard came from, about Herman's and my involvement, but he gave her his anonymous blessings to use it. She was free to do so as long as she didn't disclose the fact that the information came from FBI lab results.

Thorpe knew that the DNA on the fetus was accurate and he was confident regarding the materials Herman and I had collected from Menard at the castle. If Joselyn used the DNA findings to expose Ricardo and he sued her for defamation, the only way he could do so was by putting at issue the precise profile of his own DNA. Thorpe was sure that subsequent tests would serve only to confirm that he was the father.

He also relayed to Joselyn in confidence information that the hammer might be about to drop on Menard. He explained that local authorities had intelligence videos of a place in the hills outside Las Vegas where nefarious activities took place between wealthy, powerful men and young women. According to Thorpe, Ricardo Menard was a frequent visitor. If they were lucky, they might get him.

For Joselyn, this involved too many ifs or mights. She was looking for something involving words like *definite* and *certain*. She would have bombed the Bavarian hideout had I told her where it was. As it turned out, she has something more surgical in mind.

Two months ago, on a quiet Monday afternoon, one of Herman's investigators delivered a sealed envelope addressed to Paige Menard under the caption "PERSONAL & CONFIDENTIAL."

Inside the envelope was a carefully censored copy of the FBI's lab report on the DNA from Sofia's unborn fetus and Ricardo Menard. The chilling effect of the cold, clinical findings and the undeniable conclusion that Ricardo was the father was amplified by the disclosure that the information was about to start making the rounds of the various social networks, including several exclusive Internet sites frequented by Mrs. Menard and her circle of friends.

As far as Ricardo's fortunes were concerned, the envelope dropped on his wife had the same effect as the bomb they called "Little Boy," which was dropped on Hiroshima. It produced an instant mushroom cloud of lawyers hired by Paige rubbing Ricardo's nose in copies of their prenuptial agreement. Within a month Ricardo was back in Costa Rica picking fruit, hiding from creditors, and wondering who now held the keys to his spiffy new boat.

As for Emma, her trial and tribulations are over. The news following Tony's death, that conclusive evidence linked him to the murders of two people, Sofia Leon and Nino Toselli, started a cascade that eventually unraveled the state's case. Reports of Robert Brauer's involvement with Edward Pack on the counterfeit Blood Flag, including details of the contract they signed, caused prosecutors and police to start backpedaling in Emma's case.

The disclosure by the FBI that they had reason to believe that Tony Pack was responsible for three other murders, including that of Robert Brauer, put the final stake through the heart of their case. Three weeks ago, the district attorney dismissed with prejudice all charges against Emma Brauer. Tonight she sits at home on a quiet street in San Diego, relaxing and watching reruns of *I Love Lucy* with her dog, Dingus.

ACKNOWLEDGMENTS

There are a number of people who provided encouragement and support and who made the writing of this book possible.

Most of all I wish to thank my assistant, Marianne Dargitz, who for more than two decades has provided not only her energy and unflagging support for my work, but her encouragement, which has guided me through difficult periods. Without her constant efforts and attention to detail, none of this would have happened.

Thanks to Josh Davis for his advice and editing regarding all things high-tech and, in particular, elements of the story concerning computer technology.

Among others, I wish to thank my publisher, William Morrow, and all the people at HarperCollins, without whose unstinting care and love of the written word and for book publishing as we know it, my work as well as that of others would not see the light of day. Most of all I thank my editor, David Highfill, whose friendship over many years has been a constant source of encouragement and pleasure. I thank his editorial assistant, Chloe Moffett, who, over the course of this work, fielded my phone calls and handled many technical aspects during the transition from paper to digital editing.

I thank my agent, Esther Newberg of International Creative Management, and my New York lawyers, Mike Rudell and Eric Brown of Franklin, Weinrib, Rudell & Vassallo, for their constant attention and guidance to the business aspects of my publishing career.

For their caring interest, love, and constant encouragement I thank Al and Laura Parmisano, who have always been there for me during good times and bad. Last but not least, for her constant and unconditional love, I thank my daughter, Megan Martini, who for me makes all things possible.